Get It How I Live

Written by C."Bones" Walker

Published by: Mijini Publishing

mijinipublishing@gmail.com

This novel is a work of Fiction.

The situations and characters described in this novel are not intended to refer to specific places or living persons.

ISBN13: 978-1535223836

ISBN10: 1535223839

Dedication

This book is dedicated to the main women in my life, my mother and daughter. Ma, nothing I've done reflects you, I chose my path and stayed too true to it... Baby girl, the decisions that I've made landed me in prison when you were only 3 months old, now you can drive... wow, I want you to know that you are what I'm most proud of, the purest part of me...?

I'm swift with my word play and still I can never find enough words in the dictionary to adequately express my love for
you so I'll simply say it the easiest and clearest way, I LOVE YOU DEUVION....

Acknowledgements

First, I got to acknowledge my lil' bro B, the owner of Bz Cutz barbershop because without you and your wife (my lil' sis Moe) I know I'd be back on wild west times trying to take over.

Hollins Street, thanks a million... To my sis Tiny (Tawanda) despite being small in statue, you jumped on deck and played it like a giant regarding getting my work published, good looking out!
To a true homie, more like my brother, lil' Black, you did my whole bid with me, it doesn't get no realer then that, f*** 100 you kept it 1 billion. You already know I'm forever loyal to you playboy. To Jelly and all my homies from H & P, (Hollins & Pulaski nigga). To my homies from B & G, (Baltimore & Gilmore), Low Low you opened the door with your novel, good shit playa. Mook we been 100 since day 1, good looking on getting me sis number... To my nigga Robo (Greenmount), all my 037 homies (037 is the fed code for Baltimore nigga's), Green eye Mike (Jefferson),
Black Jerry, Fat Keith (down the hill), Leon, Bok, Lil' Tiger (Lafayette Projects), Bobby Steels, Tom Cat, buddy Love, Pop, Coo-Don (North Ave.), Payton(you still can't fuck with me in handball), BooBoo (E.A), Black Rodney, Dirty Wallace, Moo-Moo (east side sharp young nigga) Bird, Jordo, Jeez Nuts, Chim, Dre Mumbles, Turk, Keon (L T), Dime, Lando, Stover, Levi, Fat Craig, Oakie, Fat Tony (Mount & Mosher) Cruddy, Lil' Black, Dimir, Black Mouzon, Playboy, Cheese, Church (Westport), Jermaine/Hova (R & G), Sterlin, Shonn Eubanks, Naheem (Harlem & Dukeland), Dice, Twon, Enzo,

Chuck (L.A.C.), Fatz we rapped a lot when I was writing this book, Jake (Park Heights), lil Marty, Smackdown, do your rap thing young nig, Smurf, Lamont (Hoffman & Holbrook), Big Zee, "L" (Lisa love you Shorty lol.), Cheese, Sleepy and the Nickle bag boys, Wami (whats up homes), Lamont Allen, 100 Grand, Namond, Sweendy and all those I rubbed shoulders with in the feds who are still stuck.

To my comrades, the list is too many to name, but E.B., Kev-bo, Nel, Diesel, lil' Dave, Slay and Fat Relly. Nice, if you still trying to push your book get at me. I know sis will jump on it. To my D.C. homies, Den-Den, Goo, Nut, Block, Fatz, Smoke, Gee, Lil Ed, B.D., Ciroc, Sharod, Donnie Hart, and Erky Berk, Don Martin and JV, you are great homies, Don you polished me up some, showed me how D.C. and B-more supposed to ride together in the feds, JV you were the icing on the cake slim, cold blooded... Tim be easy playa ...Rock (Celebrity Chef Stew), Donnie, Lil' E (cuzo), Wayne and East Rock...
To my homegirls who kept up with me when I was down, Ikesha, Puddin, Squeaky, Roteacha, Peaches, Kanawaha, Tasha (Houston), Angie (the twins mother), Tasha (my daughters mother- you did a good job raising her, I'm proud of you yo, thanks) Sunitha, Bridgette Thomas, Crystal Frazier (good woman) .... It's a million names in my mind, if I missed you blame it on the mind not the heart....

Introduction

It was a breezy dusky evening, the sky still and starless as Lil' Al and two of his close homies (Mal and Dee), all dressed in designer clothing with jewelry on their necks, wrists and fingers exited a shoe store on Park Heights Avenue. They had just finished shopping and were all carrying bags containing new sweat suits and footwear, as they made their way to Lil' Al's money green 1993 Acura Legend that was parked at the curb up the street from the storefront.

Mal and Dee remained on the sidewalk near the car waiting for Lil' Al to unlock the passenger doors. Rounding to the front of the car Lil' Al inserted his key into the driver door, unlocked and opened it. He was just about to step into the car when two stick-up boys, high off willie blunts (a mixture of crack and weed rolled in cigar paper) ran up on him and his two homies, catching them totally off guard.

Universe, the shortest of the two stick-up boys snuck up behind Mal and Dee with a black hood pulled tight on his head, a Tech-9 pistol in his hand trained on their backs. His partner Baz approached Lil' Al from behind also with his 9mm aimed at Lil' Al's frame.

"Yo! Money, you know what time it is, kick dat shit out!", spat Baz eyeing the saucer sized lionhead medallion hanging from the huge gold Cuban link chain glistening around his neck.

Lil' Al froze in his tracks, his heart racing, he stared down at the black gun aimed at him with a bewildered look on his face. Frightened he panicked and foolishly tried to leap into his car... Blap! Blap! Blap! Baz squeezed the trigger three times causing a chain reaction as Mal and Dee tried to run then Universe let off a rapid burst of shots. Blaw! Blaw! Bla-Bla-Bla-Bl-Blaw!

The bullets from the Tech-9 Universe was spraying cut Mal and Dee down, riddling their flesh. Once they hit the pavement Universe quickly began to search Mal's bloody person, confiscating all his valuables before moving on to Dee. Likewise, the three shots Baz fired cut Lil' Al down. He fell halfway into the car, the upper part of his body laid awkwardly across the tan leather driver seat, while the rest of his body remained hanging out of the car. In a flash, Baz grabbed Lil' Al's pants at the waistline with his left hand and roughly snatched him completely out of the car and began stripping him of his valuables.

Lil' Al stared up at Baz with wide glassy eyes, gasping for air, his white, green and yellow Nautica jacket and matching rugby shirt were soaked with blood which turned the clothing a deep crimson red.

Staring up, his entire life seemed to flash before him on a projectile screen. His body became cold and his eyelids became heavy as he slipped into the hereafter.

After stripping the bloody corpse of all its valuables, Baz took the car keys and hopped into the Acura. Sitting his hot pistol on his lap he stuck the key in the ignition and started the car. Honking the horn, he shouted to Universe,

"Yo B lets be out!". Universe finished searching Dee then raised up, grabbed the passenger door handle and lifted it. It was still locked and didn't open until Baz leaned over the seat and unlocked it, then Universe lifted the handle again. He opened the door and flung Mal and Dee's shopping bags into the car before he climbed in. No sooner than he'd sat in the car Baz whipped out of the parking space and raced recklessly down Park Heights Avenue, leaving three murdered teens in their wake. A simple robbery turned into a triple homicide…

Welcome to the slums!!!

Chapter 1

And 10, 20, 30, 40… damn $3,240.00, not bad for a week day, thought Dirty having just recounted the proceeds from the previous night. After putting rubber bands on each G-stack ($1,000) he stood on top of the old oak nightstand next to his bed, using one hand he pushed the dingy white drop ceiling panel up, using his other hand he put the three G's up in the ceiling with the other $5500.00 he'd manage to save. Replacing the panel, he hopped down, grabbed the remaining $240.00 off the bed and stuffed it in his pocket. *I'ma have to call Block and re-up with another eighth (a kilo) soon cause its only seven fifty packs (fifty vials-dimes) left,*

He thought as he walked downstairs to chill in his grandmothers living room until his homies stopped by.

Just as he came down the stairs there was a knock at the front door, "Who is it?" asked Dirty approaching the front door.

"It's me yo!", stated a distorted voice.

"Who the fuck is me?!" asked Dirty already knowing the answer.

"Bucky, Yo open the door!".

"I knew it was your ugly ass knockin' all soft like you Peaches", said Dirty laughing as he opened the door.

Bucky is my man, but he's one ugly nigga for real, he looks just like Buckwheat with crooked yellowish horse sized teeth and poppy eyes, thought Dirty as he extended his hand to give his partner dap.

"What's up nigga? Where Mookie, Squirrel and the other homies at? Yall running late today Cutty", said Dirty as if he was the general of the clique.

"Smurf and em' went to school I think, Mookie and Squirrel are around the corner, we just came from down Lombard Street, you know it was a big ass fire round' there and an infant and a five years old girl died in the fire", said Bucky shaking his head from side to side.

"Dayum! Two babies died, that's fucked up yo", said Dirty.

"Tell me about it, the whole house was up in flames, shit it might still be on the news", said Bucky picking up the remote control off the couch using it to change the television to channel 13.

"See yo, they still round there!" exclaimed Bucky pointing at the television.

"That's fucked up, I'm glad it wasn't this house", said Dirty sparking up the blunt he'd rolled earlier and inhaling deeply.

Dirty's grandmothers house was an old one and some of the white paint had begun to peel and crack over the doors and near the corners, however aside from that the house was in good shape and the interior was superb by ghetto standards.

“Uuuugh, Uuuugh, dayum this dat shit Bucky”, said Dirty in a slightly hoarse tone trying to muffle a cough. “Here yo hit dis’”. Dirty attempting to hand Bucky the blunt, but Bucky was transfixed into the news causing Dirty to look also as the news broadcaster spoke.

“Pertaining to the triple homicide last night in the Park Heights community where Dwight Cook, Albert Clark Jr. and Jamal Smith were allegedly gunned down in a drug robbery gone bad, there still hasn’t been any arrests, however police believe the incident to be connected to a string of robberies committed on local drug dealers by the “New York stick-up boys”. Anyone with information concerning this incident is strongly urged to call 410-555….”.

“Dayum Dirty, Them New York cats been slumpin’ shit like crazy”, said Bucky grabbing the blunt and inhaling it, holding the smoke in his lungs for as long as he could before exhaling.

“Man, fuck them New York niggas and any other stick-up boys, I wish them niggas would come around here, I bet I give them what they lookin’ for”, said Dirty pulling out a Glock 9mm from his waistband giving inference to his statement.

“Hell, yeah yo, them whores deserve to be bodied tryna terrorize Baltimore”, said Bucky blowing smoke out of his nostrils.

“Yoooo-ho! Yooooo-ho!”, shouted a familiar voice from outside. Hearing the hood-cry Dirty pulled the black curtain on the front window to the side just enough to peep out and see Mookie’s light skinned, freckle face, red head, little body posted up on a chrome freestyle GT bike dressed in a black Levi jean set. *Mookie is only 5' feet tall, weighing ninety pounds soaked and wet but he has a lion heart and stays on his grind,* thought Dirty as he walked over and unlocked the front door, allowing Mookie to come in.

"What's up Mook?" asked Dirty.

"Ain't shit, Dirty, "replied Mookie getting off his bike and climbing the front steps to enter the crib.

"You know me Dirty, just trying to feed my son. Where the packs at anyway, it's a mob of fiends outside tryna cop. I told Bucky ugly ass to come get a couple packs about twenty minutes ago", said Mookie looking over at Bucky with a slight mug.

"My fault yo", said Bucky getting up off the couch and running upstairs to Dirty's room to retrieve two fifty packs from out of the third shoe box on the second-row lining Dirty's bedroom wall.

By the time that Bucky had rejoined Mookie and Dirty in the living room they were puffing on another blunt listening to Biggie's song "Things Done Changed", on the stereo. "Remember they use to thump/ but now they blast right/" went the lyrics being expelled from the stereo speakers. Standing, Dirty passed the blunt to Bucky as soon as he entered the room.

"Here yo, yall go ahead and walk with this", said Dirty brushing ashes off his new Coogi sweater. "After I clean up I'll be around the block yo".

"Alright yo", said Mookie taking the blunt Bucky passed to him and heading for the front door followed by Bucky.

After Mookie and Bucky left, Dirty proceeded to clean up, vacuuming, dusting and spraying air freshener everywhere. Dirty respected his grandmother's wishes and all she asked was for him to keep the house clean, take the trash out and write to his mother once a week, so this is something he's always done. Having cleaned up, Dirty was just on his way out the door when the telephone began to ring. Bliiiiiiiiing! Bliiiiiiing! Picking up the cordless phone, Dirty answered in a mild manner just in case it was his grandmother, "Hello".

"Hey Baby, what you up too?", whined Dirty's girlfriend Peaches sounding like the singer Michel le'.

"What's up Peach, what you doin' out of school so early?" asked Dirty in a concerned tone.

"Boy, school let out thirty minutes ago. I just got home and seen Mookie and them on Hollins Street and they said you was in the house so I decided to call. Why you still in the house anyway? It better not be no bitch round' there", she said firmly expressing a little bit of jealousy.

"Girl ain't nobody round' here stop acting crazy", replied Dirty laughing.

"What's so damn funny Antonio? Don't make me come around there", snapped Peaches.

Still laughing Dirty said “I wish you would so I can get some of that good stuff between your legs before my grandmother gets off work”.

“Heh, Heh, Heh, boy you crazy”, laughed Peaches “don’t worry though I’ll be around later alright baby!”

“Mmmm”, just thinking about his girl’s beautiful oval face, soft caramel colored skin tone, semi chinky almond colored eyes and her jet-black hair made Dirty fantasize. Peaches favored “Ashley”- Tatiana Ali from the T.V. sitcom “Fresh Prince of Bel Air”, starring Will Smith, except her body was fully blossomed, nice thighs, round hips, grapefruit shaped breasts and a firm flat stomach. Dirty and Peaches had been boyfriend and girlfriend since they were in third grade. “Yeah, I need to see you today so I can taste those lips”, said Dirty blowing Peaches a kiss,

“mmmttwwaa!!!”. Boom! Boom! Boom! “Man, what the fuck!” yelled Dirty walking towards the front door.

“What’s wrong baby?” asked Peaches.

“I don’t know, somebody’s banging on the door!” Boom! Boom! Boom! “Y, who the fuck is it?” shouted Dirty still holding the phone in one hand, he grabbed his gun with the other aiming at the door.

“It’s Mookie yo, open the door, hurry up and open the fucking door!” Tucking his gun back in his waistband, Dirty unlocked the door, opening it just about to bark on Mookie for beating on the door like a mad man when Mookie blurts out, “Yo, the stick-up boys got Squirrel and Bucky hemmed up round’ the corner!” Without thinking Dirty flung the cordless phone onto the couch, ran upstairs to his room, flipped his mattress over grabbing a Taurus 9mm off the box spring, running back downstairs he gave Mookie the Taurus, pulled his Glock out and he and Mookie both ran down Hollins Street, turning left on Pulaski Street, guns already drawn.

As they turned the corner their hearts pumping fast, everything seemed to intensify almost as if moving in slow motion, they spotted two dudes wearing black hoodies, running to a parked late model dark blue Chevy Caprice classic. Stepping into the street they began to fire at the stick-up boys. Blow! Blow! Blow! One of the stick-up boys stumbled, almost falling but somehow managing to catch his balance using one hand, stopping himself from hitting the ground, still trying to maneuver to the car although he was apparently hit in his upper back. The other stick-up boy started firing aimlessly over his shoulder, Blow! Blow! Blow!

The one who had stumbled made it into the hooptie first, snatching the car door open and jumping in causing his partner who was a step behind him to be stuck momentarily trying to get in the same door his partner had entered. All it took was that brief second for Dirty to level his Glock, firing Blow! Blow! Hitting the stick-up boy smack dab in the center of his back knocking him off his feet and throwing him to the ground. Apparently, there was a driver in the car because it sped off a mini second after the second stick-up boy was shot.

Scuuuuuuuurrrrrrdd!!!!!! Almost crashing, the car raced down Pulaski Street leaving the individual who had been shot for dead. Dirty ran out into the middle of Pulaski Street shooting at the car as it fled, turning left on Pratt Street. Once the car had turned the corner and was no longer in sight Dirty turned around to see Bucky and Squirrel both standing over a figure on the ground looking down. It took a few seconds for it to register that the figure was Mookie.

"What the Fuck! Nooooooooo!!!!!", shouted Dirty running over to where Mookie laid. He kneeled and grabbed Mookie's lifeless body, tears streaming down his face. Still clutching the Taurus in his small hand Mookie laid there in a pool of blood with his eyes still open with a bullet hole lodged perfectly between his eyes.

Having dropped his gun Dirty snatched the Taurus out of Mookie's lifeless hand, stood up and walked across the street to where the stick-up boy laid on his stomach trying to crawl and drag himself up the sidewalk. Bleeding profusely from the gunshot wounds in his back, leaving a trail of blood on the concrete as he crawled. Numb to the world, with blood in his eyes Dirty, no longer seeing all the people who were standing around, the cars driving pass, nothing…stood directly over the mangled stick-up boy and with no remorse, he pulled the trigger repeatedly until the chamber locked back, empty, at which time he bent down and repeatedly struck the dead, bloody, lifeless body with the empty gun.

Dirty would have probably stayed there, pistol whipping the lifeless form until the police arrived had it not been for Bucky and Squirrel grabbing and practically dragging him off the murdered stick-up boy.

"Come on yo!", shouted Squirrel pulling Dirty.

"Let um' go and come on before five-o comes yo", shouted Bucky helping Squirrel pull Dirty off the dead stick-up boy.

Unbeknown to Dirty, somehow, he wound up around Ms. Cynthia's house. Ms. Cynthia is Peaches mother. Peaches stayed in the basement of her mother's house. The basement was like a home within a home, thanks to Dirty.

Still Shaken by the incident Dirty sat on the edge of the bed with his head down, babbling incoherently. Cradling his head to her breasts, Peaches repeatedly kissed his forehead telling him that everything would be alright.

"It's going to be alright baby, it's going to be alright", said Peaches kissing his forehead all the while, "I love you Antonio, I love you..."

Those were the last words he recalled before drifting off into a fitful sleep. Peaches removed his clothes and tucked him in under the covers the best she could, climbed into the bed, wrapped her arms around Dirty, holding him she cried, afraid of losing her man. She wanted so desperately to reverse the hands of time, to change the events of the day but in her heart, she knew such things were impossible. *What can I do?* She wondered as she held her man. *All I can do is be strong for my man I guess,* thought Peaches as she kissed Dirty on his neck and cried herself to sleep.

Chapter 2

Early the following morning Dirty awakened to the sound of familiar voices. It was Bucky, Squirrel, Smurf, Fatz, Shy, the twins (Snuggles and Fatty-Pooh) and of course Peaches. They'd all hooked school and were discussing the previous day events when Dirty came to. Rising, Dirty sat up on the edge of the bed, wiped the cold out of his eyes, stretched and spoke for the first time that morning.

"Yo, what the fuck all ya'll niggas packed up in here for?"

"Damn yo, that's how you greet your homies first thing in the morning?", asked Smurf. "We just came around to check on your White ass".

"Yeah yo, niggas been worried about' you White", chimed Squirrel.

"My fault yall, yall know a nigga a little discombobulated after yesterday", stated Dirty glancing around the basement at each of his homies before finally allowing his eyes to rest on Peaches who was sitting on the far corner of the bed with her legs curled under her, wearing a long white and pink T-shirt, frowning he said

"Peaches, if you don't get your ass up and go put some pants or somethin' on… you know Bucky little perverted ass probably tryna sneak a peek up under dat T-shirt".

Everybody began to laugh at the statement about Bucky as Peaches stood up, grabbed a pair of her gray cotton shorts out of the top chest drawer and headed up the stairs to put them on under the oversize T-shirt that she usually only wore when only her and White was in the basement alone.

"Bring me some Orange Juice when you come back down baby", shouted Dirty as Peaches ascended the stairs.

"Okay Pookie", replied Peaches over her shoulder using her little nickname for Dirty.

Once Peaches was out of sight Dirty turned to his homies. "Yo, what's the deal yall?" asked Dirty, eager to know the word on the streets.

"Ain't nothing nice" said Smurf frowning. "Your name ringing like a muthafucka right now Dirty".

"You were on the news and some more shit and homicide was round' grandma's house too", interjected Dirty's cousin Shy.

"For real yo?" asked Dirty already knowing his fate would be the Maryland Penitentiary if he didn't get out of Baltimore soon, "Fuck it, I did what I had to do yo, ya know? Anyway, what's up with Ms. Cookie, Mookie's baby mother Keisha, Lil' Mookie and Munchie, yall been round' there?" asked Dirty.

"Yeah yo, Ms. Cookie and Munchie seem to be holding up fairly well. I ain't seen Keisha and Lil' Mookie yet but I'ma go 'round there when I leave here", said Squirrel.

"Oh yeah, Ms. Cookie said to tell you she loves you and if you need anything just holla and she'll be there running".

"Yeah Dirty, Ma Ma said she love you too and lay low until she can contact Aunt Jackie and arrange for you to go down North Carolina", interjected Shy.

"I heard dat yo" replied Dirty. The thought of his grandmother attempting to help him become a fugitive made him smile. "Tell Grandma I love her too and I'ma call her job", said Dirty.

"Alright Yo, I got cha" replied Shy.

"Plus, keep an eye on Keisha, Lil' Mookie, Munchie and Ms. Cookie". "Shy you keep an eye on grandma", said Dirty.

"No doubt Cuz!" replied Shy.

"Yeah yo, that goes without saying", said the twins simultaneously.

"Cold blooded!" chimed Bucky, Squirrel and Smurf as Fatz shook his head in agreement.

"I heard that, where the smoke at though yo?" asked Dirty eager to get high and set his mind at ease.

Bucky responded to the question by pulling out a box of Philly blunts and three dime bags of light green Marijuana. Dumping the contents of each bag onto the nightstand, splitting a blunt down the middle, removing the tobacco, then evenly placing the Marijuana up and down the length of the gutted blunt and hurriedly twisting it back into a smokable cigar as he licked the blunt paper to keep it stuck together after it was rolled. Squirrel and Snuggles also rolled up blunts.

"Yo, get them incense out of that top drawer", said Dirty pointing at the dresser. "Light up a couple before we spark up". Shy grabbed the incense out of the drawer and lit six of them. He placed one in each corner of the room and two at the foot of the stairs. At which time Bucky passed Dirty the blunt he'd rolled.

"Yo, spark this", said Bucky turning to see if Fatz had already sparked the blunt Snuggles rolled. "Damn Fatz, your big stinkin' ass don't never want to cop no smoke but you always the first to spark up." Everybody started laughing at the truth Bucky had just spoke, Fatz was a black Jew, tight as fish pussy and as his nickname suggested he was fat, he sported a bald head, his skin tone was that of a copper penny and he was the only one in their clique to have gold teeth. Despite being tight Fatz was a center piece to their clique, not only was he a comedian, he was also always ready to fight an outsider for any of his homies and he could rumble too.

"Yo, pass the blunt nigga", shouted Snuggles looking at Fatz. Snuggles and Fatty-Pooh were identical twins, both were stocky, light brown skinned, bowlegged and stood 5'9". The only difference between them was Snuggles kept a low fade where Fatty-Pooh rocked a small semi-curly blow out.

"Uuuugh-Uuuugh, damn this some killer smoke", said Squirrel to no one while trying to muffle a cough. Squirrel had a reddish-brown complexion, slender, tall and looked just like a squirrel in the face thus earning his nickname. "Here yo", said Squirrel passing the blunt to Smurf. Smurf taking the blunt inhaled deeply and blew out a cloud of smoke. Smurf was short, 4'10" with big feet, big ears and had a darkish bluish black complexion.

Everyone was in a zone feeling the effects of the weed. Fatz being his usual self, began cracking jokes about Bucky.

"A Bucky", said Fatz attempting to get Bucky's attention.

"What's up Fat ass", replied Bucky still hitting the blunt.

"Yo, you my nigga and all but you ugly as fuck. You sure your mother wasn't fuckin' Mr. Ed the talkin' horse when she got pregnant", said Fatz blowing a cloud of smoke from his lungs, he laughed.

"Hell yeah, your teeth big as shit Eddie, I mean Bucky", said Snuggles jumping in on the joke.

"Fuck you Fatz nigga!" said Bucky exposing his teeth as he spoke causing everyone in the basement to laugh uncontrollably, except Dirty.

Dirty's mind was elsewhere and even with the Marijuana in his system he was unable to catch the "laughy-jokey" vibe, so he got up off the bed, fumbled with a few tapes that were lying on top of the dresser. Finding the tape that he was looking for, he walked over to the stereo and put the tape in, hit rewind, then pushed play. The lyrics to Tupac and M.C Breed's song, "You Gotta Get Yours, I Gotta Get Mines" flooded the basement. Feeling the effects of the weed and vibing with the song Dirty began to rap aloud with Tupac: "I live the life of a hustler, high to I die/ finger on the trigga hand on my 9/ smoking blunts of skunk/ putting holes in punks, that's that shit right there yo", said Dirty feeling the verse.

Just then Peaches came down the stairs with a glass of Orange Juice, a plate of pancakes and some scrambled eggs for Dirty White.

"Here Baby", said Peaches handing Dirty the food she'd prepared.

"Thanks Peach", said Dirty taking the glass and plate out of her hands. Smelling the pancakes and eggs coupled with the effects of the marijuana made everyone hungry causing Fatz to speak up.

"Yo, let me taste them pancakes", said Fatz looking at the plate Dirty was holding. "why you ain't make us none Peaches?".

"Fuck you mean why she ain't make yall none, she ain't no maid or cook nigga, you better carry your fat ass up on Edmondson and Pulaski to the breakfast spot if you hungry", interjected Dirty staring at Fatz. "Matter fact yall gotta go yo, me and my wife need to be alone", said Dirty looking over at Peaches who looked gorgeous sprawled out on the bed.

"Come on yo!", said Fatz smiling.

"You putting us out Dirty?" asked Bucky.

"That's fucked up yo!", said Shy.

Everybody protested, but nonetheless one after another they began to ascend the stairs heading for the front door understanding that Dirty needed to be alone with Peaches.

After letting his homies out and locking the door Dirty returned to the basement. Climbing into bed with Peaches he immediately began to run his hands up and down her back, massaging up and around her shoulders and neck as she laid on her stomach with her head turned to the left watching TV Leaning down, Dirty kissed Peaches on her neck. Then using his right hand, he pushed her long silky black hair to the side and began to lick around her ear lobe causing her to moan softly.

"MMMM, boy you better stop before it's too late", moaned Peaches rolling over on to her back and looking up at Dirty.

"I wanted it to be too late as soon as I let Squirrel and them cut out" said Dirty, smiling as he leaned down kissing Peaches soft succulent lips. Sticking his tongue into her mouth they began to French kiss. Responding to Dirty's touch Peaches reached up and ran her hands up and down Dirty's back.

"Take your clothes off Boo", said Dirty as he leaned up allowing Peaches to get up off the bed. She did as her man asked and took her T-shirt, shorts and red panties off, she wasn't wearing a bra. She climbed back into the bed lying on her back as Dirty White put on Jodeci "Forever My Lady" and took his sweatpants and boxers off and crawled into bed right between

Peaches firm out stretched legs. Accepting him between her legs Peaches grabbed her man's manhood and guide him into her warm wet vagina. "Ooooh Antonioooo, MMMM Baby", moaned Peaches raking her nails across her man's back as he pushed his manhood into her awaiting pussy.

"Aah, Peaches", murmured Dirty kissing his girl as he thrusted in and out of her tight womanhood.

Finding their rhythm, they made love for what seemed to them like hours, though actually only being a little over a half an hour, finally Dirty began to thrust harder and faster as Peaches moaned.

"Oooh My GOD!!!, Ah Baby, Ooooh, MMM", scooting backwards she accidentally hit the top of her head on the beds headboard.

"MMMM", shouted Dirty, biting Peaches on the neck as waves of pleasure jolted though his entire body as his cum squirted into Peaches Pussy.

"Damn girl I love you", he said still lying on top of Peaches, spent as she stroked his hair, his dick still engulfed inside of her.

"I love you too Baby, I love you too", said Peaches knowing in her heart that Antonio Lord was the love of her life, her first and only boyfriend and lover. She loved everything about him from his head to his feet, his yellow complexion, to his curly dark brown hair, his mesmerizing light brown eyes, his trim athletic frame and his pearly white teeth. Everything about her Antonio screamed perfection in her mind.

Antonio Lord or Dirty White as everyone called him was a real pretty boy by the standards of most, but beyond the physical attraction Peaches was also in love with his heart and mind. He always made her feel like a queen, he was her knight and shining armor. When her mother would go on drug escapades for days, sometimes weeks at a time without bothering to think of Peaches, Dirty would be there for her. Dirty had been there for Peaches for what seemed like forever. He'd feed her, clothe her, love her and was sure to shed blood for her or over her, he truly loved Peaches with a burning passion.

Peaches was torn by the death of Mookie, knowing that it could have just as easily been her man who was killed instead of her cousin Keisha's. *What would I do without my man,* thought Peaches. Interrupting her thoughts Dirty rolled off her and grabbed the phone on the nightstand, picking it up he dialed several numbers, on the third ring a polite female answered.

"Good afternoon, Manor Care Nursing home, how may I help you?"

"Ah, I'd like to speak to Mrs. Gladice Jones please", said Dirty in a cordial tone.

"Certainly Sir, I'll connect you, please hold", said the polite woman, there was a brief pause then Dirty's grandmother picked up on an extension line on the third floor where she was catering to a patient.

"Hello Gladice Jones, speaking"

"Hello Ma Ma How you feeling?", asked Dirty.

"I'm OK Baby, how about you?", questioned his grandmother knowing Dirty's voice.

"I could be better, but for what it's worth at least I'm still alive", replied her grandson, Dirty.

"I know that's the truth chile them peoples was around the house all last night, they wanted to search your room but I told 'um to come back when they had a warrant. Why don't you call your cousin Marvin and have him pick you up and you go over his house until I can arrange for you to go down North Carolina with Jackie", his grandmother recommended with concern. "It's only a matter of time before those people come looking for you round' Peaches house".

"I know Ma Ma, I'ma call Block, oh and I'ma send Peaches round the house to get me some fresh clothes alright?", stated Dirty looking down at Peaches as she laid in bed.

"Okay Pumpkin, you be careful and no matter what, know that Grandma loves you, right or wrong you still my grand baby", said Gladice Jones meaning every word she spoke.

"I love you too Ma Ma, I'll call later", said Dirty as he and his grandmother discontinued their call and he hurriedly dialed another number, calling his cousin Marvin like his grandmother suggested. Block answered on the first ring.

"Yo, who this?".

"It's White yo, what's up cuz?", replied Dirty.

"Ain't shit, I heard you was on Rambo times on your side of town", joked Block. "Your little big head ass done gone crazy, huh?"

"Naw yo, I just did what I had to do, anyway I'm trying to come over East with you yo", said Dirty in a serious tone.

"I feel you cuz, don't worry soon as I'm finished taking care of this business I'll come scoop you up. Where you at anyway?" "I'm round' my girl house 2112 Baltimore Street, right down the block from Bon Secour Hospital, on the right-hand side". "Bet yo, I got you cuz", said Block.

"Good looking out cuz", said Dirty feeling a blast of relief after having hung up the phone and putting it back on the nightstand, he nudged Peaches. "Let's go take a bath together Boo, I need you to wash my back", he said smiling, "then I want you to go around my grandmother's and get me some fresh clothes, get that sky blue, royal blue and white Coogi, those light blue stone washed Guess jeans and those white and sky-blue Nike air max I just bought. Oh, and get $500 out of the ceiling for me, you know where it's at, the keys are on the dresser".

"Alright Baby", replied Peaches getting out of bed she walked over to the chest, opened the third drawer and grabbed two towels and two wash cloths.

Together her and Dirty went upstairs to the top floor to take their bath. After bathing, Peaches went back in the basement, got dressed, picked up Dirty's keys, ready to go around Mrs. Gladice's house.

"Damn girl, you getting all dressed up like you going down Hammer Jacks or some shit, you only going around the corner, what you trying to catch a nigga?", teased Dirty grabbing her and squeezing her in an affectionate manner, "Sike, Boo give me a kiss, you looking good girl".

"I know I look good nigga, trust me I know", said Peaches cocking her head to the side and smirking trying to be sarcastic, then she laughed and gave Dirty a kiss. "I'll be right back in a couple minutes, if my mother comes home though I doubt she will but tell her I went around Keisha house, okay Baby?", said Peaches running up the stairs and heading out the front door.

"Alright Boo", said Dirty getting a blunt, splitting it, he emptied the tobacco and using the remaining weed Bucky had left on the nightstand he rolled a blunt, lit a couple incense and sparked up, inhaling deeply.

Walking over to the stereo, he grabbed a tape off the top of it and inserted it into the tape deck and pushed play. Turning the volume up, he plopped on the bed, kicking back he listened to the silky vocals of Toni Braxton singing "Another Bad Love Song". He thought about Peaches, his grandmother and his man Mookie, Mookie loved Toni Braxton. *Damn, my man is dead… but at least I got the dude that killed him,* thought Dirty dozing off as Toni Braxton sang: "It's just another sad love song wrecking my brain like crazy…".

A half hour later Dirty was awakened by the sound of Peaches giggling as she tickled his feet. "Get up sleepyhead, I got the clothes and money you told me to get", said Peaches tossing the bag containing the clothes onto the bed, handing him the money and then sitting on the edge of the bed next to Dirty.

"Thanks Boo", said Dirty giving Peaches a kiss. "Did you see anybody on the block?"

"Yup, everybody was outside, Shy said he was handling them packs for you and Squirrel and them said they'll stop by later. I didn't know if you wanted them to know that you were going over East so I just said alright".

"That's cool", replied Dirty getting up off the bed and putting on his clothes and shoes. Once he was finished he dialed Block's car phone number. Block picked up on the second ring,

"Yo, who this?"

"It's White, cuz you still coming this way?"

"Yeah yo, I'll be over there in about 5-10 minutes I'm in route now", replied Block.

"Bet, I'll see you when you get here cuz" exclaimed Dirty hanging up. "Baby you got your beeper in case I got to hit you on the box?", asked Dirty looking over at Peaches as she sat on the edge of the bed.

"Yeah, I have it", she said pointing at her waist.

"Make sure you keep it on, even when you go to sleep clip it to your panties", said Dirty smiling but none the less wholeheartedly meaning what he said.

“Boy I know, I’ma sleep with it and the phone in case you try to reach me, don’t I always have my beeper Pookie”, smiled Peaches.

Just then there was a loud crash above their heads. KABOOM!!! The front door flew off its hinges as police swarmed the house running through the entire house with guns drawn, shouting.

“POLICE! POLICE! We have a warrant for the arrest of Antonio Lord relating to a double homicide!”

Dirty and Peaches could hear the rumbling of feet above their heads, upstairs in the house. Startled Peaches looked like a ghost as Dirty knowing there was no escape simply stood up and grabbed Peaches embracing her firmly, he told her he loved her.

“I love you Tynisha Coleman, be strong for us Baby, be strong!”, he said as several police entered the basement. One after another they came down the stairs aiming guns at both Dirty and Peaches.

“Freeze, don’t fucking move!”, shouted a burly white officer, “Keep your hands where we can see them”. Dirty and Peaches stood there frozen as the officers surrounded them.

“What’s your name son?” asked an officer whose name plate read ‘D. Jackson’. White simply looked at officer Jackson and the rest of the officers who’d cluttered the basement with hate in his eyes and a mug on his face.

“Boy, I said what’s your name?”, asked officer Jackson again pointing his finger into Dirty’s chest. Seeing the officers questioning and harassing

Peaches, Dirty spoke up. “Antonio Lord, my name’s Antonio Lord man and yall don’t have to fuck with her”, he said looking over at Peaches, “she doesn’t know shit and don’t got shit to do with this!”

“Listen here Boy, don’t worry about her, we have her and besides you have enough to worry about as it is smart ass” stated a blonde headed white officer twisting Dirty’s hands behind his back and handcuffing him, squeezing the cuffs until they dug into Dirty’s flesh.

“Whatever man, she ain’t got shit to do with this shit!”, snarled Dirty.

“Look you’re under arrest for double homicide, you have a right to be silent, anything you say can and will be used against you…”. The blonde hair officer ranted on and on as he escorted Dirty to and up the stairs.

Looking over his shoulder as he was being escorted away from Peaches, seeing tears rolling down her cheeks, Dirty mouthed the words, I Love You, be strong and blew Peaches a kiss. White was in a zone as the Blonde hair officer followed by several other officers pushed him through the kitchen, dining room, living room and finally over the toppled front entrance and down the steps leading him into the police cruiser. Reality began to sink in. *What the fuck have I gotten myself into,* thought Dirty seeing 15-20 police cars and damn near the whole neighborhood on the street from one end to the other. Seeing him the crowd that had gathered outside began to roar,

“Be strong...Keep your head up...It’s gonna be alright…” Stone faced Dirty walked to the paddy wagon with his head up and chest out. The words be strong and keep your head up, were shouted repeatedly as he climbed in the wagon. *That goes without saying,* he thought as he sat in the wagon, *I gotta keep my head and be strong.'*

■■■

"A Lucky Al", exclaimed Antmoe walking down the tier pushing a broom with a Baltimore Sun newspaper hanging out the back of his blue jeans pocket. Antmoe was 6'2", weighed 210 pounds, was dark skinned and wore his hair like Farakhan. He was the tier runner in housing unit 6 at M.C.T.C (Maryland Correctional Training Center).

Antmoe and Lucky Al were like brothers having been co-defendants in 1974 when Antmoe being a loyal friend accepted a plea for 35 years which enabled Lucky Al to beat the murder case that Al and Antmoe were arrested for in which a successful number runner and dope peddler by the name of Mickey Stokes was robbed of an estimated half of million dollars. Lucky Al, would go home and using remains from the take would cop some raw heroin, eventually becoming one of the most successful hustlers in the history of Baltimore's drug trade as the story goes in the ghetto folklore.

Reaching Lucky Al's cell, peering in, Antmoe saw his partner lying on the small bunk bed that nearly ran the length of the right wall resembling an army cot, watching a 13' inch color TV which sat on top of the locker. Tapping on the door Antmoe spoke.

"Lucky Al', what's up cutty, what you watching?" asked Antmoe.

"Ain't nothing Ant, just watching The Young and The Restless", said Lucky Al standing up and walking the short distance to his cell door to holler at his longtime comrade.

"What's up Ant?" "Ain't much man, have you read the Sun today?", asked Antmoe. Lucky Al' shook his head from side to side indicating he hadn't. "There's an article in the Maryland section about some young kid from around my way who dusted one of them New York stick-up boys who had something to do with your son getting killed", said Antmoe taking the paper out of his pocket and sliding it under the cell door to Lucky Al'.

"Oh, yeah", exclaimed Lucky Al' bending down to grab the paper.

"Look I'ma finish sweeping, go ahead and read that joint, I'll be back" said Antmoe pushing the broom up the tier as he walked away from Lucky Al's cell.

"Alright Ant, good looking out", said Lucky Al' as he walked over to his bunk, sitting down he opened the paper and began to read:

"Boy Arrested, Double Murder"

A 15 years old Antonio Lord of the 2000 block of Hollins Street was arrested yesterday evening for his involvement in the death of 16 years old Elijah Watson, of the 2100 block of Hollins Street and 28-year-old Shabazz Carpenter of the 100 block of Atlantic Avenue, Brooklyn, New York police said. The suspect in this case has been charged as an adult and is currently being held at the Baltimore City Detention center without Bail.

Damn, that's fucked up shorty got hemmed up, I hope he makes out, thought Lucky Al' folding the newspaper and laying it down on the bed next to him.

Chapter 3

"Twenty-two for intake", shouted the balding dark skin transportation guard, at which time the intake entrance door began to open.

After all the inmates were escorted into the sally port and the intake door was secured the transportation guard handed a stack of manila envelopes to a light skinned well-built female C.O (correction officer) who was stationed in the intake booth.

"Damn that bitch phat as shit!", stated one inmate.

"Hell yeah yo, I'd drink that bitch bath water right about now", shouted another inmate causing the inmates to erupt with laughter.

"Listen up, listen up", exclaimed the female C.O in the booth trying to get the inmates attention to no avail. BOOM! BOOM! "can y'all quiet the fuck down and listen for your name?", shouted the female C.O in the booth banging on the plexiglass window that in cased the booth. Shocked by the unexpected outburst the inmates quieted down momentarily as the female C.O spoke. "When you hear your name called, step up to the window and give me your name and ID number, then go over and give your print", she said pointing to her left where there was a short dark-skinned female C.O with an unkempt weave standing in front of an electric fingerprinting machine.

After all the inmates were processed, they were each given individual hygiene kits that consisted of five stamped envelopes, several sheets of writing paper, a pencil, razor, shampoo, toothpaste and a toothbrush all packaged in a small clear zip lock bag, then escorted five at a time down an eggnog colored corridor by passing four bullpens on the right side of the corridor as they made their way to the clothing room.

Dirty was amongst the third group of inmates to be escorted to the clothing room. The corridor was filled with a hideous odor, a mixture of stale urine, feces, vomit and musty dope fiends, crack heads and homeless whinos. It was a gut-wrenching odor that almost caused Dirty to gag as he was escorted from the intake to the clothing room. Upon entering the clothing room, the first thing that Dirty noticed was a 6'5" pot belly, bumpy faced, peanut butter brown skin male C.O. The C.O handed him a dingy white towel, a bar of Lisa soap and a small bottle of green liquid.

"What's this officer?", asked Dirty holding up the bottle containing the green liquid.

"It's Quell, it's for crabs and stuff", stated the C.O who'd given it to him in a husky feminine voice.

What the fuck is yo a fag or something, thought Dirty as he was being told to strip.

"Y'all strip, put your clothes on the counter, then facing me open your mouth and lift up your tongue... Lift your arms above your head, run your hands through your hair if you have some... Turn around facing the wall, lift your feet one at a time... Now turn back around facing me grab and lift your nuts... Okay, squat and cough", said the seemly homosexual C.O staring at the inmates with lewdness in his eyes.

This big ugly motherfucker gotta be a faggot, what kinda man wants to work watching niggas strip all day, thought Dirty as he followed through with the procedures.

Once the inmates were strip searched they were instructed to take showers. The shower room was a dirty gray color, it was connected to the clothing room that contained eight rusty shower heads and had the smell of amp concrete, mildew and musty body odors.

"Y'all go ahead and get in the shower, make sure y'all put Quell everywhere there's hair", whined the homo C.O. "I don't want y'all bringin' no crabs or lice in my jail."

I wish this faggot motherfucker would shut the fuck up and stop watching me, thought Dirty as he washed up as best as he could without a washcloth. After showering, drying off and getting dressed back in the same clothes they'd just stripped off, the inmates were instructed to go to the bullpens.

"Go out that door, make a right and find a seat in one of the two large bullpens", whined the homo C.O as he pointed at the door through which the inmates had initially entered. Eager to get out of the presence of the faggot C.O, Dirty hurriedly made his way out of the clothing/ shower room, made the right and went into the first bullpen he came to. There were several guards in the corridor and the grill to the bullpen was open.

Stepping into the bullpen Dirty quickly scanned the contents around. The bullpen was a dirty gray with peeling paint that had graffiti scrolled everywhere. There were three wooden benches, a toilet that was apparently out of order because there was a big blue spot a pot in front of it that filled the bullpen with a hideous smell. There were at least 90-100 individuals sprawled out everywhere in the small holding cell that couldn't have been no larger than one third of a basketball court. There were dope fiends, crackheads, homeless men, drunks, hustlers, thieves, etc. that were laying and sitting everywhere.

On the benches, under the benches, on the floor, leaning against the bars and against the walls. The spot a pot left no room for Dirty to sit so he just stood up by the front grill trying to deal with the horrible smell.

I wish these motherfuckers would come and take me where the fuck I'm going so I can get the fuck up out this bullpen, thought Dirty looking at the C.O.'s lingering in the corridor all dressed in dark blue uniforms, just then somebody in the bullpen called his name.

"A Dirty", said a raspy voice. Turning around, Dirty White had spotted Squirrel's uncle Blu making his way over to him. Blu was a shade darker than Squirrel and stood 6'2", he was stout and had big boxing glove hands, the result of being an intravenous drug abuser.

"What's up nephew?", said Blu extending his hand to Dirty. "I heard what happened shorty, you carried that shit like a soldier". Accepting Blu's out stretched hand Dirty gave Blu dap,

“Yeah, I did what I had to do”, said Dirty shrugging off the compliment. “What’s up with you Blu?”, asked Dirty relieved to be in the presence of someone he knew.

“Ain’t shit, I just got picked up on a humble for loitering and a bullshit F.T.A for a young ass theft charge that popped up. I’ll be out in about a week”, said Blu use to the occasional brushes with the law.

Shit, I wish I was getting out in a week, thought Dirty keeping his thoughts to himself though he decided to ask Blu how jail was.

“Yo, how is this joint Blu?”

“Shorty, this jail shit ain’t nothing, you a soldier, just carry it like you carry it round’ the way. They gonna send you up on T section with all the hoppers, niggas your age 15, 16,17. The hopper tier is wild, but once you set an example you’ll be straight. Shit, first nigga get you wrong punish his ass like you’d do a junkie if you caught him hittin’ your stash, you feel me?”, said Blu trying to both school and read Dirty at the same time.

“Yeah, I feel you Blu”, said Dirty understanding.

“Look White remember this”, said Blu looking Dirty directly in the eyes. “In here you’re either da predator or da prey, ain’t no halfway shit, take your pick, the choice is yours”

“I heard dat Blu”, said Dirty.

“Don’te Smith, Antonio Lord, Marcus Lewis”, shouted a guard. “Y’all come with me”

"Up nephew, dat's you", said Blu giving Dirty dap again, "Be cool shorty and remember what I said, keep your head up and your chest out".

"Alright, Blu, I will, keep your head up too", said Dirty as he exited the bullpen.

After being given bedrolls that consist of one wool blanket, two sheets and another bar of Lisa soap, Dirty White and a chubby brown skin adolescent with a missing tooth and an ashy face dark skin adolescent who had a nappy beard and a mustache were escorted by two C. O's to a grill which led to another grill, then a stairwell to T-section. One of the C. O's was medium built, stood 5'10", was clean cut and black as tar. He took up the rear of the escort as the other C.O who looked to be fortyish had a reddish-brown complexion was short and had a slight belly that protruded from his uniform, lead the three inmates. The C.O bringing up the rear of the escort spoke to the officer at the grill first.

"A Mac, we got 3 for T-section"

"What's up Coleman?", asked a big husky brown skin C.O who looked like a former football player, as he approached and unlocked the grill.

"Ain't shit, just trying to get these eight hours over so I can get home to the misses", said Coleman.

"I hear ya, what about you Jones, you thinking about working another double this week?", asked Mac speaking to the reddish-brown skin C.O. "I heard they need somebody down on K."

"Nah Mac, not tonight I'm trying to get the fuck up out of here today", laughed Jones.

"I know that's right", said Mac in a jolly tone.

"A look y'all go ahead and walk down there past the gym and Tier S, give officer Green y'all name and he'll tell y'all which cell y'all in", said Mac pointing to his right, then returning to his conversation with officers Coleman And Jones.

The three inmates proceeded to walk down the two-toned hallway passing a gym to their right, then S-section to their left, finally coming to and stepping into the entrance of T-section. There was a large metal desk to their right, behind which sat officer Green, who was brown skin with gray hair, obese and looked as if all he did was sit around eating, giving credit to this assumption was an open box of white powdered doughnuts and a large Styrofoam cup of some kind of beverage sitting on the desk. Looking up officer Green spoke in a burly tone.

"Give me all of your names and I.D numbers", he said grabbing the logbook and a pen, scrolling a few words in the logbook. "Don'te Smith, 391-192", said the rough looking adolescent with the beard and mustache. "You're going in cell 19 with Lewis, which one of y'all is Lewis?", asked C.O Green. "I'm Lewis", said the chubby adolescent with the missing front tooth, speaking up. "Well you and Smith are in cell 19 and you, you must be Lord", said C.O Green looking up at Dirty White. "Yeah", replied Dirty nodding in agreement. "You're in cell 15" said the C.O, getting up from behind the desk with seemingly difficulty, wobbling over he unlocked the grill. “All of you sleep on the bottom tier, the doors will be opened when you reach them and don’t stop or linger on my tier”, he said as the three inmates walked onto the tier, he slammed the grill, relocking it behind them.

What the fuck is this, thought Dirty as he walked down the gloomy gray tier bypassing a dayroom to his left, some steps, a shower and a closet all to his right, noticing four phones running along the left wall he thought of Peaches and his grandmother, wanting to grab a phone however deciding against it he continued down the tier. Bypassing several cells before reaching his own, in each cell he passed he could see a stone-faced adolescent or two mugging him.

First nigga that get my pretty boy image fucked up and try me like a sucker I’ma smash his ass and I put that on my man Mookie, thought Dirty as he entered his cell.

“What’s up yo?”, said a frail muddy-brown, bumpy faced adolescent as he sat up on the bottom bunk.

“Ain’t shit”, replied Dirty sizing his cell mate up.

“What’s your name?”, asked the adolescent.

“Dirty White”, replied Dirty flat and dry still trying to read his cell mate, as he tossed his bedroll and hygiene kit up onto the top bunk…

“Where you from Dirty White?”

“Westside, Hollins and Pulaski, yo”, said Dirty with bass in his voice.

“A Weasel!... A Weasel, I know you hear me yo!”, shouted someone in an aggressive tone from one of the cells towards the back of the tier.

“A Weasel, I know you ain’t sleep yo”, shouted someone in a burly tone.

“Yooooooo, what’s up Lex?” asked Dirty’s cell mate getting up off his bed and walking towards the front of the cell where bars made up a door, as Dirty stepped to the back of the cell and leaned against the toilet/sink.

“What the fuck, you ignoring a nigga now Weasel”, barked Lex accusingly.

“Nah yo, I’m just rapping with my cell buddy”, said Weasel timidly.

“Tell your cell buddy come to the grill”, shouted Lex.

“Yo, they want you”, said Weasel turning around to look at Dirty then looking down at the ground. Brushing by Weasel, Dirty made his way to the front of the cell and hollered out the bars.

“Yeah yo, what’s up?”

“A main man, what’s your name?”, asked Lex.

“Dirty White”

“Dirty White, huh? Where you from slim?”, asked Lex as a few adolescents began to snicker

“Hollins and Pulaski”. “Oh, you the dude was in the paper and on the news for 2 bodies, huh yo?”, interjected someone in a voice unknown to Dirty.

"Yeah", replied Dirty.

"Man, fuck that murder shit Black", said Lex directing his words to the adolescent who'd just spoke known as Black. "Ain't no guns in here Yo and I want dat Coogi Slim got on yo."

"A Slim you hear dat", exclaimed Lex.

"I want dat Coogi tomorrow when grills pop or you know what time it is".

"And I want them Air Max you got on Slim", shouted another voice unknown to Dirty.

"Man, fuck y'all niggas", exclaimed Dirty turning red from anger. "I wish I would let one of y'all niggas take something from Antonette Jones son", he said turning away from the grill, as the adolescents on the tier continued to hoot and holler.

"You know Lex and them gonna try to rob you and run you around R tomorrow", said Weasel looking nervous as if he might catch some drama just for being Dirty's celli.

"Man, they got me fucked up, ain't no nigga gonna take shit from me or run me nowhere", exclaimed Dirty. "What the fuck is R anyway?"

"R section is P.C, protective custody, that's where niggas go when they get stabbed, banked or just don't wanna be in population", explained Weasel.

"Oh yeah, well where do they send a nigga who ain't going for shit? Cause that's where I'ma be for killing one of them whores if they try me", barked Dirty. Weasel didn't reply, instead he just laid back on his bunkbed staring at Dirty as he paced back and forth in the small confines of their cell. Finally, a verse from Snoop Dog's song "Murder was the case" struck Dirty.

"Late night I hear toothbrushes scrapping on the floor/ niggas getting they shanks just in case war pops off.

Grabbing his hygiene kit off the top bunk, he dumped the contents onto the bed, finding the toothbrush he removed it from the plastic wrapping and squatting down in the corner of the cell, he began to scrape the toothbrush against the floor fashioning one end into a point, tearing a small piece of sheet off one of the dingy sheets he'd been given in his bedroll, he wrapped it around the bristles of the toothbrush making a greppable handle. Holding the make stiff knife in his hand, he jigged at the air a few times imagining he was facing off with someone. Finally, Weasel spoke up,

"Yo, them niggas got real steel man", he said looking petrified.

"Man, fuck them niggas" said Dirty. "Come my way I'ma hold my own. I put that on my man Mookie".

"Alright yo", said Weasel looking away.

Yo a real whore. Ain't no way I'ma live like that, fuck that, predator or prey, if it gotta be that way I'ma be a predator, cold blooded, thought Dirty.

Unable to sleep, Dirty stayed up all night anticipating the inevitable confrontation he faced when grills opened. Several hours had passed when the grills opened for breakfast, at which time all the inmates made their way up the tier to the day room where trays were being passed through a slot in the day room door. The tray consisted of greenish yellow scrambled eggs, a small clump of oatmeal and a rock hard imitation English muffin. Also, given to the inmates were an 8oz. carton of milk and an optional coffee.

Dirty stepped out of his cell, on point expecting “Lex and them” to be at his door with “steel”. Seeing no one waiting on him he eased up the tier taking his surroundings in as he received his tray and made his way back down the tier to his cell. He wasn’t hungry so he gave the tray away.

“Yo, you want this?”, asked Dirty extending the tray to the chubby missing tooth adolescent who came up with him as he walked by.

“Yeah yo, you don’t want it?”, said the chubby adolescent in a rapid dialect, hurriedly accepting the tray as if Dirty might change his mind. “Good looking out yo”.

“Ain’t nothing yo”, mumbled Dirty dismissing the gratitude from the chubby youngster and walking back to his cell.

“Yo Weasel, when they gonna let us out to use the phones and shit?” asked Dirty speaking to his cell buddy after the grill to their cell was secured.

“In about a half an hour they gonna pop the grills, but you probably gonna have to wait to get on the phone though cause’ niggas be hawking them joints up, try to run them and shit”, said Weasel.

"What you mean they be hawking them up and try to run them?", asked Dirty. "What that got to do with me making a quick call?"

"Yo, if you not wit Lex and em' they be trying to whore niggas when it comes to the phones, charging niggas and some more shit", said Weasel shrugging his shoulders.

"Man fuck all dat I'm getting on the phone as soon as these doors crack", exclaimed Dirty White. "And what's the address and the visiting day?"

"401 East Eager Street, Baltimore Maryland 21202, you gotta put your I.D number on the envelopes and visiting days are on Thursday", said Weasel.

"Hold up yo", said Dirty grabbing the pencil and a piece of paper off his mattress handing the pencil and paper to Weasel. "here, write the address down for me so I don't forget". Accepting the pencil and paper Weasel wrote down the address and gave it to Dirty. "Good looking out", said Dirty taking the paper and putting it in his pocket, he sat on the toilet waiting for the grills to pop as Weasel went back to sleep.

After what seemed like an hour the grills popped. Standing Dirty cautiously walked out of his cell looking from side to side anticipating someone to be waiting on him. Seeing no one, he proceeded to walk down the tier heading straight for the phones. Three of the phones were occupied, the fourth phone was empty and the receiver was dangling down so Dirty picked it up and dialed Peaches number. Peaches answered on the first ring in a groggy voice.

"Hello"

"You have a collect call from... Antonio, do you accept?"

"Yes"

"Hey Boo, what's up sexy?", asked Dirty.

"Oh, my god Heeey Baaabbyyy, I'm so glad you called, I miss you like crazy", said Peaches, fully awake now. "You alright over there, Baby?"

"Yeah, I'm cool Baby and I miss you too, look get a pen and write this address down", said Dirty reaching in his pocket for the piece of paper with the address on it. As he did so, he could feel the shank he'd made.

"I already got the address and your ID number Pookie, Ms. Cookie called over there like you was her son and got it for me, plus she said she'd bring me over to visit you on Thursday", said Peaches in a cheerful voice excited by the thoughts of seeing her man.

"I know that's right, you on top of your shit, huh Baby?"

"Nigga you know I ain't going to miss a beat when it comes to you", said Peaches giggling.

"I know that's right, that's why I love you", said Dirty White sincerely meaning the words he spoke.

"I love you too", said Peaches.

"A main man, that's my phone", said someone standing behind Dirty in a familiar voice. Turning around still clutching the phone Dirty spotted a dark skin, stocky, tall, bald head adolescent with his mug broke down. He was accompanied by five other youngsters.

"Yo, you heard me slim, that's my phone and you need to get up off that joint", said the stocky dark skin adolescent whom Dirty presumed to be Lex.

"I got you in a minute Yo", said Dirty returning to his conversation with Peaches.

"Look Baby, make sure you check on my grandmother, write me and send me some pictures."

"I already put 2 letters in the mail with some pictures and a money order last night. I went around you grandmother's yesterday and she gave me the money order. She told me to tell you she loves you if I talked to you before she did", said Peaches.

"A yo, I told you to get up off that phone", shouted Lex.

"Who's that Baby? Is he talking to you?" asked Peaches concerned.

"Some dude talking about get off the phone", said Dirty sizing Lex up.

Yo, jive big but I think I can smash him if I strike first, thought Dirty.

"Go ahead and get off the phone and just call later, don't get in no trouble Antonio", pleaded Peaches with her voice cracking a little.

“It’s alright Baby, he just going to have to wait ‘til’ I’m finished, you done already accepted the collect call now”, said Dirty.

“What the fuck did you say?”, asked Lex walking up closer to Dirty as his boys watched still standing where they had been.

“Either you gonna get off that phone or I’m hanging that joint up on your ass”.

“Whatever Slim”, said Dirty about to return to his conversation with Peaches when Lex reached over and disconnected the phone. Without thinking, in one swift motion Dirty smacked Lex square in the face with the phone receiver, hitting him so hard it broke his jaw.

Craaaaack!!! Blood splurged out of Lex’s mouth as he stumbled back a few steps trying to gain his composure to no avail.

“You bitch ass nigga!” shouted Dirty, jumping on Lex with the swiftness of a Panther, swinging a flurry of blows to his face and head. Lex somehow managed to swing a haymaker at Dirty completely missing him as he ducked down. Grabbing Lex by his lower legs Dirty White scooped him up in the air using his shoulder pushing forward power slamming Lex to the ground knocking the wind out of him. As Lex laid on the ground Dirty White hit him with a flurry of punches, then pulling out the shank out of his pocket that he had made he began to stab Lex repeatedly, not really causing much damage, but nonetheless allowing him to release the built rage. Roughly 2 minutes had passed when several C.O.’s rushed onto the tier tackling and restraining Dirty as they escorted him to L section in handcuffs (L section is segregation/lockup). Lex was taken to medical and would eventually end up on R section.

Chapter 4

"Blessed is he whose transgression is forgiven, whose sin is covered. Blessed is the man the Lord imputeth not iniquity and in whose spirit, there is no quill…'", shouted the clean cut, forty-two years old, chocolate brown skin Pastor dressed in an exquisite navy-blue two-piece Italian made suit.

He stood at the oak podium and read the scriptures from his opened Bible to the family and friends of Elijah "Mookie" Watson, who'd come to pay their last respects to the slain teen.

Despite having been shot in between the eyes, Mookie was still able to have an open casket at his funeral. Though he looked a bit pale and slightly bloated around his cheeks, everyone agreed that the mortician had done a fairly decent job. Ms. Cookie had chosen to bury her son in a marble gray colored casket and instead of the typical suit favored by families of the deceased, Ms. Cookie buried her son in a multi-rainbow colored Coogi sweater with a matching hat, black Guess jeans and some black Timberlands, knowing that's what her son would have chosen for himself if he was alive.

Nearly everyone in the neighborhood attended the funeral; men, women, teens and children all dressed to impress in designer clothes and footwear. Everyone in attendance showed some form of sympathy and grieved to a degree as they passed the casket surrounded by flowers. Mookie laid in the casket as if he was at peace. However out of all the people in attendance Keisha was by far the most dramatic. She screamed at the top of her lungs and cried, throwing herself onto the casket causing the line viewing the body to pull her off and away from Mookie.

That's one phony bitch. She didn't even really love my brother but look at her performing like a fucking actress, ooohhh I hate her freak ass, thought Munchie as she looked over her shoulder back at Keisha who was being carried away from her brother's casket kicking and swinging.

What's next god? First my father gets killed then my brother gets killed and even Dirty White gets taken from me, every male figure I love or care for is taken from me, thought Munchie as tears ran down her cheeks.

Bucky had a serious crush on Munchie and seeing her vulnerable he rushed over to console her.

"It's gonna be alright Munch", said Bucky wrapping his arms around her as she wept. "Be strong Munchie, Mookie wouldn't want you all broke down like this".

"I know Bucky, I'ma be strong", said Munchie using the palms of her hands to wipe her face.

"Munchie, you alright Baby?", asked her mother approaching her and Bucky, followed by Peaches.

"Yeah, I'm alright Ma, it's just hard, Daddy, Mookie, Dirty White… Why Ma Why?", cried Munchie breaking down.

“I know Baby, I know”, said Ms. Cookie hugging her daughter as she stepped away from Bucky and buried her head into her chest.

“I love you Baby, be strong for me, okay sweetie”. Mookie’s mother was trying to stay stern and mask her emotions but inside she was devastated. She had cried herself to sleep for the last few nights. Still holding her daughter, she tried to reframe from breaking down.

Looking over to Peaches she spoke: “Peaches Baby, did you get an obituary for Antonio?”

“Yes Ma’am”, replied Peaches.

“Make sure you send it to him, I know he’d want one, okay Sweetie?”

“Yes, Ma’am I will”.

“Yes Ma’am, thanks Ms. Cookie”, said Peaches smiling inside.

“You don’t have to thank me, it’s the least I can do for Antonio”, exclaimed Ms. Cookie feeling obligated to do what she could to assist Antonio for avenging her son’s death.

■■

“Lord, you got a visit”, shouted the C.O in charge of L section for the 3 to 11 shift. “I’ll be down to get you in 5 minutes, be ready”. Hearing his last name called for a visit, Dirty sat up on the flat well-worn down mattress, swung his feet around and stood up. Where he'd been lying at reading the mail that the tier officer had passed out ten minutes before. Letter still in hand he laid it on the empty top bunk as he went over to the sink to brush his teeth. Once he finished, he put on the yellow jumpsuit issued to all inmates on segregation. He slipped into his Air Max and paced the cell for about a minute, he picked up the letter from Peaches and started reading where he had left off.

"Lord, you ready?", asked the C.O as he approached Dirty's cell.

"Yeah, I'm ready?", replied Dirty.

"Turn around so you can be cuffed", stated the C.O holding a pair of handcuffs in his hands.

Dirty turned around with his back to the grill and took two steps back enabling the C.O to reach into the food slot on the grill and cuff him. After Dirty was cuffed, the C.O shouted to another C.O to Pop 32 open. The grill slid open and Dirty stepped onto the tier.

"Lord off L, for visit", shouted the officer escorting Dirty.

Central control responded by opening an electrical grill to their left which led to a flight of stairs. Dirty and the escorting officer walked down a few steps and pass a bullpen and stopped at the red door which was the entrance to the visiting room. Dirty was uncuffed and told to enter the visiting room.

"You can go on in there, find your visitors and sit down", stated the C.O.

"Alright", replied Dirty walking down the congested visiting area which consist of several semi-sectioned booths with stools bolted to the ground. At the sixth booth, he spotted Peaches and Ms. Cookie sitting down as Munchie stood close behind them. Peaches looked gorgeous, her hair was in a wrap, cascading down and around her face, she wore the jewelry Dirty White had bought her and she had on an air brushed T-shirt that had 'Tynisha loves Antonio' written on it. Ms. Cookie who favored Pam Grier in her prime had her hair in a short Toni Braxton styled do and Munchie looked like a light skin version of Ms. Cookie with long braids.

"Damn girl, I miss you like shit ooh oh, excuse me Ms. Cookie, how you doing? How was the funeral?", asked Dirty as he sat down on the stool looking at Ms. Cookie.

"The funeral was nice, everybody showed up. I took some pictures, I'll make sure you get some okay? Anyway, I'm alright Sweetie, I guess. What about you? I heard you got into a fight or something. What happened?", asked Ms. Cookie trying to steer the conversation away from her deceased son.

"Some dude was trying to run the phones and I wasn't going for it so I got on one and the dude hung up on me while I was in the middle of a conversation with Peaches", said Dirty looking over at Peaches with love and admiration in his eyes.

"You know I went off and put that phone receiver on his face then I beat his ass, I meant butt".

"Um Um Um, why that child hang up on you and your Peaches, he must've been crazy", said Ms. Cookie shaking her head. "I'm surprised you ain't kill him".

"How about that Ma?", chimed in Munchie, in agreement causing everybody to start laughing.

"What's up Munch? Why you ain't write me yet?", asked Dirty.

"I did write you!"

"Yeah right, I ain't get no mail from you".

"Oh' my goodness, I did write you Boy", said Munchie looking to her mother. "Ma didn't I write him?"

"Yes Munchie", said Ms. Cookie "Yeah Antonio, she wrote you".

"I told you, now!", said Munchie folding her arms cross her chest and rolling her eyes while twisting her head slightly as if she was offended that he doubted her love.

"I wrote you too Baby", interjected Peaches "Did you get my mail, I been writing everyday".

"Yeah I got two letters and some pictures today. I was just reading one of them when they called me for a visit. What's up with you though baby, you been going to school and being strong?", asked Dirty.

"Yeah, I been going to school and I'm being strong but I ain't gonna lie, I miss you like crazy. I sleep in your T-shirts every night just so I can feel close to you", said Peaches blushing as she looked out of the corner of her eye at Ms. Cookie.

"Girl, don't pay me no mind, say what you feel, go ahead and enjoy your visit Sweetie", said Ms. Cookie sympathizing with Peaches because she'd been in a similar situation as a teen when her children's father was incarcerated.

"Okay Ms. Cookie, Yeah Baby like I was saying I miss you and I've been miserable since you got locked up, but I'm alright for now while I'm seeing you", said Peaches lashing a beautiful smile.

"You're miserable, imagine how I feel, my man gets killed, I get charged with his murder for killing the coon that killed him, so not only am I locked up on a double homicide but on top of being locked up, I'm on lock up in here, I can't even touch you and you're right in front of me, man, man, man", exclaimed Dirty shaking his head in frustration as he blew out a gust of air making a slight hissing sound.

"Yeah Baby I read that in the paper", said Ms. Cookie "How'd they charge you like that?"

"I don't know, I haven't figured it out and I ain't seen no lawyer or nothing yet", replied Dirty.

"Don't worry about Mookie's death, I know you ain't kill him and everybody in the neighborhood knows too, so you'll beat that. I'll come to court and testify in your defense, maybe you can get self-defense or something", Ms. Cookie said hoping for the best.

"Yeah Maybe, back to you though Peaches, what's up with Ms. Cynthia?", asked Dirty.

"I don't know, I haven't seen her since before you got locked up".

That's a damn shame, thought Ms. Cookie, *how could a mother leave her teenage daughter alone for weeks at a time, that's crazy and it's sad because Peaches is such a good child, she's an honor student, she's beautiful and she's very respectful…'*

"I heard that, have you been around my grandmother's lately?", asked Dirty.

"Yeah, I go around there every night around 7 o'clock and check on Ms. Gladice, she makes me eat dinner, then I help her clean up and we'll watch a little TV and talk. She said she'll bring me next week, she had to work a swing shift this week but she gets off at 3 o'clock Thursday coming up".

"What do you mean she makes you eat?" asked Dirty

"Nah, I haven't really had no appetite since you got locked up, that's all", replied Peaches.

"What you mean you ain't really had no appetite as greedy as you are? Peaches you got to eat, I need you to be strong and take good care of yourself, you're my backbone right now Baby, understand?", exclaimed Dirty almost as if he was scolding her.

"I will, I'ma be strong and take care of myself, I promise", whined Peaches tears welling up in her eyes.

"Peaches, don't start crying Baby", said Dirty putting his hand on the chicken wire and glass partition wanting so desperately to hold his girl and wipe away her tears as he'd done many of nights when she'd cry for her mother when she disappeared.

Ms. Cookie being a mother understood the situation, wrapping her arm around Peaches she pulled her to her breast.

"It's going to be alright Peaches, shhhh don't cry Sweetie", said Ms. Cookie.

"Wrap it up, visits are over", shouted the C.O.

"They just said visits are over ya'll, look I love ya'll, make sure ya'll write me, send me some pictures and come see me next week, alright? Oh, and make sure I get some underclothes and stuff and Peaches be strong Baby", said Dirty standing about to depart from the visiting room. "I love you Peach".

"I-I-I love you too Antonio", said Peaches still shedding tears as her and Ms. Cookie stood.

"We already dropped a package off for you when we came in it'll be in your property when you come off lock up, Sweetie", said Ms. Cookie.

"Oh, and my girlfriend Denise works over here, her last name is West, I told her you were my godson and to look out for you so if you need anything in her power let her know okay".

"Okay I will, I know who she is, she the one that got me another towel and hygiene kit and stuff, thanks Ms. Cookie", said Dirty grateful for the support she was providing.

"it's nothing Sweetie, Ms. Cookie will always be here for you".

“Let’s go, visits are over!”, shouted the C.O.

“alright, look I love ya’ll, Peaches be strong, I’ll call when I can”, said Dirty as he put his hand on the chicken wire and glass partition. Munchie, Ms. Cookie and Peaches all returned the gesture and one at a time put their hands on the partition directly in front of his. Dirty felt tears welling up in his eyes so he hurriedly stepped away from the visiting booth in route back to the gloomy confines of his cell as his visitors departed.

Chapter 5

"Yo, I'm about to take this $250.00 around the corner to Peaches for Dirty, then I'ma run down my crib for a minute, plus I'ma call Block so we can re-up. A Fatty, come on and walk with me real quick yo", said Squirrel knowing Fatty-Pooh was strapped and would not hesitate to shoot.

"Alright yo", said Fatty-Pooh getting up off the upside down milkcrate, that he was sitting on in the shabby living room of their stash house, smoking blunts with Smurf, Fatz, Bucky, Lil' Gizmo, Squirrel and his brother Snuggles. He walked out the front door with Squirrel.

"Yo, we'll be back in about 15 minutes ya'll", said Squirrel over his shoulder. "Lock the door and make sure ya'll put da 2x4 on the door too".

"Gotcha Cutty", said Snuggles getting up off the old beat up couch and locking the door as his brother and Squirrel and Fatty-Pooh departed.

"A Snug, make sure you put the 2x4 on the door", shouted Smurf. "I know, I did yo. A Giz pass the blunt Cutty", said Snuggles reaching for the blunt Gizmo had between his lips as Gizmo twisted his head to the side slightly enabling Snuggles to take the blunt out of his mouth, all the while keeping his eyes on the 19" TV as he worked the control buttons on the joystick connected to the Sega video game.

Taking the blunt Snuggles flopped down onto the couch next to Fatz. Once he was comfortable he put the blunt to his lips and inhaled deeply, holding the smoke in his lungs until he started gagging.

"Damn Yo, you alright?", asked Fatz reaching for the blunt in Snuggles hand while patting his homie back.

Bucky and Gizmo were consumed in their battle playing Mortal Combat while everyone in the living room watched the scrimmage when out of nowhere there was a loud thunderous crash at the front door, followed closely by a second thunderous crash as the front door on the stash house flew inward off the hinges toppling to the floor, undercover and uniformed police rushed into the small rowhouse taking the occupants by complete surprise.

"Police! Police! This is a raid, don't nobody move", shouted the Baltimore City Police Officers as they entered the row house with guns drawn.

To stunned to speak and momentarily frozen by shock, no one attempted to move as the police stormed the house handcuffing all the occupants, including Blu and Dot who were upstairs in their bedroom. The officers made everyone stay in the living room while they ransacked the house retrieving a chrome 357 python hand gun, a 9mm Beretta handgun, a sawed-off Mossberg shotgun, 6 glassine bags containing Marijuana, 31 vials of powder cocaine, a small amount of heroin on a mirror and a total of $532.00 in U.S currency. Gizmo being just 13 years old knew he'd only go to Boys village or Charles hickey for a few months tried to do the honorable thing by speaking up for his mother, father and homies, claiming that everything in the house was his.

"A Police man, them is my guns and drugs, I snuck them in here", said Gizmo, who only stood 4'2", was brown skin, had poppy eyes and a gray patch of hair thus earning him his nickname. "Didn't nobody know that stuff was in here but me".

"Nice try son, but all of ya'll are going down, especially the adults", stated the police officer, looking over at Blu and Dot as they were escorted out of the house, followed closely by all the teens and put into the back of a patty wagon.

■■

"Lord, pack up, you're going back to T section", shouted a C.O. at the top of the tier as he popped Dirty grill open.

Damn, it's about time they let me off this bullshit lock up, I been over this dirty motherfucka for 60 days, thought Dirty as he hurriedly packed his personals. Tossing everything onto the bed he wrapped the sheet up around his personals, tied a knot in the sheet securing his stuff, then swung the bundle up and over his shoulder and rushed out of segregation and back to T-section knowing his homeboys were on the section because of the house raid 3 weeks ago, that Peaches and everyone he communicated with had vaguely told him about. After being given his clothes and shoes out of the property room, Dirty was escorted to T section by a middle aged attractive mocha complexion female correctional officer who so happened to be C.O West.

“Hey Antonio, I see they’re finally letting you back into population, huh?” asked C.O West

“Yes Ma’am” replied Dirty.

“That’s good, just make sure you stay out of trouble this time. You already let them hoppers know you ain’t having it, they respect violence so they gonna stay out of your way. Me and your godmother are like sisters so if you need anything I can help you with, let me know. Officer Green is cool and so is Smith they work with T, have either one of them call me if necessary, okay Sweetie?”, said C.O West.

“Alright Ms. West”, replied Dirty as he crossed the threshold to T section.

“Hey Smith, this is my nephew”, lied C.O West handing Smith Dirty’s Q card. “If he needs anything call me, k?”

“No problem Denise”, said C.O Smith as he stood and walked around the desk to the grill and unlocked it.

“You’re in 21.” “Take care Sweetie”, said C.O West once Dirty stepped onto the tier and the grill was relocked and secure.

“I will, thanks Auntie”, said Dirty rolling right into the lie C.O West told, as he smiled and walked on down the tier immediately spotting Snuggles on the phone in what appeared to be a deep conversation staring down at the ground as he talked into the telephone receiver.

"Yo Snug, what's up nigga?", shouted Dirty happy to see his homie. Knowing the voice Snuggles looked up.

"Yoooooo, Dirty, what's the deal nigga?", shouted Snuggles looking towards the back of the tier he yelled for the rest of the homies, still clutching the phone receiver in his hand. "A Fatz, Smurf, Bucky...Dirty White down here yo!", turning back towards Dirty he asked,

"Yo, what cell you in Cutty?"

"I'm in 21... who in there?", asked Dirty.

"Damn 21, dat's next to Bucky and Fatz cell, oh that's the dude from over East, he's cool. "Hold on ", said Snuggles returning to his phone conversation. "Look Meka Dirty White just came on the tier off lock up, I'ma help him carry his shit to his cell and get him right, I'll call back later, alright?"

"Yo, tell Meka I hollered at her", interjected Dirty.

"A White hollered at you Baby...She hollered back yo...", said Snuggles looking as Dirty. "Alright then, yeah tell my brother I'ma call tonight. Yeah, I love you too", said Snuggles hanging up the phone, letting the receiver drop and dangle as he took the bundled wrapped in sheet out of Dirty hand and lead him down the tier.

The grill to cell 21 was wide open and looked identical inside to cell 19 where Dirty was for his first night in B.C.D.C except there was a 12" TV sitting on top of 2 up-side down milk crates against the wall and there was a small black radio on the shelf. Dirty's cell mate wasn't in the cell as he and Snuggles stepped in and tossed his belongings on the empty bunk.

"Come on, let's go fuck with Fatz and Bucky, they sleep right next door, Smurf probably in there too", said Snuggles leading the way as Dirty followed. "You can straighten your shit later".

The grill to Fatz and Bucky's cell was open but they had a wool blanket hanging down in front of the entrance so you couldn't see into the cell. Pushing the blanket to the side Snuggles ducked into the cell followed by Dirty. Once in the cell the first thing Dirty noticed was Bucky laying on the top bunk listening to a Walkman and Fatz sitting on the bottom bunk with no shirt on in just his boxers, drinking an orange can soda with a half empty pack of oatmeal iced cookies on his lap watching TV.

"Man, what the fuck, your greedy ass always eating Fatz", said Dirty laughing.

"White", said Fatz and Bucky almost simultaneously, sounding exuberant. "What's up nigga?", asked Fatz scooting over on his bunk so Dirty could sit down as Bucky jumped down and gave Dirty a hug while Snuggles made himself a seat out of the toilet.

"Ain't shit yo, just happy to be off that hammer, L section is a bitch", said Dirty hugging Bucky then sitting down next to Fatz. "Yo, where Smurf at?"

"He's probably sleep, I'ma go get um', I'll be right back", said Bucky slipping his boots on and disappearing under the wool blanket.

"Alright Bucky", said Dirty. "Yo, I never did find out exactly what happened with the house raid shit."

"Shit ain't much to it, the peoples kicked the door in round' Blu and Dot house while we were in there and found 3 guns, some pills, some smoke and some dope. Blu and Dot was upstairs. They locked everybody in the crib up. Lil' Gizmo tried to take the charges, but they weren't going for that shit. My brother and Squirrel would have got knocked too if they hadn't had just went around the corner to give Peaches some money for you", explained Snuggles.

Just then Bucky and Smurf appeared, one after the other, they slipped under the wool blanket and squeezed into the cell. "What's up Dirty?", said Smurf giving Dirty White dap.

"Ain't shit yo, what's up with you?"

"Same ol' same ol', A yo what's up with the smoke?", asked Smurf pulling out a pack of top paper from the pocket on his red Nautica sweatpants. Snuggles doubled over on the toilet lifted his black jeans pant leg pulling out a glassine bag containing what looked like a quarter ounce of marijuana from his sock.

"Here yo, roll something up so we can get Dirty right!", said Snuggles tossing the bag of weed to Smurf.

"Damn ya'll niggas got smoke, get the fuck outta here", exclaimed Dirty.

"Yeah yo, my brother and Squirrel be getting at us, sewing the shit into our clothes and gluing the shit in our tennis shoes. We catch every week, H.P nigga", said Snuggle breaking his mug then laughing.

"That's what I'm talking about", said Dirty impressed. "So, Squirrel and Fatty still holding shit down, huh?"

"Hell yeah yo, your cousin Block be hitting them niggas real heavy", replied Smurf passing Dirty a toothpick sized stick of marijuana rolled up in top paper.

"I heard that", said Dirty accepting the stick of marijuana then looking at it with bewilderment. "Yo, what the fuck is this? How a nigga gonna get high off this little shit?" Dirty was use to smoking blunts so the jail-house jay looked foreign to him, however everyone else in the cell knew that a couple of jail-house jays being passed amongst them would have all 5 of them twisted (high as a kite), so they all bust out laughing.

"Yo, you gonna be fucked up Cutty, trust me!", said Snuggles passing Dirty the lighter. "Spark up nigga!"

Dirty, accepted the lighter, put the jay between his lips, lit it, inhaled deeply and passed the lighter to Fatz who lit a jay and passed the lighter to Smurf who lit the jay he had.

"Yo take two and pass", said Snuggles speaking to everyone but really directing his words to Fatz knowing Fatz would smoke close to the whole jay before he passed it.

As the jays circulated around the cell, Dirty began to feel the effects of the weed as the munchies crept up on him causing him to pick up the iced oatmeal cookies that were sitting between him and Fatz on the bunkbed.

"Damn dis' smoke is alright", said Dirty between bites of the cookies. "Yo, what else ya'll got to eat?"

"Whatever you want nigga", said Bucky. "We got everything commissary got, matter fact why don't you make a hook up for us tonight Fatz?"

"what the fuck is a hook up?", asked Dirty

"A hook up is a couple cups of soup, kipper snack, steak fish, tuna, mayonnaise, cheese, boiled eggs, hot pickles, honey, hot sauce and onions all mixed together. Yo, it's good, you put it on crackers and smash", explained Fatz.

Frowning, Dirty said, "What kina shit is dat yo? Man, fuck all that just give me a couple Snickers and a Pepsi or something'".

"Yo, you'll like that hook up shit", said Bucky. Reaching under the bunk bed and sliding a big bag full of snacks out. Get what you want Dirty".

"Yo, don't take my iced oatmeal joints Dirty", said Fatz watching Dirty as he leaned forward and reached into the bag pulling out 2 Snickers and some red-hot potato chips and a Pepsi.

"Man, fuck Fatz yo, get what you want Dirty. Why don't your fat ass put on a shirt anyway, titties hanging out and shit looking like Big Shirley on What's Happening", said Snuggles, causing everyone to erupt with laughter.

"Hell yeah!", said Bucky co-signing Snuggles remark all the while laughing.

"Fuck you mean, hell yeah Bucky your lil' ugly ass always co-signin' shit", said Fatz as he stood up and started doing a little dance step shaking his upper body while snapping his fingers. "Yeah me, Fat Daddy get your guns out blow! Get your guns out". Everybody fell out laughing, they were feeling the effects of the weed.

"Yo, what's up with the phone?", asked Dirty once the laughing and clowning had died down. "You know I gotta call Peaches".

"Oh, that phone I was on when you came on the tier that's Hollins & Pulaski's phone. That's why I left it off the hook. You can go get it we the only ones use that joint unless a nigga asks us", stated Snuggles.

"Man, get the fuck outta here", said Dirty doubtfully.

"Shit, H.P. strong on this block nigga. Your cell buddy and his little squad got a phone, Murphy Homes and Lexington Terrace got one and the other joint is for stragglers and off brands, that's how it's goin' over this bitch", stated Snuggles.

"Yeah nigga we heard you wrecked a nigga over the phone your first day on the tier so you know we had to secure a phone, shit our man went to the hammer for 60 days behind one of those phones, we pose' to have one", interjected Smurf.

"And we got steel if a nigga act like he trying to go", stated Bucky flipping his mattress back and pulling out a jail house ice pick about the size of a kindergarten pencil that was rusty with a point on one end and masking tape wrapped around the opposite end.

"Yeah yo, we got 6 bangers", said Smurf, "I'll get you one before the night over".

"Cool yo, ya'll already know it's whatever, one for all, all for one, same way on the bricks", said Dirty standing up and giving his homies dap. "I'ma go call Peaches, alright yo?"

"Don't forget to hook up, Fatz", said Smurf leaving Bucky and Fatz cell also. "Alright ya'll, A tell Peaches to holler at Kim on Wheeler Ave. for me and get her to come see a nigga", said Fatz as Dirty and Snuggles one after another disappeared under the wool blanket out of Fatz view.

"I got cha Fatz", replied Dirty.

Dirty White having talked to his grandmother, Peaches and Mrs. Cookie on the telephone, decided to go straighten his belongings up in the cell he'd been assigned and then take a shower. When he reached the cell, there were two individuals in the cell smoking a cigarette, one had a peanut butter brown skin complexion with an athletic figure slightly thicker than Dirty and was sitting on the bottom bunk, the other one was black as tar, stout and had 8 cornrows in his hair and was sitting on the toilet.

"What's up Yo, you in here?", asked the adolescent on the bottom bunk.

“Yeah”, replied Dirty staring at the two adolescents trying to read them.

“I heard that, Yo my name is Nah, I sleep in here too, that’s my man Black”, said Nah motioning his head towards the adolescent sitting on the toilet. “What’s your name?”

“Dirty White”.

“Oh yeah, you were on the tier before and punished Lex over the phone, damn they just letting you off lock up?”, stated Nah.

“Yeah Yo”.

“Damn, well look I’ma go ahead and give you the cell so you can get yourself together, I’ll holler at you later. Come on Black, let my celli get the cell yo”, said Nah as him and Black stood and left the cell allowing Dirty to make his bed and put his stuff away.

After straightening his cell Dirty took a shower at the front of the bottom tier in the filthy one-man shower. Having showered, dried off and put deodorant on, he got dressed. Feeling fresh he went up the tier and picked up the Hollins & Pulaski phone and called Peaches and they talked for a while. Snuggles approached Dirty about an hour or so later.

“A Dirty, let me get a call into Tameka before lock-in Cutty”, said Snuggles.

Shaking his head up and down at Snuggles, he spoke into the phone. “Look Baby I love you, I’ma let Snuggles call Tameka, alright? Be strong and take care”, said Dirty.

“Okay Pookie, I love you too, make sure you call tomorrow and don’t get into no more trouble”, replied Peaches.

“Alright Baby, give me a kiss”, said Dirty.

“MMMMMTTTWWWAAA! I love you Antonio”.

“Love you too”, said Dirty hanging up the phone and handing it to Snuggles.

“Good looking out, yo go get your bowl from Fatz before he eats your shit Cutty”, said Snuggles as he dialed Tameka’s number.

“Bet yo!”, said Dirty strolling down the tier to Fatz and Bucky’s cell.

The wool blanket was pulled back and tied to the bunkbed so no one could see into the cell.

“Yo, where my bowl at Fatz?” asked Dirty.

“It’s right there”, said Fatz pointing to a plastic gallon jug that had been cut in half and turned into a bowl which was sitting on top of the TV with a roll of crackers next to it. Picking up the bowl Dirty squeezed onto the bottom bunk next to Fatz, sitting down as Fatz scooted over.

Hungry as an Ethiopian Dirty started eating the hook up while watching ‘The Simpsons’ with his homies.

“Yo, this shit alright Fatz”, said Dirty finishing the remains of the food in the bowl.

“I told you White”, said Bucky “Fatz be putting that shit together”.

“You know that fat ass nigga knows how to cook, all fat people can cook” added Smurf.

“Damn right, the fat daddy gotta know how to cook, got to be able to fill the dumpster”, said Fatz with a shit eating grin on his face as he used both of his hands to juggle his belly causing his homies to laugh.

It was nearing lock down when Snuggles finally hung up with Tameka and made his way to Fatz and Bucky’s cell.

“Yo they about to lock down, roll up a couple joints for Smurf, one for me and you for the cell, one for Fatz and Bucky, and one for Dirty”, said Snuggles entering the cell, throwing Smurf the bag containing the weed. As he untied the string that was holding the blanket to the bunk allowing it to fall back in front of the entrance to the cell.

“Yo, Dirty wait till after they take count before you spark up alright yo?”

“I heard that Cutty”.

“Lock down in 10 minutes, be in your assigned cell when the grills lock”, said a C.O racking the grills twice.

“Here yo,” said Smurf handing Bucky a jay for him and Fatz once he’d finished rolling them. He also handed Dirty one along with a banger/shank which he concealed in his dip.

“Yo, I’ll catch ya’ll in the A.M”, said Smurf giving everyone dap as he exited the cell.

“Yeah, I’m out too, holler in the morning”, said Snuggles giving his homies dap. “I put some food n your bunk for you. Oh, and Fatty said what’s up and him Squirrel got us this week on the smoke tip.”

“Alright yo, good looking out, I’ll holler at ya’ll tomorrow”, said Dirty to Fatz and Bucky as he followed Snuggles and Smurf out of the cell and walked next door to his own cell.

Entering his cell Dirty peeped Nah sitting on the bottom bunk with a yellow writing pad on his lap writing something which he put under his mattress when Dirty walked in the cell. Taking his sweatshirt off Dirty wrapped the banger Smurf had given him in it and threw it on his bunk real swift so Nah couldn’t peep it, then he stood at the toilet and relieved himself, wiped the toilet seat and washed his hands, out of habit.

“Yo, you got any matches?”, asked Dirty turning away from the sink and looking at Nah as the grill locked.

“Yeah, I got some”, replied Nah.

“I’ma need one after the C. O’s take count.”

“No problem yo. Ain’t you from Hollins & Pulaski?”, asked Nah.

“Yeah”, replied Dirty.

“You know a girl over there name Pumpkin, she light skin, phat as shit and bowlegged?”, asked Nah.

“Yeah, I know Pumpkin she lives three houses down from me, what’s up with her?”, asked Dirty.

“Naw ain’t nothing, I just be hollering at her, she be coming to see me that’s how I got alright with Snuggles and them, she asked me about you a while ago that’s all”, replied Nah.

“Oh yeah, Pumpkin cool, next time you holler at her tell her I said what’s up. Where you from anyway yo? I thought you lived over East.”

“Yeah Pumpkin’s grandmother lives on my block that’s how I met her. Yeah, I’m from East. I live on Barkley and 20th up by Greenmount”, replied Nah.

“Oh yeah, you might know my cousin Block with the gray Acura Legend and the burgundy 300z joint”, said Dirty.

“Hell yeah yo, Block is my muthafuckin nigga. Yo be giving my sisters and my mother money for me all the time. He a real nigga, I was hustling for him when they raided my man Black, upstairs house and locked us up. That’s your cousin for real?” exclaimed Nah getting all animated.

“Yeah, I’ma call him tomorrow and let you holla at him”, said Dirty as a C.O peeped in the cell and kept walking followed two seconds later by another C.O who repeated the first C.O moves.

“Do that yo, that’s my nigga for real. Yo, love me I’m telling you”, said Nah in an ecstatic tone.

“Yo, you think the C. O’s finished with count?”, asked Dirty.

“Yeah, what’s up?”, asked Nah.

“Let me get a match. You smoke trees?” Dirty asked Nah.

“Do I, shit like a chimney”, replied Nah.

“I got a little toothpick jay, you trying to go?”. Asked Dirty.

“No question, hold up”, said Nah getting off the bottom bunk and putting a wool blanket across the whole grill. “Here go the matches.”

Taking the matches Dirty put the jay between his lips, sat down on the toilet, lit it, inhaled deeply as he leaned back on the toilet, he tilted his head back and closed his eyes… as he blew out a cloud of smoke, then inhaled again, held the smoke in his lungs as he leaned forward and passed the jay to Nah. Nah taking the jay, hit it soft two times real quick, then took a nice long hit, nearly filling his lungs, he made a shallow choking sound as his shoulders heaved a little, a result of holding the smoke in his lungs and trying to suppress the cough.

When they finished smoking the jay Nah put a little baby powder in a sock and swung the sock in the air propelling the fragrance throughout the cell, then he wiped deodorant on the walls and lit a cigarette.

“Yo, you want one of these fugs?”, asked Nah offering Dirty a cigarette.

“Naw I’m cool, I don’t smoke cigarettes”, said Dirty grabbing a bag of Red Hot potato chips and a warm Pepsi off the top bunk when he stood up. Sitting back on the toilet, him and Nah watched ‘Martin’, then he kicked his shoes off and hopped up on the top bunk and laid back. Nah turned on his radio and him and Dirty listened to 92Q's 'Quiet Storm' until they dozed off to sleep.

Chapter 6

The following afternoon shortly after lunch Dirty was escorted to the visiting hall for an attorney visit, however instead of making a right once he'd reached the visiting area, he was directed to go left and placed in one of the lawyer booths. Stepping into the lawyer booth Dirty, whom was expecting to see a middle aged white man like Matlock or Perry Mason was surprised to see such a beautiful, young looking ebony toned sister. To him she looked like a goddess with her soft looking mahogany skin, almond brown sensual eyes, full luscious lips and shoulder length black hair that had streaks of almond dye in it which set off her eyes.

"Damn!", mumbled Dirty under his breath.

"Excuse me, did you say something?", asked the beautiful sister.

"Ah, naw, well ah, how are you doing?", asked Dirty trying to recuperate as he stumbled over his first few words.

“I’m okay and you?”, said the beautiful sister staring in Dirty eyes.

“I could be better”, said Dirty.

“I’m sure you could. Well my name is Patricia Smallwood, I’m with the office of Public defenders, I’ve been assigned to your case, you may have a seat Mr. Lord.”

“Oh yeah, thanks”, said Dirty, still mesmerized by his attorney. As he was sitting down he could see the ample cleavage peeking out of the red silk blouse she wore with the first two buttons unfastened, causing him to get a mild erection.

Damn I been locked up too long, thought Dirty as he tried to think of something to get his mind out of the gutter.

“Well, first I apologize for not making it to see you sooner but I have a very hectic case load”, said Patricia Smallwood apologetically

“I understand”, replied Dirty.

“Okay with that said, I must say this is a very bizarre case, I spoke to Pamela Watson and from what I gathered the victim Elijah Watson was her son, your best friend and was actually shot by the other victim in this case, Shabazz Carpenter. How is it that you were charged with both homicides?”, asked Patricia looking up from the papers she’d been fumbling with.

“I don’t know”, replied Dirty.

“well, how about you give me your side of the story”, stated Patricia.

“What chu mean give you my side of the story?”, asked Dirty with a puzzled look on his face.

“Mr. Lord, first let me assure you that nothing we discuss will be used against you in anyway, you have to trust me to some degree and help me make a defense for you, understand?”, stated Patricia as she smiled attempting to dis-alarm her client.

“Yeah, I guess I understand”, replied Dirty.

“Okay, well can you please give me your side of the story?”

“Alright, the dude who got killed came around my way and tried to rob my homies and I saw it and came to their aid, the dude started shooting back, Mookie got killed and that dude got killed, but I didn’t kill Mookie and that’s my word. I was just being a true homie aiding my homeboys”, explained Dirty as he told the public defender the half-truth.

“I see, so you didn’t shoot Mookie who is Elijah Watson, right?”, asked Patricia.

“Right, Mookie was behind me when he got shot.”

“Okay, how about the other young man, Shabazz Carpenter, did you shoot him?”

“Yeah, I shot him but he was shooting too, I was just holding my own, you know defending myself”, said Dirty trying to justify his role in the homicide.

“I understand, but unfortunately there is no self-defense law in the state of Maryland, so the best we can hope for is a manslaughter case with Carpenter and I'm pretty sure the Watson homicide will be a knoll prosequi or dismissed if…"

"What's pross-a-what?", interjected Dirty cutting his Public Defender off in mid-sentence.

"Knoll Prosequi is when there isn't enough evidence for the case to stand trial on that particular count or charge", explained Patricia.

"Oh okay, so I'll beat Mookie's murder and get a manslaughter for the other dude?", asked Dirty.

"No, not exactly, we can try to get the prosecutor to agree to dismiss or knoll pros the Watson count if you'd agree to plead down to manslaughter in the Carpenter case", explained Patricia.

"Then what?", asked Dirty.

"Then being as though this is your first brush with the judicial system we could get you a deal and you could very well be home in a couple of years, which looks a lot better than life without parole which is what you're facing for both homicides as it stands", said Patricia hating to have to reveal the horrible truth to the handsome young man, as he sat there staring at her with his adorable eyes.

"What about probation?", asked Dirty in a hopeful tone.

"Being honest Mr. Lord, you don't stand a chance of getting probation for such a hideous crime, in fact if you get a single digit sentence consider yourself blessed", stated Patricia flatly.

Damn that sounds so harsh, she thought knowing she was only being honest, though trying to clear her conscious she spoke again before Dirty had a chance to rebuttal a word. “Look on the bright side Mr. Lord, you’re still very young and have a lot of life left to live”, said Patricia trying to sting out of her words while giving the handsome young man a positive way to look at the bleak situation.

“Yeah, I understand”, said Dirty knowing he was in between a rock and a hard place, the infamous catch 22. “Well, see what you can do for me Ms. Smallwood, thanks okay?”

“No problem, I’ll do what I can just try to stay out of trouble, you don’t need to go on segregation anymore, okay?”, said Patricia feeling sympathy for Antonio Lord.

“Yes Ma’am”, replied Dirty.

“Well I’ll see you again as soon as I know something. Oh, plus you have a court appearance on October 13th at 9:30, okay?”, Patricia stated as she stood, turning her back to her client, she bent over to pick her briefcase up and gathered her belongings.

Good god almighty, she wearing them black slacks, MMMM look how she setting that ass out like she doing it on purpose, she a stallion for real, she even phatter than Mary J. Blige, I’d have a ball with her, thought Dirty as she finally straightened up and waved to him with her elegant manicured hands.

“Be good Mr. Lord”, said Patricia exiting the lawyer booth.

“I’ma try!”, said Dirty.

Once Dirty was escorted back to T-section, he called his grandmother, Peaches and Ms. Cookie and informed them that he'd had an attorney visit and what had been said, then he smoked a little weed with his homies and ran the news down to them, played a couple games of spades(cards), took a nice shower and went to sleep.

Chapter 7

It had been nine months since Antonio Lord a.k.a Dirty White was arrested and sent to the Baltimore City Detention Center on charges of double homicide. Over the course of those desolated months he'd grown to be a no non-sense predator and violence became as easy as breathing.

Aside from the incident he was involved in with Lex, he had also been involved in two other separate incidents. The first of the two incidents evolved after two adolescents were caught cheating in a spades card game, trying to swindle Dirty and his partner Nah out of the two packs of cigarettes they'd bet on the game. Having caught the opposing team cheating Dirty and Nah, looked at each other with frowns on their faces and understanding the unspoken they both whipped out shanks and repeatedly stabbed the two adolescents. One of the adolescents had to be rushed to Shock Trauma for medical attention having almost died from excessive hemorrhaging. The other adolescents, wounds were less severe resulting in him only going to the jail infirmary.

The second incident evolved when an adolescent sitting next to Dirty on a visit unconsciously mumbled that Peaches was "Phat as shit". Dirty having overheard the disrespectful comment waited until they had returned to T-section, then roughly two hours later he caught the dude on the phone and walked right up on him and split his head with a vicious blow from the mop ringer he clutched in his hand. Using all his might he swung the mop ringer, Crack! The impact of the blow caused the adolescent to drop to the ground unconscious as blood oozed from the gapping gash in his head. As he laid there shaking involuntarily Dirty struck him again in his face with the mop ringer.

“Bitch ass nigga”, spat Dirty walking away calm and collected.

Miraculously Dirty managed to avoid being apprehended by the C. O’s in either incident and remained on T-section for the duration of his stay at B.C.D.C where he ruled with an iron fist. His homeboys, Smurf, Snuggles, Bucky and Fatz had all been released due to a technical defect with the warrant issued for the house raid. The warrant was for 2013 West Booth Street instead of 2113 West Booth Street. Due to the error, the state was forced to dismiss all charges.

■■

Dirty cell mate and new-found comrade Nah had received his sentence of six years and was transferred to M.C.T.C in Hagerstown, Maryland. With his homies and Nah no longer on T-section Dirty pretty much rolled solo, but even alone he remained the uncontested ‘shot caller’ on T-section.

Finally, after nine intense months of prepping at the gladiator school known as "City Jail", the time had come for Dirty to graduate to the actual gladiator pit, prison. He was due to appear in court the following morning where he'd be sentenced to the seven years he'd agreed to accept for the murder case of Shabazz Carpenter which had been reduced to manslaughter.

I wonder where they going to send me. I wonder how shits going to be, who I'ma know... then again fuck it, it don't matter, anywhere I go I'ma put in work and carve my name in the scenery. Like Blu said, "either you the predator or the prey", and make no mistake about it I'ma always be the predator, thought Dirty as he laid on his bunk looking up at the bunk over top of him when his thoughts were interrupted by a love dedication on 92Q's Quiet Storm playing on the radio in his cell.

"This is Peaches, I'd like to give a love dedication to my husband Dirty White over City Jail, I love you Baby, be strong, we'll see you in court tomorrow", exclaimed Peaches sounding like a mature woman instead of a sixteen-year old teenager.

I love you too Boo, thought Dirty as he rolled over on to his side attempting to get comfortable on his bunk, closing his eyes he attempted to get some rest before court in the morning.

"Lord, Court!", shouted a C.O from the top of the tier having opened the grill in Dirty cell.

"Alright Man!", retorted Dirty as he came to, still a bit disoriented having only slept for five hours he stood up and got himself together.

After getting himself together Dirty and two adolescents off T-section were escorted to the bullpens on the ground level of B.C.D.C where they were given brown paper bags that contained their breakfast of two stale pieces of bread, one boiled egg, a carton of milk and a small orange. Once in the bullpen they tarried around until the transportation C. O's arrived. Two hours later, transportation arrived and the C. O's called off a list of names. As the inmates heard their names called they stepped out of the bullpens, were searched, then put in a three-piece restraint set. Once all the inmates were suited in the restraints, they were escorted to the van.

The journeys to and from court in the caged van were down right deplorable, however there was a bittersweet side to the journeys, that being, being able to glance out of the caged windows seeing the streets of Baltimore and especially being able to lull at the many females of all shapes, colors and sizes as they made their ways through the streets on route to work, school, home, etc.

“Oh my god yo, you see shorty with that green skirt on”, shouted a light skinned inmate on the first row looking to his left as he mashed his forehead against the metal caging trying to get a better view.

“Man, shorty phat as shit, MMM MMM MMM”.

“She aint fuckin' with shorty right there in them blue jeans, look at the ass on that woman yo”, exclaimed a young-looking inmate on the row in front of Dirty.

And so, went the conversation for the entire ride, there was a comment made by someone on the van about nearly every woman the van passed in route to the court house, even though only a third, if that many of the women were dimes, attractive and voluptuous bodies.

"Wooo! Man, look at shorty right there", said the older brown skin inmate sitting next to Dirty as the van past a woman who favored Adina Howard standing on the corner of the Old Post Office Court house building.

Finally, we here, thought Dirty who was stuffed between a musty old dope fiend, a foul breath obese man and wanted badly to get out of the sardine can van.

The transportation officer navigated the van into the underground parking area, parked and he and his partner unlocked the van door enabling the inmates to exit the van. Soon as all the inmates were out of the van the transportation guards lead them into the court house towards the metal detector to be uncuffed and searched before being placed in the bullpens.

I wish this clumsy motherfucka would hurry up and get these tight ass handcuffs and shackles off me, thought Dirty squinting his eyes and mugging the C.O as he fumbled with his keys before finally uncuffing Dirty. Having uncuffed Dirty, the C.O patted him down, had him take his shoes off, searched them then directed him to step through the metal detector after he handed him his shoes.

"Go ahead and step through the metal detector and stand right there beside officer Dickerson", said the transportation guard motioning to a tall slender C.O. Officer Dickerson was standing in front of a wall that made up the lower part of the Control Center booth. The Control Center booth sat up several inches off the ground thus enabling the C. O's in the booth to look down on the inmates as they were escorted into the holding cell area through the plexiglass window that made up the upper part of the booth.

The holding cell area consist of four bullpens that formed a L-shape. There was a bullpen for women and a juvenile bullpen along the left-hand wall of the corridor which connected to the men and federal bullpens along the back wall.

After all the inmates had passed through the metal detector they were placed in one of the bullpens. Dirty being an adolescent was directed to go into the juvenile bullpen along with three other adolescents, two of whom slept on T-section with Dirty, the other having slept on R-section.

The juvenile bullpen was extremely clean in comparison to the bullpens at B.C.D.C. Once the holding cell was secured Dirty, taking off his jacket off and turning it into a makeshift pillow, he laid it on the concrete and sat down. Having made himself comfortable he laid down on his back staring up at the ceiling with his arms folded across his chest. Just as he blocked the voices of the other adolescents out and closed his eyes the bullpen door opened and he was called for court.

“Lord, let’s go buddy they just called for you upstairs”, said the C.O standing in the doorway of the bullpen.

“Alright, here I come”, replied Dirty as he rose, swung his feet around, slid his shoes back on and stood.

Walking over to the sink he pushed the water button then cupped his right hand under the faucet catching the cold water he splashed his face twice, wiped his face with his hands, then he cupped a little water in his hand and drank it, swishing it around in his mouth for a second before spitting it into the toilet and walking towards the bullpen door. “I'm ready”.

“Sit right there so I can put these shackles and handcuffs on you”, stated the C.O. pointing to a concrete slab in the center of the holding cells area.

Stepping over the concrete slab Dirty was shackled once he sat down, then standing he was handcuffed and escorted through a door, passing several doors and foggy tinted window panes on each side of the hallway before finally coming to a set of elevators. A minute or so passed by before the elevator doors opened. Stepping onto the elevator along with Dirty the C.O pushed the number six on the panel as the elevator door closed and the elevator proceeded to the sixth floor.

Reaching the sixth floor, the elevator doors opened as the hallways were almost identical to downstairs, yet the only difference is that this hallway was filled with family and friends of the women and men due to appear in court today. In the distance, just down the hall Dirty could see his immediate family (excluding his parents), and his friends waiting in front of the courtroom he was scheduled to appear in, all there to support him. Upon seeing him everybody stood up and began smiling, whistling, cheering, etc.... as if he'd just returned from a war. The show of support warmed him causing him to smile.

“White we love you!”, screamed Peaches and her friends.

“Keep your head up Cutty!”, remarked another of his supporters.

“Hold your head up Baby, it’s gonna be alright”, exclaimed a feminine voice.

Everybody made some kind of affectionate remark as Dirty nodded his head in response all the while smiling as he entered the courtroom. Dirty was led into the courtroom and to the table beside where Patricia Smallwood was seated looking stunning in a two-piece cream skirt set with a pearl white satin shirt.

“Good morning Antonio, how are you feeling today?”, asked Patricia as Dirty was being unhandcuffed.

“I’m alright I guess”, replied Dirty staring at his public defender with lustful admiration. *Man, she fine,* thought Dirty.

“That’s good, you can have a seat right here”, said Patricia patting the seat next to her.

Before sitting Dirty glanced towards the back of the courtroom, seeing all the pews were packed and people were even standing, all here on his behalf caused a surge of pride to sweep over him. As he sat down he glanced up at the white ceiling above his head and mumbled a few words.

“Rest in peace Mookie! Slim dead, I got his bitch ass yo!”

“Antonio, are you okay?”, asked his public defender having heard him mumble something inaudible.

“Yeah, I was just thinking out loud, I’m cool”, replied Dirty.

“Okay, do you understand what’s going to take place in a few minutes?”, asked Patricia as she swirled around in her chair facing her client.

“Yeah, I’ma plead guilty and get seven years for manslaughter, right?”, stated Dirty.

“Well for the most part yes, but you’re also…”

“Everybody please stand”, said a middle aged white female standing in front of the judge’s booth as she addressed the people in the courtroom.

Everyone stood as the judge entered the courtroom. The judge was a white man in his mid-fifties. He was frail and the black robe he wore engulfed him, he looked almost like an elf as he sat in the enormous brown leather chair.

“You may be seated”, said the court clerk as she sat down next to the stenographer.

“State of Maryland verses Antonio Lord case docket number 943774539A. Mr. Lord has been charged with two counts of murder in the first degree. To my understanding a plea has been agreed upon. Mr. Livingston would you like to address the courts?”, stated the judge as the prosecutor stood to address the court.

“Yes, your honor, the state of Maryland is here to offer a plea to the defendant in this case, Antonio Lord. The plea is as follows; the first-degree murder of Elijah Watson would be knoll pros, while the first-degree murder of Shabazz Carpenter would be reduced to manslaughter. Manslaughter carries a maximum sentence of ten years. The maximum sentence would be imposed, suspending three years to be served on probation upon the defendant's release. The state feels this would be a sufficient penalty enabling the defendant to pay his debt to society and be rehabilitated", stated the prosecutor.

"I see, okay, now would you like to address the court Ms. Smallwood?", asked the judge.

"Yes, your honor", replied Patricia Smallwood as her and Dirty stood to address the court. "My client and I agree with said plea and I'd like to ask that your honor take into account while passing judgement on my client and sentencing him that at the time of the incident he was only fifteen years old and prior to this incident had never had a single brush with the law, not even so much as truancy."

Nodding his head up and down slightly the judge spoke to Dirty. "Mr. Lord, please state your entire name, date of birth and address for the record".

"My name is Antonio Marcus Lord. My date of birth is 7-21-78 and my address is 2008 West Hollins Street, Baltimore Maryland".

"Do you understand the charges set against you Mr. Lord?", asked the judge.

"Yes"

"Have you been promised anything outside of this plea?", asked the judge.

“No”, replied Dirty.

“And how do you wish to plea to the agreed upon count of manslaughter?” questioned the judge.

“I plead guilty”, stated Dirty suppressing the lump in his throat.

“Do you understand that by pleading guilty you waive all rights to appeal?”

“Yes”.

“Do you also understand that you could have selected to go to trial where you could have chosen to have had a jury of your peers or judge to oversee your case where the prosecutor would have had to prove beyond a reasonable doubt that you committed the crimes you’ve been accused of?”, questioned the judge.

“Yes, I understand.”

“The defendant Antonio Lord has agreed that he clearly understands his rights and has pleaded guilty to the count of manslaughter. I accept the plea and hereby sentence the defendant Antonio Lord to ten years suspending three years which is to be served on probation upon his scheduled release date. The defendant will also be giving three years for the handgun…”

“What does he mean three more years?”, asked Dirty frowning at his public defender.

“SSSH, it’s a concurrent sentence so it’s only seven years Antonio”, explained Patricia Smallwood in a hushed tone as she grabbed Dirty hand in her own trying to calm him without disrespecting the courts.

“…I hope you will use this time to further your education so you maybe a productive member of society when you are released Mr. Lord. Court is hereby adjourned”, stated the judge as he banged the gravel on his desk top.

Chapter 8

Got damn! That was a long motherfuckin' ride, but I'm glad to be up out of D.O.C, thought Dirty as the Bluebird (Prison bus) pulled up to a fourteen feet high electrical fence topped with razor wire which had an identical fence about thirty feet behind it.

The first fence slowly slid open with a loud clicking sound allowing the Bluebird to move forward once the fence had completely opened. The second fence was still secure so the bus had to stop in between the two fences. After the first fence was secured, the transportation officers checked their guns into the guard tower which was about twenty feet high and sat to the left of the bus.

Having checked their guns in, the C. O's climbed back aboard the Bluebird as the second electrical razor wired fence slid open, allowing the Bluebird to pull into the huge college campus like compound at the Maryland Correctional Training Center in Hagerstown. Parking in front of Receiving and Discharge the transportation C. O's from Maryland Reception Diagnostics Correctional Center began to take the 10 inmates designated to M.C.T.C off the bus. Piling them into the reception area where there were at least twenty white racist looking hillbilly correctional officers standing about.

A few C. O's were posted up in front of several large caged storage bins, while a few leaned against the waist high counter. The inmate restraints were unlocked, then they were directed to go to the back of the reception area and prepare to be strip searched.

"Okay ya'll boys find yourself a table and take them clothes off and put them on the table to be search", said a potbelly redneck.

Each inmate complied with the instructions and made their way to one of the twenty tables, stripped and placed their clothing and shoes on the table. The clothing and shoes were searched as the inmates were directed to open their arms above their head, turn around lift their feet one at a time, turn back around lift their testicles, squat and cough.

After every inmate was thoroughly searched they were instructed to get dressed, given their identification cards and a brown paper bag containing their necessities.

"You boys who just arrived grab a bedroll right there and go to unit six. Returnees you know where you sleep. Make sure you don't walk on the grass and don't be eye fuckin' our women either, now get…", stated the redneck C.O as he pointed to the door through which they'd entered and we departed.

"Yo, how we get to unit six?", asked a young-looking brother once the inmates had exited R&D.

"I'm in seven, I'll show ya'll", replied an older inmate who was wearing a black, green and red Kufi.

Following the older inmate in the Kufi they walked to the end of the R&D building and made a left. Walking pass the kitchen and a guard station they made their way down a tar covered path. To their left was an eight feet high fence that lead to several vocational shops and to their right a few steps down was several buildings; education, the Chaplin, medical, central control and commissary. To their left there was six housing units that made up a horse shoe… Across from unit six there was a large gymnasium, behind which sat housing unit seven, next to which was the courtyard.

As the inmates neared unit one, two inmates who had returned from court made a left and walked in that direction. The remaining eight inmates continued to make their way across the compound. At night M.C.T.C looked like a decent college with its well cared for green grass and freshly trimmed shrubs. It appeared to be a calm and peaceful environment, but in reality, the appearance was but an illusion. M.C.T.C or the new jail as it was referred to by convicts was a gladiator pit where only the strong survived.

“That’s six right there”, said the older inmate in the Kufi pointing to the building they were nearing. “Walk down there, make a right and you’ll be in six.”

“Good looking out Ock”, said the youngster who’d asked for directions.

“No problem”, replied the older inmate as he continued down the walkway that lead to unit seven.

Reaching unit six all of the inmates climbed the few concrete stairs in front of the building and entered it where they were met by three hillbillies C.O.’s in the hallway in front of B&C tiers dayrooms.

"Allen, Smith, Martin", you come with me ya'll sleep on B-tier", said one of the C.O.'s as the three inmates followed him turning left, after a few steps they made a right and disappeared.

"Johnson, you're on A-tier", stated another C.O. as inmate Johnson was lead in the same direction the other inmates had just traveled straight to A-tier.

"Lord, Bullock, Colts, you come with me, ya'll sleep on C-tier", said the dirty blond head C.O. who lead the three adolescents to C-tier, just around the corner in the opposite direction of where the other inmates went.

"Green you're in cell four, Lord you're in fourteen and Colts you're in twenty-three. You all sleep on the bottom tier", stated the C.O. as he turned to the control box to the inmates right and opened the three cells.

Stepping on the tier the inmates walked through a large grill, across a small landing and down six concrete steps to the bottom tier where their cells were located.

Dirty's cell was the third from the end of the tier. Reaching the cell, soon as he stepped in the door it was immediately secured with a loud clang.

"What's up Joe?", asked the onyx black adolescent lying on the bottom bunk as he sat up.

"Ain't shit Yo", replied Dirty tossing his hygiene bag and bedroll on the top bunk, sizing his new cell mate up.

“Where you from young?”, asked Dirty’s new cell mate.

“Hollins and Pulaski!”, replied Dirty.

“What’s that East or West B-more?”

“It’s West, why? Where you from yo?”

“I’m from D.C. Joe, over South East, I got locked up in P.G county though”.

“I heard that, what’s your name yo?”, asked Dirty out of curiosity.

“Everybody call me Go-Go, what they call you?”

“Dirty, how long you been up here yo?”

“About eighteen months, I only…”

“You should know my man Nah then, he came up here like two or three months ago, but I don’t know…”

“Yeah, I know Nah. Youngin’ be going hard, he sleeps in…damn hold up”, said Go-Go as he shouted out the door breaking the silence on the tier. “A Nah… Yo, Nah come to the door… A Nah, I know you ain’t sleep yo.”

“Yo, who dat”, replied Nah not noticing the voice immediately.

“Fuck you mean who that nigga you forgot my voice yo”, shouted Dirty.

“Yo Dirty, what’s up nigga? I ain’t forgot your voice yo it’s just one o’clock in the morning and you woke a nigga up hollering it's all good though. Damn my nigga up here now, yeah Son!!", exclaimed Nah.

"What's up though?", asked Dirty.

"Ain't shit you know me just keepin' it gutter!"

"Yeah yeah yo, I was hopin'..."

"Quiet the fuck down before I come snatch a few of you's out them cells and rush you's asses over to lock up!", shouted a hillbilly C.O from the top of the tier.

"Fuck you whore!", shouted an unknown adolescent.

"Suck a fat dick you redneck bitch!", shouted another.

"Look Dirty these crackers be on some shit so go ahead and step back, we'll rap in the morning, ain't no sense going in the hammer for no bullshit", explained Nah shouting over the adolescents who were cussing the C.O. out.

"Make sure you get up for breakfast Dirty".

"Cool, in the morning yo!", shouted Dirty as the tier lights came on and the C.O. stepped on the tier silencing the ranting.

"Now quiet the fuck down and I mean it", shouted the C.O. as Dirty stepped away from the cell door to make his bunk at which time his cell mate spoke.

"Young, Nah your man for real?", asked Go-Go causing Dirty's alarm button to go off, he looked at Go-Go with his eyes squinted and his head tilted slightly to the right.

“Yeah that’s my man, why? What’s up?”, asked Dirty looking at Go-Go with indifference plastered across his face.

“Nah, youngin just a zap out, he be leanin’ on these niggas and ain’t got no problem swinging that knife that’s all”, informed Go-Go trying to put his celli on point.

“Oh, yeah I’m hip to Nah, we were partners over the city jail, that’s my dog, for real!”, said Dirty cracking a half ass smile.

Having finished making his bed he kicked his shoes off, pulled his pants off, folded them, placed them at the foot of his bed and hopped up on the top bunk.

“You can cut the light out when you ready. The buttons on the left”, said Go-Go.

The rectangular light fixture was located directly above Dirty’s head. Being exhausted because of the nearly three-hour ride to Hagerstown from Baltimore Dirty spotted the off and on button on the light, reaching up he pushed it, turning the light off. Making himself as comfortable as he could on the thin mattress, pulling the top sheet and wool blanket up over his shoulder he closed his eyes and drifted into a light sleep lying on his left side.

The following morning Dirty walked to breakfast with Nah, Black and several other adolescents he knew. There were at least thirty adolescents on C-tier in unit six from over B.C.D.C that he knew who all held him in high regard. Once all the adolescents reached and entered the mess hall(kitchen), they were directed by the C.O. to either go left or right. Nah, Black, Dirty and roughly twenty-five other adolescents wound up on the left-hand side of the mess hall. Halfway through the line Dirty was confronted by an older convict who was sitting at the second table away from the line.

“A lil' homie with the gray D.O.C shirt on”, said the older convict looking at Dirty who was dressed in clothes given to all new inmates.

“Where you from?”

“Who me?”, asked Dirty pointing to himself.

“Yeah, where you from lil' homie?”, asked the older convict.

“I'm from Hollins and Pulaski yo, why? What's up?”, asked Dirty staring at the older convict stone faced as he tried to place who he was.

“Yo, who dat?”, questioned Nah looking back at Dirty he whispered, “You know I got a banger right now, with me and I'm for whatever.”

“A I'm Antmoe, I'ma holla at you in the yard later”, replied the older convict.

“What you mean you gonna holla at me later, what's up? You can holla at me now Slim”, stated Dirty squinting his eyes and curling up the corner of his mouth staring at the old head completely stopping in line.

“What's up Dirty?”, asked Nah ready to put in work as about eleven other adolescents stood still in line.

"Nah Youngblood it ain't like that, we from the same block. You know Cookie? She asked me to look out for you if you come this way. I know Antonette and Ms. Gladice also. Your grandmother use to babysit me when I was a kid", explained Antmoe respecting how the youngster from his neighborhood was ready to get down for his if necessary.

"Oh alright, I'll holla at cha later then", replied Dirty nodding his head once as he moved forward in line.

Shorty must be a thorough lil' nigga cause several of them hoppers looked like they were ready to roll with him if it come to it, thought Antmoe as his row was directed by a C.O. to depart from the kitchen.

Dirty, Nah, Black and an adolescent name Mike-Mike from Nah and Black's neighborhood all sat at the same table to eat their breakfast of waffles with syrup, oatmeal and butter and drank their milk, orange juice and coffee.

"Yo they feed a nigga good up this bitch", said Dirty, use to the horrible food at B.C.D.C, as he put another spoon of the waffles in his mouth.

"No bullshit this shit way better than over the jail", replied Nah agreeing with Dirty White.

"Yo, you know the old head you were just talking to?", interjected Mike-Mike out of curiosity as he looked at Dirty.

"Naw, I don't know yo, but he named my godmother, grandmother, and my grandmother's daughter all by name so he must know me or know about me, why?

What's up?", asked Dirty with a puzzled look on his face.

"Yo, you know slim Jive run all them old heads. He be catching blow and shit, yo a thorough O.G for real. If we would've jumped out there them old heads would've tried to murder us up in here", explained Mike-Mike in between spoons of oatmeal not out of fear but simply trying to put his niggas on point.

"Man, fuck them old heads", interjected Nah. "Me and Dirty will punish them old niggas like we did them niggas who tried to cheat us over the jail. Huh Dirty?"

"Ain't no question, you know I aint got no picks Cutty", replied Dirty.

"Yo, them niggas zap out Mike-Mike", interjected Black looking at Mike-Mike when the C.O. directed their row to stand and exit the mess hall.

Having ate, all the adolescents walked back to unit six and locked in their respected cells where they remained until lunch, unless they had a job or went to school in the A.M... After lunch, the inmates locked back down until 12:30 which was recreation time.

Prior to going to the yard while in the dayroom waiting to be called out Nah pulled Dirty to the side and slipped him a rusty old butter knife with a well sharpened blade that had probably been stolen out of the kitchen years ago.

"Here yo, case shit jumps off", explained Nah as he pulled the shank out his dip and handed it to his partner. "Keep it tucked Dog!"

“Bet yo, Good looking’ out!”, replied Dirty as he put the shank in his waistband and pulled the strings, on the gray Russell sweat pants Nah had given him at lunch time, tight and tied them in a knot holding the shank in place.

“C-tier rec!”, shouted the C.O. working C-tier for the 7-3 shift as he opened the tier grill.

Several adolescents scurried out of the unit in hopes of getting some weights or a spot on one of the basketball courts. Nah and Dirty just casually strolled to the yard as Dirty observed and took in his surroundings.

Stepping into the yard he noticed there were eight C.O.’s lingering around the entrance to the yard, beyond them he could see a basketball court. To the left of the basketball court there was a baseball diamond next to which sat a weight pit complete with several weight benches and dozens of weights (pig iron). There was also a waist high concrete section that held a toilet, a urinal and a water fountain just to the left of the weight pit. Across the three-foot wide track, also to the left of the weight pit sat a yellowish colored concession stand where ice cream, snacks and beverages could be purchased with canteen tickets sold on commissary.

Crossing the gravel track Nah treated Dirty to a pint of vanilla ice cream from the concession stand and brought himself a butter pecan ice cream, then they proceeded to stroll the yard, kicking it, while they ate their ice creams. They passed two more basketball courts one after another to their right, further down in the far-left hand corner of the yard there was a huge gun tower to their left and another baseball diamond to their right.

“Yo, them motherfuckers got pumps and some more shit up on that gun tower”, exclaimed Dirty as he marveled up at the two redneck C.O.’s posted up on the tower with pump action shotguns.

“Yeah, this the big house, Dirty. They aint letting no nigga escape up out of here if they can help it”, stated Nah, continuing around the track they came to and passed a sand clad volleyball court, dug into the greenery of the large field, sitting on the far-right hand corner of the yard.

“Yo, they out that bitch playing volleyball like they on a beach, with no shoes on and shit. What the fuck kind of shit is that?”, asked Dirty laughing at the volleyball players.

“That’s how them crazy ass white boys and homo’s’ is Yo”, explained Nah referring to the predominately white group of men who sprinkled with a few black homosexuals were playing volleyball in the sand pit.

They continued strolling around the track passing another baseball diamond to their left before turning the corner leading back to the first basketball court one saw upon entering the court yard. Nearing the basketball court Antmoe called Dirty.

“Hey Antonio, let me holla at you for a minute”, shouted Antmoe approaching Dirty and Nah as they slowed down.

“What’s up yo, asked Dirty sizing Antmoe up, *Yo, a big dude, but I’ll put this knife in his ass quick,* thought Dirty as Antmoe neared him and Nah.

“Aint too much young blood. What’s going on with you?”, replied Antmoe in a smooth laid-back tone.

“Aint shit just chillin’ with my partner”, replied Dirty flatly.

“I feel ya, you cool though, you need anything?”, asked Antmoe.

“Nah, I’m cool, I don’t need shit!”, stated Dirty leery of accepting anything from anyone he didn’t know due to the stories he’d heard about convicts trying to bait you in to rape you by offering you stuff.

“Have you spoke to Cookie or your grandmother yet?”, asked Antmoe sensing what the youngster was probably thinking.

“Nah I ain’t been on the phone yet. I can’t call until tonight, why?”, asked Dirty trying to figure Antmoe out as Nah continued to stare Antmoe up and down, having tossed his ice cream in the grass Nah now had his hand under his shirt clutching the shank in his dip.

“Look, when you get on the phone just ask your grandmother, mother or Cookie about me alright Antonio?”, Antmoe said.

“Alright cool! And you can call me Dirty yo”, he stated in a stern voice.

“No problem Dirty, be easy and don’t forget to ask your peeps about me and tell them I send my regards", said Antmoe as he turned around walking away.

I like shorty style. He kind of reminds me of myself when I was his age, thought Antmoe as he returned to where he'd been to finish watching the basketball game with his partner Lucky Al'.

"What's up with shorty?", asked Lucky Al' once Antmoe was again standing next to him.

"I don't know. He seems like he cool, and on the surface, he seems like a thorough cat and so far, I like him", stated Antmoe shrugging his shoulders, flipping the palms of his hands up, and tilting his head to the right on a slight angle.

While Lucky Al' and Antmoe were discussing Dirty, Dirty and Nah were discussing Antmoe.

"Yo, what's up with slim", asked Nah.

"I don't know, but I'ma find out tonight when I get on the phone", rebutted Dirty.

"Yeah yo, do that so we know what's up, he might know the chump you killed and be trying to rock you to sleep so he can bring you a move", said Nah. "Shit, if that's the case we going to have to bless his ass and send him up and out of here".

"No doubt Cutty, no doubt!", exclaimed Dirty smiling devilishly.

At 2:30 the yard was closed and all the inmates returned to their tiers and lingered around until 2:45 when they had to lock back in their cells until dinner. Later that evening after dinner Dirty managed to get a fifteen-minute call. He called his grandmother. There was an answer on the third ring.

“Hello, how may I…”

“You have a collect call from ‘Antonio Lord’ at the Maryland Correctional Training Center. If you accept this call do not use three way or call waiting features or you will be disconnected, to accept dial one now… thank you, said the automated computerized voice.

“Antonio?” “You there?”, asked Gladice having pushed one to accept her grandson’s call.

“Hey Ma Ma! How’s my loving grandmother doing?”, asked Dirty smiling.

“I’m alright child, how about you Pumpkin?”, replied his grandmother.

“I’m okay, holding on with both hands, I got transferred yesterday, now I’m up Hagerstown”.

“How is it up there?”, questioned his concerned grandmother.

“It’s cool so far, I know a few people”, he replied, then as an after-thought he asked his grandmother about Antmoe. “Oh, Ma Ma do you know a dude name Antmoe? He said he knows you, Ms. Cookie and Antonette and he told me to give you his regards.”

“Antmoe, Antmoe… Oh yeah Anthony Jenkins I use to watch him before you were even born. He’s been in jail for nearly twenty years and he still sends me a card every Christmas, Easter and Birthday. Let him know I said Hi and take care”, said Gladice.

“Alright, A MA MA, I need you to write my new address down, you got a pen and paper?”

“Hold on Pumpkin”, said his grandmother fumbling around in the kitchen drawer where she kept her coupons retrieving a pen and some paper. “Okay Pumpkin what’s the address”.

“It’s 18800 Roxbury Road Hagers…”

“Slow down child, spell Roxbury”

After Dirty spelled the address out for his grandmother he ran down a couple of things he needed her to get.

“I already got most of the stuff in my room and all my clothes are like new so I’m only going to need some new underclothes, shoes, boots and shower shoes.”

“Child, you got seventy-eight pair of shoes up in that room of yours, you don’t need no more shoes”, refuted his grandmother.

“Just tell Bloc to get them for me Ma Ma”, pleaded Dirty.

“Okay child, Oh, speaking of Marvin he said call him if you need anything so go ‘head and call him and let him know what you want”, replied Gladice knowing even if her grandson Marvin didn’t get the shoes, etc.… for her Antonio she would, she never seemed to deny her favorite grandbaby.

“A Ma Ma, have you heard from Peaches lately?”

“Yeah, she should be walking through the door any minute. I sent her to the store about five minutes before you called”.

“Oh, have you talked to Antonette lately?”, asked Dirty inquiring about his mother whom he never referred to as mom or mother.

“Yes, she called the other day she should be home next month. I hope she’ll have herself together this time, those drugs ain’t for her”, replied his grandmother as tears welled up in her eyes from the thoughts of her daughter who’d become a drug addict and had been in and out of prison since Antonio was seventeen months old.

“Yeah, hopefully she will”, replied Dirty dryly.

“I don’t understand why she won’t just do right. Hold on Pumpkin somebody’s at the door”, said his grandmother as she sat the phone on the kitchen and went to answer the door.

“Hey Baby!”, shouted Peaches a couple seconds later picking the phone up off the counter having run to the kitchen after Ms. Gladice let her in and told her Antonio was on the phone. “If I would’ve knew you was calling I’d would’ve waited to go to the store for Mrs. Gladice”.

“I know that’s right. What’s up though, you being good and taking care of yourself?”, asked Dirty, envisioning Peaches in his mind.

“Yes Pookie”, whined Peaches “I’ve been going to school, coming home and chillin’ with Ms. Cookie and Munchie.”

Click! Click!

“Look the phone just clicked so it’s about to hang up, I love you, tell Ma Ma I love her and write me, you write me too. Oh, and I sent you a letter so you’d know what I want in my package.”

“Alright Baby, I love you too”, replied Peaches, her voice cracking a little.

“Baby holla at everybody for me and try to get Ma Ma or Ms. Cookie to bring you up here to visit me, the visits are contact so we can hug and kiss, you know I miss that!”

“I miss that too, I’ma ask Ms. Cookie to bring me…”

Peaches was unable to finish her sentence because the phone had been disconnected by the automatic timer. Dirty placed the phone receiver on the hook and walked to the dayroom to play cards with Nah, Black and lil’ Alfie.

Chapter 9

The next few days were uneventful as Dirty settled in at M.C.T.C. Everything was as well as it could be under the circumstances until Nah started arguing with an adolescent who also slept on C-tier and had been in M.C.T.C for two years. His name was Roc and he thought he was a shot caller. He was a muscular youngster of about six and a half feet tall and ran with a thorough little clique, but Nah could care less about Roc and his clique, wasn't nobody going to treat him like a chump or wrong him.

"Yo, don't foul me like that no more Roc!", shouted Nah, Roc having nearly knocked his head off while he was attempting to lay the basketball up.

"Or else what nigga?", retorted Roc as he grabbed the ball and checked it at the top of the key.

"Like I said, don't do that shit no more yo! We cool, but don't do it no more", warned Nah holding the ball cuffed in his left arm against his left side with his right hand balled up into a fist.

"Come on Nah, let's play ball yo", said Black as he walked over and stood between Roc and Nah, intervening.

"Cool, check it up?", said Roc cracking a half ass smile.

The basketball game continued. Dirty and Lil' Alfie were posted up on the side line with bangers watching the game.

Nah was a show-off on the court, he could play and continuously made fancy moves aggravating the opposite team. About nine possessions later Nah crossed Roc up something vicious and when Roc reached for the ball Nah shot it through Roc's legs stepped around him grabbing the ball still in stride he went straight to the hoop with a finger roll... Roc came out of nowhere and swatted Nah's right arm scratching him badly causing a fine bloody welt about six inches long to appear on his forearm. Angrily Nah picked up the ball and flung it at Roc's head barely missing him as Roc quickly jumped out of the way.

"Fuck is wrong with your bitch ass yo!", shouted Nah as he charged at Roc but was grabbed and restrained by Black and a few other youngsters.

"Nah you a bitch! Your whore ass don't wanna fight for real!", rebutted Roc as he advanced on Nah but was also grabbed.

"Yo, get the fuck off my man?", said Dirty as he approached Nah and the adolescents who were holding him. "Man, we can punish his bitch ass right now in the yard Cutty, what's up?"

"Chill don't worry I got his bitch ass, bet that!", exclaimed Nah as he grabbed his shirt from Lil' Alfie using it to wipe the sweat off his face then putting it on.

"Gimme that banger Alfie!"

Looking around Lil' Alfie pulled the nine-inch ice pick looking nail out of his dip and slipped it to Nah real quick. Nah taking it, cuffed it and putting it in his hip he began to stroll around the courtyard with Dirty, Black, Alfie and Mike-Mike.

“Yo, I’ma get Roc bitch ass on the tier first chance I get!”, stated Nah, temper flaring.

“Shit you know I’m for whatever”, said Dirty.

“Fuck that shit Nah”, said Black trying to be a peacemaker.

Once the yard had closed everybody returned to their respected tiers. Roc, Q and Nardo all hurriedly jumped in the shower to get a quick bird bath in before lockdown at 2:45. They had roughly ten minutes give or take a few. Nah seen Roc, Q and Nardo in the shower when he entered the tier. Roc was washing his dreads under the middle shower head, without saying a word Nah pulled his shank out followed closely by Dirty who seeing Nah whip his shank out, followed suit and together they stormed the shower swinging them.

Catching Roc off guard Nah stuck him first, hitting him in his upper back, tensing up Roc jerked forward as Dirty sunk his shank into Roc’s side pushing the rusty butter knife in him to the hilt, before pulling out and plunging it back into Roc, hitting him this time just under his arm pit puncturing his lung causing him to scream as he tried to twist and turn to ward off the attack.

Nardo closest to the exit, seeing all the blood and commotion frantically ran out of the shower area nearly falling, he left Roc for dead. Q, on the other hand attempting to assist Roc hit Nah with a sharp right-hand causing Nah to turn from Roc, focusing on Q he swung the nine-inch nail hitting Q in his right eye. Blood oozed from the socket where his eye had been. Q, hollered because of the blow to his eye and tried to back pedal in the small confines of the shower area to no avail. Nah stuck him again in his right collarbone, then in a rage he repeatedly stabbed Q a total of thirteen timed before Dirty grabbed his arm and pulled him away having already stretched Roc out, leaving him bloody on the concrete shower floor.

"Come on yo, let's get rid of these bangers Cutty!", exclaimed Dirty, pulling Nah away from the bloody shower area.

Roc and Q were a bloody mess as they laid in the shower ass-naked, water still, running, riddled with multiple puncture wounds. Roc was having complications breathing with one punctured lung and Q was in a state of shock having lost his right eye.

Dirty and Nah passed Lil' Alfie the bangers as soon as they entered the dayroom, then they undressed, putting on robes and shower shoes, which they obtained from two inmates in the dayroom to make it appear as if they'd taken showers and was just relaxing.

Lil' Alfie, wrapped the shanks in the bloody shirts Nah and Dirty had taken off and banged on the wall that separated C and B tiers dayrooms.

"Yo, somebody call Roscoe, tell him hurry up and come to the window", shouted Lil' Alfie as he stood in the far-right hand corner in the dayroom hollering out the window while banging on the wall.

“Yoooo, what’s up cuz?”, hollered Roscoe on the other side of the wall on B-tier about ten seconds later.

“Yo, stick your arm out the window and grab these bangers real quick cuz!”, exclaimed Lil’ Alfie as he stuck his arm out of the dayroom window and passed the shanks wrapped in the bloody shirts to his cousin Roscoe on B-tier.

“I got them shorty, what’s up yo?”, asked Roscoe as he pulled the shanks in the window on his side.

“I’ll holla at you at dinner cuz, one!”, replied Lil’ Alfie as he walked away from the window and went to a card table as if he’d been playing cards the whole time.

The whole bloody incident had taken place in less than five minutes. The C.O. on duty didn’t even know the stabbings had occurred until he came out of the office where he’d been on the phone and was about to lock down. Realizing that it was abnormally quiet on the adolescent tier he peered in the dayroom, seeing nothing, he walked around where he could view the tier and walked down to the grill peering in the shower he saw two inmates stretched out bleeding excessively.

“What the hell!”, exclaimed the C.O. using his walkie talkie to call for assistance.

“This is Cox, unit six, Charlie tier, I have two inmates stretched out in the shower bleeding pretty badly. They appear to have been stabbed.”

It didn't take long for assistance to come. The C.O.'s locked all the inmates in the dayroom as the two inmates in the shower were carried out on gurneys covered with blood soaked white sheets appearing deceased, though neither adolescent had died. Soon as the two adolescents were rushed off the tier on route to the infirmary the C.O.'s could look for wounds on the inmates in the dayroom which may infer that they were involved in the melee.

Nah, having a small lump under his eye from where Q had hit him, coupled with the long welt on his right forearm from the basketball game was handcuffed and escorted off the tier. He was placed on A-tier in housing unit five on administrative segregation pending an investigation. Dirty, managed to stay in population and the double stabbing propelled him up the ladder as a predator and a shot caller on the adolescent section and gained him recognition throughout the entire institution.

Chapter 10

The past five and a half months had been good to Dirty if such could be said about life in prison. He'd been enrolled in G.E.D. classes and was nominated the tier runner. He and Antmoe had formed an alliance that quickly blossomed into a close-knit bond, almost as if the two were blood relatives.

Antmoe taking a great liking to Dirty explained all the in's and outs of life in the belly of the beast to him. He passed everything he'd experienced directly or witnessed over the seventeen years he'd been incarcerated on to Dirty, the robbing, raping, stabbing, murdering, gambling, loan sharking, hustling and peddling drugs.

Dirty could recall vividly the day Antmoe put him on with the "Dope game" as if it had been yesterday rather than the actual four months that had elapsed.

"See nephew, in here everything revolves around fear, respect and power. The physically weak will be victimized by the physically strong, but brute strength cannot compare to mental strength... The thinking man, the mentally strong is who controls and rules over all", explained Antmoe as he and Dirty strolled around the track in the courtyard. "Learn to out think these niggas and you can control them without having to resort to physical violence, feel me nephew?"

"Yeah, I'm with cha!", stated Dirty absorbing Antmoe's every word like a sponge absorbs water.

“You already possess two of the three most sort attributes behind these walls, that being fear and respect. Those who don’t fear you, respect you. The only remaining sort after attribute you lack to a degree is power… On the streets money is power, but in here this is power... On the streets money is power, but in here this is power”, explained Antmoe passing Dirty a crumbled-up Newport pack, accepting it he held it in his hand with a perplexed look on his face as Antmoe spoke.

“That’s a gram of raw heroin, the street value is one hundred dollars, in her it’s worth a G. I put a paper in there also so you can estimate the weight of a quarter, a twenty-five dollar piece, use magazine paper to bag up, it has a waxy finish on it so the blow won’t stick to it, feel me?”

“Yeah Yeah, I’m wit cha’, so you said this is worth one hundred dollars on the streets and a G in here, right?”, asked Dirty.

“Yeah, you can make roughly a thousand dollars”, replied Antmoe staring at Dirty trying to read his mind.

“Okay, now let me ask you this, how much do I owe you for this?”, questioned Dirty as he stuffed the package in his sweatpants pocket.

“You don’t owe me shit, just get on your feet nephew and make sure you get everything you need”, stated Antmoe.

“I heard that, good look’ out!”, exclaimed Dirty intending to do just that.

Three days later during night yard after given Antmoe dap he handed him the same crumbled up Newport pack he'd given him, accepting it Antmoe was baffled as he spoke.

"What's this, what you couldn't get rid of it nephew?", questioned Antmoe.

"Naw I got rid of it the..."

"If you got rid of it, what's this then?", asked Antmoe cutting Dirty off in mid-sentence.

"That's three hundred dollar bills, so you tripled your money with what you gave me, good lookin' out unc!", stated Dirty.

"Naw shorty I told you that you aint' owe me nothing", protested Antmoe attempting to give him back the crumbled Newport pack containing the three hundred dollars.

"Naw Unc, I'm cool! That's you man, go ahead and keep it"

"I told you it ain't about that with me, besides you my lil' partner I wouldn't tax you like that anyway, if anything I would've told you to give me what I paid for it", explained Antmoe still attempting to return the money extending it to Dirty who refused to accept it.

"Well, how about this, consider me paying you the street value on what you gave me and just put me in the car with you next time you cop if that's possible", stated Dirty in a practiced tone having already anticipated that Antmoe would refuse to accept the money. “Plus, I got my man Nah a carton of cigarettes how much you think it’ll cost me to get them to him?”

“You a sharp lil’ nigga”, laughed Antmoe taken back by the way the youngster thought and maneuvered. “I respect that, you in the car on the next trip. Oh, and don’t worry about the transportation fee on the cigarettes just get them to me and I’ll make sure he gets them”.

Dirty hadn’t looked back since and now he was flipping three grams a month, plus he’d started a jailhouse store on his tier. The store contained nearly every item sold on the institutions commissary which he lent to inmates; one item for two items in return payable on state day (when everyone who worked or went to school was paid for the month). The store was doing well and he had to use Lil’ Alfie and Black’s cell to store some of his commissary.

Finally, after six wretched months Nah was allowed back into population. Dirty being tier runner could pull a few strings, getting Nah put in his cell. He couldn’t ask for much more under the circumstances, he had everything one was allowed in prison, he was receiving a visit every weekend, mail nearly every day, could use the phone at will, he was making money, his partner was his cellmate and time was flying by, everything was flowing smoothly, until…

“Oh Bloc, um Bloc- Bloc- Bloc mmm- yes aaah!”, moaned Tish as Bloc continued to thrust in and out of her wet pussy from behind, doggy-style.

“Whose pussy is this?”, bellowed Bloc as he repeatedly smacked Tish’s soft red ass cheeks.

“Ooooh, it’s your pussy Bloc! Mmmm, it’s your pussy- damn your dick is sooo big…mmmm-oooow boy- aaah, fuck me Bloc-oow, yes!”, moaned Tish as Bloc grabbing her on both sides of her waist, pulled her to him, slamming his dick in and out of her wet pussy, their bodies slapping together. “Oooooh, mmm, I’m bout’ to cummm, AAAAAHAHH!”, groaned Tish burying her face in her pillow she screeched at the top of her lungs, her pussy muscles contracting as she reached her climax causing Bloc to explode, cumming inside of her.

“Auuugh! Damn you got some good pussy girl, um- um-um!”, bellowed Bloc he held Tish’s waist for a couple of seconds, before playfully pinching her on her ass and sliding out of her sloppy wet pussy.

Getting up he headed towards the bathroom, while Tish rolled over and answered the phone which had been ringing continuously the whole time her and Bloc were having sex.

Stopping at the linen closet Bloc grabbed a towel and a washcloth before stepping into the bathroom. Adjusting the water to the temperature he desired he stepped in and began to lather up.

A few minutes passed before Tish stepped into the shower with her man. Taking the washcloth out of his hand she began to wash his chest and stomach, then using the lather from the soap she massaged his manhood.

“Yo, who was that on the phone Tish?”, questioned Bloc as his dick began to rise.

“Dumb ass Marlin talking crazy! I don’t know why he keeps calling, I told him it was over. He acts like he don’t get the message. This my man right here, he need to move on”, said Tish as she squatted before Bloc putting his semi-erect penis in her mouth, she sucked it moving her head back and forth, he lips wrapped around Bloc’s dick.

Shit, I see why slim don’t want to let go, good as this pussy and head is, thought Bloc as he tilted his head back while Tish attempted to deep throat him.

Tish was what men and some women considered a dime. Her mother was white and her father was black, she was a light skin stallion with wavy black hair that flowed down her back, she stood five feet nine inches tall and was thick in all the right places like Ebony Ayes the porn star in her prime. She was twenty-five years old, childless and had a good job. She had met Bloc a few months back at ESPN zone and since then the two had been inseparable, the only problem was her deranged ex- boyfriend that she dumped several months before her and Bloc met. He continuously stalked her, she wanted to put a restraining order on him, but Bloc being anti-police kept her from doing so. After showering Bloc got dressed.

“Look, I’m about to go take care of a few things, I’ll holla at you tonight. Call my cell phone if you need anything", shouted Bloc as he floated down the steps still feeling spent from the sex, shower and oral sex. He was feeling good though.

"A Baby hold up a minute!", shouted Tish as she sprinted down the hall and steps dressed in nothing but a thigh high pink robe. "Can you pick up my brown suede Chanel outfit from the cleaners in Fox Ridge before you head in town? Your white and red Pelle is in there too."

"Yeah, I got you", replied Bloc taking the cleaners stub out of her hand as he leaned in to kiss her on her forehead.

"Thanks, be careful Baby!", said Tish as she held the door open watching Bloc walk to his car.

Stepping out of Tish's townhouse Bloc pushed the alarm button on the key ring he had in his hand deactivating the alarm system. Lifting the car door handle, he blew Tish a kiss just about to step into the car he heard footsteps as if someone was running up behind him, turning quickly, all he saw was a flash, as gunfire leaped from the muzzle of the nine millimeter Beretta Marlin was clutching, Boom! Boom! Boom! Bloom!

The first bullet hit Bloc in his chest, the second one caught him in his throat, the third slug hit him in the jaw and the fourth and final bullet caught him in his head, blowing his brains out, blood and brain fragments splashing all over his car. He'd been shot four times at pointblank range and was dead before he hit the ground.

Marlin fled as Tish stood in her doorway in shock screaming at the top of her lungs,

“NOOOOOOO!!!!!!!!!!!”

■■

“Lord you have to go to the Chaplin”, stated the tier officer who’d just motioned Dirty over to the grill after tapping on the dayroom window to get his attention.

“What do I have to go to the Chaplin for?”, asked Dirty with a quizzing look on his face.

“Beats me, I was just told to have you report to the Chaplin”, explained the C.O.

“Do you need to get in your cell for anything?”

“No, I’m straight”, replied Dirty as the C.O. opened the grill and he started on his way out of the unit.

Nah seeing his man about to go somewhere, jumped up from the card table and hurried over to the dayroom window.

“Yo, what’s up, where are you going?”, mouthed Nah banging on the window.

“The Chaplin!”, retorted Dirty shrugging his shoulders implying that he had no idea what was going on.

“I’ll holla at you when you get back”, mouthed Nah throwing his right fist up in a swift motion saluting his comrade.

Dirty nodded his head in agreement, returning Nah’s salute with the same closed fist gesture. As he exited Unit 6, he noticed the stillness of the compound, the sky was a dreamy grayish color and the normal everyday sounds of life in prison seemed to be on mute. *Somethings wrong,* sounded the alarm in his mind as a chill ran up his spine causing him to jerk involuntarily when he crossed the threshold to the Chaplain's building, where he was greeted by a pale faced, gray haired, elderly man.

"How are you doing, sir? Your name is Antonio Lord, right?"

"Yeah", replied Dirty as he was led to the Chaplain's office which was located to the left of the entrance on the right side of the off-white hallway.

"Please have a seat", stated the Chaplain as he himself sat down. "Your grandmother's name is Gladice Jones, right?"

"Um-hum", replied Dirty as he sat down trying to brace himself for what was to come.

"Well, she called a little while ago… I hate to have to inform you of this but, uh, your cousin Marvin Jones Junior was shot to death this morning", said the Chaplain compassionately, picking up the phone on his desk he offered Dirty a call, "If you'd like you may use the phone…"

"No, I'm cool, I just want to go to my cell", said Dirty his whole being numb, his stomach had dropped and his head was pounding frantically.

"I understand", stated the Chaplain to Dirty's back as he walked out of his office.

"If I ever cross the path of the nigga or niggas responsible for slumpin' you cuz, I promise you I'ma send them where you at Bloc or die tryin'... Rest in peace cuz!!!", exclaimed Dirty looking up at the gloomy grayish sky, a single tear trickling down his left cheek as he made his way back to Unit 6.

■■

"Yo, you going to the yard, Dirty?", asked Nah tapping his partners foot jarring him awake. "Come on and spin the track with a nigga so we can put this smoke in the air Cutty. I got a fat ass King Edward rolled up."

Dirty came to opening his eyes he peered at Nah and spoke for the first time since his visit with the Chaplain the previous night.

"Yo, what time is it Nah?"

"It's almost time for rec.! What's up yo? You aint been right since yesterday, you aint even get up for the fried chicken at lunch, what's the deal?", questioned Nah worried about his partner.

"Yo, I'll put you on point after we put that smoke in the air", stated Dirty still trying to accept what the Chaplain had told him as he sat up on his bunk.

Rubbing his eyes, he stretched, swung his feet around and stood. Stepping over to the locker where his C.D. player sat on top, pushing play, 2pac's song 'Shed so many tears' filled the cell. He brushed his teeth, washed his face and put on a sweat suit and his New Balance before the cell doors opened.

While waiting in the dayroom for the yard to be opened Dirty didn't indulge in the small talk conversation Nah, Black, Lil' Alfie and Mike-Mike were engaged in. About five minutes passed before C-tier was finally called to the yard.

They headed to the yard, disbanding from their clique Nah and Dirty hit the track. When the two neared the volleyball court Nah bent over, pulled the left leg of his sweatpants up and retrieved the blunt he'd stashed in his sock.

"Here, spark up Cutty", said Nah extending the blunt to Dirty who responded by accepting it, putting it between his lips and striking two matches simultaneously, covering the flame he cuffed his left hand in front of it until he lit the blunt, then he tossed the matches. Inhaling deeply, he held the smoke in his lungs, then exhaled a gust of smoke. They'd smoked two thirds of the blunt before Dirty dropped the bomb on Nah.

"Yo, Nah, you know why I had to see the Chaplain yesterday?", he asked taking another drag on the blunt before passing it back to Nah.

"No yo, I was going to ask you last night but you were zoned out! What's the deal Cutty?", asked Nah genuinely concerned.

"Yo, Bloc got killed yesterday", stated Dirty in a low murmur still trying to cope with the loss of his cousin.

"Man, get the fuck out of here!", exclaimed Nah. The revelation having hit him like a ton of bricks he took a few steps back and looked at Dirty in disbelief. "Nooo, not Bloc yo!"

"Yeah Man, I'm fucked up about that Nah! Yo, raised me. Antonette has been a dope fiend since she gave birth to me and I never knew my father so Bloc held a nigga down like a father while my grandmother was Ma-Ma… I just want to smash a nigga to relieve my frustration and anger", explained Dirty with blood in his eyes and murder in his heart.

"No bullshit, I feel you yo! I can't believe a nigga killed him. Did you find out who did it, why, where, anything?", questioned Nah also in an emotionally charged mood.

"No, I was so fucked up in the head when the Chaplain told me what was up that I didn't even take the call he offered me", said Dirty. Having discarded the roach from the blunt, they began to stroll the yard lost in their own thoughts, wanting a reason to brutalize someone, anyone.

Bending the corner of the track near the entrance to the yard Dirty locked eyes with an older convict. He'd been watching Dirty constantly since he arrived at M.C.T.C nearly a year ago.

"Yo, Nah, I'm about to step to that old head right there in that Coogi sweater with them glasses on", stated Dirty looking in the older convict's direction. "That motherfucker been watching me since I got here yo."

“I see him”, said Nah looking over at the older convict also. “Hell yeah, he staring at you right now, what’s up? My joint in my shoe lets go sit by the basketball court real quick so I can get my shit then it’s whatever yo. You strapped, right?”

“Make no mistake about it”, said Dirty touching the shank in his dip. “Get your joint and I’ma pull dude up, if he so much as smile sideways I’ma bless him”.

Nah was always game to put in work so as soon as he felt safe enough to remove his shank from his shoe without being detected by a C.O. in the guard towers he quickly did so and slid it up his right shirt sleeve and he and Dirty approached the older convict. Dirty was so set on him he didn’t even notice Antmoe standing off a couple steps to the side with his back turned talking to a convict in a black Kufi.

“Yo, slim why the fuck you always watching me?”, barked Dirty nearing the older convict, Nah right at his side. “Ever since I been here your old ass been sneaky-eye ballin’ me. What the fuck you know me or you like me?”

Antmoe spinning around to assist Lucky Al, seeing it was Dirty who was ranting, quickly intervened before Lucky Al’ could respond.

“Whoa! Whoa! Whoa! Hold up nephew! What’s going on shorty?”, questioned Antmoe stepping in front of Lucky AL. “Calm down nephew, come on walk with me, let me holler at you, you too Nah.”

Both youngsters respected Antmoe’s status as a thorough convict so they walked with him.

“Now what’s going on nephew?”, questioned Antmoe once they’d walked a few feet.

“Man, that bitch ass nig…”

“Whoa, slow down with the bitch ass nigga thing, talk to me like a man, like I talk to you nephew”, retorted Antmoe cutting Dirty off in mid-sentence.

“No unc, that dude been sneaky-eye ballin’ me since I got here like he a gump or something so I was about to pull him up and see what’s on his mind”, explained Dirty with his adrenaline pumping.

“Look, let me pull you and Nah’s coat to this, that dude you referring to is Albert Clark- Lucky Al- one of the richest and thorough-est gangster to ever walk the streets of Baltimore. His name rings like Lil’ Melvin, Peanut, Joe Dancer, Rudy, Liddy and all the old Baltimore legends. Slim a real good nigga for real! Me and Al go back a long way. He was my co-defendant on the case I got this bid for, I cut him loose and copped to thirty-five so that should tell you what kind of regards I have for him. As far as him watching you, maybe he digs your style, maybe you remind him of himself, or maybe you remind him of the son he lost about two years ago. I don’t know, but I can assure you he ain’t no gump, no faggy, or no shit like that. He a real man and he ain’t on no bullshit. Whatever’s on your mind let it go for me and trust me when I say Lucky Al is a good nigga”, explained Antmoe never once telling Dirty that Lucky Al’ secretly held a special interest in him and had advised Antmoe to look after him, groom him and give him his first gram hoping he would do just as he did. “And that goes for you to

Nah, I know your lil' sneaky ass probably got ten knives on you ready to go".

Dirty and Nah laughed at Antmoe's last statement despite the state of mind they were in because of Bloc's death. They gave Antmoe their word it was over and agreed to leave the situation alone as he requested.

"You got that, Unc, it's dead".

"Yeah, it's dead", chimed Nah.

"Cool, ya'll straight, y'all want an ice cream or something out the stand, look like y'all might have the munchies, eyes all red and beady", laughed Antmoe.

"Yeah get me an orange sherbet", requested Dirty.

"Me too", chimed Nah.

"I got y'all", replied Antmoe strolling to the concession stand.

Bloc was buried in style three days later at Marc Funeral Home on North Avenue. Due to the disfigurement of this corpse he had to have a closed casket at his funeral. The casket was marble green with gold fixtures on it. On top of the casket sat a blown-up picture of Bloc with Chunk gold jewelry adorning his neck, wrist and fingers like Slick Rick. He was in his prime on the picture clutching a wad of money in each of his hands. Bloc had always been about a dollar so it was only natural that the funeral color code was green. Everybody wore green to symbolize what Bloc represented, money.

The same day that Bloc's funeral was held, Lucky Al stepped out of M.C.T.C in grand fashion, a free man. When he stepped onto the tar paved black top in M.C.T.C parking lot, there was a white, chauffeur driven, stretched limousine waiting on him. He'd been incarcerated for two and a half years and was now ready to reclaim his throne.

They took two and a half years of my life for that trumped-up ass gun charge, thought Lucky AL as he climbed into the back of the limo making himself comfortable he sat in the plush black leather seat. *Had I been on the streets, maybe my son wouldn't have gotten killed,* thought Lucky Al as he reflected on the night he was arrested…

He was cruising on Route 40 on his way to Tiffany's house, when a racist white county police officer signaled him to pull over. The police officer alleged that he'd been speeding, which somehow lead to the illegal search of his car. A 44 Magnum Smith and Wesson handgun was recovered under the driver seat. Falsifying the police report the officer claimed that the handgun was in plain view when he pulled the motorist over for a traffic violation. The false report and the handgun gained a conviction against the seemly untouchable Albert 'Lucky Al' Clark resulting in a three-year sentence on which he served two and a half years. He could have been home in two years had he earned his maximum amount of good days by working in the institution, but Lucky Al refused to work for 'the man'.

"I'm back to claim my crown. Baltimore belongs to me, it's time I put shit back I order", stated Lucky Al aloud talking to himself as he reached for the car phone and began dialing numbers.

In Maryland, a person convicted of a crime and sentenced prior to November 1995 was eligible for parole after having served a fourth of his/her sentence. Dirty was sentenced in 1994 and now had just over twenty-one months incarcerated. He went up for parole and was denied due to the 'nature of his offense'.

Having set his heart on receiving parole, initially he was gravely disappointed after being denied. But he soon accepted reality and continued serving his sentence. He occupied his time by reading. He read everything he could get his hands on from Donald Goines and Charles Avery Harris to Sun Tzu and Machiavelli. He began to lust after knowledge because it is making him feel superior and enabled him to escape from the stone and steel that held him captive. His mind was free when he read books.

Chapter 11

"Yellow Dot out y'all! Dot's out! Hittin' in the hole!", shouted Snuggles who was posted up on the corner of Harlem Avenue and Dukeland Street.

All of the dope-fiends who'd been lingering around on the intersecting blocks of Harlem and Dukeland since the 'Yellow Dot Boys' had sold out thirty minutes ago, hurriedly bum rushed the hole, the alleyway on Harlem Ave. that lead to Rayner Avenue. Eager to cop some of the scrambled heroin that had been cut(mixed) with fentanyl so they could be on their way. The dope fiends cluttered in a cluster in a small alley way. Yellow Dot was rumored to have caused nine dope fiends to die from overdoses in the past month which had every dope fiend in Baltimore City and the surrounding counties craving it, wanting it and chasing it.

"Get the fuck in line and get ya money out, we ain't takin' no shorts!", shouted a youngster as he crossed Harlem Avenue and stepped into the hole, followed closely by Smurf.

Like trained soldiers being given orders by the drill sergeant the dope fiends snapped to attention and stood in a single file line. With their money out of their hands followed closely by Smurf who gave them the amount of gel capsules containing the heroin they'd paid for.

"Baby can I get three for $28. 00? asked a light skin former beauty queen who'd succumbed to heroin by way of the needle. She now looked like a zombie with pale spotted skin, dark rings around her eyes, sunk in cheeks, badly chapped lips, filthy unkempt hair and the few teeth remaining in her mouth were yellow and rotten.

“Bitch I said No Shorts! What part didn’t you understand!”, retorted the youngster in green.

“Please Baby, I’ll bring the two dollars back, I promise”, pleaded the woman.

“What the fuck I say Bi…”

“Hold up Rah-Rah, that’s my man’s mother, go ahead and take the short”, interjected Smurf recognizing the woman’s face.

“Thank ya Baby! I’ma let Antonio know you looked out for me”, lied Antonette who hadn’t spoke to her son since she’d been released from jail.

“Alright yo, but she owes two dollars”, said Rah-Rah taking twenty-eight dollars and stuffing it in his pocket with all the other crumbled up bills he’d just collected.

“Here Ms. Antonette”, said Smurf handing her three gel caps.

“Thanks Baby!”, replied Antonette grabbing the three gel caps, she bolted out of the hole in a hurry to get around to the ‘Shooting Gallery’.

Clutching the three pills in her hand which was balled into a tight fist, she briskly walked down Harlem Avenue. There were people sitting on the steps adjacent to their rowhouses and children were playing ‘it’s’ running around parked cars and up and down the street. Antonette paid them no attention as she turned on Claymount Avenue and bee-lined straight to the 'Shooting Gallery' on Edmondson Avenue.

Sweating she hammered on the dingy yellow door at the 'Shooting Gallery'. Her hands shaking, she used her blue shirt sleeve to catch and wipe away the snot that was trickling from her nostrils.

I know somebody in here, she thought banging on the door again.

"Hold the fuck up, got damn it… I'm coming shit!", shouted a grumpy man from just behind the closed door. Peering through the peephole in the door, seeing it was Antonette the grumpy man removed the two-by-four off the back of the door, unlocked it and swung it open.

"Hey Fly, how you doing?", asked Antonette brushing by him as she entered the house eager to get high so she could get rid of the sickness that plagued her from not having put her midday fix in her system yet.

"Say excuse me ya ol' crowfoot heifer!", barked Fly to Antonette's back, turning he shut and secured the door.

Paying him no attention Antonette continued down the dimly lit hallway. The basement door was to her right, opening it, she entered the basement and descended the creaky wooden stairs. The basement was filthy and smelled of stale urine, mildew, wet concrete, aged liquor, blood and vomit. Old clothes and garbage were everywhere, covering nearly the entire floor.

Stepping over the trash on the floor Antonette tiptoed to the front part of the basement. There were two filthy piss stained mattresses in the front part of the basement and several milk crates scattered about. Antonette spotted the guy Doc immediately, he was hunched over with a needle in his hand, sitting on a crate. In front of him on one of the piss stained mattresses lied a dark skin woman Antonette knew to be named Fay. Fay was on her back with her skirt hiked up around her waist, legs spread wide apart as Doc peered at her vagina area with an expert eye searching for a vein. Finding one in her vagina he inserted the needle and injected the heroin into her bloodstream. Fay closed her eyes and licked her bottom lip instantly feeling the warm soothing comfort the drug brought her.

Doc, was the undisputed 'hit-man'. Whenever junkies were unable to find a vein they'd pay Doc to do so for them. Antonette having abused her veins always had to seek Doc's expert assistance.

"Doc, Baby I need you to look out for me. I'm ill as a motherfucker!", exclaimed Antonette pulling her syringe and 'cooker' out of the Royal Crown bag she had secure in her bra. "I got a pill for ya, alright Baby?"

"Yeah, go ahead and get ready I got you Netta", said Doc putting the blast Fay had given him in his arm.

Antonette quickly poured the heroin out of both gel caps she had for herself onto a large metal spoon. Seeing Doc was working the needle in his own arm Antonette quickly shook a little heroin out of the pill she had for him on to her own spoon also. Sticking her hypodermic needle into a blue cup containing water that sat on the coffee table next to where she'd sat her 'cooker'. She sucked water into her spike then squirted it onto the 'cooker' with the heroin. With a steady hand, she lifted the 'cooker' and placed it over one of the lit candles on the table until the heroin melted into liquid. Pulling the spoon away from the fire she sat it down on the table careful not to tip it over. She then put a small piece of cotton on the spoon and picking up her needle she stuck the point into the cotton on her 'cooker' and drew the clear liquid up into the syringe. Her mouth-watering she smacked her lips and turned to Doc.

"Come on Doc Baby I'm ready", whined Antonette in her most persuasive voice handing Doc the needle containing the liquefied heroin along with his doctor's fee, the pill of heroin she'd tampered with.

"Where we goin' Netta?", asked Doc knowing Antonette's veins were worn out, even the veins in her vagina were hard to hit, having been abused for so long.

"You know I gotta go in my neck Doc?", stated Antonette as she sat down on the milkcrate in front of Doc.

Closing her mouth held her breath blowing her cheeks out and tilting her head to the side exposing her neck. Standing over Antonette, Doc tapped her neck twice with his free hand aggravating the veins in her neck causing them to bulge a little, lining the needle up with her jugular vein he inserted the point into the flesh of her neck. Drawing back on the syringe he saw blood and knew he had a direct hit so he applied pressure to the syringe pump slamming the liquefied heroin into Antonette's bloodstream.

"Aaah! Yesssss!", hissed Antonette biting her bottom lip, she scratched her neck, then feeling the effects of the drug she closed her eyes and nodded off into total darkness...

Hours had passed before anyone even noticed Antonette had overdosed and wasn't breathing. Monk-man trying to get Antonette to go stealing with him called himself waking her by rattling her arm as she sat slumped over on the milkcrate appearing to be in a vicious dope-fiend nod.

"Antonette, I got a sweet sting for us... Antonette! An-to-net-te!", said Monk-man his voice going up a few notches as he continued to shake her arm until he shook her a little hard causing her body to topple over. "What the fuck! A Doc I think she dead man."

Doc reached down and felt for her pulse, first feeling her wrist then her neck. Not feeling her pulse, he smacked her face several times while shouting her name.

"Antonette!... Antonette!... Antonette!... Somebody get some ice water."

Moments later Monk-man returned with Fly and several trays of ice. Cracking the ice trays, they place ice down her pants, down her shirt and Doc held ice under her arms to revive her, but their efforts were useless. Antonette had already passed on to the unknown, she was dead.

“Man, the heifer dead ya’ll, aint no since in wastin’ no mo’ ice on her stinkin ass”, stated Fly. “Come on and help me get the heifer upstairs Monk-man”.

Monk-man shaking his head at Antonette’s demise grabbed her legs while Fly grabbed up under her arms. Doc lead them up the stairs as they picked her up and carried her up the basement stairs and straight to the back door.

“Open the backdoor Doc”, stated Fly.

Doc did so and Fly and Monk-Man carried Antonette’s deceased body down the back stairs through the backyard, out the fence which had no gate, up the alley and tossed her lifeless form amongst some garbage near the basketball court.

“Better she be found in the park than up in my crib”, reasoned Fly after disposing her body. ‘she already done fucked my high up. I’ll be damn if the worthless heifer gon’ fuck up my crib by having them crackers snoopin’ all through my shit!”

“How about that”, agreed Monk-Man as he headed in the opposite direction. “I’ll catch you in a minute Fly I’ma run around Harlem and Dukeland to cop me summa dat’ shit dat’ killed Nette. That Yellow Dot a motherfuckin bomb!”

■■

It had been over two years since Bloc was killed, however Dirty could still vividly recall the seemingly long gloomy walk to the Chaplain building on that dreaded day, today felt no different. When he was instructed to report to the Chaplain's office he knew to expect the worst. His only fear was that it may be his grandmother.

Anybody but Ma Ma... Anybody but Ma Ma, he thought as he sat before the Chaplain, his heart racing.

"How are you doing Mr. Lord?", questioned the Chaplain looking up from the papers he had sprawled out on top of the oak desktop.

"I'm alright I guess", replied Dirty.

"Mr. Lord I hate to inform you this, uh (Dirty's heart was thundering and he had butterflies in his stomach), Antonette jones passed away two days ago... I now this may be quite a revelation, if you need to talk, that's what I'm here for... Or perhaps you may wish to make a phone call. Do you have anyone you'd like to call?", asked the Chaplain.

"Yeah, I'd like to call my grandmother", requested Dirty needing to hear her voice.

The Chaplain dialed his grandmothers number for him, then handed him the phone. He was relieved to hear her voice. He could tell she was still emotionally rattled behind her daughter death, he tried to console her verbally as best he could. Before they said their 'I love you and hung up Dirty managed to calm his grandmother and stop her from crying.

Sadly, the fact that his mother was dead had no effect on him emotionally. His heart was black when it came to her. In his eyes, she'd died years before her actual physical demise. The only emotion he felt at the time was a joyous relief knowing his grandmother was alive and well.

Things had changed a lot over the course of the four years and five months he'd been incarcerated. His grandmother who he loved with all his heart had been diagnosed with sugar diabetes, but she was a strong woman and continued to take good care of herself. His cousin Shy having been scared straight by Mookie death and his incarceration steered him clear from the streets. He had finished high school, had a part-time job and was doing good for himself.

Peaches had also completed high school and was in her first semester at Georgia Tech. She'd been given a nice scholarship from the N.A.A.C.P. She was still madly in love with Dirty and wrote him frequently. Even from prison he still found a way to assist her, sending her $500.00 a month from the heroin he sold in the joint. The money he sent her coupled with the check and tips she received as a waitress enabled her to maintain well while in Georgia.

Ms. Cookie still wrote and visited him regularly. She did everything in her power to keep him abreast with the status of his homeboys and the happenings in the neighborhood. She'd told him that Fatty-pooh and Squirrel were still hustling on Hollins and Pulaski, they were doing okay. They stopped past her house every couple of days to check on her and give her fifty to sixty dollars to send him. Snuggles, Smurf and Fatz were now hustling up on Harlem and Dukeland working for Freeze selling Yellow Dot. They collectively stopped by on occasions to check on her and give her a hundred dollars or so also to send Dirty. Bucky and Lil' Gizmo had recently been arrested for armed robbery and copped to a plea of three years to the reduced charge of robbery.

Her daughter Munchie was running the streets heavy. She'd had twin sons named Tywon and Kywon by an older hustler everyone called White Folks, he was said to favor Dirty. She hadn't written Dirty in over a year. Lil' Mookie was in the second grade now and still lived on Smallwood Street with his mother Keisha. Lil' Mookie wrote Dirty when Ms. Cookie did, the letters touched Dirty, he always addressed him as Uncle White, putting his letters in the envelope with hers.

While everybody was living and learning beyond the stone and steel that held Dirty captive, he was steady conditioning himself for his up and coming release. He'd learned well how to be both the fox and the Lion; the fox when cunning craftiness was necessary and the Lion when brute force was necessary.

He'd become a young master mind with amazing leadership qualities. He'd learned to save and manage money he obtained via hustling in the joint. He lived off his hustle and hadn't spent one penny out of his account in nearly two years. All the money his family and friends sent him went untouched, plus he made it his business to add five hundred dollars a month to his account balance.

He wanted to step out of the joint with enough money in his account to get on his feet. He wasn't trying to go out like Lil Alfie who'd been released six months earlier with nothing. So out of desperation he robbed a hustler to get on his feet. He came off, bought a Q45, sent Dirty, Nah, Mike-Mike and his cousin Roscoe all five hundred dollars and started flipping the money; only to be killed two months later right in front of his baby mother house because of the robbery.

Had he had a few dollars saved up when he touched down maybe he wouldn't have been killed, reasoned Dirty.

"A Unc, when I touch down I'ma get that money for real!", said Dirty as him and Antmoe stood on the side line by the first basketball court watching Nah do his thing.

"I feel you nephew, just take your time and carry it like you carry it in here", replied Antmoe taking a sip of the Pepsi he had in his hand. "You definitely got the potential to get money, but getting' money aint hard, it's what you do with the money once you got it. You got to invest in shit, buy houses, a barber shop, clothing stores, a car-wash, something, feel me?"

"Yeah I feel you. I'm going to invest in some shit. I'm a buy a bunch of cheap rowhouses and fix them up… you know renovate them and resell them. Plus, I want to open a club or something. Trust me I'm on top of my shit. By the time that I'm twenty-five I'ma be finished with the streets", boasted Dirty confidently.

"I hear ya Neph, just make sure you don't forget the O.G. cause I'ma still be up in here…", replied Antmoe.

"Come on Unc, don't play me like that, I'm a real nigga. I'm going to always keep it real… Loyalty is Everything!", said Dirty aggressively.

"Yeah, I know Neph, I know, I was fuckin with ya", confirmed Antmoe remembering how every time Dirty made a move while Nah was on lock up he would send him a carton of cigarettes and fifty dollars' worth of commissary.

Shorty a good kid, thought Antmoe as they finished watching the basketball game.

■■■

"Hello, Hell…"

"You have a collect call from' Anthony Jenkins', at the Maryland Correctional Training Center. If you accept this call do not use three-way or call waiting features or you will be disconnected. To accept this call please dial one now… Thank you.

"Hey Ant, what's going on Comrade?", questioned Lucky Al.

"Ain't too much man just taking it easy. What's up with you?", replied Antmoe.

"I'm moving in slow motion, I just came back from down Florida. I sent you a post card, plus I put a couple rolls of film in the shop today so soon as I get them out I'ma send them to you. Those Florida broads are the truth, Moe."

“Shit I bet they is, what’s up with Los did he hang out with you down there?”, asked Antmoe.

“Oh, you know slim was with a nigga, shit he still down there… He closing a contract with a dude we supposed to be building a club for”, explained Lucky Al choosing his words carefully.

“I feel you, make sure you holler at him for me next time ya’ll rap”, said Antmoe understanding that Los was still tying up the loose ends on some illegal business.

“Hey Ant, what’s up with Nephew?”, questioned Lucky Al.

“Shorty doing good. You know his mother just died from an overdose. He handles it well on the surface though. We were rapping earlier today. He got some shit on his mind. All the lil’ nigga do is read, workout and try to call shots. He thinks he’s the don or some shit”, said Antmoe sharing a laugh with Lucky Al. “No bullshit man, that lil’ nigga gonna storm Baltimore if he stays grounded.”

“He ready, huh? Shit I hope so because I’ma cold blooded bless him when touch down. Make sure you give him the number to the construction company so he’ll have a job when he come uptown. When he supposed to touch anyway?”

“He touches down in about six months and you know I’m going to give him the number”, Antmoe replied.

Click! Click!

“Yo my phone clickin’ and it’s Los so I’ma catch his call, hit me whenever. Alright Comrade, continue to look out for shorty, love ya Comrade.”

“I love you too Big Homie, be cool”, replied Antmoe hanging the phone up.

Chapter 12

Dear Antonio,

How are you doing? I hope fine. Me, I'm still having a hard time dealing with what happened to Marvin. I don't think I will ever get over losing him... Anyway, I'm just writing to let you know that the coward who killed your cousin was sentenced to thirty years and may be coming your way. I know Marvin probably wouldn't have wanted me to testify against Marlin, but I had to. Marlin killed my son father. My son will never have a chance to know his father and his father never had a chance to know his son, he didn't even know I was pregnant all because of Marlin's sorry ass, FUCK HIM, I hope he dies in jail. Look, I'm for becoming so emotionally worked up, I have tears running down my face and everything. I'm about to depart, so I can pull myself together, take care and be strong.

Keep your head up,

Latisha Davis

P.S here's a recent picture of Lil' Marvin and an old picture of Marlin in case he comes your way, just so you know, his whole name is Marlin Chambers.

After reading the letter Dirty sat it on top of his TV and looked at the pictures. One of the pictures was a small professionally taken picture of a little Marvin with blocks sitting in front of him. He was looking just like his father. The other picture was of Marlin, Dirty studied Marlin's face and stored it in his memory bank before putting the picture on top of the TV with the letter.

Don't worry Tish, if he comes this way he gonna die in the joint, thought Dirty as he nudged Nah attempting to wake him.

"Yo, it's almost time for chow nigga, get the fuck up!", said Dirty jokingly.

He then turned his C.D. player on blasting Jay-Z's song 'Hard Knock Life'.

"SSH7…SSH8…SSH9…SSH10!", exclaimed Dirty as he racketed the 225pound weight bar he'd been bench pressing, then stood.

"Yo, spot me Mike-Mike", said Nah sitting on the weight bench, he laid back getting comfortable.

"I got you yo", said Mike-Mike walking to the top of the weight bench standing over Nah head so he could assist him if the bar became heavy.

Nah began pressing the weights, doing his set. Dirty stood at the foot of the weight bench stretching his arms and rotating his neck from side to side when a familiar face caught his eyes. Squinting his eyes, he stared at the familiar face briefly trying to register where he knew the guy from.

“Yo Dirty it’s your go. This the last set right here so burn out”, stated Nah when Mike-Mike rose from the weight bench having just completed his set, he was leading the pack. Nah’s statement momentarily broke Dirty’s train of thought.

“Oh, yeah yo”, replied Dirty, sitting on the weight bench, he laid back, grabbed the bar and pressed it sixteen times before his arms burnt out.

When he finished, Nah did his burn out set. Soon as Nah was finished Dirty spotted the familiar face again out of the corner of his eye. The familiar face had circled the track and was nearing Dirty. Turning his head in the direction where the familiar face was Dirty tried to place who it was.

Finally, it hit him like a bolt of lightning. *That’s that bitch Marlin,* thought Dirty with his thoughts involuntarily transforming into words, escaping his lips.

“What you say yo?”, asked Nah looking at Dirty.

“Yo, that’s the bitch ass nigga that killed Bloc. I almost didn’t recognize him, the whore ain’t have dreads in the picture I got”, explained Dirty, his upper lip curling up.

“Where yo?”, asked Nah and Mike-Mike simultaneously looking around.

“Right there”, shouted Dirty pointing at Marlin.

"Chill yo, don't point at the nigga, we gonna get his ass just chill", said Nah stepping in front of Dirty.

"Yeah yo, chill don't put slim on point by pointing at him", agreed Mike-Mike.

"Man, fuck that bitch ass nigga!", ranted Dirty who was emotionally charged.

"Come on Cutty, think nigga! What's the George Jackson type of shit you always tell me, don't let your emotion govern your intelligence or some shit. Yeah apply that now! You gotta be smart and think, you touch down two months after me, we gonna get him let's just do it right, feel me?", questioned Nah.

"Man, fuck a release date, I'm trying to kill slim bitch ass right now", exclaimed Dirty who was due to be released in sixty-nine days.

"Yo, I'ma ride wit you regardless, but let's just plan shit and strike right. Come on yo, think nigga. Why be reckless Cutty?", asked Nah grabbing Dirty by his head pulling him to himself in a brotherly/homie type of embrace. "Yo, we definitely going to get him!"

"Yeah yo, you right", admitted Dirty reluctantly.

Immediately he began to conjure up a way to murder Marlin as soon as possible...

By the time, the yard was closed Dirty had found out that Marlin slept in Unit 6 on B-tier and was cellmates with Roscoe's partner Bo. He planned to move on Marlin at breakfast since the compound was usually still dark and semi-deserted at that time. He sent word by Roscoe for Bo to see him on the walk to dinner.

At dinner time, Dirty pulled Bo to the side and offered him a half of a gram of heroin to be Marlin's alarm clock for breakfast. Marlin having just come from M.R.D.C.C. where food was of a poor quality was almost guaranteed to go to breakfast for the pancakes in the morning, especially if Bo awakened him so he didn't oversleep. Bo quickly agreed to do his part, accepting the pay off.

During night Rec. while in the dayroom, Dirty ran his plan down to Nah and Mike-Mike in full detail. Nah and Mike-Mike in turn put the plan in motion by spreading the word to all the stand-up adolescents who were to assist with the plan. Everything was understood before lock down.

That night Dirty couldn't even sleep, he was too charged up. All he could do was think of avenging his cousin. He sat up listening to music all night until the doors opened for breakfast.

When the cell doors opened for breakfast nearly everyone who slept on C-tier stepped out. Most them were dressed in state issued blue jeans and coats with gray skull caps on their heads. They all walked to the mess hall in a loose cluster.

Once they reached the mess hall they split up. Dirty and several adolescents went on the left side, just in case Marlin wound up on that side. Nah and the remaining adolescents went on the right side in case Marlin wound up on that side.

Soon as Dirty sat down with his tray at a table on the third row he spotted Marlin in line to be served talking to Bo and Roscoe. A smile formed on his face as he nodded his head slightly to Bo and Roscoe. Then looking up at the mess hall ceiling he mumbled a few words.

I got him cuz, I'ma bless his bitch ass, cold blooded!

Dirty didn't touch his food and was relieved when the C.O. finally directed his row to depart from the kitchen. Once outside of the mess hall, Dirty lingered around for a minute or so before walking down the compound at a snail's pace. Everybody off C-tier loosely gathered around him and Nah.

Marlin stepped out of the mess hall walking with his head down trying to strike a match to light the cigarette he had between his lips, unaware of his surroundings.

By the time he'd lit his cigarette and was half way to the unit a crowd of adolescents all dressed in state issued denim outfits with knitted skull caps on their heads had formed around him. Nah who was ten feet in front of Marlin bent down in the crowd on one knee appearing to tie his shoe. Smoothly he slid the long metal shank he had up his right sleeve out and clutched it, still appearing to tie his shoe.

Marlin neared Nah as Dirty allowed him to pass himself and slid up behind him with ease. Dirty using his right hand slid the long metal shank he had in his dip out and held it at his side cuffed in his hand the blade running up his forearm. Closing the gap between Marlin and himself, Dirty reached out with his left hand grabbing a handful of Marlin's dreads he snatched his head back and in one fluid motion he brought his right hand up and around sticking the shank in Marlin's neck.

"This for Bloc you bitch ass nigga!", spat Dirty.

Marlin gagged, trying to jerk left to get away, it was useless. Nah who was still kneeling just a foot in front of Marlin when Dirty made his move quickly rose in a spinning motion and thrust the shank he held in hand into Marlin's mid-section. Nah could see the look of bewildered horror on Marlin's face as he repeatedly jammed the shank into Marlin's stomach. Dirty snatched the shank he held in Marlin's neck. Blood poured out like a running faucet. Marlin attempted to holler but only made a goggling noise as he choked on the blood that filled his mouth.

"Uuuugh!"

Dirty plunged the shank he held back into Marlin's frame, hitting him in his right temple, instantly killing him. Feeling his body go limp Dirty released his dreads and Marlin fell forward, his body hitting the ground with a thud.

The cluster of adolescents just stepped around Marlin's lifeless body as he laid face down on the tar pathway in a puddle of blood. The sticky glistening fluid leaking out of the multiple puncture wounds that stole his life from him, Dirty and Nah passed their shanks off to an older convict name Mousey who slept in unit 5 with Antmoe.

Once they entered Unit 6 Dirty and Nah hurriedly removed their state issued coats and passed them to Roscoe and Twon, who disposed of them on B-tier in the big barrel trash cans under the stairs. That way if the blood-stained coats were recovered the administration would assume the individuals responsible for the act slept on B-tier.

Fortunately, everything went according to plan and no one was apprehended for the stabbing death of Marlin Chambers. A local newspaper ran a short article on the murder the following day.

'A 28-year-old man Marlin Chambers was pronounced dead yesterday at the Maryland Correctional Training Center after being stabbed multiple times, officials said. At Approximately 5:45am Correctional Officer R. Thorton noticed a crowd of inmates returning to their unit after breakfast, when the crowd past an inmate was lying face down on the walkway. The only description he could provide of the culprits was that they were dressed in state issued coats and jeans with gray knitted hats on their heads, officials said. No apprehensions have been made relating to the incident, however the prison administration is still investigating.'

Chapter 13

Anxiously Dirty paced back and forth in the small cell, deep in thought. At last the big day had arrived, in a matter of hours he'd be back on the streets of Baltimore. *It's your turn Dirty White, Hollins and Pulaski is yours for the takin'…,* he thought as he paced the cell for the umpteenth time.

He'd mastered the laws of prison and not only had he survived amongst the cesspool of predators, he'd done so impressively, not a single blemish on his jacket. He'd reached the pinnacle of respect in prison, being well respected by both the young and old convicts alike. *I did my thing in the joint it ain't no way I aint gonna do my thing on the bricks…,* thought Dirty steady pacing the cell.

Instead of prison rehabilitation Dirty, it had made him shrewder, more manipulative and colder hearted. Having become a power figure in prison he now craved power.

I should be able to employ the velvet glove when I take over on H and P, but if the velvet glove doesn't work then I'ma resort to the iron fist. Either way Hollins and Pulaski is mines…, thought Dirty as he sat on his bunk and stared at the wall.

He was young, black, intelligent and ambitious. Coupling those attributes with nearly seventeen grand he had in his account, it was safe to say he would come up and be successful. *I'ma cop a quarter brick (nine ounces), a little hooptie and grind hard…,* he thought.

Nah had informed him that he was getting a little money, hustling, but didn't go in depth on the phone. Dirty was certain that his niggas and Nah was gonna roll with him. Dirty had it all mapped out.

Having spent the last five years and twenty-three days of his life in prison he was unsure of what to expect when he returned to his old neighborhood. One thing for certain though, by any means necessary he intended to get his lion's share.

I've been locked up since I was fifteen, I got a lot of catching up to do. It's all or nothing, either I'ma get rich or die trying…, thought Dirty. Just then the cell door opened with a loud cling.

"Lord, pack up and report to the administration building", shouted the tier officer.

Dirty had given all his belongings to Mike-Mike and Bucky so he didn't have anything left to pack up. Aside from the things he had on and the photo album and phone book he'd grabbed when his door opened. He looked around his cell one last time and stepped out on to the tier.

Antmoe stood at the top of the tier with a yellow push cart. He'd made a way to see his young protégé off. Dirty spotted Antmoe, but took his time strolling up the tier, briefly stopping at Mike-Mike's cell he banged on his door.

"Yo, be cool Cutty, keep the store up and make sure you call my grandmother's in a week or so alright yo?", stated Dirty.

"Yeah son, take it easy and send a nigga some flicks of some bitches when you get right", replied Mike-Mike standing at the cell door he watched Dirty step across the tier to Bucky's cell.

"I got cha nigga", said Dirty over his shoulder to Mike-Mike, then hammered on Bucky's door. "Yo, get the fuck up nigga. I'm out yo! Be cool and make sure you call Ma Ma or Ms. Cookie this week."

"Yo, I'ma call this weekend, make sure you holla at everybody for me", said Bucky hopping down off his bunk he made his way to the cell door. "Yo, I know you gonna get money Dirty just be careful and have a spot for me when I touch, I'll be home in about five months. Oh, and get me a couple flicks of Munchie."

"Nigga want for something else, you know you always got a spot with me Cutty", said Dirty stepping away from the door he added, "I love ya Buck, be cool yo!"

"I love you too Dirty White", replied Bucky shaking his head wishing it was him that was being released instead of Dirty.

Nearly the whole tier had awakened and were banging and kicking on their doors as they whistled and yelled, "Be cool Dirty!", "Hold ya head up nigga!", "Don't come back!", and so on went the chanting until he exited the tier.

"Alright ya'll I'm out!!!", shouted Dirty White turning to Antmoe he gave him dap and they strolled to the front door of the unit. "What's up Unc?"

"Aint too much, just came to see you off. You got your thoughts together right Nephew?", quizzed Antmoe.

“Yeah, I got my shit in order”, replied Dirty side by side with Antmoe up the compound. “I’ma make it happen Unc, believe that! “

“I know you are Nephew just remember what I always say…”

“I know, if you can out think them you can control them”, said Dirty finishing Antmoe’s sentence for him causing both men to chuckle lightly before Antmoe spoke again.

“Make sure you call that number I gave you. You still got it right?”

“I got the number right here”, replied Dirty holding his phonebook up

“I’ma call soon as I get home.”

“For real Nephew, you need a job when you touch, plus the person whose number that is can assist you however you wanna move, feel me?”, stated Antmoe in a serious tone.

“I’m wit cha Unc, you said call say no more I’ma call”, said Dirty reassuringly.

“My man, look I can’t go out the fence wit cha so we gotta depart here. Get your lion share Nephew and try not to come back. Use your head!!”

“I’m wit cha Unc and I want you to know I appreciate all you done for a nigga, good lookin’ out! If it’s ever a way I can repay you just holla and it’s done”, stated Dirty as he and Antmoe embraced.

"Just call that number Neph and stay in touch and that's repayment enough", replied Antmoe patting Dirty on his back before they broke their embrace.

"Go ahead and get gone, I'll be in touch"

"I heard that be cool Unc and keep your head up", said Dirty turning into the administration building.

"You do the same", replied Antmoe turning on his heels he returned to his unit.

After what seemed to Dirty like hours he was processed out and given directions to R.C.I business office where he'd have to pick up his check. A blonde haired green eyed female C.O. escorted him to the visitor's waiting lobby just beyond two electrical fences and pointed him in the direction of the double doors leading to the parking lot.

"The person who came to pick you up is parked just outside those doors. She opts to wait in her car instead of sitting in this empty lobby", stated the female C.O.

"Good Luck."

"Thanks!", replied Dirty dryly exiting the lobby.

Soon as he exited the lobby he spotted his grandmother's 1988 Cadillac Coupe Deville. Seeing the car instantly brought back memories, Dirty thoughts traveled back to when he was just twelve, right before he started hustling....

… It was a warm summer evening. Bloc had given Ma Ma the car for her birthday a week or so before. Leaving her the keys on the table Dirty who'd been stealing cars to joyride in with his homies for about a year decided to steal the keys and take Ma Ma's new car for a quick spin down to the shopping center and back. Grabbing the keys, he crept out of the house. Looking around suspiciously to see if anyone was watching him, content seeing no one he walked over to the car parked directly in front of the house unlocked the door and hopped in behind the steering wheel.

Sticking the key in the ignition he revved the car up, adjusted the electrical seat and maneuvered the car out of the tight parking spot pulling off. He drove around for ten minutes or so before he decided to return the car and creep back into the house his grandmother none the wiser. Unfortunately for him things didn't go as planned. When he turned onto Hollins Street to park the car he was totally dumbfounded.

"Aw shit!", cursed Dirty at the sight of the neighbors' old LTD parked where the Cadillac had been.

Forced to park down the street he did so and crept back into the house placing the keys back where they'd been. Then he went to his room to get some rest. Bright and early the following morning Ma Ma literally woke him with a belt. She beat him until he was blue and purple, his high-yellow skin badly bruised. The neighbor had seen him take the car and parked into the spot intentionally then notified his grandmother that Dirty had stolen the car, that would be the last time he ever stole a car...

“Boy why you just standing there looking crazy? Bring your narrow behind over here and give Ma Ma some sugar”, shouted Ma Ma standing outside of the parked car, with the door wide open.

Dirty snapped out of the daze and looked at his grandmother. She hadn’t aged a bit and still possessed the beauty of a thirty-eight to forty-year old woman, though she was in her early sixties. He smiled then spoke.

“No, I was thinking about when you whipped the skin off me for stealing your car”, explained Dirty approaching his grandmother he hugged her firmly and kissed her on her cheek, “I love you Ma Ma!”

“I love you too Pumpkin”, replied Ma Ma climbing back into the car. “Come on let’s get out these mountains, I can’t stand these racist ass hillbillies.”

“I know that’s right Ma Ma”, agreed Dirty walking around the car, he climbed in and shut the door.

The car smelled of strawberries and still looked new on the outside but the inside was a bit worn, the seats slightly faded. As Dirty leaned back in the passenger seat observing the interior he had it set in his mind to buy his grandmother a new car as soon as he got right. Ma Ma turned her radio up, Al Green’s ‘Love and Happiness' filled the car. She adjusted her seatbelt and pulled off.

"Oh, Ma Ma I gotta go cross the street to R.C.I to get my money."

"Okay Pumpkin", replied Ma Ma following the direction to R.C.I he gave her.

They stopped at the gas station once they left R.C.I filled the tank and began the two-hour trip back to Baltimore City. They listened to the radio while conversing in a little small talk. It wasn't until they were fifteen minutes from Hollins street that the conversation became heavy.

"Antonio, listen… I've seen a host of young men get killed on Hollins Street, too many to name, I've had to bury your mother, your uncle Marvin, your cousin Marvin… I don't wanna have to bury you Pumpkin", stated Ma Ma with tears welling up in her eyes.

"You aint gotta worry about that Ma Ma, I'ma be alright", replied Dirty trying to soothe his grandmother.

"Antonio, I raised you, I know how you are. You've always been drawn to the streets I expect that out of you. As intelligent as you are, you could have been a doctor, lawyer or even a judge but that wasn't your calling. You were put on this earth to be who you are nothing else, I understand that everybody can't be a doctor or lawyer, that's why I always allowed you to pretty much chose your own path I want you to follow a straight and narrow path, but you're your own man so you're going to do what you choose. Only you know what's best for you. I'm not going to preach to you about what to do and don't do, you do whatever works for you Pumpkin. Just give it your all and be the best at doing it that you can possibly can", stated his grandmother turning onto Lombard Street.

"Don't worry Ma Ma, I'm definitely gonna give my all to whatever I do", replied Dirty sitting up in his seat he stared at the filthy slums known as Baltimore where he was born and raised as they rode in silence for the remainder of the ride.

Dirty sat on the edge of the passenger seat viewing the scenery. West Baltimore looked congested and even filthier then he'd remembered. Nearly every other rowhouse was abandoned with boards on the windows and doors. The houses that weren't abandoned looked shabby with cracked windows, peeling paint, missing steps and side railings. Even the side of the church on the corner of Mount Street and Lombard had been vandalized. Someone had sprayed paint on the side 'Hittin in the hole! No Shorts!!', read the large white letters. Heaps of trash and broken glass littered the streets.

As Ma Ma turned onto Hollins street, parked the car and then climbed out. Dirty surveyed the block. Hollins Street was still an open-air drug market. People were loitering everywhere. At least twenty hustlers stood on the corner of Payson Street, 'touting'.

"Blue tops ya'll", shouted one youngster.

"Red tops, pass me by you won't get high!", shouted another as three junkies approached the corner.

From where Dirty stood he could see Pulaski Street which appeared to be flooded with hustlers also. His grandmother had just stepped in the house when someone yelled his name.

“Hey Dirty White!”, shouted a feminine voice having spotted him from the corner where she’d been standing. “Oh, my God, when did you come home yo?”

Squinting his eyes, he looked in the direction where the voice came from. It took a couple of seconds for him to recognize the face. *Damn is that Tracy? She looks different if it is her,* thought Dirty as the big-boned light-skinned female approached him. Yeah, it’s Tracy.

“Yo, what’s up Tracy?”

“Ain’t shit yo! When you come home?”, asked Tracy.

“I just got out today”, replied Dirty looking Tracy up and down.

“Damn yo, you were down for a while. You got big as a motherfucker and your hair long as shit now. Your shit longer than mines”, stated Tracy laughing. “You saw Squirrel and them yet?”

“No, you the first person I’ve seen, I’m supposed to go to Ms. Cookie house a little later for a little coming home party.”

“Oh yeah, can I come? I got some bitches probably kill to get their hands on your red ass”, laughed Tracy before adding. “Yo, Squirrel and Fatty-Pooh they doing jive alright, but now you home I know ya’ll getting’ ready turn it up.”

“Girl you crazy, I’m chillin”, lied Dirty, then out of curiosity he asked, “What you doing out here anyway?”

“Yo, I gotta feed my kids and pay the rent”, replied Tracy dryly shrugging her shoulders.

Understanding Tracy was implying she hustled he pried no further, instead he asked her, “yo, you got your own crib?”

“Yeah, I live around the corner on Frederick Ave.”

“Oh yeah, I heard that, look I’m about to go up in here and rap with my grandmother. Be cool Tracy and come down Ms. Cookie’s later, bring them broads too”, said Dirty jogging up the steps he went in the house.

“Alright, I got cha”, replied Tracy returning to the corner, before he’d shut the door she was touting again, “Red tops Baby, Red tops right here”.

Tracy got her own crib, huh? That’s a potential stash house right there, thought Dirty as he locked the front door, his mind already in the gutter.

The inside of the house looked exactly how he remembered, with the exception that it appeared to be smaller as a result of his years spent in M.C.T.C. His grandmother had already gone up to her room to get a few hours of rest before work. She had to be to work at 4:00pm. While Ma Ma slept Dirty made a few phone calls. First calling Peaches, they talked for a good thirty minutes, she’d be home in fifty-three days on summer vacation. Neither one of them could wait to be in each-others presence.

After talking to Peaches, he called Ms. Cookie and spoke to her briefly. Everyone had promised to show up for the party, he told Ms. Cookie he'd be around the house once his grandmother went to work.

Hanging up with Ms. Cookie he called Nah's house. Nah wasn't home so he left a message with his sister Ra'jah who assured him she'd relay it before they hung up. Last, he dialed the number Antmoe had gave him. A female answered on the second ring.

"Hello, Clark and Son Construction, how may I help you?", said a soft-spoken female.

"Yeah, this is Dirty White, uh I mean Antonio Lord. Anthony Jenkins told me to…"

"Oh, yes Antonio, I've been expecting your call. Do you think you'll be able to make it here today? If need be the company will pay for your transportation, just catch a cab…"

Pulling the phone away from his ear Dirty looked at the receiver for a split second in bewilderment before returning it to his ear and speaking.

"No, I don't think I can make it today. How about tomorrow, can I come tomorrow?"

"Certainly, the office is opened from 9am to 5pm, the manager is looking forward to seeing you."

"Okay then I'll be by tomorrow, thanks."

"No, thank you", replied the soft-spoken female before hanging up.

Man, what the fuck is that all about… I guess I'll find out tomorrow, thought Dirty placing the receiver on the cradle.

Hungry he went to the kitchen making himself two turkey and cheese sandwiches, he poured himself a cup of extra sweet red Kool-Aid and grabbed an open bag of plain UTZ potato chips that were rolled up sitting on top of the refrigerator. Tucking the chips under his arm he returned to the living room. Sitting his food and drink on the table, he turned the TV on and begin to flick through the channels until he reached B.E.T. He ate and watched music videos until his grandmother had to leave for work.

Before he knew it, his grandmother appeared in the living room dressed in her white nurse outfit prepared to leave for work. Bending down she kissed her grandson before she left.

"I'll see you tonight. Have fun at the party. Oh, and here's your keys, I almost forgot", said Ma Ma handing Dirty three keys on a key ring.

"Thanks Ma Ma, be safe", said Dirty accepting the keys he stood, walked his grandmother to the door and gave her a hug and pecked her on the cheek before she walked down the front steps to her car and climbed in. "I love you Ma Ma".

Soon as she pulled off, Dirty turned back into the house, cut off the TV and left being sure to lock the door. Putting his game face on, Dirty strutted towards Ms. Cookie's house in the 2100 block of Hollins street.

As he crossed the street, coming to the corner he saw a host of familiar faces and some not so familiar. Everyone who knew him spoke and gave him a pound, hug or dap. Those who didn't know him seeing the attention he received whispered to those who knew him inquiring about him. He even heard one individual ask Rico who he was when he passed them.

"Yo, who slim? Ol' pretty boy ass nigga walking through here with his mug twisted up like he a serious nigga or some shit."

"That's Dirty White yo, slim just came home off a body. Yo is 'bout it", replied Rico.

Dirty had been tempted to show the individual that Rico was talking to who he was, but thought better of it and continued to Ms. Cookie's. In the short distance between his grandmother and Ms. Cookie's he'd spoke to and shook hands with two or three dozen people. *I aint been forgotten, it won't be hard to squeeze back in,* thought Dirty as he walked up the steps to Ms. Cookie front Door, he knocked.

The door flew open, it was Ms. Cookie. She smiled from ear-to-ear before she spoke with her arms open to give Dirty a hug.

"Hey Baaaay-Be! It's good to see you home Sweetie".

"And it's good to be home", replied Dirty giving Ms. Cookie a hug before she led him into the house.

Ms. Cookie rowhouse could only be described as 'ghetto fabulous'. In the living room, there was charcoal gray leather furniture and nearly every wall was covered from floor to ceiling with huge mirrors. The carpet was a plush dark gray that matched the gray big screen TV. Everything was just matched and exclusive.

Few people were in attendance when he arrived but the later it became the more people popped up and stopped by. Everybody seemed to show up. Several people even slipped Dirty money. The party was a blast. The music blared, people danced, clowned around and all in all had a nice time partying until the wee hours of the morning. Those who drank alcohol enjoyed everything from Jack Daniels to Remy Martin. The buffet of food consisted of fried chicken, crabs, shrimps, barbecue spare ribs, hamburgers, hot dogs, potato salad, collard greens, macaroni and cheese, corn on the cob, ice cream, watermelon and a host of finger foods and beverages. Dirty couldn't have asked for more, the party was wonderful up until 3:15am when the *police* arrived, shouting and claiming, 'People in the neighborhood were calling Southwestern District Police Station complaining'.

The party pretty much disassembled and everyone went home. Dirty waited until virtually everyone had departed before giving Ms. Cookie a bear hug and thanked her for the party and all the support she'd given him over the years, then he headed to his grandmother's. That night he slept in his old bed and for the first time in years he felt safe, sleeping like a baby. *Damn it feels good to be home,* was the last thought that crossed his mind, he then slipped into a peaceful sleep.

Chapter 14

'THE COME UP'

Bright And early the following morning Dirty woke up, brushed his teeth and washed his face. Dressed in the outfit he'd been released in, his grandmother drove him to the bank so he could cash his institution check, withdrawing six thousand seven hundred fifty-three dollars. Once they left the bank they headed to Mondawmin mall where Dirty ran in and purchased a few outfits while his grandmother waited in the car while he shopped. Before leaving the mall, he stopped at 'The Great Cookie" and purchased some snicker doodle cookies for his grandmother. In total, he spent nearly a thousand dollars, but it didn't put a dent in his pockets because he had received around two thousand dollars from his friends and associates at the party.

Having taken care of the business, he needed to attend to that morning he and his grandmother returned home. Taking a hot bath, he soaked in the tub for a while before getting out and getting dressed. Reluctant to call the number Antmoe had given him he put it off most of the morning, but being a man of his word, he finally called. The feminine voice answered the phone on the second ring.

"Hello, Clark and Son Construction, how may I help you?"

“This is Antonio Lord, I was ‘pose to come up there today…”

“Oh yes, Antonio, how are you doing?”

“I’m alright I guess”

“That’s good. So, do you need me to send a cab for you at the company’s expense or do you have transportation?”, she asked.

“I have transportation”, lied Dirty. “where I gotta come too?”

“Do you have something to write with?”

“Hold on”, replied Dirty fumbling around in the kitchen coupon drawer where he found a pen and a piece of paper. “Alright I’m ready”.

“Okay we’re located right off Howard and 25th Street, travel about a block and make the second right you come to, there’s a large parking lot with a gray aluminum paneled trailer, you can’t miss it.”

“Thanks, I think I got it, I’ll be there in an hour or so.”

“See you then, have a nice day”, said the feminine voice before hanging up.

Dirty put the phone receiver on the cradle and made his way up the stairs to his grandmother’s room. When he reached her room, the door was closed so he tapped on it.

“Come in Pumpkin”

“A Ma Ma”, said Dirty opening her bedroom door and stepping in. “I’m about to go up Howard and 25th to check on this job. I'll be back later. If anybody call for me take a message..."

"Boy I ain't no secretary", said his grandmother her eyes glued to the TV watching the Young and the Restless.

"Come on Ma Ma", pleaded Dirty.

"Alright Boy!", replied his grandmother looking up from her bed. "Be safe, okay?", she said looking her grandson directly in his eyes.

"I will, I love you Ma Ma", said Dirty closing the distance between the door and his grandmother's bed he leaned down and pecked her on her forehead.

Before she had a chance to respond her grandson had dashed out of her room closing the door behind him. In a flash, he hit the stairs and slipped out the front door. Before heading up the block he checked his pockets to be sure he had his keys and a few hundred dollars he'd kept out when he stashed his money in his old hiding place, the dingy drop ceiling.

Walking towards Pulaski Street he spotted Smurf, Snuggles, Squirrel and a few unknown faces standing on the corner. The corner store they stood in front of was boarded up and had graffiti covering the walls, one tag read 'R.I.P. Bud', a local homie who was gunned down by police.

Dirty stopped to 'kick it' with his homies, he couldn't help but acknowledge how torn down the hood looked. Trash, broken glass and drug paraphernalia littered the sidewalks. The streets were riddled with potholes and nearly all the houses looked shabby. Though the block looked raggedy he could tell from the constant flow of junkies that H and P was still a 'gold mine'.

"Look yo, I'm bout' to go catch a hack up on Baltimore Street so I can make a run, I'll holla at ya'll when I get back, we gotta rap", stated Dirty after kickin' it with his homies for ten minutes or so.

"I'll walk you up. Hold the fort down ya'll", said Squirrel over his shoulder as he and Dirty walked up Pulaski Street.

"Alright White", chimed his homies when they walked away.

"I'll holla later".

Once they reached Baltimore Street Dirty immediately flagged down a hack. The hack pulled over and idled at the curb until Dirty and Squirrel exchanged handshakes and Dirty walked over to the car. Leaning down he peered into the opened passenger window. The driver was an older man.

"Where you trying to go young blood?", asked the hack exposing uneven yellow teeth he leaned over the passenger seat and opened the door.

"Over off Howard and 25th to Clark and Son Construction", replied Dirty climbing into the call he pulled the door closed.

"Oh, I know where that's at... that's going to be nine dollars, young blood."

“Alright I got you”, replied Dirty.

“I’m going to need that up front”, said the hack sternly.

Dirty shot him a sideways look his brow wrinkling and the corner of his lip curling up.

“It ain’t nothing personal young blood, but motherfuckers a have you drive them all around Baltimore then fuck around and jump out on a nigga wit’ out giving you shit”, explained the hack.

“I feel you”, replied Dirty dryly, reaching into his pocket he pulled his money out and handed the hack a ten-dollar bill. “Here man take the whole ten”.

“Thanks, young blood”, said the hack driver accepting the money, he stuffed it in his pocket, turned the radio up and pulled off.

They drove in silence. The weather was nice so Dirty kept the window down and stared out at the attractive woman they passed. He longed to hold a woman, to get inside of a woman and feel the warmth of some juicy pussy, but pussy would come he knew, his main objective was to stack some funds.

The block still looks profitable but it’s way too many niggas ‘round there. It’s more top colors ‘round that bitch then in a rainbow, thought Dirty as they pulled into the parking lot at Clark and Son Construction Company.

“This the spot young blood”, said the hack stepping on the break.

“Good lookin’ out”, said Dirty, opening the door, he climbed out and slammed the door behind him.

The trailer looked exactly as the lady on the phone said, with gray aluminum siding. Dirty climbed the few wooden stairs, knocked on the door, then entered when the feminine voice shouted, “Come in!”. Soon as he stepped into the trailer he spotted an attractive cinnamon complexion woman with shoulder length hair sitting behind a large gray metal desk with a computer sitting on top it.

“How may I help you Sir?”, she asked in the velvet smooth voice Dirty recognized from the phone conversation.

“I’m Antonio Lord, we spoke on the phone.”

“Oh, hold on for one second”, replied the secretary smiling. She picked the beige phone receiver up, dialed a couple numbers, paused for a second then spoke, “Albert, Antonio just arrived… Umhm, okay”. She hung up the phone, “Go ahead back to the manager’s office right there”, she said pointing to a wooden door.

Dirty stepped over to the door and knocked on it.

“Go ‘head in, he’s expecting you.”

Dirty twisted the brass door knob and entered the office. He was instantly taken back by the figure he saw posted up behind the large oak desk with his black reptile skin shoes kicked up on the table as he leaned back in a plush leather office chair. The figure before him was Lucky Al.

“What’s up Antonio”, he asked standing he extended his hand to Dirty who still weary accepted it. “I didn’t think you would call, let alone come, but I’m glad you did. How does it feel to be back in the free world?”, asked Lucky Al as he sat back in the leather office chair.

“Everything jive cool so far I guess. It beats being in the joint, that’s for sure”, replied Dirty, looking Lucky Al’ directly in the eyes. He didn’t really feel at ease knowing he’d had a verbal confrontation with Lucky Al once. Nonetheless he rode the wave and decided to play the meeting by ear.

“I can attest to that, go on have a seat”, said Lucky Al motioning to the leather chair in front of his desk.

“So, what’s up, you ready to work?” asked Lucky Al putting his hands together in a one clap motion allowing his hands to land on his desk.

“Yeah, I guess so”, replied Dirty nonchalantly.

“You don’t sound to convincing… you aint really wit’ that work shit for real, huh? Questioned Lucky Al hitting ‘the nail on the head’.

“No not for real but I’ma do what I gotta do so the law won’t be breathing down my back.”

“I feel ya, Antmoe figured such that’s why he asked me to do him a solid and give you a job. Just out of curiosity if you not really trying to work then what are you trying to do with yourself?”

“Shit I’m trying to come up. I just did five years and some change, I’m trying to make it happen now that I’m out”, explained Dirty.

“Well look I know some people who know some people what do you think you can handle and where would you go if you get right?”, questioned Lucky Al studying Dirty face trying to read his mind.

“Shit I’d go around my block, Hollins and Pulaski and I…

“You been gone five years and you just going to pop up on a block, Hollins and Pulaski is an open-air drug market. You think niggas going to just go for you coming out and postin’ up?”, said Lucky Al cutting Dirty off in mid-sentence.

“Man, Hollins and Pulaski is my hood, I was born and raised on that block, I went to prison for that block and I rep’d that block while I was locked down. In my heart that’s my block and I got the heart and brains to control that whole area. Niggas either going to roll with me, get out of my way and respect me, or get from around there. I mapped this shit out the whole-time I was down and I intend to put clamps on H and P”, stated Dirty sternly, offended that Lucky Al second guessed him and his potential.

“I feel ya”, said Lucky Al with a smile on his face. “You sound focused, what do you think you can handle?”

“What’cha mean what can I handle? I deal wit’ girl and I’m only in position to cop a quarter bird, from there I’ma grind…”

"A quarter? What are you going to do with a quarter? That ain't even lawyer money. You think got to think big, besides I ain't ask you what you can cop, I asked you what you can handle", scolded Lucky Al as if he were talking to his own son.

"Man, I'ma handle whatever I get or die trying", snapped Dirty becoming offended by the way Lucky Al seemed to be talking down on him.

"Now that's what I'm talking about, in this game you have to be ambitious and hungry. Ain't no half way shit if you really trying to come up. Look, like I said I know a few people, I'ma make a call on your behalf for Antmoe. If you blow consider it Antmoe you crossed, not me", stated Lucky Al bluntly. He then picked up a pen and jotted a number down on the back of a business card.

"Here call this number at 3:30, ask for Los."

Without any questions Dirty accepted the card and put it in his jacket pocket.

"By the way how did you get over here? Can you drive?", asked Lucky Al.

"I caught a hack over here, but I can drive though."

"You caught a hack over here, how you getting back over West?", questioned Lucky Al.

"Same way I got over here, catch a hack", replied Dirty.

"Don't worry, I'll run you over and let's see why we can't get you a hooptie or something cause' you're going to need some wheels", said Lucky Al as he stood and stepped around his desk towards his office door.

Dirty also stood, he then opened the office door and he and Lucky Al filed out.

“Tiff, I’m going out for lunch, you want me to grab anything for you?”, asked Lucky Al stopping at Tiffany’s desk.

“No, I just ate a McDonalds salad, thanks anyway Sweetness”, replied Tiffany smiling.

“I’ll see you when I get back”, said lucky Al over his shoulder exiting the trailer a few steps behind Dirty.

At the bottom of the stairs Dirty stepped to the side and stood still allowing Lucky Al to take the lead. They walked over to a champagne colored Cadillac Deville. Lucky Al popped the doors, unlocking them with the remote on his keychain. He then climbed behind the wheel and Dirty climbed in on the passenger side inhaling the smell of new leather.

When he started the car up, the smooth tunes of Sade pumped out of the speakers. As they headed towards over West Baltimore, both men were consumed in their own thoughts so neither man spoke a word until the car reached the corner of Hollins and Pulaski Street.

“Which way from here, left or right?”, asked Lucky Al sitting at the stop sign on Pulaski street.

“This cool right here”, said Dirty seeing his homies posted up on the corner he opened the door. “Call this number at 3:30 right?”

“Yeah, be safe Antonio and use your head, shit will work out for you”, stated Lucky Al extending his hand, they shook hands. “I’ll be in touch.”

“Bet, good lookin’ out”, replied Dirty sliding out of the car.

Lucky Al pulled off honking his horn, he threw his fist up in a homie salute. Dirty returned the gesture, crossing the street.

“Yo, who that Dirty?”, asked Squirrel giving him dap.

“That’s this old head I was in the farm with”, said Dirty nonchalantly.

“I heard that, what’s up though? What was you talkin’ about before you left?”, asked Squirrel out of curiosity.

“I’m trying to put things in motion now, I’ll fill ya’ll in later, I just hope ya’ll niggas with me”, stated Dirty trying to draw a reaction.

“Nigga we wit cha”, hollered Fatz and Smurf simultaneously, they were back on Hollins and Pulaski selling coke, small time.

Dirty took notice that Squirrel didn’t give his word of alliance, but he didn’t probe further and instead switched the subject, “Yo, where the twins at?”

“Fatty-Pooh had to go over Guilford to see his P.O and Snug…”

“Five O yo, knockers coming up Hollins!”, shouted a look out man when he spotted the crown Victoria speeding towards Pulaski.

A few people scattered as Dirty strolled towards his grandmother's. Hearing the Crown Victoria screech to a halt, he stopped and looked back. The Crown Victoria was halfway up on the curb with all four doors wide open and five undercover cops were out with guns drawn harassing the individuals on the corner diagonally across from where Dirty and his homies had been standing. The suspects were made to assume the position, hands on the wall facing the wall, legs spread apart and searched. Knowing the procedure, he was content knowing that it wasn't any of his homies, he stuck his key in the door, opened it and went in to relax until 3:30.

At exactly 3:30 he called the number Lucky Al had given him. The phone rang four times, he was just about to hang up when a male with a heavy baritone answered the phone.

"Hello"

"Can I speak to Los?"

"This him…"

"Lucky AL told me to call."

"Oh, this Antonio?"

"Yeah"

"Look, you know where the Renaissance Hotel at, cross from the Harbor?"

"Yeah"

“Meet me there at 5 o’clock. Don’t change clothes, walk through the front door and make a left as if you’re going to get on the elevator, I’ll see you there.”

The phone had gone dead in his ear. The Renaissance Hotel, 5 o’clock, don’t change clothes, go left towards elevator, he ran the directions over in his head a few times. Then he dialed Nah’s sister number. A female answered the phone on the second ring.

“Hello”

“Can I speak to Naheem?”, asked Dirty

“Hold on”, said the soft voice. “Naaahh Phooneeee!”

Dirty could hear the soft voice screaming for his partner. A few seconds passed before Nah picked up the phone in a different part of the house.

“I got it, hang the phone up Ra’jah”, said Nah. She hung up. “Yo, this Nah, who this?”

“It’s Dirty yo, what’s up nigga?”

“Yooooo, what’s up? Where you at?”

“I’m at my grandmother’s. Yo, why you ain’t call a nigga back? I told your sister to tell you to call me yesterday”, said Dirty.

“Yeah, she just told me like an hour ago, I called then and ain’t nobody answer the phone, check the caller I.D”, replied Nah.

“Nigga I believe you, fuck I need to check the caller ID for?”, stated Dirty.

“What’s up though, what you up too?”

“Shit, I’m just chillin’, I just got finish fucking this little bitch Tee Tee. Why? What you got planned?”, asked Nah.

“I gotta take care of something at 5 o’clock, then I’m free.”

“What’s up, you need a nigga to strap up?”, asked Nah thinking, ‘taking care of something’ may mean blood needed to be shed.

“No, it ain’t like that yo. I just gotta catch a hack and go hook up with somebody”, replied Dirty.

“Man, fuck that hack shit, I’ma swing by and pick you up in bout’ twenty-five to thirty minutes.”

“You got a whip?”, asked Dirty.

“Yeah, I got a hooptie, it’s an old box Crown Vic.”

“I heard that yo. Look if you gonna come hurry up, I don’t want to miss this meeting. You know the Street and my address is 2008.”

“Cool yo, I’ll be there in bout’ twenty-five or thirty, one!”

“One”, replied Dirty.

It took Nah twenty minutes to reach Hollins Street. When he did he parked, climbed out of his car and knocked on Dirty grandmother’s door. Dirty answered the door.

“Who is it?”

“It’s Nah yo”

Snatching the door open Dirty shouted, “What’s up Cutty?”, both men embraced briefly.

“Aint shit nigga. What’s up wit’cha”, replied Nah. “You ready to roll?”

“Yeah”, answered Dirty checking out the dark blue Crown Vic with the crud ball, pitch black tinted windows, “That’s you right there, huh?”

“Yeah, yo I copped that joint about two weeks ago, a nigga need them wheels”, replied Nah glancing at his black Ironman watch. “Yo, it’s four something if we gonna go, let’s get gone nigga.”

“No question, I definitely aint trying to miss this”, said Dirty locking his grandmother’s door and following Nah to his car, they both climbed in.

“Yo, you know where the Renaissance Hotel at downtown? That’s where we gotta go”, said Dirty leaning back in the already reclined passenger seat.

“Yeah, I know where it’s at, it’s right next to the Gallery”, replied Nah revving his car up and pulling off.

Juvenile’s 400 Degrees Cd blasted in the car as Nah floored his car east bound on Pratt St. They made it to the hotel in no time. Unable to find a parking spot Nah circled the block, came up on Lombard and parked in a private parking lot across from the hotels entrance.

“I’ll be back in a minute yo”, said Dirty getting out of the car.

“I’ll be right here”, said Nah leaning back in his seat and he bobbed his head vibin’ off the Mannie Fresh produced track.

Downtown was busy, people were everywhere as Dirty strolled over to the hotel. Several bus boys were standing in front of the lobby doors and Dirty couldn’t help but to smile because the outfits they wore reminded him of Curious George’s outfit. Dirty took note to the waterfall in the middle of the lobby and all the plants decorating the lobby when he entered it. To his right there was the lobby desk and to the left there was a large arched throughway. He couldn’t see any elevators but walked in that direction nonetheless figuring the elevators were beyond the throughway.

Suddenly out of seemingly nowhere he was approached by an older gentleman.

“Antonio”, said the older gentleman in a very subtle voice.

Startled, Dirty looked to the man giving him a quick once over, then replied. “Yeah that’s me.”

“I’m Los”, he said sticking his hand out to Dirty, they shook hands firmly.

Then in a whisper he spoke again, “There’s a set of keys over there in the second phones coin dish. The keys go to the sky blue Grand Marquis in the underground parking lot, it’s parked on the first level. The stub so you can get out of the lot is in the glove compartment along with the title, the car is yours to keep. Also, there’s a duffle bag in the trunk, you owe forty-two and remember I never saw you and you never saw me. You feel me?"

Dirty nodded his head that he understood and with that confirmation Los stepped off, not bothering to look back. His job was done.

Dirty waited a few seconds, scanned the lobby to assure he wasn't being watched, then walked over to the second phonebooth. He picked the phone up, motioned as if dialing the number, pretended to talk for a minute or so and swiftly removed the car keys from the coin dish, then casually strolled out of the hotel.

He jaywalked across the street and cut through the parking lot, stopping at Nah's car. He climbed in and ran everything down to Nah in a quick chopped version.

"Yo, I just hollered at my plug. I got a whip in the underground parking lot with some work in it. I'ma get the car and drive to my grandmother's house, meet me there yo"

Nah didn't ask any questions, he just agreed to meet his partner at his grandmother's, "Alright yo, I'll see you when you get there."

"My nigga", said Dirty getting out of the car after giving Nah dap.

Nah pulled off and Dirty made his way over to the Renaissance underground parking lot. It didn't take long for him to locate the car. He looked around in every direction before approaching the car. Satisfied that no one was watching him he walked up to the trunk and opened it removing the duffel bag. He closed the trunk, walked around to the driver's door, sat the bag on the car's roof, unlocked the door, grabbed the bag off the roof, opened the door and climbed in sitting the duffel bag in his lap. He closed the door, looked in the rearview mirror seeing the parking lot empty and immediately unzipped the bag to examine its contents.

"Damn!", he exclaimed grabbing the huge black 45. Hi-point automatic handgun sitting on top of the two-silver duct taped square blocks inside the bag. He held the gun up, twisting it from side to side before placing it back in the bag and touching the two squared blocks.

What the fuck is this, wondered Dirty having never seen kilograms before in whole. Using the car keys, he ripped a hole in the tape revealing a white compressed powder substance. Licking his fingertip, he touched the powder then tasted it, it instantly numbed his tongue. *Damn, this is two bricks of Yay",* sighed Dirty. *I'm thinking forty-two hundred, they talkin' forty-two grand, shit, it's on.*

Excitedly Dirty sat the duffel bag on the passenger seat, put the key in the ignition, started the car and pulled off. Breaking at the toll booth, he used the stub from the glove compartment, paid the toll and drove up the ramp on route to his grandmother's. Parking directly in front of his grandmother's he slid out of the car, bag in hand and bee lined straight for the shelter of 2008 Hollins Street. He was half way through the door when Nah jumped out of his car on the opposite side of the street and shouted to him.

“Yo Dirty, everything, everything?”, asked Nah crossing the street.

“Yeah come on”, replied Dirty over his shoulder stepping all the way in the house, followed by Nah. “Lock the door and follow me”.

Nah locked the door, then followed Dirty upstairs to the second level of the house. Once upstairs they went directly to Dirty’s bedroom. He tossed the bag on his bed and turned to Nah with a ‘shit eating’ grin on his face.

“Yo, we on Cutty”, shouted Dirty unable to conceal his excitement, “I just got blessed wit’ two mothafuckin bricks my nigga!”

“Man, get the fuck outta here”, replied Nah in disbelief.

“No bullshit, look”, said Dirty as he unzipped the bag and flipping it upside down the contents falling onto the bed. “What the fuck you call this my nigga?”

“Oh Shit! Damn yo”, shouted Nah, realizing he was being loud he lowered his voice. “My fault yo, who else up in here?”

“Nobody, my grandmother at work. What’s up though nigga, are you ready to get this money or what?”

“Motherfuckin’ right, we bout’ to lock Baltimore down”, exclaimed Nah.

“Ain’t no question, walk me down the block so I can holla at my homies”, said Dirty putting the two kilos back in the duffel bag. He pushed the bag under the bed and stuck the 45. In his waistband pulling the drawstring tight, securing the gun.

Emerging from the house together Dirty and Nah headed for the corner of Hollins and Pulaski. The block was flooded in all its ghetto glory, people were everywhere, sitting on their steps, leaning against parked cars, hanging out their second-floor windows, kids were running up and down the block, junkies were coming and going and the hustlers were hugging the corners getting money.

“Yo, what’s up ya’ll”, said Dirty addressing his homies standing in front of the abandoned corner store. “I need to holla at ya’ll real quick, it’s important”.

“What’s up Dirty?”, asked Squirrel first basically speaking for the whole clique.

“I need to rap wit ya’ll in tight”, explained Dirty, motioning with his hands for them to walk with him. “Come on yo, walk up my grandmothers with me for a couple of minutes. Dirty started back towards his grandmothers, followed by Nah. Everybody else just stood still for a second exchanging curious glances before shrugging their shoulders and following their homie Dirty and Nah up the street. Once they entered the house, they followed Dirty up to his room and squeezed into it. In a total, there were seven individuals in the room.

Dirty gave everybody the once over then spoke, “Yo, I’ma cut straight to the chase, I’m back and I’m tryna take over around here", he pauses letting his words sink in then added, "and I got all the yay we need to start".

"Oh yeah, huh, what you think we gonna need? I mean this damn near the year 2G it aint 93, 94", said Squirrel in a jive sarcastic tone.

The sarcasm was caught by Dirty who shot him an icy glare, then responded, "Yo Squirrel, what you working with?"

"What you mean, what I'm working with?", replied Squirrel.

"You know what I mean nigga, what you copping?", asked Dirty stone-faced staring at Squirrel.

"Me and Fatz copping a quarter, why what' up?"

Dismissing Squirrel's question Dirty looked to Smurf and asked him the same question, "Yo, Smurf what you copping?"

"I ain't really nowhere, I just fuck wit' Squirrel and Fatty"

"How about you Fatz, what you look like?"

"I'm just flipping an ounce, bullshitting waiting on Freeze to come back out with the blow.

"How about you Snug, how you looking?", asked Dirty looking at Snuggles.

"I'm like Smurf, I help my brother and Squirrel, but for real I'm waiting on Freeze too."

"I see... look I ain't trying to shine on my homies, but I can triple what ya'll copping right now", said Dirty bending down, he reached under the bed and pulled the duffel bag out. Unzipping it he dumped the contents on the bed. That's two bricks right there. Ya'll my niggas so I'm trying to do this with ya'll like a true team playa, but with or without ya'll me and Nah gonna lock shit down around here and over East. So, what's up ya'll with a nigga or what?"

No one said anything for a few seconds. They just stared at one another, then glanced down at the bricks on the bed, as if stunned. Finally, Smurf broke the silence.

"Yo, I'm with you, you always been real and about money. You and your cousin Bloc got all us in this room hustling when we were kids, I'm with you"

"Yeah, fuck waiting on Freeze, I'm ridin' wit you Dirty", chimed Snuggles.

"Shit ain't no since in bull shittin', Fat daddy gotta eat, I'm down. Let's make it happen", added Fatz.

Neither Squirrel nor Fatty-pooh had replied or made a comment so Dirty questioned them, "What's up Squirrel and Fatty? Ya'll gonna roll with the clique like back in the day or what?".

"Yo, let me finish what I got left, then I'll let you know something", said Squirrel not wanting to flat out refuse Dirty.

"Yeah, yo when we finish this work we got, then we gonna holla at you", agreed Fatty-pooh.

“That Isn’t the answer I was looking for, but I respect it for now, but next month this time it’s only going to be one color top around here and that’s gonna be White tops”, snapped Dirty unzipping his jacket exposing his 45. Handle. “Mark my words.”

Everybody in the room knew Dirty White meant the words he spoke and wouldn’t hesitate to use the gun sticking out of his waistband. So, no one challenged what he said.

Sticking the two kilos back in the duffle bag, he placed the bag under his bed. Then everybody stepped out of his room and made their way back down the stairs.

“Yo, I’ma holla at ya’ll Squirrel and Fatty. Be easy and think about what I said I really need ya’ll on the team”, said Dirty opening the front door so they could leave. “Ya’ll still my niggas and ain’t no hard feelings”, he said as he secured the door behind them.

“Alright now, this is our team right here we about to build an empire but it’s going to take a little grinding from the gate. Now first off, how many guns ya’ll niggas got?”, asked Dirty addressing his team.

“We got four joints, a 44., two techs and a bullshit 32. Revolver”, said Fatz “They really Freeze joints but they at my crib.”

“Good! What about you Nah? What you workin’ with?”

“I got this”, replied Nah pulling a chrome nine milli-meter from his waist, “and I got a double barrel sawed-off.”

“That’s a nice little arsenal to start off with”, said Dirty, then he asked his next question of importance, “What size vials niggas using?”

“Everybody using twenty-five to thirties, except the nigga Orko, yo got thirty-five’s”, replied Fatz.

“What you think Orko seeing a day?”, asked Dirty.

“Yo, probably doin about nine to ten G-packs on a regular day, and twelve to fifteen when it’s pumped. Slim jammin’ for real”, said Fatz.

Dirty white sat silent for a minute digesting the information, then “Yo, what a nigga vial up off an ounce, if we use forty-fives?”

“I don’t know, depend, probably about $1500”, guessed Fatz.

Dirty put his right hand on his chin and calculated in his mind the possible outcome of using forty-five vials. Multiplying seventy-two times fifteen hundred, he quickly figured he pull in over one hundred grand and ran with it.

“Look, we gonna bust out with forty-fives and take over. We gotta grind, but by next month all of us should have big whips, tight lil’ cribs and a lil’ change stacked up. If slim and them doing damn near ten on a regular with twenty-fives, thirties and thirty-fives, then we should be able to shut them down with forty-fives and do ten ounces or so a day. Shit this shit a be gone by next week. We about to turn it up around here.”

“Ain’t no question”, agreed Fatz.

“Niggas gonna be mad with us”, added Snuggles.

“Who gives a fuck, we out for the bread”, said Nah always ready for beef.

Everybody laughed.

“Yo, what’s up with Tracy? Can she be trusted?”, asked Dirty thinking of using her house.

“I don’t know about the trust thing but she cool. Why what’s up?”, replied Snuggles who was cool with her.

“I’m trying to use her crib to vial this shit up, we gonna be all night doing it”, said Dirty remembering how long it use to take him to vial up an eighth, “and we ain’t doing it up in here”.

“Oh yeah, she’s cool for that, just give her a few dollars and she’ll be happy”, said Snuggles.

“Do you know where she lives at?”, asked Dirty.

“Yeah, she lives right around Frederick Avenue”.

“Alright cool, A Fatz, do they still got that vial store on Frederick Avenue?”, asked Dirty.

“Yeah, it’s still around there”.

“Hold up, I’ll be right back”, stated Dirty darting up the stairs to his room. Standing on the old dingy nightstand, he pushed the dingy drop-ceiling panel up and removed two G’s from his stash. Jumping down he hurried back down to the living room.

“Yo, here go twelve hundred dollars Fatz, get a hundred and twenty boxes of vials”, said Dirty handing Fatz crisp one hundred dollar bills straight from the bank, along with the keys to his car. “Take my car, it’s the sky-blue Marquis out front”.

“Damn, nigga you got a gun, yay, a whip, fresh big faces, who the fuck you meet in the joint, Escobar?”, asked Fatz joking as he accepted the keys and money. Niggas laughed. “Come on Snug ride with me…”

“No, Smurf can ride with you, I need Snug to help me find Tracy”, said Dirty cutting Fatz off. “Check day is this Saturday, that’s three days away by then I want shit on lock. Get white tops yo.”

“What if they don’t have white tops?”, asked Fatz over his shoulder as him and Smurf headed out the door, Dirty, Snuggles and Nah on their heels.

“Get clear”, replied Dirty, then added, “I’ll meet ya’ll back here in like twenty minutes.”

“Bet!”, said Fatz as him and Smurf climbed in the car.

“Come on Nah, ride us around Tracy’s. You know what house it is right Snug?”

“Yeah, yo”, replied Snuggles as they crossed the street to Nah’s car.

Climbing in Snuggles gave Nah directions. He followed them, driving around the corner to the 1900 block of Frederick Ave., where Tracy lived.

“Pull over right here”, it’s a house full of bitches. I’ma run in and see if she in there”, said Snuggles easing out of the car.

Dirty and Nah waited in the car and watched as Snuggles approached the house. He knocked on the slightly ajar door causing it to open. Peering into the front room Snuggles spotted Tracy sitting next to lil' Chrissy on the couch smoking a blunt and watching TV. The house reeked of burning weed and hair being hot combed.

"Yo, what's up Tracy?", asked Snuggles stepping into the house from where he now stood he could see the source of the burning hair. Keisha was in the kitchen straightening Big tittie Nay-Nay hair with a hot ironing comb.

"What's up Snug? Where Fatty at?", asked Tracy flicking the blunt ashes in the ashtray.

"He around Hollins and Pulaski", Snuggles offered before calling her to the side.

"Come here Tracy, I need to holla at you about some business real quick".

Tracy grabbed the arm of the couch and used it as leverage to stand. Once on her feet she hit the blunt, inhaling deeply, then blowing out a cloud of smoke. Snuggles lead the way out of the house and stopped outside on the curb, Tracy right behind him.

"What's up Snug? Asked Tracy inhaling the blunt again.

"Yo, Dirty tryna vial up in your crib, he gonna look out for you", explained Snuggles.

"How long ya'll gonna be?", asked Tracy exhaling a gust of smoke.

“I don’t know, it’s going to be a minute though”, huffed Snuggles.

“Where Dirty at?”, asked Tracy leaning back on her legs with her hand on her hip.

“He right there in the car”, replied Snuggles pointing in the direction of the car.

“Call him for me”, said Tracy smiling.

“Man, fuck all that Tracy, you gonna let us use your crib or what”, snapped Snuggles.

“Just call him real quick Snug, dag”, whined Tracy.

“A White! Come here yo!”, shouted Snuggles motioning with his hand for Dirty to get out and come to see what he wanted.

Seeing the motion, Dirty climbed out of the car and approached Snuggles and Tracy, “What’s up Cutty?”, he asked when he reached them.

“She wanna holla at cha yo”, said Snuggles motioning Tracy with his head., then stepped around her and entered the house to go holler at Keisha.

“Snug give this to Chrissy for me”, said Tracy catching him before he was all the way in the house, she handed him the blunt. “Thanks, yo”.

“What’s up Tracy?”, asked Dirty.

“What are ya’ll tryna do?”, she asked.

“Didn’t Snuggles tell you? We tryna use your crib to vial up. I’ma look out for you”, replied Dirty.

“What are you going to give me?”, inquired Tracy

“What you want?”, asked Dirty.

“I want you”, said Tracy laughing. “Sike yo, just give me a couple dollars. My homegirl Nay-Nay want you for real though.”

“I ain’t looking for no broad right now, my focus is this bread, bitches will come”, said Dirty pulling out a knot of money from his pocket, he peeled several bills off and handed them to Tracy. “Here yo, that’s two hundred dollars, is that cool?”

“Hell, yeah nigga, I thought you was talking about maybe one hundred, shit damn right two hundred dollars cool, good lookin’ out. When ya’ll coming?”, asked Tracy folding the money she stuffed down in her shirt into her bra.

“We’ll be around in ten to fifteen minutes. Tell Snug, we’ll be right back”, said Dirty walking over to and climbing into Nah’s car.

Tracy tried to tilt her head on an angle so she could see who was driving but the windows were too dark. She watched the car disappear onto Monroe Street, then turned on her heels and went in her house.

Dirty and Nah circled back around to Hollins Street. Spotting Fatz and Smurf parked, he told Nah, “Pull up beside them Cutty”, and rolled his window down also.

“Yo, ya’ll get the joints?”, asked Dirty.

“Yeah all he had was a hundred and thirteen boxes, we got them all”, replied Fatz.

“That’s cool, go ahead around Tracy house, we’ll be right around there”, said Dirty.

“Alright yo”, agreed Fatz, nodding his head, he rolled the window up.

Nah put his car in reverse. Fatz pulled off and Nah pulled into the parking space Fatz left.

Dirty opened the car door and stepped onto the curb, “Yo, I’ll be right back!”, he said over his shoulder disappearing into his grandmother’s house.

In a flash, he emerged from the house carrying the duffle bag. Climbing back into the car, he and Nah drove back around to Tracy’s house. Parking directly behind Dirty’s car, Dirty and Nah exited the car and darted into Tracy’s house, the door was already open.

“Yo, ya’ll ready?”, asked Dirty soon as he and Nah entered the house.

“Yeah, we ready?”, confirmed Fatz, Smurf and Snuggles in unison.

“Where we goin’ Tracy?”, asked Dirty looking in Tracy’s direction.

“Upstairs to the third floor, in the front room. It’s a glass table up there. Ya’ll gonna have to grab them chairs and take them with ya'll", replied Tracy pointing to the four black metal chairs surrounding her kitchen table.

Grabbing the chairs, they headed up the narrow dark brown wooden stair way. The stairs creaked under their weight. Once on the third floor they entered the front room. There were two windows overlooking the front of the block. Sitting in the center of the room there was a broken glass table, one end held up by milk crates. Blunt fillings, chicken boxes, brown paper bags, aluminum foil, soda bottles, liquor bottles and all kinds of trash covered the table and floor.

"Damn, this bitch junky as shit", said Dirty sitting the duffel bag down he swept the table with his arm knocking everything onto the floor, off the table.

"Yo, help me flip this glass over".

Nah grabbed one end, Dirty grabbed the other end and together they flipped the glass over and sat it back on the table frame. Then Dirty bent down, unzipped the duffel bag, and pulled out the kilo's. ripping it open, he put the chalk like block on the table. Fatz passed out the boxes of vials, bags of tops, and single edge razors. The cocaine was so compressed that Smurf had to get a steak knife from the kitchen to saw the brick into small pebbles. Then they stuffed the pebbles into glass vials, a little larger than a BIC pen top and sealed the vials with plastic white tops.

'Vialing up', packaging the cocaine, required time and patience. They had started the process just after

8:00pm, now roughly ten hours later they, half asleep on their feet, stuffed their last boxes.

“Damn, this shit takes all fuckin’ night. Next time we gonna pay Tracy and em’ to do this shit”, huffed Dirty.

“Fuck yeah Cutty, I’m tired as shit”, agreed Nah.

“Ya’ll a get used to it. Shit we use to be at the table for hours helping Freeze shift and cap-up that blow”, explained Smurf, then laughing added, “Ya’ll niggas look exhausted as shit”.

“Fuck you yo, exhausted or not I bet I hit Hollins Street when we finished and start pumpin’”, stated Dirty, hunger in his eyes.

“Shit, me and you both”, agreed Fatz. “I got’s to get that paper yo”.

“Ain’t no question”, agreed Snuggles.

Just before 6:00 am they had finished vialing up. In a total, there was one hundred thirteen G-packs, one hundred thirteen thousand dollars’ worth of cocaine. Dirty scooped the remaining powder off the table and put it into one of the Ziploc bags, left over. He eyed the bag, estimating there was about an ounce or so left, before putting it in his pocket. Leaving thirteen G-packs on the table he packed the rest into the duffel bag.

“Yo Fatz, take them packs and ya’ll hit the block after ya’ll get some rest”, said Dirty looking at Fatz.

“Man fuck that rest shit. I’ma put the bulk of packs around my crib then I’ma find lil’ Moo-Moo and Dirt-

Dirt and hit the block right now", said Fatz speaking like a true hustler.

"Smurf can hang with me while everybody else get some rest then we can switch shifts later, that way we pumpin' around the clock".

"Fuck it, I'm with it", agreed Smurf.

"Shit that sounds like a tight plan. I'ma run ya'll 'round Fatz house, then I'ma run this work out to my stash spot", lied Dirty not wanting anyone to know he was keeping the drugs in his grandmother's house.

"What's up Nah? You wanna try your hand over East or you wanna help us get shit off the ground over here first then shoot over East?"

"It's up to you Dirty, but we'd probably move faster with two spots. My lil' cousin Shyheem and a few lil' niggas 'round 20th and Barclay a help me and wit' them big ass vials I can easily do five to ten 'round my way'", replied Nah.

"Cool I'ma give you ten and tomorrow, I mean later today we all gonna have to get cell phones so we can communicate", stated Dirty.

"Yo, Black Derrick got the Nextel connect, the joints two hundred a piece and the bills one or two hundred a month unlimited", said Snuggles.

"So, that's a G, huh?", said Dirty doing the math in his head. "Look, when you see yo tell him give us five of them".

"I Got cha", replied Snuggles.

With everything pretty much said and done the clan descended the stairs to the first floor. In the living room laid a brown skin female with micro-mini braids in her head curled up on the love seat in a deep sleep and on the couch laid Tracy stretched out, sleeping with her mouth slightly open. Dirty tapped her on her thigh, awaking her.

“Yo, Tracy get up”, said Dirty tapping her thigh again.

Squinting her eyes, she arched her body, stretching. Her face looked as if she'd eaten something sour, her voice was groggy, “What's up?”, she asked once she'd gotten herself together a little.

“I'm about to bounce, here go an extra hundred dollars, see to it that room we were in get cleaned up and don't let nobody up there, that's going to be my room. Don't worry from here on out I got you”, stated Dirty in a brotherly tone handing her the money.

“Alright, thanks. Next time you come it will be clean”, replied Tracy accepting the money.

“Oh, you got any bags?”, asked Dirty.

“What kind of bag?”, asked Tracy wiping her face as she sat up.

“Like a shopping bag or something”, replied Dirty.

“Yeah, it's some grocery bags under the sink”, said Tracy pointing toward the kitchen.

In the kitchen, he looked in the broken cabinet under the sink and retrieved two grocery bags. Doubling the bags, he then unzipped the duffel bag and placed 10 G packs in the bag. Closing the cabinet and zippering the duffel bag up he swung it over his shoulder and with the grocery bag in hand, he headed to the car.

"I'm out Tracy", said Dirty exiting the house.

The clan having already exited the house stood out front awaiting Dirty. When he came out he immediately passed Nah the grocery bag and gave him dap.

"Yo that's ten, I'll talk to you later, be safe Cutty".

"Aint no question", replied Nah with the bag in hand, he stepped over to his car and crawled in, fatigue weighing him down.

Pulling off he honked his horn and drove down Frederick Avenue, turning left on Fulton Avenue, disappearing.

"Come on ya'll, I'm tired as shit and I still gotta make a run", stated Dirty.

Piling up into Dirty's car, Dirty drove around Fatz house on Baltimore Street where he dropped his homies off. After giving each one of them dap he sped off. Driving straight down Baltimore Street giving the illusion that he was going somewhere other than his grandmother's, but after traveling four blocks westbound he made a left turned and circled around, back to 2008 Hollins Street.

Dirty parked then glanced in all directions, scanning the block. Satisfied that no one had their eyes on him, he hopped out of the car, carrying the duffel bag and snuck into his grandmother's place discreetly as possible.

Safely in the confines of his bedroom Dirty stashed the bag containing the narcotics in his closet under a couple black trash bags that were filled with his old clothes and shoes from before he went to prison. With the duffel bag camouflaged in the closet, he shut the door, turned around and dived right onto the bed. There he slept, arms stretched out over his head, legs spread eagle, fully clothed, too tired to undress.

Chapter 15

Awakened by the sound of sirens nearby Dirty rolled over and climbed out of the bed. Still fully dressed he slipped out of his room and down the hallway to his grandmother's bedroom to ask her if anyone had called for him while he was asleep. Finding the door shut he knocked on it. When he didn't get a response, he decided to turn the knob, cracking the door he peered in, the room was empty, the bed made. Looking from the bed to the digital clock on the nightstand, he was shocked to see that it was 4:17pm.

"Damn, I ain't know it was that late", he mumbled turning on his heels he headed to the bathroom.

After urinating, brushing his teeth and washing his face he skipped downstairs to the kitchen. Raiding the refrigerator, he grabbed a cold slice of pizza and a can of orange soda. Then called Nah while eating the rubbery pizza. Ra'jah answered on the second ring.

"Hello".

"Yo, where Nah at?", asked Dirty in a muffled tone, his mouth full.

"He not here. Who this Dirty White?", asked Ra'jah.

"Yeah, this Dirty, where he at?"

"He around the corner. He told me to tell you to come over and stop by Safeway to get some food cause' the fridge almost empty or some crazy ass shit", stated Ra'jah.

"I know what he talking about, thanks and tell him I'll be over soon as I make a few runs", said Dirty stuffing the last of the pizza into his mouth.

"I'll tell him, but ya'll gonna have to pay me to be relaying these messages", cracked Ra'jah jokingly.

"Don't worry I got you", laughed Dirty hanging up the phone, he guzzled down the soda and tossed the can in the trash.

That nigga Nah jammin', thought Dirty smiling with that thought in mind he decided to go check on Fatz and them. He left his grandmother's house and headed down to the corner of the block. The strip was cluttered with people. A crowd was gathered around the steps of a rowhouse in the middle of the block gambling, shooting dice. Stepping around the crowd Dirty spotted Snuggles sitting on the steps in front of the abandoned corner store counting a wad of money.

"Yo Snug, what's up Cutty, said Dirty.

"Yooo, what's up nigga?", asked Snuggles sticking a balled-up fist out, clutching the money, he gave Dirty a pound, hitting his knuckles against Dirty's.

"Ain't shit, I just woke up. What it look like out here?", asked Dirty eager to get a report on the progress being made.

"Yo, it's jammin', we almost done them packs, we gonna need some more soon. Fatz already got damn near ten G's in the crib and here go six hundred right here. Shit movin' like a motherfucka", said an animated Snuggles.

Soon as he made that statement a white van pulled up to the corner. A middle-aged white man was driving, Dot, Gizmo's mother, jumped out of the passenger door in flip flops and cut off stonewashed shorts.

"Go ahead and circle the block', said Dot to the driver of the van waving him off as she stepped up onto the sidewalk.

"Hey, Snuggles Baby, can I get thirty-three for this three hundred?"

"Yeah, give it here", said Snuggles taking the money from Dot, he called out to a young frail kid "A Moo-Moo, give Dot thirty-three".

Moo-Moo pulled a Ziploc bag from his dip as he hopped up off the steps next to where they were shooting dice. Reaching in the bag he came out with four bundles, handed Dot three, then removed three vials from the fourth bundle and gave them to her also. Dot stuffed the three bundles down the front of her shorts and put the three loose pills in the coin pocket on her shorts.

"A Snuggles, why don't you let me tout for you? You know all them white people down pig town fuck with me. All I want is a dollar off a pill and I ain't gonna come for no less than ten pills at a time", stated Dot trying to sell herself so she could get a touting fee and a copping fee.

“You got that Dot”, said Dirty speaking for Snuggles, “But we ain’t gonna be keeping track of the two’s and few so you got to cop at least a bundle to get your touting fee”.

“Alright Baby, I’ll see ya’ll in a little while”, said Dot stepping into the street when she spotted the van coming down Hollins Street, having circled the block. She waved back to Dirty and Snuggles, then climbed into the van and was gone.

“That’s all day Dirty, Dot cop bundles constantly, she plugged with all of them white people down pig town because she won’t burn them and she always get them the best for their money”.

“See that just goes to show, loyalty is everything yo. Dot get hers every day because she loyal to the people she fucks with, feel me?”, asked Dirty.

“Yeah, I feel you Cutty. A yo, we gonna need some more packs. Why don’t you go holla at Fatz? I got around here, Moo-Moo and Putt gonna hold it down with me”, stated Snuggles.

“Bet, I’ll be through later, Fatz gonna have the joints when ya’ll need’um believe dat!’”, said Dirty about to walk up the block.

“Oh yeah, Derrick going to bring the phone’s around later, he giving us five for eight fifty”, said Snuggles as a junkie approached him trying to cop a few pills.

“Fatz will have the dough for the phones. Go ahead and handle your business, I’ll holla later”, said Dirty leaving Snuggles to tend to the corner, he retracted his steps.

Back in his grandmother's house, he hit his closet and grabbed the duffle bag. Removing twenty G-packs he tossed them on his bed and concealed the duffle bag where it had been. Grabbing the shopping bags containing the outfits he had purchased at the mall, he dumped them out on his bed and used the empty bags to put the packs in, putting ten G-packs in each bag.

Before leaving the house, he tucked the 45. Hi-point in his waistband and concealed it with his jacket. Then he grabbed the two bags with his left hand and eased out of the house. From the door way, he glanced up and down the block, then casually strolled over to his car locking the house door behind him.

At the car he unlocked the door, climbed in, started the car and shot around Fatz house. Stopping in front of Fatz house, Dirty parked and climbed out of the car carrying both bags. Walking the short distance to the front of Fatz mother house he knocked on the door. A couple minutes passed before Fatz answered the door.

"What's up Dirty?", asked Fatz soon as he opened the door, yawning he rubbed his eyes.

"Ain't shit", replied Dirty giving Fatz dap as he squeezed by him and stepped into the house. "Snuggles told me ya'll needed some more work".

"Yeah yo, shit jammin'! I know Orko and em' mad as shit cause' ain't nobody been getting' no money but us", said Fatz cracking a toothy grin and grabbing Dirty in a one arm embrace. "Nigga you a motherfuckin genius, those big ass pills shuttin' shit down. Come on and get this bread I got for you."

"Yeah nigga, I told you we gonna take over", gloated Dirty right on Fatz heels as he made his way towards the basement, where he sleeps.

The basement was a mess, typical of Fatz. Clothes laid everywhere in the dimly lit basement, along with shoes, empty pizza boxes and an assortment of food wrappers. When Dirty reached the bottom step he made a comment about the mess.

"Damn Fatz, your dirty ass need to clean up, yo".

"Fuck all dat'", snapped Fatz bending down to retrieve a purple Pokémon bookbag from under his unkempt bed. "I'm on the grind right now, when I blow up, I'll clean up".

"Nigga you crazy", replied Dirty shaking his head.

"I know that's why the ho's love me", said Fatz with a chuckle… "Sike yo, here this is $9600, it would a been 10 G's but with shorts and shit it's off a couple hunnid", explained Fatz handing Dirty the Pokémon bag. "The G stacks are rubber banded flat, the $600 is rubber banded in a roll".

Dirty accepted the bookbag and handed Fatz one of the bags.

"Here put this up, its ten more. You want me to give you the money for the phones out of this or you think you'll have it by time Derrick swing through?"

"We'll have it when he come, just go ahead and take all that and stash it", advised Fatz.

“Bet. Look I gotta shoot over East to holla at Nah, he almost done too. Y’all cool?”, asked Dirty.

“Yeah everything everything, be safe yo and lock the door behind you, I’m going back to sleep”, said Fatz pushing the bag under the bed then flopping down on it.

“Alright Fat Daddy, I’ll holla later”, said Dirty skipping up the stairs, he dashed out of the house, making sure to lock the door behind him.

Hopping back into his car, he tossed the Pokémon bookbag and the bag for Nah on the passenger seat, started the car and made a U-turn in the middle of Baltimore Street, coming out of the U-turn he headed straight for East Baltimore.

Roughly twenty minutes later he reached 22 ½ Street. Unable to recall the exact address to Nah’s sister’s house, he drove down Grenmount Avenue, located a phonebooth. He called Ra’jah and found out the address, then drove to her house. Parking in the small one way alley street his car half way on the curb he climbed out. Clutching the two bags in his left hand, he knocked on the flimsy door.

“Who is it?”, shouted Ra’jah from behind the door.

“it’s Dirty White yo”.

Ra’jah answered the door looking sexy dressed in a pink Polo Sports bra, with light stonewashed Capri’s which were unbuttoned, the zipper down an inch or so revealing the top of her pink panties. Ra’jah had a beautiful toffee colored skin, light brown eyes, standing 5 feet 5 inches and her body was covered with soft fine hair.

Dirty unconsciously stared at the trail of fine hair running from Ra'jah's belly button down south to her pink panties, mesmerized, he thought of Peaches.

"Well, you gonna come in or not?", asked Ra'jah sarcastically.

Her words brought Dirty back to the present and he responded by entering the small nicely decorated house.

"You can have a seat. I sent Ta'jay to get Nah when you called", said Ra'jah tucking her right foot under her as she sat down on the loveseat returning her attention to the movie she'd been watching.

Dirty sat on the couch and laid the two bags on the coffee table in front of him. Then out of habit he slouched back, stuck his right hand in his dip and in silence watched TV with Ra'jah. They both were into the shooting scene involving Method Man in the movie 'Belly' when Nah and Ta'jay showed up. Entering the house seconds apart.

"Yo, what's up Cutty?", asked Nah when he entered the house, walking right over to Dirty he gave him dap.

"Ain't shit, just trying to get shit right", replied Dirty watching as Ta'jay whom was attractive like her sister but darker sashay over to the love seat and sat next to her sister. "What's up wit'cha? Ra'jah told me to swing by".

“Shit movin’ White. I got a few stacks for you, hold up”, said Nah disappearing up the stairs located just outside of the living room. Reappearing a couple minutes later he handed Dirty a white Foot Locke bag.

“Yo this $7500.00, I got two packs on the block now and I got some pocket change. Yo, the white tops crushin’ the comp.”

Dirty accepted the bag of money. He wasn’t too fond of talking business in front of Nah’s sisters so he didn’t say much when he spoke. “I heard that. Yo that’s the same from last night”, he said handing Nah the bag he brought with him off of the table.

“I’ma swing back later with your phone, the dude supposed to have them tonight”, said Dirty getting on his feet he stuffed the Foot Locker bag into the Pokémon bag and zippered it up.

“I’m about to shoot back West, you cool, right?”, asked Dirty ready to leave.

“Yeah, I’m cool, I got my cousin Shyheem, Lil’ Ty, Skiddie Box and Brisco on the block, they all hungry young niggas. We about to be rich nigga”, exclaimed Nah.

Dirty shook his head in agreement while checking Nah’s sisters out. Ra’jah was eavesdropping discreetly, staring at the Tv, but Dirty could tell she overheard every word spoken. Ta’jay also eavesdropped, but she did so openly, staring at Dirty and her brother clinging onto every word.

“Yo, next time you come over I’ma show you the block and introduce you to niggas”, said Nah enthusiastically.

“Cool, I’ll holla at’cha later, I’m out”, replied Dirty exiting the house clutching the Pokémon bookbag, he looked around precociously before getting into his car and heading back to West Baltimore.

Hollins Street looked like Lexington Market during lunch hour. People were everywhere when Dirty pulled into the block. He parked and sat in the car for a few seconds observing the crowd. Content that nothing looked out of place or suspicious he slung the bookbag up on his shoulder and hopped out of the car with his right hand up under his jacket gripping the handle of the 45., in his left hand he held the key to his crib.

In the blink of an eye he’d made it to the front steps, unlocked the door, stepped in the vestibule and locked the door behind him. In his room, he emptied the book bag on top of his bed, emptied the Foot locker bag, sat down and began to count the money he’d collected, the total was $17,100.00. jumping up on the nightstand he retrieved his stash from the drop ceiling which equaled $6000.00.

He added $4900.00 of the $6000.00 to the $17,000.00 he collected making it $22,000.00 on the bed, he putting 5’s with 5’s, 10’s with 10’s and so forth, all the bills facing the same way, wrapping rubber bands around each of the 22 G stacks.

“It ain’t been but a day and already I got 22 G’s and counting, that’s half my bill and some… shit I’ma go see Lucky Al first thing Monday morning. At this rate, I should be ready to cop a brick or so myself when I take him what I owe", said Dirty excitedly to himself as he stuffed the G stacks into the bookbag.

With the bookbag in hand he walked down the narrow hallway to his grandmother's room. In her room, he picked up the black cordless phone off the charger on the nightstand next to the alarm clock. Using it he dialed Ms. Cookie's number.

"Hello", she said answering on the second ring.

"Hey Ms. Cookie, what ya up to?", asked Dirty.

"Nothing just relaxin' watching 'Don't be A Menace While Drinkin' Your Juice in The Hood', why, what's going on? Everything alright?", asked Ms. Cookie with motherly concern.

"Oh, ain't nothing goin' on like that, I just want to holla at cha' about something important. Who home with you?"

"Nobody, but my grandbabies Tywon and Kywon, you can come over, I'll be waiting for you", replied Ms. Cookie.

"Alright I'm on my way, love ya!"

"I love you to Sweetie", replied Ms. Cookie, hanging up.

By the time that Ms. Cookie rose off her couch, walked to the kitchen to grab another Jack Daniels cooler out of the refrigerator and returned to the living room to finish watching the movie Dirty knocked on her front door. Walking over to the door she placed her hands on the door and stood on her tiptoes peeping out of the glass panel at the top of the door. Seeing her sweetie Antonio, she opened the door with a smile.

“Hey Sweetie”, said Ms. Cookie giving him a motherly hug before closing and locking the door behind him. “Come on and watch some of this movie with me, it’s funny as shit. You ever see it?”

“No, I ain’t never see it”, replied Dirty following her into the living room where they sat down on the couch to watch the movie.

“Boy what in the world is your grown ass doing with a Pokémon bookbag?”, asked Ms. Cookie noticing the bag in his hand when he sat down.

“That’s what I came to talk to you about, I need you to do me a favor. You know outside of my grandmother and Peaches you the only one I trust…”

“Boy stop sugar coating and beating around the bush and spit it out. What’s going on?”, stated Ms. Cookie cutting him off.

“I, ah, I need you to hold this money for me”, said Dirty stumbling before blurting the words out.

“Boy, you act like you was ready to ask me to kill the president or something. How much money is it?”

“It’s 22 G’s”, mumbled Dirty.

“What you just say?”, asked Ms. Cookie, not believing what she thought she heard.

“It’s $22,000”, Dirty repeated a little louder.

“Whoa! How you get that kinda money?”, asked Ms. Cookie, then she held her hand up like a crossing guard. “Then again, I don’t even want to know. Just give it to me, I’ll hold it for you”.

“Here”, said Dirty passing her the bookbag, she took it. “Even though you said you don’t want to know where the money came from I’m going to tell you anyway, I’m hustlin’ again”.

“Um-hum”, said Ms. Cookie tightening her lips. “I understand, just be careful and use your head”.

“I am, you see I ain’t bull shittin’, uh I mean bull jivin’, I only been home three days and I’m already jammin’. For five years I’ve plotted on coming home and shining and I got a good connect so I’ma ride til’ the wheels fall off.”

“I hear you sweetie, just don’t wreck while you ridin’, okay?”, stated Ms. Cookie.

“I won’t”, replied Dirty leaning over he gave her a hug and a kiss on the forehead. “Thanks Ms. Cookie, I love ya!”

“I love you too sweetie”, she replied standing. “Let me go put this up, I’ll be right back”

“I gotta make some runs so I’ma leave, I’ll call you tonight to give you my cell number, Snuggles ‘pose to get me a phone”, said Dirty standing and walking towards the front door.

“Alright sweetie”, said Ms. Cookie following Dirty to the door, she locked it behind him when he left and went to stash the money he’d given her.

From Ms. Cookie house, he walked to the corner of Hollins and Pulaski, speaking to Pinky, Toya and Pebbles along the way, they were sitting on Pinky's steps. The first one of his homies he spotted was Fatz, posted up on the corner with a sub sandwich in one hand a large whit cup in the other, directing traffic as he ate and touted.

"White tops yall! Big white's out!", shouted Fatz.

"What's up Fat Daddy? How shit lookin' out here?", asked Dirty when he neared Fatz.

"Shit everything, everything, we been jammin'..."

"Yo, where Snugs and Smurf?", asked Dirty not seeing either of them on the block.

"They walked to 'Bay Island' to get something to eat", replied Fatz biting his sandwich, then talking with his mouth full he added. "I got Moo-Moo and Dirt-Dirt out here wit' me, they hittin', I'm just watching for 5-0. We gonna feed em', make sure they smoke and pay em' on salary. They thirsty so they with it, plus them lil' niggaz hustle their ass off. Oh, and before I forget I got the phones for you and Nah 'round the crib, plus it's about 5 more G's 'round there too. Yo, I ain't never seen coke pump like this since when we was kids.

Niggas who nickel and dime on different strips coppin' our shit by the bundle and breakin' em' down and some mo' shit. Yo we gonna be rich."

"I told you yo. I could've tried to stretch them 2 birds and made 150 G's, but we'd a been forever movin' dat shit, right now it's about the quick flip and the takeover", said Dirty smiling at his own cleverness.

"Soon as Smurf and Snug get back I'ma run around the crib and get the phones for you and give you dat... Hey Baby, right here, white tops, big whites", said Fatz to a white female looking in their direction as she drove by at a snail's pace in a purple Ford Mustang with the passenger window rolled down.

Hearing Fatz, she held up 4 fingers implying that she wanted four pills and stopped in the middle of the street. Dirt-Dirt, short with nappy hair, seen the car stop and bolted over to it. At the car, he reached around his back with his right hand sticking his hand down the back of his filthy blue jeans he retrieved a bundle of pills having had them concealed between his ass cheeks. He pulled the four pills off the bundle, stuck his hand in the car, grabbed the $40 from the white lady and handed her the 4 pills. When he stepped away from the car an old black man approached him with crumbled up bills in his hand, he purchased 2 pills and put them in his mouth hurrying on. Then a light skin frail man asked could he get 8 pills for $77, Moo-Moo served him and a young-looking female who wanted 5 pills.

"See yo, shit jumpin' 'round this bitch", stated Fatz.

"Yeah, I see", replied Dirty taking note that in 10-15 minutes it took Smurf and Snuggles to return from 'Bay Island', Moo-Moo and Dirt-Dirt sold at least 8 bundles.

When Smurf and Snuggles returned to the strip they were carrying food that Dirt-Dirt and Moo-Moo requested and sodas. They gave the youngsters their food. Happily, they accepted the food and sodas, taking a brief intermission to wolf down their food, drink their sodas and puff a blunt.

Dirty and Fatz left Smurf and Snuggles to oversee the corner. They strolled down to Dirty car and got in. Dirty drove around to Fatz house. He parked and Fatz wobbled into the house to get the phones and money. Returning within a couple of minutes, he climbed back in the car.

“Yo, here go the phones”, said Fatz attempting to hand them to Dirty.

“Put them in the glove compartment.”

“Plus, here go 5 more G’s”, said Fatz reaching into the big pocket of his gray hoodie he pulled the money out.

“Put it in the glove compartment with the phones”, said Dirty looking into his rearview seeing the street was clear he grabbed the steering wheel and stepped on the gas making a U-turn.

“yo, just drop me off on the corner”, said Fatz when they neared Pulaski St. “The phones already programmed, so just hit me on the CB thing”.

“What the fuck is a CB thing?”, asked Dirty not knowing because he’d never owned a cell phone and had just spent the last 5 years in prison.

“It’s right here, watch”, stated Fatz pulling his phone from his waistband, he flipped it open, pushed a couple buttons, then held one of them until the phone crackled. “Yo Snug pick up your phone…”, he released the button.

‘Bit.Dit. Dit...’ was the sound that came from Fatz phone and then Snuggles voice could be heard, like a walkie talkie effect.

“Yo what’s up?”

Holding the button on the phone Fatz spoke back, “Ain’t shit I’m just tryna show Dirty how to work the joint”.

“Oh, damn yo don’t know how to work the joint”, laughed Snuggles, “I’ll holla”, he said then clicked off.

“Did you follow me?”, asked Fatz.

“Hell no, I don’t know what the fuck you just did, but I’ll figure it out”, replied Dirty honestly.

“Alright, I’ma get back ‘round the block, be cool yo”, said Fatz giving Dirty dap he slid out of the car a split second before the light had turned green.

Fatz started back towards the block and Dirty honked the horn as he turned left and headed towards over East Baltimore to give Nah his phone. When Dirty turned on Nah’s block he could see the silhouette of 5 people in front of Ra’jah’s rowhouse. As he got closer he could make out Ra’jah lounging in a chair next to her front steps, on the steps sat 3 unknown attractive females of various skin tones, looking at Ta’jay who had the flor standing in the street talking with her hands and rolling her head. Seeing the car coming down the street she stepped on the curb so the car could pass. As she did so Dirty couldn’t help but gawk at her frame, her jeans were fitting her a latex glove. Slowing to a stop in front of the girls Dirty leaned up and hit the button to roll the window down halfway.

"Yo, where Nah at?", asked Dirty speaking to the group of females.

"Hey Dirty White", shouted Ta'jay recognizing him. "He around the corner, I'll show you".

Before Dirty had a chance to respond Ta'jay had pranced around the front of his car and grabbed the passenger door. Instead of protesting he just hit the button and unlocking the passenger door. She hopped in smelling sweet like she'd recently bathed in something from the Bath & Body Works Shop.

"You go girl!", shouted one of the females sitting on the steps causing the whole little bunch to snicker.

"Girl go 'head", replied Ta'jay dismissing her sister and girlfriends with a wave of her hand as Dirty pulled off. "Oh, this my song!", screamed Ta'jay turning the volume up on the car stereo. Juvenile's 'Back Dat Ass Up' filled the car as Ta'jay directed Dirty to the corner of Barclay and 20th Street.

"There he go right there", stated Ta'jay pointing at her brother.

Nah was posted up on the corner looking like a thug. Dirty honked the horn to get Nah's attention. Seeing the car, Nah held up 1 finger indicating to give him a minute. Then he turned to a slim dude with spike dreads, said a few words and strolled over to the car.

"Yo, what's up Cutty?", asked Nah when he reached the car.

“Ain’t shit just came to check on you and give you your phone”, replied Dirty, then he turned to Ta’jay. “Give me one of those phones out that glove compartment.”

The money that Fatz had put in the glove compartment had slipped his mind momentarily. When it dawned on him Ta’jay had already opened the glove compartment.

“Yo, hit the back door and ride with me ‘round the corner real quick, I got a few more stacks for you”, said Nah then turning to the teenager with the spiked dreads he shouted. “Yo, Shy hold shit down ‘til I get back”.

Nah climbed in the back seat and Ta’jay passed him one of the phones. Dirty pulled off and drove back to Ra’jah’s house, parked and the 3 of them stepped out of the car.

“Come on yo”, said Nah over his shoulder trying to make his way up the front steps. “Get the fuck out of the way Lisa, you too Meka, damn yall see a nigga tryna get in the house and the only one that got sense enough to get up is Tee-Tee, ya’ll two dizzy bitches.”

“Fuck you Nah, you the one dizzy nigga”, snapped the lightest of the two females as they stood enabling Nah and Dirty to enter the house.

“Dis dick ain’t dizzy”, cracked Nah without missing a beat.

“That lil’ ass di…”

They were in the house and Nah had slammed the door behind them before she'd finished her sentence. Nah ran upstairs and Dirty waited in the living room until he returned. When he did return, he handed Dirty a wad of money.

"Here yo, this is $4500. Make sure you hit me first thing in the morning".

"I'ma definitely do that, I'm out", said Dirty putting the money in his pocket he gave Nah a homie hug before turning on his heels, opening the door and leaving.

Once in his car Dirty honked the horn and sped off. Glancing in his rearview mirror he could see Ta'jay step into the street and using her hand she blew him a kiss. The other females doubled over in laughter.

If nah wasn't my man I'd be at his lil' sister…she phat and she sexy, thought Dirty just as quickly pushing the thought out of his head and replacing it with thoughts of Peaches. He turned the volume up, cranking Juvie's C.D...

Back in West Baltimore Dirty stashed the money he'd collected from Nah and Fatz in the drop ceiling in his room intending to take it to Ms. Cookie House in the morning. After stashing the money, he used his Nextel to call Peaches, they talked for a while before hanging up. Bored, Dirty walked down to the corner to oversee the block and kick it with the homies. Business was good and five-o was nowhere in sight so Dirty remained on the strip until the wee hours of the morning. His eyes became heavy from fatigue around 3 A.M so he finally went in the house to crash, leaving Smurf, Dirt-Dirt and Putt on the block.

Chapter 16

It was a breezy Monday morning when Lucky Al' pulled into the parking lot at his construction company. Normally the parking lot would be empty until 8:30 or so, but today there was a car already in the parking lot. Lucky Al's eyes instantly became wide at the sight of the sky-blue Grand Marquis he'd told Los to give Antonio. Having begun his lucrative hustling career with the proceeds from a robbery, the sight of the car with an occupant behind the wheel set off an alarm in his mind.

What Shorty here for this early in the morning? Why he ain't call first? He can't be finished yet; all kinds of crazy thoughts ran through Lucky Al's mind as he parked.

Seeing the Cadillac when it pulled into the lot Dirty slid out of the car and started towards Lucky Al's car. Dressed in the same outfit he'd had on Wednesday when he and Lucky Al' met. Nearing the Caddy Lucky Al' became further alarmed at the sight of the bulge in Antonio's waist. He knew the bulge was the imprint of a pistol. Lucky Al stared into Antonio's eyes, they were bloodshot red, but he couldn't read anything menacing.

With the car still running, the gear in reverse, Lucky Al kept his right hand on the steering wheel just in case Antonio made a sudden move. If he did Lucky Al reasoned he'd be able to step on the gas and with luck whip out of the parking lot without being shot. Hitting the button on the steering wheel, the driver's window slid down a little less than halfway.

"Hey Antonio, what's going on? What brings you out this early in the morning?", asked Lucky Al in a subtle tone.

"I got that bread for you", replied Dirty.

"You mean you finished already?", asked Lucky Al suspiciously.

"Yeah, the money in the trunk, plus I'm trying to cop somethin' too", said Dirty turning on his heels he went to the trunk of his car to retrieve the duffel bag Los had given him.

"Leave that other thing and come on and get in with me", said Lucky Al to Dirty's back.

Dirty knew he had to be referring to the gun and nodded his head in agreement. Popping the trunk, he turned to the side and in one swift motion snatched the 45. from his waistband, laying it in the trunk of the car. Then he grabbed the duffel bag and slammed the trunk shut before returning to the Caddie. He climbed into the passenger side, placed the duffel bag between his feet on the floor and sat back. Lucky Al pulled off in silence.

Once they were out of the parking lot, Lucky Al broke the silence. "What you selling weight?", he asked.

"Naw, I went to the block wit' everything", replied Dirty proudly.

“That explains why you look haggard, you ain’t getting the proper rest”, stated Lucky Al navigating through traffic.

“I can’t afford to rest right now, I gotta make moves. When my money, get right I’ll rest, until then I gotta grind”, explained Dirty.

“I feel ya!”, said Lucky Al admiring Antonio’s means of thinking he smiled. “I can’t argue with that at all. So, what you tryna do? You want something else, huh?”

“Yeah, I got what I owe you, plus I got 42 for myself, this 84 G’s right here”, boasted Dirty grabbing the duffel bag, he sat it on his lap and unzipped it revealing stacks of green. “I need two more birds”.

“So, you need two more, huh?”, asked Lucky Al glancing at the bag while keeping his eyes on the road. His chest filled with pride as if Dirty was his son and had just graduated from high school.

“How ‘bout I give you five and you owe me sixty, no make it fifty-eight since you giving me forty-two, from now on they twenty for you. How that sound? Can you handle that?”

“Ain’t no question, I got two spots already, one over my way and one over east, I can definitely handle it”, boasted Dirty confidently.

“I hear ya… Oh, plus from now on whatever you cop, I’ma front ya, so if you get five, I’ma give you ten and you just owe me the difference”, said Lucky Al using his left hand to steer the car while dialing a number on his cell phone with his right hand. He paused for a second then spoke into the phone, “Hey Los, how you feeling this morning?... That's good, A look you know the new project Antmoe had us working on… Yeah, look the first two turned out well, I'm thinking about trying to renovate five more in the same neighborhood… let's discuss it at the job site in an hour… Alright then peace."

Lucky Al had just told Los he'd received the payment from Antonio for the first two kilos and to bring five more to the construction company in an hour. Los understood the coded conversation and an hour later he pulled up in the parking lot of Clark & Son Construction Company. Parked his Chevy pick-up truck and entered the office.

Lucky Al and Dirty were inside his trailer office waiting on Los when he entered dressed in a black and blue dusty lumberjack shirt with ashy denim jeans and dusty wheat colored construction boots carrying a large red metal tool box.

Lucky Al had already put the money Dirty gave him into a red tool box identical to the one Los carried and sat it on his desk top. Without saying a word Los approached the desk, made eye contact with Lucky Al, nodded his head, exchanged the tool box in his hand for the one on the desk top and departed.

"Go ahead and take that tool box, it's for you, and for future reference, whenever you come over here wear construction clothes and bring your tool box. No more sweat suits and duffel bags, this ain't no gym, feel me?", explained Lucky Al, once Los departed, trying to polish his young protégé.

"Yeah, I feel you! Good looking out. I'll be in touch as soon as possible", said Dirty, standing he grabbed the toolbox, he and Lucky Al nodded to each other and then Dirty departed.

Once outside of the trailer, he strolled over to his car, put the toolbox in the trunk and discreetly retrieved his pistol, tucking it in his waistband. Hopping in his car he cruised over to West Baltimore straight to Tracy's house, his day just beginning.

When he reached Frederick Avenue, Dirty parked and eased out of his car stepping over to Tracy's crib. He knocked on the door and waited until an unfamiliar voice shouted from inside the house.

"Who is it?"

"It's Dirty White, where Tracy?"

At the mention of his name a brown skin teenager with huge breast swung the door open flashing him a smile. "Hi Dirty, Tracy's upstairs, come in I'll go get her for you."

Dirty stepped into the house. The huge breast teen started to shut the door, but Dirty stopped her, "Leave it open so I can watch my car", he said wanting to keep an eye on his car because the five kilos were still in the trunk.

"Oh, alright", said the teen as she turned on her heels and skipped up the steps to get Tracy.

Two minutes later Tracy appeared followed by the teen who'd answered the door.

“Hay White what’s up?”, she asked clearing the last step, her head wrapped in a gel stained multi-colored scarf.

“Yo, I need to rap wit’ you ‘bout some business”, replied Dirty.

“Sure, what’s up?”, asked Tracy crossing the living to turn on the stereo sitting on top of her TV.

Dirty didn’t speak, instead he looked over at the teen who was staring down his throat and then back at Tracy. Understanding the unspoken Tracy told her to go upstairs.

“Go ‘head upstairs for a minute Key-Key so I can holla at White, alone.”

Without protesting Key-Key turned around and skipped back up the stairs. With her gone Dirty spoke,

“Yo I need you to do me a favor and go get all the 45 white top vials you can buy, I’ma give you the money for them and I’ma look out for you. Plus, I got a job for you if you up to it, but you gonna need some help”, he explained.

“I’ll go get the vials on the strength you aint gotta look out for me doing that”, replied Tracy.

“But I do need a job, so what you got for me on that tip?”

“I need you to vial up for me and like I said you gonna need help. I’ll have Smurf sit around here with you, but you gonna need more than just him” replied Dirty looking from Tracy out to his car and back to her.

“Oh, shit I’ll definitely do that for you Yo and I already got some people to help me. I just gotta give them a couple dollars”, replied Tracy.

“I’ma give you $750.00 a bird and you going to the table wit’ two at a time, that’s $1500.00. Plus, I’ma pay all the bills in here for you, rent gas and electric, everything, just keep this between us and don’t let nobody on the third floor in that front room. Matter fact I’ma buy a lock for that room and a new glass table set, alright?”, asked Dirty.

“Hell yeah it’s alright nigga, shit I can give five of my lil’ homegirls a ball a piece and still make a G and I ain’t gotta worry about no bills, shit hurry up and get Smurf and that work around here for you change your mind”, said Tracy excitedly smiling from ear to ear.

“Bet, here’s $4500.00, use 3 G’s to get all the vials you can and the $1500.00 is yours. I’ma go wake Smurf up now, he’ll be round in about 30 minutes and remember don’t discuss our business with nobody, not even my close homies, feel me?”

“Yeah Yo, don’t worry as real as you keepin’ it you don’t have to worry about me saying shit, I ain’t tryna fuck my good thing up”, she said tilting her head back, laughing.

“I know that’s right. Be cool, I’ll holla at ya later, I gotta go get Smurf up and then I gotta take a shower and put on some fresh gear”, stated Dirty exiting Tracy’s house.

“Bye White”, said Tracy shutting the door.

"I'ma have to get Ms. Cookie to help me get an apartment first thing smokin' so I'll have a place to keep shit, thought Dirty on route to Smurf's house.

After picking Smurf up he explained to him that he expected no less than $55,000.00 off a kilo. Then he gave him two kilos and dropped him off at Tracy's.

■■

Things were flowing smoothly for Dirty. Not only did he have a car and a townhouse in Baltimore County, but he also had several thousand dollars saved up and two flourishing drug corners. In just three weeks he'd established a stronghold on Hollins and Pulaski, West Baltimore and Barclay and 20th Street, East Baltimore.

Having finished the five kilos, he had he linked up with Lucky Al again four days ago for the third time. Paying the $58,000.00 he owed, he gave Lucky Al and additional $100,000.00 for five more kilos and true to his word Lucky Al matched what Dirty purchased, giving him five kilos on consignment. His new bill was $100,000.00.

After this flip, everybody in the clique were going to the auction to purchase vehicles. The thought of getting whips motivated everyone. Even Dirty was holding shifts down on both sides of town. This day he was posted up on Hollins Street overseeing Putt, Moo-Moo and Dirt-Dirt.

Couldn't nobody sell a single pill, except white tops. Squirrel and Fatty-Pooh accepted the fact and moved to a new location, they hadn't been seen in a week or two. Orko and his crew on the other hand still came out and tried to hustle but made virtually no money. So, one day out of frustration Orko and two of his boys, all dressed in black decided to confront Dirty. Crossing the block, they approached him.

"Yo, main-man, let me holla at 'cha real quick, said the short, stocky and curly head dude Dirty knew to be Orko pointing at Dirty.

"Who me?", questioned Dirty pointing at himself.

"Yeah you, let me holla at you Main-man!", said Orko with a little bass in his tone.

"My name Dirty White Cutty, not Main-Man!", he replied giving Orko a cold stare.

"Look Yo, something gonna have to give, ya'll niggas ain't letting nobody else eat. Either yall gonna have to make yall pills littler or move around Calverton road or something", said Orko in a false stern voice, his two henchmen at his side.

"Do what nigga?", questioned Dirty with a baffled look on his face.

"I said yall gonna have to move from 'round here", stated Orko his confidence mounting due to the baffled look on Dirty face he mistakenly read as fear.

"Nigga you got me fucked up", responded Dirty breaking his mug. "I wish the fuck I would let a nig…."

CLICK! CLICK!, the sound of the two henchmen cocking the automatics they'd whipped out cut Dirty's sentence short. He looked down at the guns then up at the faces of the men clutching them. He stored their faces in his mind.

If these whores don't kill me, I'ma sure make'um wish they would have, thought Dirty, his heart thumping, sweat forming on his brow as he stared directly in Orko's eyes, his jaw muscles clinched.

"Like I said Yo, you gonna have to get away from here or we gonna send you away", threatened Orko shrugging his shoulders. "You make the call".

"I heard that, ya'll got that Cutty", said Dirty knowing he didn't have a win even though he was strapped. "Yall got that", he repeated backing away with a smirk on his face.

Orko and the two gunmen allowed him to back away keeping their guns leveled at him they walked the opposite direction. Just before they turned off Hollins Street onto Pulaski they tucked their guns.

When they did so pride made Dirty pull out the 45. from his waistband and sprint up Hollins towards Pulaski to shoot, but it was too late. When he reached the corner Orko and the two gunmen were driving down Pulaski in Orko's car.

▪▪

"I'ma kill that bitch ass nigga Orko", said Dirty for the umpteenth time, pacing back and forth in front of Snuggles who was getting his hair braided by Tracy I her living room. "I can't believe them niggas pulled out on me and ain't bust me! I'ma kill that bitch!"

"Yo, just chill! We gonna handle it", said Snuggles calmly.

"Yeah White, you can easily get Orko, he goes up in the barber shop on Payson and Pratt damn near every day, he fucks with the girl who be braidin' up in there", explained Tracy as Dirty turned to walk out of her front door.

"Yo, where you goin' White? Don't go do no crazy shit in the..."

Dirty slammed Tracy's door behind him and jumped in his car peeling off in a rage. Heading East he used his Nextel to call his trusted comrade Nah.

"Yo, what's up Dirty?", asked Nah when he answered his cell phone noticing Dirty's number on the face of his Nextel.

"Yo, I gotta holla at ya, you ain't going to believe what just happened", said Dirty in an agitated tone.

"What's up Cutty?", questioned Nah sensing that something was on his partner's mind.

"Yo, just meet me around your sister house in about 15 minutes, I'm on my way over", replied Dirty.

“I’m there!”, stated Nah immediately heading towards his sister’s house.

“I’ll holla at ya when I get there Cutty”, said Dirty hanging up.

When Dirty reached 22 ½ Street Nah and his cousin Shyheem were sitting on the steps in front of Ra’jah’s house smoking a blunt. Pulling his car half way on the curb, he parked and climbed out, a look of indifference plastered his face.

“Yo, what’s up Cutty?”, asked Nah standing when Dirty exited his car, he gave him dap.

“Yo, I need to rap wit’ cha”, said Dirty then turning to Shyheem he said, “What’s up Shy, let me holla at Nah for a minute yo”.

“Oh, alright Dirty”, said Shyheem, he stood and strolled down the block taking the blunt with him, his oversized blue jeans hanging down to his knees.

“What’s up Cutty?”, asked Nah once Shyheem was out of ear shot.

“Yo, where that sawed off at?”, questioned Dirty.

“It’s upstairs in Ta’jay’s room, why what’s up nigga?”, replied Nah stone faced.

“These cowards over my way flashed on me talkin’ ‘bout a nigga can’t hustle ‘round there. I’ma kill dem niggas, cold blooded!”, exclaimed Dirty.

“Say no more, I’ll be right back”, replied Nah dodging into Ra’jah’s house he reappeared in no time with the sawed off shot gun in a green bookbag with his chrome 9 millimeter.

“Come on Yo, let’s do this you know where the niggas at?”

“Yeah, one of them fuck with a bitch that work in the barbershop around my way. If necessary I’ma snatch that bitch up and make her show me where a nigga live. He gotta go!”, replied Dirty as he and Nah climbed into the car.

“Yo drive around the corner so we can get my whip. Leave your shit over here, that way we can creep on them. They don’t know my car, but they might know yours, feel me?”, reasoned Nah, making sense.

“Yeah I feel ya”

“Yo make this right… make this left, alright park and come on”, said Nah.

Dirty followed Nah’s directions and after parking they switched cars getting into Nah’s car. Nah drove while both men sat in a trance, listening to Juvenile on route to West Baltimore.

Nah broke the silence, “Yo, we should go to H&H and cop some black gloves, ski masks and shit”, he suggested.

“Yeah let’s do that”, agreed Dirty.

Nah drove to a surplus store in downtown Baltimore called H&H. Leaving the guns in the car they strolled into the store to purchase the needed gear. H&H carries all kinds of outdoor accessories, boots, coats, jackets, hats, hunting supplies, fishing supplies, etc.

They bought black long sleeve Dickie shirts with matching pants, black knitted gloves and black knitted skullcaps that could be rolled down into ski masks, then they headed for West Baltimore.

“Yo Fatz, it’s White, pick up...”, shouted Dirty on his Nextel walkie-talkie.

“Yooooooo-oh, what’s up White?”, answered Fatz his voice coming across clearly.

“Yo, meet me around your crib in five minutes”, said Dirty.

“Bet, I’m on my way now”, replied Fatz.

“See ya when I get there”, stated Dirty, hanging up then turning to Nah.

“Shoot by Fatz crib so we can put this shit on.”

Nah pulled up in front of Fatz house a couple minutes later and parked. Seeing the Crown Vic pull up Fatz opened the front door and peered out. Sure, that they saw him he left the door ajar and turned back into the house.

Dirty and Nah exited the car and walked straight into Fatz crib carrying the H&H bags and the green bookbag. Dirty entered the house behind Nah so he closed the door. Looking to his left he saw Fatz slouched back on the tan sofa in the living room, his left hand in his dip the other clutching a cheesesteak sub sandwich.

“Yo, what’s up yall?”, asked Fatz with his mouthful.

“Ain’t shit”, replied Nah.

“Yo, we just came by to change real quick Cutty”, explained Dirty as he kicked his boots off and began to strip down to his boxers in the hallway, laying his 45. At his feet. “Yo get me that D.E. Fatz”.

Fatz stood and went to retrieve the Desert Eagle without asking any questions. Nah also got undressed. Once they’d stripped down to their boxers and wife-beaters, they hurriedly draped themselves in the garments. By the time Fatz returned with the grayish silver Desert Eagle, Dirty and Nah were fully clothed in black.

“Here Yo”, said Fatz extending the gun to Dirty.

“Give it to Nah”, said Dirty picking the green bookbag up off the floor.

Unzipping the bookbag he removed the sawed off double barrel shot gun. Then bent down and picked his sweatpants off the floor and used them to wipe the shot gun down, freeing it of all fingerprints. He laid it on top of the coffee table. Next, he wiped off his 45. Off and stuck it into his right pant pocket, he picked the sawed off up and put it in his dip, it ran down his thigh halfway. Nah also wiped his 9mm and the Desert Eagle down and placed them in his waist line tightening his belt.

“Yo you aint seen me Fatz”, said Dirty as he and Nah left the house. Fatz nodded his head in agreement.

With the sawed-off shotgun in his dip, Dirty walked a bit awkward as he strolled to the car. Nah right in front of him. At the car, he had to grab the sawed off and re-adjust it so he could climb in. Once in the car he directed Nah to the barbershop on Payson and Pratt Street.

Nah followed his directions, made a U-turn on Baltimore Street, drove eastbound to Payson Street, made a right and drove southbound. Dirty's heart began to race, his hands becoming clammy inside the knitted gloves at the sight of Orko's black Acura Legend parked on Payson, on the barbershop side.

"Yo, this bitch think shits a game! That's the whore car right there", exclaimed Dirty his adrenaline flowing.

"Yo, what the nigga look like? I'ma go peep in the joint to make sure he in there, then I'ma signal you over", explained Nah pulling over to the curb across from the barber shop and Orko's car, he parked.

"He about Ra'jah complexion with jive curly hair and he short and stocky like lil' Alfie was", replied Dirty, Nah nodded his head and slid out of the car.

Leaving the keys in the ignition with the car on Nah walked over to the barber shop and peered in, he spotted the individual Dirty described. Turning towards the car he motioned with his hand for Dirty to 'come on'. Seeing the signal Dirty pulled the mask down, slid the sawed off shot gun out of his dip and looked around, before satisfied that the coast was clear he eased out of the car. The atmosphere seemed to become subtle and things appeared to be moving in slow motion as he crossed the street.

Once Dirty stepped out of the car, Nah pulled his mask down and whipped both guns he had from his dip and held them at his sides, “He sitting in the second chair”, whispered Nah when Dirty was in earshot.

Storming pass Nah, Dirty kicked the red door inward, it swung open and leveling the sawed-off shotgun he stepped into the crowded barber shop. Followed closely by Nah who caught the door with his foot stopping it from closing. His two guns were extended out in front of him trained on the occupants in the barber shop, his eyes were sweeping the room. Everybody in the small confines of the barber shop were frozen in silence, mouths open. Orko himself sat paralyzed unable to move a single muscle, fear on his face as he stared wide-eyed at the gunman aiming the double barrel shot gun at him. He wanted to plea for his life but the words were stuck in his throat.

“Don’t bluff’um, bitch bust’um”, barked Dirty pulling both triggers on the double barrel simultaneously.

B-BOOM!, the sound of the explosion was deafening as a full side of pellets from the buckshot’s tore into Orko’s upper torso at point blank range.

Orko didn’t stand a chance, the impact of the shot gun blast ripped clean through him and the barber chair, killing him instantly. Blood, shredded leather and flesh flew everywhere covering the mirrors along the wall behind the barber chair and the white and gray tile floor. Screaming replaced the echo of the blast. Dirty dropped the shotgun and in a fluid motion whipped the 45. Out of his dip scanning the barber shop for Orko’s cohorts. They weren’t there so he backed out of the door gun in hand.

Spinning on his heels he calmly strolled over to and jumped in the car on the driver's side. Nah bringing up the rear of the getaway emptied the 9mm into the barbershop ceiling causing all the occupants to hover in fear, hands over their heads curled up in fetal positions. He called himself instilling fear in them so they wouldn't jump right up and call the police or try to get the make of his car or tag number.

After he unloaded the 9mm he jogged over to the car and hopped in on the passenger side, Dirty pulled off before Nah had even shut the door. Word on the streets surfaced claiming Dirty and the 'White top boyz' were responsible for the gruesome slaying of Orko. No one could prove the claim, but the accusation nonetheless propelled the 'White top boyz' up the ladder as a force to both fear and respect.

Chapter 17

Blingggg…..Blingggg..Bli-

"Yo, who dis?", questioned Dirty answering his cell phone.

"You have a collect call from 'Anthony Jenkins' at the Maryland Correctional Training Center. If you accept this call do not use three way or call waiting features or you will be disconnected. To accept this call dial one now… Beep! Thank You."

"Antmoe, damn, what's up Unc?"

"Ain't too much Neph, just taking it easy. I didn't think I was going to be able to catch up wit cha in the house…"

"Naw I ain't in the house, I just forwarded my house calls to my cellphone. What's up though? Did you get the money and the pictures?", asked Dirty as he navigated through the rush hour traffic on Green Street.

"Yeah I got everything today. I like the car, what kind is it?"

"it's a 1997 Acura NSX, this joint mean as shit Unc", stated Dirty speaking on the car he had purchased from a Nigerian Lucky Al introduced him to. It cost him 43G's and he'd had it for about ten days, having bought it when him and his clique went to the auction in Elkridge, Maryland.

“Remember what we talked about far as investing your bread, don’t get side tracked splurging”, warned Antmoe.

“I feel ya Unc, I definitely gotta do some investing”, agreed Dirty. “By the way what’s up with my lil’ man’s Bucky and Gizmo? I sent them over too, did they get it?”

“Most likely they did. I really don’t dig Bucky, I just get a bad vibe from shorty but I’ll ask em when I go out to da yard. The other lil’ dude real laid back, he on the Muslim thing since he came off lock up”, explained Antmoe.

“Oh yeah, what about my partner Mike-Mike? I sent yo some bread and about sixty thong shots of these lil’ broads that be with my homegirl Tracy. I know yo gonna love that.”

“I don’t know if shorty got them cause they shipped him down Jessup to the cut two days ago. He got hooked up in some B.G.F shit. He’ll be cool down Jessup though cause they deep down there and it’s more serious, plus the cut better for him wit that fifty years on his back, feel me?”

“Yeah I’ma must get a broad to go see my nigga, I heard you can get some pussy down there if your money right”, laughed Dirty.

“Speaking of broads, what’s up with your girl? You still holla at her?”

“Make no mistake about it, I’m on my way out BWI to pick her up right now. She coming up for summer vacation today. You know that’s wifey Ant, ain’t nothing change. These broads out here can’t hold a candle to my baby”, boasted Dirty.

“I feel ya neph, you definitely need to keep shorty, she a good woman and they hard to come by”, stated Antmoe. “Look I’m about to get off this phone so I can hit the yard, I just wanted to touch bases wit cha to let you know I got the flicks and dough, good lookin’. Be cool Neph and keep your head up. Tough love.”

“Yeah Unc, tough love. Make sure you call from time to time and don’t hesitate to hit me if you need me to handle anything”, stated Dirty pulling into BWI airport’s compound.

“Alright Neph, I’ll be in touch”, stated Antmoe hanging up.

Pulling into the parking garage Dirty parked on the second level, then got out. Smoothing his shirt and pants over, he lifted his left pant leg up so it would fall behind the tongue on his brand-new Butter Timberlands, like his right pant leg. Looking down at himself, content with his appearance, he stepped in the direction of the airport. Crossing the street, he entered the huge duplex leveled airport, walking through the electrical sliding doors.

Peaches should be arriving any minute, thought Dirty glancing down at his watch. In a brisk stride, he made his way towards B-pier. Stopping at the metal detector he placed his belt, phone and the contents in his pockets into the small blue basket. After passing through the metal detector he continued through the airport passing several food chains, before reaching B-pier's landing where passengers board and depart.

When he reached the gate for South West Airlines, people were already disembarking from the plane. Butterflies fluttered in the pit of his stomach, anticipation mounting as a sea of people exited the plane. Nearly fifty people exited the plane before Peaches appeared, her beauty breathtaking.

Scanning the waiting area her eyes searched for and found Dirty. Her heart skipped a beat, a huge Colgate smile formed on her face lighting up the entire terminal.

"Oh my God!", screamed Peaches sprinting over to Dirty she threw herself into his arms, tears of joy running down her cheeks. "I missed you sooo much baby!"

"I missed you too Baby", replied Dirty wrapping his arms around her waist he pulled her to himself.

Palming her soft ass, he kissed Peaches intimately, sticking his tongue into her mouth. Kissing, they held each other in a passionate embrace for several long minutes, resembling a 'Big Red' chewing gum commercial. After a while they reluctantly released each other and Dirty just wrapped his right arm around her neck and she wrapped her arm around the small of his back. Together they slowly strolled to and boarded the escalator, taking it to the first floor to retrieve Peaches' luggage.

They stood by the conveyor belt until Peaches spotted her luggage and pointed the two black and tan suitcases out. Dirty grabbed them. Then the couple returned to the upper level, exited BWI and strolled to the car. The words of Sade's song "is it a crime" filled the car as he backed out of the parking space and pulled off.

Stopping to pay the parking fee before exiting the garage and cruising to Vellegio's, a cozy little restaurant in the little Italy section of downtown Baltimore. The seafood lasagna had been recommended to him by one of Ms. Cookie's friends, so he ordered it with garlic bread, lemonade and cheese cake for dessert. Peaches ordered the same. Conversations was light as they waited for their food and through-out the meal but what they failed to express verbally could easily be understood through their body language and constant eye contact. Having enjoyed the candle lit meal, Dirty paid the tab and left a generous tip then he and Peaches walked to the car hand in hand, embracing and kissing again before getting in the car, on route to Dirty's townhouse in Baltimore County.

When they arrived in the tucked away townhouse development a smile formed on Peaches face as she marveled at the light brown cobble stoned and tan storm siding townhouse which was now her crib. She could hardly believe her eyes, the townhouse looked beautiful and was a far cry from the slums where her and her man were raised. Keisha had told her that her husband was getting money hustling, but the car and crib were more then she'd anticipated. She looked like a deer caught in a spotlight as she admired the house. Dirty's voice snapped her out of the daze.

"Peaches, Peaches, come on, you gonna have to open the door while I grab your suitcases", said Dirty handing her his keys.

By the time he'd retrieved the suitcases out of the trunk Peaches had already ran up the few steps leading to the house. Opening the door, she stepped in the front room and stopped short, turning back to Dirty with a puzzled look on her face she stepped out of the house.

"Why you looking all crazy?", asked Dirty when he reached her.

"The house is empty", replied Peaches looking from Dirty into the house seeing nothing but bare off white walls and wall to wall tan carpet.

"Oh, yeah I only put furniture upstairs", explained Dirty stepping into the house he sat the suitcase down in the living room.

"Aint no reason for me to decorate the joint when I'm the only ever come out here and when I'm here I just sleep".

"Well 'least you could have brought a couch or somethin' for downstairs, all you got is curtains", said Peaches stepping ack into the house and locking the door behind her.

“if you want a couch and shit we can take 10-15G’s and go furniture shopping tomorrow, dat ain’t nothing heavy”, replied Dirty over his shoulder as he skipped up the steps to the second floor, Peaches right on his heels.

“Nah I was just sayin’ you could…”

“like I said we’ll go shoppin for furniture tomorrow and you can get some summer shit while we out too, alright Boo?”, stated Dirty crossing the threshold of the master bedroom he turned around, and held his arms out.

“Come here Baby, damn I missed you. You don’t know how many nights I’ve dreamed of this union”.

“The hell I don’t, I did those five years and twenty-three days wit’ your red ass”, snapped Peaches stepping into his arms, they embraced and found each-others lips, kissing passionately.

“MMMM I missed you soo much Antonio”, said Peaches in between kisses her nipples becoming hard, her vagina throbbing, becoming moist.

“Please don’t ever leave me again Baby, I need you here wit’ me to hold me like this all the time.”

“Don’t worry I don’t intend to ever leave ya Boo”, said Dirty palming Peaches by the ass pulling her to himself his manhood erect, pressing up against her leg as he sucked on her neck.

“Damn it feels so good being able to hold you.”

Removing his right hand from her ass he ran it up her stomach a began massaging her breast all the while sucking on her neck. Peaches began slipping into an ecstatic state tilting her head back, her eyes close, she ran her tongue over her lips, a soft moan escaping them. The soft moan coupled with the heat Dirty felt radiating from Peaches pushed him over the edge. Unable to stand the foreplay any longer he roughly tugged at her Capri's attempting to unfasten them, he accidentally snapped the button and broke the zipper.

"Damn baby calm down", laughed Peaches stepping back she looked at her man.

"Take your time I ain't going nowhere".

"Fuck all dat calm down shit, I'm bout' ready to rape yo' ass up in here", joked Dirty playfully grabbing her he slung her on the king size canopy bed and half heatedly dived on top of her tickling her.

"Boy…stop…playing so much", laughed Peaches squirming around on the bed as Dirty attacked her.

"Let…. Me…up Baby!"

"You gonna take your clothes off if I let you up", asked Dirty having pinned her down he nibbled on her neck.

"Yes Baby…Yes", replied Peaches in a fit of laughter.

"Say you promise"

"I-I-I promise Bay-Be", stuttered Peaches unable to stop laughing.

"Alright then, get your ass up and strip", demanded Dirty jokingly. Standing he helped Peaches to her feet, "Take that shit off."

“I aint takin’ nothing off”, said Peaches playfully swinging at his head, he ducked right before she connected and scooped her up, tossing her back on the bed.

“Alright, alright I’ma do it Baby I promise”

“Fuck dat I’ma do it for ya”, quipped Dirty grabbing her Capri’s at the waist he yanked them down revealing her smooth firm caramel colored hips and thighs, she grabbed them so he couldn’t get them all the way down.

The red thongs she wore only covered a portion of her soft pubic hair, the sight caused Dirty’s dick to grow stiff as a board. Kicking frantically, she tried to hold her Capri’s up and ward off the attack at the same time, but eventually loss the battle as Dirty snatched the Capri’s completely off her. He then held them over his head triumphantly like a prized championship belt before turning to put them on top of the black and gold mirrored dresser. Just then Peaches jumped up, hopped off the bed and leaped on his back wrapping her arms around his neck and her legs around his waist, locking onto him.

“Alright Boo, you win”, laughed Dirty looking at his girl’s reflection in the dresser mirror.

“Naw nigga, don’t Boo me now”, said Peaches shaking her head from side to side,

“You take your shit off!!”

“Shit, you aint said nothin’”, replied Dirty using his hands to balance himself on the dresser, kicking his boots off one at a time, he undid his pants in lightning speed and stepped out of them once they fell to his ankles.

“Now get off my back so I can take my shirt off before I toss you somewhere”

Peaches released him and stepped to the side. Dirty finished undressing, discarding his clothing in a heap on the floor, then he laid across the bed on his back. He watched lustfully as Peaches removed her jewelry, shirt and panties. He couldn’t help but marvel at how much she’d developed over the years. Not only were her breast larger but so was everything else from her waist down to her ankles, ass, hips, thighs and calves.

After she stepped out of her panties she crawled onto the bed, laying on top of her man. She grabbed his face in her hands and kissed him passionately, parting her lips as Dirty darted his tongue into her mouth. Closing her eyes, she could feel tingling chills of pleasure running up and down her spine, as her man gently ran his hands down her back and palmed her soft rear end.

A surge of lust and desire caused Dirty to flip Peaches over onto her back and rolling with her he came up on top of her, their hormones were in over drive. Peaches shifted her hips, spread her legs agape and drew her knees up to her chest revealing all her goodies. Dirty hurriedly positioned himself between her legs on his knees. Grabbing his dick, he rubbed his fully erect manhood against her sensitive clit and moist, slippery, hot vagina opening. She sighed deeply.

“Oooooh, ummmm… put it in me Bay-Beee!”, moaned Peaches biting down on the corner of her lip.

Complying with her wishes he pushed forward, the head of his dick penetrated the tight walls of her steaming wet pussy. She wrenched from the pain of being stretched open after having practiced celibacy for over five years, her face contorted, she groaned loudly and dug her nails into Dirty’s back.

“Ooooooh, aaaah, be eaaaasssyyy, oooooh”, moaned Peaches attempting to scoot back.

“MMMM, I am Baby”, coaxed Dirty running his hands under her back, he cuffed her shoulders so she couldn’t move and continued to work his dick in and out of her tight pussy in a slow motion.

“Damn I missssed you Boo mmmmm!”.

“Oh Antonioooo”, moaned Peaches her pussy muscles clenching Dirty’s dick like a vice grip.

Rotating his hips in a circular motion with each thrust he stretched her pussy causing electric volts to run up and down her spine. It didn’t take long for the pain of having her pussy filled after so long to subside, replaced by pleasure.

“Oooow yesss, make ahhh love to me Baby, oow make your pussy feel good, aww yes”, moaned Peaches, finding her rhythm she began to rotate her hips also matching her man’s thrust.

“Ooooh, it feels sooo good Antoniooo, ooow,um aaah”.

“Mmmmm Peaches, this pussy good as shit girl. Damn I love you girl”, exclaimed Dirty steady gliding back and forth, in and out of the tight confines of Peaches love tunnel.

“Ooooow, I love you too Baby, ah, ah, ah”, moaned Peaches as electrically charged sparks shot through her entire body.

“Ooooh my God, faster, oooow, faster, ooooo I’m about to AAAHHHHHH, Antonioooooo!!!”

Waves of pleasure rippled through her as she climaxed. Clinging to Dirty she wrapped her legs around his waist and dug her claws into his back. With her head twisted to the left, her eyes closed as she bit down on her bottom lip and shuddered in ecstasy. She laid still for a moment, then once she pulled herself together she began to match Dirty’s thrust again.

“MMmm...that’s right Boo, give Daddy that pussy”, urged Dirty speeding up as a thunderous electrical urge overcame him, all his nerves on end, his toes curled, his eyes rolled up in his head, he exploded inside of Peaches.

“AAAAAHHH!!!”

Globs of hot cum spurted into Peaches pussy triggering her second orgasm,

“OOOOOWww Antoniooooo!!”, she screamed digging her nails deeper in Dirty’s back.

Spent, they laid still for a while overcome by sweet lassitude. Then Dirty reached over and began to kiss on Peaches neck again, running his hand between her legs he stuck his finger inside of her and round two began. After round two came three and four, they made love in all kinds of positions before they fell asleep utterly relaxed, content and satisfied. Dirty slept like a baby as did Peaches who felt safe and secure in her man's arms.

■■■

Bliiiiinnnngggg…Bliiinnnnngg…Bliiiinnngggg……

Dirty opened his eyes and squinted in the ark trying to read the digits on the clock. It read 3:47.

Bliiiiinnng…Bling…Bling.."

"Man, who da fuck callin' me this fuckin' early", griped Dirty rolling over he leaned out of bed balancing himself with one hand on the floor he fumbled for and found his phone with the other hand.

"Yo who dis?", asked Dirty his voice heavy with fatigue he pushed himself back onto the bed and laid back.

"It's Snug yo, my fault for wakin' you up but Squirrel and Fatty told me to hit ya immediately 'cause they locked up. They got locked up in a house raid wit some shit and a hammer, they bail 100G's a piece and they tryna get out before the check on the hammer come back 'cause it might be a body on it", explained Snuggles in rapid dialect.

“Oh yeah? They locked up and now they wanna call a nigga, huh? Where they bail money at? They aint wanna fuck wit’ a nigga because they supposed to been jammin’, but now they over the bookings and can’t even pay their own bail”, ranted Dirty knowing he could spring them with one phone call since the past few weeks he’d been giving a bail bondsman Lucky Al introduced him to named fat Frank a couple thousand every week or so, in case of a crisis.

“they still our homies and they’d see to it that they got you out on bail if they could if shoes were on the other feet”, reasoned Snuggles trying to be rational.

“Yo I can get Fatty wit’ the dough I been stackin’ but if I get Squirrel too my funds gonna be low as shit, feel me?”

“Yeah, I feel ya, look even though them niggas ‘posed to rolled wit’ us when I came home I ain’t gonna see’um locked up so I’ma put up the five percent on both of ‘um, my peeps a get ‘um for that and they’ll just have to owe the bail bondsman the other 5G’s a piece. You go ‘head and save your dough. If you talk to them before I do tell’um I said real niggas do real shit”, boasted Dirty.

“Look on the bright side them niggas gonna owe you.”

“Ain’t no question”, laughed Dirty, “other than that everything, everything?”

“Yeah everything Kosher, Cutty”.

“Cool, I’ma call the bail bondsman and take care of that, I’ll holla later”, said Dirty hanging up before Snuggles responded.

Then he immediately called the bail bondsman. To his surprise frank answered his phone on the second ring without a hint of sleep detectable in his tone. He agreed to post their bail with the understanding that they'd have to pay weekly payments on the balance owed, the other five percent and bring co-signers to his office later that evening. After taking care of the bail situation, he tossed his phone back on the floor on top of his pants and snuggled up next to peaches. Draping his arm over her, he kissed the nape of her neck. "I love you Boo", were the last words he spoke before dozing back off to sleep.

Chapter 18

Nearly three months had elapsed since Dirty paid Squirrel and Fatty-Pooh's bails. The $10,000 he'd come out of his pocket with proved to be a wise investment. Not only did he now employ both Squirrel and Fatty-Pooh, but he'd also inherited the corner they'd been hustling on since he took over Hollins and Pulaski.

The newest corner generated an average of $12,000 a day and $120,000 every ten days. So, in total between the three corners he controlled he sold roughly a brick a day, grossing an estimated $550,000 every ten days. Business was great and everyone on Dirty's team ate well.

Pay day came every ten days like clockwork and went as follows: Lieutenants- Nah, Fatz, Smurf, Snuggles, Squirrel and Fatty-Pooh received $10,000 to oversee foot soldiers, foot soldiers received $2500 to serve hand to hand, Tracy received $7500 off every ten bricks for packaging the drugs, fat Frank received $7500 in case bail became an issue, Warren Browno received $7500 in case a lawyer was needed and all mishaps-short money, losses, robberies, etc., fell in Dirty's lap. In all the payroll swallowed up roughly $120,000. Minus-ing payroll and the re-up money, $200,000. Dirty still cleared roughly $230,000 for himself every ten days, more than half a million a month.

The money rolled in abundance and Dirty made it his duty to bless his family and friends from his grandmother to his Comrades in the Division of Correction and everyone in between. One of his most memorable showings of blessing a friend was when Bucky came home. Bucky was released on July 18th, the following day Dirty hooked up with Cujo and the three of them went to the Auction to purchase a vehicle for Bucky, who would have been content with a hooptie but Dirty insisted that his homie get what he wanted, he chose a truck. The Tahoe he chose cost $21,000. After Dirty gave Cujo the money to pay for the truck, Cujo gave him the keys and Dirty turned the keys over to Bucky.

"Yo, this how real niggas do shit Cutty!", said Dirty handing Bucky the keys to the truck and $10,000 in cash.

"Make sure you get a Black outfit for the 'Black Out' party we throwin' at the Lava Lounge, it's for my birthday and your home coming".

"Damn White", stated Bucky accepting the key and money, he looked at Dirty. "I don't know what that fuck to say yo"

"Nigga don't say shit, just enjoy this shit, I told ya you'd always have a spot wit' me nigga", explained Dirty giving Bucky a hug.

"I love your ugly ass like a brother Cutty!"

"I love ya too White... Good lookin' out Yo", said Bucky all choked up as the two embraced.

The lava lounge is considered a 'hot spot', located in the Inner Harbor section of downtown Baltimore. To retain the club for his 'Black Out' party Dirty paid $2500 a month in advance. Word of the party leaked and spread like a wild fire through the streets and everybody of status in the slums of Baltimore seemed to show up dressed to impress from head to toe in black designer outfits.

Dirty himself showed up draped in a black Iceberg History button up short sleeve shirt with matching shorts and a pair of black Kenneth Cole soft bottom's, no socks. His hair freshly cornrowed, he smelled of Issey Miyake. Though he didn't wear flashy jewelry that screamed 'hustler' or 'money', his mannerism reeked of such and the 'dime piece' at his side spoke volumes for his status. Peaches is a 10 and she looked outstanding next to her man in a black backless form fitting Prada dress that stopped an inch above her knees with a black mink shawl draped over her shoulders and black open toe Prada heels. She smelled of Chris 1947, Christian Dior, her hair in a bun, diamonds and white gold sparkled visibly from her neck, fingers, wrist and ears.

When they entered the dimly lit club they bared to the left and climbed the black spiral stairs to the third level, VIP. The music was blaring, people were mingling, dancing, socializing and enjoying themselves. When Dirty and Peaches reached the third level all the occupants of that level shouted, "Happy Birthday!!", and made their way over to Dirty to shake his hand and exchange pleasantries. The entire team showed up for this evening. Dirty basked in the spotlight for a while his chest filling with pride.

I've come up, thought Dirty grabbing Peaches.

"Come on Baby let's dance and enjoy ourselves".

They grinded and danced for twenty to thirty minutes undisturbed, then all at once lieutenants and Tracy approached him and Peaches.

"Here Cutty, Happy Birthday from the crew", said Nah extending a platinum chain with an iced-out, diamond clustered, medallion the size of a deck of playing cards with 'Slum Lord' engraved on it and the back drop of Baltimore City's horizon.

"You on top of your game nigga, the Lord of the Slums Cutty. Happy 21st Birthday, I hope you see many more."

"Good lookin' out yall", said Dirty accepting the chain.

"Wouldn't none of this be possible without yall, everybody plays they part, we a team. Let's continue to get this money yall. Get Money!!"

"Get Money!", echoed the team in unison, each personally hugging Dirty White.

"A White, put the chain on Cutty", said Snuggles after everyone had given him a hug.

"Yeah Yo, put that shit on White", agreed Tracy.

"I ain't never seen you wear jewels."

He put the chain on, fitting it over his head, it dangled from his neck. It looked official on him, lights dancing off the diamonds, vibrant colors glistening.

"Stand still Cutty", said Nah giving Dirty White a critical once over from head to toe, "Yeah that's you nigga."

"Yo, this may sound crazy but I was just standin' here looking over the railing at the other two levels, this motherfucka packed, shit we need to open a motherfuckin' club and get rich", said Fatz out of nowhere dressed in Gucci from head to toe with shades on, an indication that he was rollin' high on Ecstasy pills.

"Open a club huh Fatz?", mocked Smurf who was standing next to Fatz also dressed in Gucci.

"Hell yeah Yo and I could be the DJ, DJ Fat Daddy on the wheels of steel", shouted Fatz licking his fingertips he rubbed them on Smurf's bald head as if he was scratching on a turntable. Smurf smacked his hand down and Fatz started doing the snake snapping his fingers then stepped back and motioned with his hand like he was DJ'ing making a turntable sound with his mouth.

Everybody burst out laughing. The team lingered around a little longer sharing small talk before blending back in with the rest of the party crowd. Peaches, Munchie and Keisha were talking off to the side and Dirty and Nah were talking looking over the railing at the other two levels.

“Maybe a club would be a good thing to invest in Nah. What you think Yo?”, asked Dirty still hanging on to Fatz words.

“Shit why not? You got the bread, do you Cutty!”, replied Nah.

“Yeah Yo, look how many people up in this bitch”, said Dirty scanning the club when two individuals at the large bar on the first level caught his eye.

‘It can’t be’, thought Dirty squinting his eyes to see if what he thought he saw was correct.

“Yo Nah, that look like them niggas that pulled them joints out on me, Orko’s homies”, said Dirty not taking his eyes off the culprits.

“Where Yo?”, asked Nah looking in the same direction as Dirty.

“Right there at the bar”, replied Dirty pointing at the two individuals. “The light skin one wit’ his hat to da back and the chump next to ‘em wit’ the braids, you see’um?”

“Yeah I see’um. You sure that’s them?”, asked Nah.

“Yo go get Tracy, I’ma keep an eye on ‘um”, replied Dirty.

“Alright Yo”, sad Nah spinning on his heels he went to find Tracy. A minute or so later returned with her at his side.

“Hey White, what’s up? Nah said you wanted me”, stated Tracy walking up next to him she looked at him smiling.

“Yo, you see them niggas at the bar right there, the one wit’ his hat cocked back and slim wit’ the braids next to him?”, asked Dirty pointed at the culprits.

“Yeah, I see um’, that’s Turtle and Fry. They use to be ‘round the way wit’ Orko”, offered Tracy, “What’s up?”

“Naw ain’t nothin’ I was just tryna tell Nah the light skin one was fuckin’ wit’ his sister. I couldn’t remember his name and I wasn’t sure if that was the dude but I knew he use to be round’ the way”, lied Dirty.

“Thanks Tracy”

“Oh, you welcome Yo”, said Tracy shrugging her shoulders, she stepped off.

“What’s up Cutty, let’s see them niggas right now”, remarked Nah soon as Tracy walked away.

“You know I got the hammers in here.”

“Naw we bigger than that now. Hold up I got a plan”, said Dirty turning to Peaches, Munchie and Keisha.

“A Munchie let me holla at cha’ for a minute”.

“What’s up birthday boy?”, asked Munchie walking over to him.

“Yo I need you to do me a favor”, said Dirty draping his arm around her shoulder turning away from Peaches and Keisha overlooking the lower levels,

“See them two dudes at the bar, the one wit’ his hat cocked back and slim wit’ the braids?”

"Yeah, I see um", replied Munchie. "What's up wit' um?"

"I need you to get one of your buddies and you and her go down there and befriend them niggas wit a bottle of Cris' or somethin' and don't let um leave the club or get out of your sight if possible. I'll send somebody to get you in a couple of minutes", said Dirty pulling out a wad of money out of his pocket he handed her ten crisp one hundred dollar bills.

"Here this is for the Cris' keep the change".

"Alright yo!!", replied Munchie accepting the money she walked over to a caramel colored skin female. They appeared to be discussing something, then they disappeared. Minutes later appearing at the bar on the first level.

They eased up on the two dudes flashing smiles, flirting and acting slightly tipsy. The dudes immediately took to Munchie and her buddy like fishes take to water. Thinking they could get the attractive females to leave the club and go to the hotel with them at the end of the night.

"Now what's up", asked Nah when he saw Munchie and her buddy start kicking it with the two dudes.

"Hold up, I'm put you on point in one minute", said Dirty turning to Peaches. "A Baby come here."

"What's up Pookie?", asked Peaches.

"Look, take these keys and you and Keisha go 'head and leave now", said Dirty handing her the keys to his car. "Call me when you get in the car".

“What’s wrong Baby?”, questioned Peaches her smile turning into a frown, her eyebrow wrinkling up.

“Ain’t nothing wrong, just do as I said”, stated Dirty looking deep into her eyes. She shook her head okay and accepted the keys.

“Give me a hug and kiss… I love you Baby”

Peaches did so, squeezing her man she fought back the tears knowing something wasn’t right.

“I love you too”. *Please God don’t let nothing happen to my man’,* she silently prayed as her and her cousin Keisha left the club.

“Yo, Nah get Dirt-Dirt and Skiddie Box lil’ asses, they in here somewhere, tell’um it’s 5G’s on each of dem niggas heads and tell’um make sure it’s done right soon as they leave the club”, demanded Dirty once Peaches left the third level on route to his car.

“Bet Yo!”, said Nah blending into the crowd he went to find Dirt-Dirt and Skiddie Box, two 15-year-old foot soldiers who’d jump at the opportunity to impress the team for the sake of loyalty and devotion to the members, the members, the money only being a bonus.

Several minutes passed before one of Dirty’s cell phones vibrated. Grabbing it off his waist he glanced at the caller ID before answering it. “Hey Boo, you straight?”

“Uh-huh, I’m about to leave the parking lot now”, replied Peaches navigating the NSX out of the parking lot and into traffic.

"Is everything okay?"

"Yeah, everything, everything, don't start crying and acting crazy I'm cool. I'll be home later okay?", stated Dirty, knowing Peaches was prone to get emotional when it came to him.

"Okay if you say everything alright I believe you just make sure you make it home to 'this' tonight", stated Peaches emphasizing the word 'this', she laughed.

"Your goodies a be waiting for you Day, mmmtttwwaaa, I love you Antonio".

"I love you Boo, I'll see you when I get home".

Closing his phone, he put it back on his hip and continued to focus on the two dudes at the bar being entertained by Munchie and her buddy.

Dirt-Dirt and Skiddie Box were standing with several other foot soldiers near the bar on the third level. The whole little squad of a dozen or so were dressed in black Dickie outfits with black Timberland boots, black Oriole fitted caps, black shades and black bandanas hanging out of their pockets or tied through the first two belt loops on their pants, like belts. Nah spotted the youngsters at the bar posted up with drinks in their hands. He approached them, pointed to them and motioned for them to follow him, they did so. Once out of earshot of the other foot soldiers he turned to them and spoke.

"Yo I need yall to put in some work for the team", began Nah looking at both teens, seeing he had their attention in full he continued, “It’s two niggas up in here that need to visit North Avenue, it’s 5G’sin it for both of ya’ll a piece”.

“Where the niggas at?”, asked Dirt-Dirt.

“Yeah point um’ out we got two techs’, a Glock and two 380.’s in the Crown Vic’ outside”, said Skiddie Box.

“Come on, I’ma show yall and make sure they twisted, feel me?”, stated Nah leading the way to the railing.

“Ain’t no question, I’da killed them niggas just because… but for 5G’s I’ll kill them and they mama”, said Dirt-Dirt in a menacing tone meaning every word he spoke.

“Hell yeah, I’ma go straight out Cycle world and cop me a new dirt bike”, added Skiddie Box already spending the money in his mind.

“See the cat wit’ the braids and slim next to em’ wit’ his hat backwards?”, asked Nah when they reached the railing.

“Un-huh”, both teens remarked nodding their heads up and down.

“Make it happen and hit me when everything’ is everything’” said Nah giving them dap before dismissing them. “I’ma holla at ya’ll later.”

“Bet, it’s a done deal”, said Dirt-Dirt as he and Skiddie Box headed for the parking lot to retrieve the guns.

Nah returned to Dirty’s side and informed him that things were in motion.

“Yo, Dirt and Skiddie on route to get the joints, everything a go”.

“I heard that Cutty. Where Bucky at?”, asked Dirty looking around the crowded third level.

“Yo was just right there… A Bucky!”, shouted Nah.

“A Bucky! Come here Yo”, shouted Dirty spotting him, he motioned him over.

“Yo go down there and get Munchie, she all hugged up wit’ them clowns at the bar”, stated Dirty pointing at Munchie, her friend and the two dudes.

Knowing Bucky had a crush on Munchie since childhood Dirty played on that.

“Get Fatz and a few homies and go get your girl Cutty. You can’t let them niggas be all at Munchie like that, they disrespectin’ you Yo, go snatch her ass up.”

“I don’t know what the fuck wrong wit her, she gonna make me kill one of dem niggas”, barked Bucky feeding into Dirty’s plan, he stormed off, rollin on the Ecstasy pill he’d taken, he went to find Fatz and go get Munchie. Minutes later Bucky, Fatz and four foot soldiers appeared at the bar. Bucky immediately began ranting, pointing his finger at Munchie and the two dudes.

Munchie looked up at Dirty who’d been watching the whole incident unfold in amusement, Nah at his side, he nodded his head at her slightly, signaling for her to go along with the flow. She understood and fell right in motion with Bucky’s deranged behavior.

Fy and Turtle didn't have their guns so they didn't want any trouble. Instead they opted to just walk away from the bar and leave the club before things got out of hand. Unconsciously playing right into the trap Dirty had set.

Dirt-Dirt and Skiddie Box were posted up just outside of the club, scanning the faces of everyone who left the Lava lounge. Both teens were now strapped with Tech 9mm's, waiting to handle their business. The soldier rags they had in their back pockets ere now folded into triangles tied around their necks. When Fry and Turtle exited the club, the teens hearts began to thump in their chest, adrenaline pumping. Unmindfully Fry and Turtle walked right pass them. Once they did the teens looked at each other, nodded, pulled the soldier rags up over the lower part of their faces and whipped the Tech's out from under their Dickie shirts. Leveling the guns at Fry and Turtle backs, they opened fire.

BLOW!-BLOW!-BLOW!- BLOW!-BLOW!-BLOW!-BLOW!-BLOW!..., a fusillade of bullets tore into both victim's backs.

The impact of the first couple of bullets knocked Turtle off his feet, his body toppled forward, blood gushing from his mangled frame. Skiddie Box ran up on him as he laid on his stomach attempting to crawl forward, blood smeared the concrete sidewalk. Once he was directly over top of him, he squeezed the trigger on the Tech rapidly, aiming from Turtle's waist up. He shot thirteen times in total, every bullet ripping into Turtle's waist up. He shot thirteen times in total, every bullet ripping into Turtle's prone body, which was now a bloody pulp.

Fry on the other hand upon the impact of the first two bullets stumbled forward but managed to keep his footing and took off in an awkward trot his hands up over his head. Dirt-Dirt right on his heels chased him down shooting repeatedly. Fry took the first eight bullets in stride, still on his feet he struggled to keep his footing. There was blood coming from his upper body, he became light headed, gasping for air, he felt as if his insides were on fire, virtually no strength left, everything turned black, Fry collapsed falling face first, dead before he hit the ground.

Dirt-Dirt finished the job when he hit the ground by running up on the corpse, aiming the Tech at Fry's head and squeezing the trigger three more times, leaving Fry's brain matter on the concrete, positive he was dead.

Satisfied with their work the teens fled to the Crown Victoria that Nah had gave Skiddie Box when he copped his gold Lexus Ls 400. Once in the car Skiddie Box dialed Nah's cell phone while navigating the car out of the downtown area up towards over East Baltimore.

"Yo, what's up?", asked Nah answering his phone.

"Everything, everything, like Pac and Biggie", replied Skiddie Box calmly.

“I heard that, I’ll see yall later, One!”, said Nah not waiting for a response he hung up and looked to Dirty smiling.

“Everything straight, Skiddie and Dirt, handled they business”.

A smile formed on Dirty’s face, he gave Nah dap and they resumed partying. Dirty later thought of a Machiavelli proverb; A prince should have no other aim or goal nor take up any other thing but war and its organization and discipline for it’s the only art necessary for one who commands… Looking down at his chain he smiled,

“Slum Lord! Yeah Baltimore is mines!!!”

Chapter 19

Three weeks after his own party Dirty paid for another extravagant birthday party, this one for his grandmother was held at 'Martin's West'. Tiffany made all the arrangements for the day at Dirty's request. The entire day was laid out, all the way until the following morning when Ma Ma and Ms. Cookie would be chauffeured to BWI airport, where they'd fly to Florida and aboard a yacht for a seven-day boat cruise, touring the Caribbean islands.

Early on the morning of the party Ma Ma and Ms. Cookie were picked up in a white limo and driven to the finest five-star hotel in Baltimore, Harbor Court. A presidential suite awaited them. They enjoyed the luxuries of the hotel, full body massages, facials, manicures, pedicure's and hair do's.

Peaches picked out their attire. After a day of pampering that evening Ma Ma and Ms. Cookie stepped out of the white limo in front of Martin's looking and feeling like movie stars, smiles plastered across their faces. They entered the huge ballroom and were greeted by a host of family and friends. The prestigious ballroom was filled with people superbly dressed and enjoying themselves. It was a nice evening. The highlight of the party was when Dirty took his grandmother by the hand and lead her to the center of the dance floor where they slow danced together. He spun his grandmother around then dipped with her causing a standing ovation, everyone cheered and applauded.

"This ain't nothin' Ma Ma, you deserve this, I wish I could do like this for you every day. I love you, here's your other gift", he added handing her a small gift-wrapped jewelry box.

"What am I going to do with all this jewelry Pumpkin?", asked Ma Ma accepting the box she opened it, stunned by the contents she looked up at her grandson then back at the set of keys with the Cadillac emblem on the key chain.

"You can get rid of that old car, those the keys to your new caddy… it's a 1999 fully loaded Deville, it's parked out front wit a big red bow on the hood. Happy Birthday Ma Ma", said Dirty hugging his grandmother. She was speechless, her head nuzzled against his chest, tears of joy stained his clothes.

In the past month or so Dirty noticed a change in Peaches. One minute she laughed, smiled and was the perfect woman, then the next minute she'd flip and turn into an evil, grumpy spiteful pest. He couldn't understand what was bothering her. He did everything in his power to keep her happy.

Even Peaches herself was alarmed, she'd never been so moody and suspicious. It seemed like everything Dirty did she questioned, nagging-ly. Some days he would purposely come in the house late hoping she'd gone to sleep just to avoid a confrontation with her, which only raised her suspicion more. All he was doing was trying to balance hustling, providing for his loved ones and tending to the renovation of 'Club 410'.

Both love birds were going through changes and doubting their mate, neither having stopped to give thought to the fact that Peaches hadn't come on her monthly menstrual cycle. She was pregnant and the mood swings were attributed to the pregnancy.

Despite the craziness Dirty still tried to shower the woman he loved with the best and make her feel like a queen. Since the end of August was near upon which Peaches would have to return to college he decided to take a trip with his wifey 'Peaches' and the whole team. Everybody agreed to meet up at Druid Hill Park early in the morning on the last Sunday of the month. From the park, they'd all drive to Adventure World Amusement Park to close out the summer and celebrate the completion of the club's renovation.

By 9:30 am everyone had arrived at the park, except Fatz. Dirty and Peaches were sitting in his Cadillac truck he'd purchased when he went to get his grandmothers new car, talking with lil' Mookie in the back Playing the game system hooked up to the TV's in the truck's head rest. Nah, Ra'jah, Ta'jay and Nah's girlfriend Tasha were all standing on the side of his Lexus talking and smoking blunts with Tracy and three of her buddies, her Acura was parked beside Nah's car. Squirrel and Fatty-Pooh were standing next to their twin Ninja Motorcycles conversating with two music video looking sisters in booty shorts with micro mini braids. Smurf had the driver's door to his truck open enjoying the blunt while talking to a mediocre red bone female. Bucjy was parked next to Dirty's NSX which Shyhid was driving. Snuggles was sitting on the hood of his Acura talking to his baby mother, Tameka. The foot soldiers were surrounding Nahs old Crown Victoria and Dirty's old Grand Marquis.

By 9:45 am everybody still waiting on Fatz gathered around the basketball court and were watching the scrimmage. East won the first game, West won the second game, they were in the middle of the tie breaker when Fatz made his grand entrance, disrupting the game.

Honking his horn, he whipped into the park and slammed on the breaks bringing his fire engine red Ford lightening pickup truck to a screeching halt, the whole truck jerked.

Everybody's heads whipped around looking in the direction of the loud screeching sound. They stared in amusement as Fatz jumped out of his truck in the middle of the street dressed in nothing but his boxers, slippers, black sun shades and his large gold chain with an iced-out Buddhist statue medallion hanging from his neck. He walked around the truck, opened the tailgate and climbed into the back of the pick-up bed.

Everyone watched him in wonder, he quickly killed the curiosity. Bending down Fatz grabbed two rolls of toilet paper from amongst the twenty or so he had, one in each hand he flung them in the air towards the basketball court.

“I’m shittin’ on the world yall. Fat daddy shittin”, he proclaimed loudly, grabbing and throwing roll after roll of toilet paper.

“Fat daddy getting’ it yall”, he continued to scream steadily tossing rolls of toilet paper. He’d popped two double stack ‘007’ Ecstasy pills and downed a fifth of VSOP, the combination had him in a zone.

“Fat daddy getting’ it and he shittin’ yall!!!”

Everybody fed into the ‘Fat Daddy show’, adding fuel to the fire, they encouraged him to keep going by clapping and chanting, “Fat Daddy gettin’ it and he shittin’ yall!!! Fat Daddy getting’ it and he shittin’ yall!!!”

When Fatz ran out of toilet paper he started dancing to the chanting and applauding, snapping his fingers while shaking his upper body he leaned back as far as he could then leaned forward. He danced until he became tired and light headed his breathing labored then he climbed out of the truck bed and hopped in the driver’s seat behind the wheel.

“Come on yall let’s get to Wild World!”, screamed Fatz out of the truck window using the original name of the amusement park ‘Adventure World’.

Everybody made their way to their vehicles and one after another filed out behind Fatz. Fatz leading the pack sped off, one hand on the steering wheel, leaning back with his mug broke pumping Nas and Scarface’s song ‘Favor for a Favor’, he put the pedal to the floor exiting the park. In a drug and liquor induced state of mind, he didn't even notice the huge pothole in the road. When 'BOOM!', the truck's front wheel hit the pothole violently jerking the steering wheel out of his hand.

The truck veered off to the left at full speed. Fatz frantically tried to slam on the breaks but it was too late the truck had jumped the curb and slammed directly into a building with a thunderous crashing sound- 'K-BOOM!'. The front of the truck instantly smashed in causing the steering wheel to crush his chest and his head lurched forward, his face smashing into the windshield. Just that quick Fatz was dead to the world.

■■

Dirty paid for all the funeral arrangements and vowed to look after Fatz's family for the rest of his life. Since it had originally been Fatz idea to open a club Dirty changed the name of the club from 'Club 410' to 'Fat Daddy's' in memory of his deceased partner in crime. The club immediately sky rocketed to a ranking 'hot spot'..........................

Chapter 20

"Damn Yo, we been out this bitch for an hour, let's go up in that mothafucka, fuck this waiting shit!", said Mikey Moe from the back of the MPV caravan.

"Chill Yo, the nigga gotta come up out dat bitch soona or lata", said T.C from the passenger seat.

"Yeah Yo, he gonna come up out there den we gon' snatch'em real quick and make'em take us to dat bread", agreed J.R cocking the hammer on the .38 Smith & Wesson he had in his hand, with his thumb on the hammer he squeezed the trigger easing the hammer down, then he repeated the act.

"I'm just tryna get dis nigga and look out for my peeps for Christmas", stated Muppet sitting next to his brother Mikey Moe.

"Huh Man, a nigga need dat", agreed T.C. staring at the front of club Fat Daddy's located on Pulaski highway in a large red building up the street from the city impound.

The holiday season had everyone on the grind. The occupants of the van were plotting to snatch Dirty White and force him to tell them where his money could be located. They'd been following him all day and were anxious to make their move.

Inside the club Dirty and his cousin Shyhid rapped up the meeting they'd been having with Mr. Kenny. Lucky Al had introduced Dirty to Mr. Kenny several months ago, who at the time suffered from near bankruptcy. The two men came to an agreement three days later, Dirty would back Mr. Kenny financially and become a silent partner in the public's eyes, but between them Dirty with the help of Shyhid who he'd hired as his business consultant, would have full reign of the club and the direction it went in. the agreement thus far was without flaws and the club was booming.

"I'ma holla at cha later Mr. K. make sure we're stocked for the holidays, alright?", said Dirty extending his hand to the jazzy gray head elder black man, they shook hands, both men standing at the closure of the meeting.

"Okay Antonio, I'll call you after I finish taking inventory, on the cellular", replied Mr. Kenny turning to shake Shyhid's hand. "Yall young men take it easy."

"You too Mr. K", replied Shyhid turning on his heels he headed for the front door.

"come on White let's shoot over west to check on the house for sale off North and Eutaw."

"I'm right behind you. Yo, how the joint look?", asked Dirty as they made their way to the front of the spacious club.

“It’s big like the house on McCullough, you can probably convert it into three apartments, it’s nice”, said Shyhid over his shoulder, referring to one of the four rowhouses Dirty had purchased and renovated with the help of Lucky Al’s tutelage and Shyhid’s eye for good investments, over the past three months.

Dirty tried unsuccessfully all summer to get Shyhid to join his team in the streets but Shyhid refused him. He admitted that he didn’t have the drive and mentality to be a figure in the streets like his cousin. Shyhid hadn’t so much as had a ticket since his teens let alone indulge in crime. Finally, Dirty stopped trying to persuade him, accepted and respected the stance he took. Instead of trying to get him in the streets he put him on the legitimate side of business enabling him to make nice money, legally.

“Shit if you say it’s nice we ain’t even gotta go up there, I take your word. You been right wit’ all the other houses”, said Dirty on his cousin’s heels as he stepped out of the club’s front door.

“Man, stop tryna cut corners nigga, let’s go check da joint out”, said Shyhid paying no attention to the suspicious black MPV van parked in front of the club.

“Nigga I ain’t tryna cut corners, I just tru……”, Dirty’s words caught in his throat at the sight of the black crud ball tinted MPV van in the parking lot, the sliding door opening in a fast motion.

His eyes became big, an alarm sounding in his head- ‘Stick Up! Stick Up!’ out of reflex he whipped the .45 Hi-point out of his dip. At the same time three dudes jumped out of the van, two from the sliding door, one from the passenger door, all three waving pistols.

“Shy duck!”, shouted Dirty peeping the move.

A burst of fire came from the ‘would be’ kidnapper’s guns at the sight of Dirty whipping his gun. Dirty quickly fired back, exchanging shots with the gunmen. Hitting two of them, one in the shoulder, the other in his arm before they scurried back into the van and burned rubber, skidding off recklessly. Once the van disappeared Dirty breathing heavy looked down at his stomach which seemed to be on fire. Blood covered the lower half of the white T-shirt and peach Polo hoodie he wore, he’d been shot in his abdomen. Blood also filled his mouth, a bullet having entered the side of his jaw uprooting several of his molar teeth before exiting his mouth.

A few feet in front of him laid Shyhid a puddle of blood forming around his lifeless body. The left side of his leather jacket he wore had three bullet holes in it. One bullet hit Shyhid’s heart, the second one hit a quarter inch above that, the third one hit his collar bone. His glazed eyes still open.

Dirty kneeled down cradling Shyhid’s head, his body numb unable to speak. Blood in his eyes, a murderous mask on his face, he looked at his deceased cousin, then up at the gloomy bluish-gray sky.

Not Shy God, he the good one, damn not Shy, he thought.

“Oh my God! What the hell happened?”, questioned Mr. Kenny standing over Dirty and Shyhid clutching a .30-30 rifle.

“I called the police when I heard all the shooting.”

Dirty on the void of comprehension didn’t even respond to Mr. Kenny. Hearing the sirens in the distance Mr. Kenny bent down and slowly removed the .45 from Dirty’s hand.

Taking the gun, he disappeared into the club to hide it, returning minutes later still toting the rifle. The police and ambulance arrived minutes apart. Asking a million questions, the police hovered over Dirty while the paramedics tended to him, lifting him onto the gurney.

“Who shot you? Did you see who shot you? Why were you shot? What happened?”, asked the officer firing one question after another.

“Man, I don’t know shit, stop fuckin’ askin’ me”, spat Dirty blood dribbling down his chin as the paramedics lifted the gurney into the back of the red and white ambulance and drove him to John Hopkins hospital.

When Peaches received the news that her man had been shot and hospitalized she caught the first plane out of Hartsfield airport in Georgia on route to BWI so she could be at his side. Everybody dropped by occasionally, but it was Peaches who now had a huge belly, her pregnancy showing, that stayed at his side nearly around the clock nursing him back to health.

After two and a half weeks of being stuck in an uncomfortable hospital bed Dirty was finally discharged from the hospital. He had staples in his stomach, a colostomy bag on his side and he was twenty-one pounds lighter, but the doctor felt he was stable enough to be discharged. The doctors also advised him to reframe from strenuous activities. Peaches drove him home from the hospital and tucker him in that night. For the next few days they lounged around enjoying each others company. They talked about their child's future, their future and a host of different issues. Things seemed to be back on track, the rocky weeks in the summer before Peaches returned to school were now a thing of the past. Peaches was happy and so was Dirty until Munchie broke the peace with a phone call, four days after he'd been released from the hospital. They were snuggled up watching the movie 'Rush Hour' when the phone rang.

'Ring… Ring… Ring…'

"Yo, who dis?", asked Dirty answering the phone.

"Munchie yo, I got some serious info. For you", she claimed.

"What's up Munch? What's the info. 'bout?", asked Dirty wrapping his arm around Peaches he kissed her neck.

"Yo, I'm over Kitten house and it's a clown name J.R up in here talkin' 'bout he the one dust you, yo tryna impress Kitten", explained Munchie.

“Oh yeah?”, asked Dirty having heard the rumor that he’d been killed but in all actuality, it was his cousin. “what the nigga looks like?”

“He ‘bout six foot, got a missing tooth in the front of his mouth, jive slim”, replied Munchie nothing grabbing his attention as being memorable until she added, “The nigga got a black MPV with the crud tints.”

“Oh yeah?!”, exclaimed Dirty his brow raising at the mentioning of the MPV. “He still there lil’ sis?”

“Yeah, he tryna get some pussy from Kitten”, stated Munchie, “I stepped out front to call you, why? Yo sound familiar?”

“Look, tell Kitten give da nigga some pussy and keep ‘em there, I’ll give you a G to give her”, said Dirty in a rapid dialect. Peaches cocked her head to the side staring at him in tentatively trying to piece together the one-sided conversation.

“and don’t let Kitten know I got shit to do wit’ it, I’m on my way!”

“Alright Yo, I got’cha!”, replied Munchie hanging up.

“What was that all about Baby?”, asked Peaches running her hand softly across Dirty’s face.

“Don’t worry about it! It ain’t nothin’”, replied Dirty brushing her off as he dialed Nah’s cell phone number.

Nah his trusted Comrade who’d taken care of everything while he’d been in the hospital answered on the first ring.

“Yo, what’s up Cutty? How your stomach feel?”, he asked knowing the number on his caller I.D.

“Yo get da old Vic from Skiddie and strap up. One of the nigga’s that shot me over a bitch ‘round my way house. Munchie just called and told me da nigga braggin’ and shit”, explained Dirty.

“I’ma meet you on Tracy block”.

“Say no more, I’m on my way now”, replied Nah hanging up.

“Baby, what’s going on?”, questioned Peaches, after hearing the one-sided conversation her man had with Nah. “Please don’t go out. Let that shit go Pokie. Think about the baby.”

“Peaches, them niggas shot me and killed Shy I gotta deal wit’ dat”, replied Dirty struggling to get dressed in an all-black sweat suit. He stuck his foot in his black leather Timberlands, one after the other, stepping down he wiggled his feet into the boots, leaving the laces untied.

“You ain’t gotta do shit Antonio. Fuck them streets, you got a child on the way. Haven’t you been through enough in your life? Leave that bullshit alone. Don’t you wanna see your child born, huh? Don’t you?”, shouted Peaches ranting on not letting Dirty get a word in as tears ran down her cheeks.

“Please leave that shit alone. Fuck them streets baby. You don’t need the streets no more, you got everything niggas hustle for. Damn you Antonio listen to me!”

Dirty grabbed his car keys, then turned to Peaches to give her a hug. She shunned him, “Don’t hug me if you plan on leaving. I need you here, please don’t leave”, pleaded Peaches sobbing.

“I gotta do what I gotta do, this is who I am Boo”, stated Dirty trying to rationalize with the love of his life. “Try to understand…”

“Understand shit!”, screamed Peaches fuming. “What I understand is it’s either gonna be me and the baby or the streets, you choose.”

“what the fuck you mean by that?”, questioned Dirty dumbfoundedly, not believing his ears.

“what I said”, replied Peaches, her hand on her hip staring at him I his face, not believing what she’d said herself, but thinking it might keep her man from leaving she stuck to her guns.

“Man, I ain’t tryna hear that shit, you and dat baby in your belly belong to me aint no ultimatum type shit going on”, replied Dirty stone faced.

“We’ll see then”, stated Peaches walking to the dresser grabbing the keys to the Benz Dirty purchased for her the week before he was shot, her Christmas gift.

“we’ll see what?”, questioned Dirty staring at her.

“I’m leaving! When you get your priorities in order call me”, she said storming out of the room, down the stairs, and out of the door in her pink silk pajamas and slippers, before Dirty could protest.

The staples made it difficult for him to move fast so he couldn't chase her down. He was forced to let her go. Once she left the house so did he. Climbing into the NSX he made his way over to West Baltimore to handle his business.

Nah already parked on Tracy's block hopped out of the Crown Vic with Skiddie Box at his side when he saw the NSX round the corner. Dirty parked and eased out of the car.

"What's up Cutty?", asked Nah giving his partner dap.

"Ain't shit just tryna see dis nigga", replied Dirty.

"Yo I brought Skiddie just in case, I know you still fucked up and shorty my most trusted lil' headbusta", explained Nah.

"I feel ya! What's up Skiddie?", said Dirty extending his hand to give the youngster, who looked a little like Steve Erkel, glasses and all, dap.

"Ain't shit White, how your stomach?" replied Skiddie after they shook hands.

"It's cool, but I'm still fucked up for real", said Dirty climbing into the passenger side of the car, Nah drove and Skiddie Box sat in the back seat.

While giving Nah directions to Fairmount Avenue and Catherine Street, Dirty made a quick call to Munchie on his cell phone via speaker.

"Hello", said Munchie answering the phone.

"Yo, it's me Munch, dude still there?", asked Dirty.

"Yeah", replied Munchie flatly.

“Look unlock the front door I’m right out front.”

“Alright, I got ‘cha, hold on a minute”, replied Munchie standing to exit the small living room. She walked out of the front door before continuing the conversation.

“Yo, his man in da living room and slim and Kitten up in da room fuckin’. Where you at?”

“I’m right here”, said Dirty spotting Munchie standing on the steps in front of Kitten’s house when Nah turned on to Fairmount and Parked. “Go ‘head and leave now, Munch.”

“Alright Yo”, she agreed looking around trying to figure which car Dirty was in before she hung up and walked over to her car, climbed in and pulled off.

Once she drove off Dirty, Nah and Skiddie Box all climbed out of the car, each with hoodies and president mask on, guns in their gloved hands. They walked right passed the MPV caravan and eased into Kitten’s small rowhouse. Nah leading the pack, Dirty bringing up the rear, slipping into the living room they caught J. R’s man off guard.

“Sssshh!”, warned Skiddie Box with his finger to his lips. “Don’t say shit or I’ma put your brains on da wall.”

J. R’s man threw his hands in the air, a frightened look on his face, he kept his mouth shut. Skiddie Box held him at gun point. Nah and Dirty crept on up the stairs to the second floor. They could hear a female moaning and the bed squeaking in the front room. Nah, standing in front of the flimsy brown wooden door which was closed, lifted his right foot and kicked the door inward. 'KABOOM'! a thunderous sound echoed in the house, the door flew in. they immediately rushed into the room, guns leveled. Inside the room laid Kitten on her back with her legs spread, her feet in the air and J.R ass naked between them on a full-size mattress. J.R looked over his shoulders, his back and forehead glistening with sweat, horror plastered across his face at the sight of the two masked gunmen.

"Oh My God!", screamed Kitten when she saw the gunmen.

"Shut the fuck up bitch!", demanded Dirty then speaking to J.R. he said,

"Get ya bitch ass up Slim!"

"N-n-n-n-no pr-pr-problem yo!", stuttered J.R easing off the bed, his hands over his head.

"Wh-what's goin' on Yo?"

"Tie they asses up Cutty", said Dirty to Nah who had the duct tape in the large pocket on the front of his black We-R-One hoodie.

Nah tucked his gun in his waist, then taped J. R's hands behind his back. After taping J. R's hand, he turned to Kitten and taped her hands and feet up. Having completed that he stuffed Kitten into the small closet, placing a piece of tape over her mouth.

"Don't say shit and don't move and your life will be spared", warned Nah. Kitten shook her head up and down in agreement, tears flowing freely down her cheeks.

Nah closed the closet door leaving Kitten in there. Then he and Dirty escorted J.R down the stairs where Skiddie Box held his main-man at gun point.

“Tape dat nigga hands up”, said Nah tossing Skiddie Box the tape. He caught it, tucked his gun and did as instructed.

“Come on. Let’s take these whores to the basement”, said Dirty escorting the two hostages to the basement with Nah and Skiddie Box.

“Get two chairs yo”

Skiddie Box grabbed two chairs out of the kitchen and carried them down into the basement. The basement was in bad need of repair, the tile on the floor was dingy, the low ceiling was stained with corroded plaster, bare water pipes ran along the ceiling and the whole scenery looked gloomy.

Forcing the hostages to sit in the chairs, Nah proceeded to run tape around their torso’s taping them to the chairs. Once they were securely taped to the chairs, Dirty removed his mask. J. R’s eyes opened wide as if he were looking at a ghost.

“Remember me?” I’m the ghost of Dirty White, the nigga you killed at the club”, said Dirty as he began to pistol whip J.R.

“Where the fuck is the niggas that was wit’ your bitch ass?”

“Yo, I ain’t have shit to do wit’ dat shit, I told dem dumb ass niggas not to try you Yo”, pled J. R’s main-man at the sight of all the blood leaking from J. R's head, because of the pistol whipping.

"Shut da fuck up nigga!", spat Dirty glaring at J. R's main-man. "I'll be at you in a minute!"

Nah and Skiddie Box just stood by watching in amusement as Dirty repeatedly struck J.R with the butt of his gun. Nah already knew how Dirty worked, but Skiddie Box on the other hand was fascinated. He didn't think a 'pretty boy get money type' nigga like Dirty White had the heart to pistol whip someone.

"Now who the fuck was wit' your bitch ass when yall shot me?", asked Dirty stopping the assault long enough to see if J.R would respond.

"Yo tell' um J.R man, fuck dis, I ain't have shit to do wit dat shit mister, I swear", pled J. R's main-man, piss running down his leg, a puddle forming around the chair, when Dirty cocked the 9mm and stuck it in J. R's mouth.

"Man, it was Muppet, Mikey Moe and they cousin T.C", blurted J. R's main-man trying to save their lives.

"Who the fuck you say?", asked Dirty turning towards J. R's main-man pointing his gun at his head.

"I said it was Mikey Moe, Muppet and T.C", he replied closing his eyes, feeling the cold steel pressed against his temple.

"Yo that's who was wit ya?", asked Dirty looking at J.R who was barely able to talk from the sever beating simply nodded his head in agreement.

“Yo where they live at?”, asked Dirty glaring at J. R’s main-man poking him in the head hard with the tip of the chamber.

“Mikey Moe and Muppet live with they moms on Division Street, between Bloom and Pressman, I think it’s 1912, but I ain’t sure, the house red wit’ a white screen door”, offered J. R’s main-man.

“T.C live up Walbrook Junction somewhere. Now you gonna let us go? I told you da truth, I ain’t have shit to do wit’ it Yo”

“Fuck I look like lettin’ yall go!”, replied Dirty leveling the 9mm in his hand at J. R’s torso, he squeezed the trigger.

‘BOOM! BOOM! BOOOM!’, the bullets ripped through his body. His head snapped back, fell forward and his chin rested on his bloody chest.

“Pleeeeeeeeeease! Mister don’t kill me”, begged J. R’s main-man jerking about in the chair trying to free himself of the restraints, “I swear to God I ain’t hav....”

‘BOOM! BOOM!’, the blast silenced him.

Then Nah and Skiddie Box having watched the whole incident did a loyal deed. They both stepped forward and one after the other pressed their firearms to the dead men skull’s and fired a single shot into each of them....... A pact written in blood.

Chapter 21

In the process of pistol whipping J.R, before murdering his main-man, Dirty tore the staples in his stomach and had to be hospitalized again. With Dirty back in the hospital Nah did the honorable thing, a true Comrade would do and stepped up to the plate taking command. As a true friend, Nah put the wheels in motion to avenge the shooting of his partner and eradicate those responsible. Figuring that the task wouldn't be too hard since he had at least two of the remaining three's addresses. He called Skiddie Box and Dirt-Dirt again and put the youngsters on the job giving them the address and letting them know there was a nice price on the culprit's heads, 10 G's a piece. Skiddie Box and Dirt-Dirt hopped at the opportunity to earn some extra money while proving their loyalty. To them they were killing two birds with one stone. After talking to Nah they hooked up and set out to look for Mikey Moe and Muppet.

They stalked the 1900 block of Division Street paying special attention to the red colored rowhouse with the white screen door, the numerals 1912 written in black on the wall between the front door and the large front window.

“Yo, I bet that’s dem right there”, said Skiddie Box motioning with his head to the two dark skin dudes loitering on the steps in front of 1912 talking to two brown skin females and one light skin female, as they drove by in the Crown Victoria.

“Ain’t no question, that gotta be dem niggas”, agreed Dirt-Dirt cocking one of the twin Glock 9mm’s he had. He put the firearm in his right chest pocket on the black Eddie Bauer coat he wore, then cocked the other one and put it in his left chest pocket.

“Come on Yo let’s pull over and handle our business, dem niggas gotta pay for tryna kill White.”

“I’ma park on Pressman, then you go down Robert Street, come out on Bloom real quick and walk up Division. I’ma bend Pressman and walk down Division so we can sandwich’um in”, said Skiddie Box familiar with the neighborhood because his grandmother stayed on Gold Street, a block up.

“Yo, gimme a good minute or two to go ‘round da block”, said Dirt- Dirt as they turned on to Pressman Avenue and parked.

“Dat’s Robert Street, right?”, asked Dirt-Dirt pointing to the small alley like street.

“Yeah”, replied Skiddie Box.

Dirt-Dirt climbed out of the car and started in the direction of the alley like street, to circle the block. Skiddie Box watched Dirt-Dirt disappear onto Robert Street, then leaned over the front seat and retrieved the Mac-10, a fake baby doll and a pink and white checkered blanket off the back seat. Wrapping the blanket around the baby doll he used it to conceal the Mac-10 behind it. He climbed out of the car and using his foot he kicked the car door shut leaving the keys in the ignition. He strolled up to and the crowded dope strip of Pressman and Division. Dope fiends and hustlers were everywhere; however, they were so consumed with either buying or selling heroin that they didn't pay Skiddie Box any attention.

Once he circled around the corner he looked down Division Street spotting the occupants on the steps in front of '1912' and Dirt-Dirt in the distance making his way toward the targets. Dirt-Dirt had his hands in the chest pockets of the winter coat he wore with the fur trimmed hood up on his head. Skiddie Box looked like another teen father carrying his infant in the slums as he neared the targets… suddenly he was so close that he could hear their conversation.

"Muppet, ain't nobody suckin' your ick to hit your funky blunt. Shit you want your dick sucked eat my pussy", said the light skin female rolling her head and eyes.

"Bitch aint nobody eatin' your stinkin' pussy", replied Muppet grabbing his crotch while inhaling the blunt.

"Your dirty ass should wanna suck this big black dick on the strength ol' ugly crowfoot bitch!"

Everybody on the front laughed… just then without warning Skiddie Box dropped the baby doll, Mac-10 in hand, he started firing.

“What da fuck!”, gasped Mikey Moe abut to run as Dirt-Dirt also started firing right through his coat pockets, never pulling the twin Glocks out.

He and Skiddie Box showered the occupants of the steps with hot lead. Hitting the brothers and their female friends in the chest, stomach, arms, legs, backs and faces. Their bodies looked like swiss cheese, blood flowing freely from the multiple gunshot wounds.

Mikey Moe’s face was half blown away by a bullet that hit him in his left eye. Muppet laid twisted on the pavement, his body covered in blood the impact of the blast having knocked him off the steps. All three of the females laid sprawled out awkwardly around the steps soaked in blood. The blood stained the concrete and seeped into the streets gutter.

Having assassinated their targets, the teens fled, leaving five bullet riddled corpses on Mikey Moe and Muppet’s mother’s door steps. By the time they reached the Crown Victoria two dope fiends, who along with the rest of the block that scattered at the sound of guns being discharged, reappeared from the alley on Division Street and were searching the deceased victim’s pockets.

When the police finally arrived Skiddie Box and Dirt-Dirt were long gone. Laying in their wake were five mangled victims, stripped bare of their lives and their valuables.

■■

Pleased with the news of Skiddie Box and Dirt-Dirt's exploit, Dirty, after being discharged from the hospital, purchased twin royal blue and white 1999 Yamaha Banshee ATV's for the deadly duo as tokens of his appreciation, on top of the 10 G's a piece they received from Nah.

Dirty presented the teens with the four wheelers that very evening in the parking lot where he'd been shot. Then together Dirty, Skiddie Box and Dirt-Dirt joined Nah and the rest of the team inside Fat Daddy's. everybody showed up under the presumption that it was Skiddie Box and Dirt-Dirt's birthday party. Skiddie Box and Dirt-Dirt knew the party was attributed to the 'work' they'd put in, but they played along with the birthday theme, basking in the limelight. Both youngsters were totally brainwashed and would without question shed blood or cause blood to be shed for Dirty and the team. Total loyalty.

"Yo, White, good lookin' out wit the Banshee, that joint mean as shit", said Skiddie Box for the second time that night, extending his hand to give Dirty dap again.

"That shit ain't nothin', you came through for me, least I could do is bless you a little somethin'- somethin'", replied Dirty as they shook hands.

"You my lil' partner Skiddie Box. Shit I'm pose to be tellin' you good lookin' out for handlin' dat situation."

Skiddie Box eyes lit up, his chest swelling with pride at Dirty's praise, "Yo, anytime you need me for whateva I'm on it, just say the word", said Skiddie Box sincerely.

“Speaking of that, I do need you to do somethin’, park that Crown Vic. Keep it in the cut and go get another hooptie ‘cause niggas done used that Vic. A rack a times, feel me?”

“Yeah, I feel ya, I’ma do that.”, agreed Skiddie Box.

“Hold on Skiddie”, said Dirty grabbing his cell phone, which was vibrating on his hip. He looked at the caller I.D before answering.

“Hey Big Homie, How ya feelin’?”

“I’m cool but I need to see you first thing tomorrow, it’s important”, said Lucky Al with urgency in his tone.

“I’ma get wit’cha Skiddie”, said Dirty holding the phone away from his mouth and walking toward the back of the club before speaking further.

“What’s up Big Homie? We can hook up right now if somethin’ wrong!”

“Naw it can wait til’ tomorrow”, replied Lucky Al.

“You sure?”, asked Dirty frowning.

“Yeah I’ll see you tomorrow. I ain’t gonna rap on dis phone just meet me at the Rain Forest Café, alright?”, stated Lucky Al.

“Alright, what time?”

“’Round lunch time, twelve-ish”, replied Lucky Al disconnecting the call.

Damn I wonder what the fuck that’s all about, thought Dirty placing his phone in the clip on his hip. *Somethin’ definitely on the Big Fella’s mind……*

Chapter 22

The Rain Forest Café is a cozy restaurant located in Towson Town Center. The scenery inside of the café is tropical and tranquil, resembling a real rain forest, complete with wilderness sound effects, artificial greenery, taxidermic animals and fish tanks containing tropical fish.

When Dirty entered the café at 11:53am, he walked directly to the far-left hand corner where he had spotted Lucky Al. he was sitting with his back to the wall; typical of hustlers because it enables one to view the entrance. Lucky Al was staring at his cup of cappuccino on the table as if he was in deep thought. When Dirty reached his table, Lucky Al looked up at him and nodded his head in acknowledgement, his face blank.

“what’s going on Big Homie?” How ya feel?”, asked Dirty extending his hand across the table and they shook hands before he sat. “What’s on ya mind?”

“Antonio, I’ma get straight to the point of this meeting, Los with the Feds…”

“The Feds? What da fuck happened?”, asked Dirty paranoia detectable in his tone.

“It aint nothin’ heavy, just a bullshit gun charge. The Feds picked it up, he’ll be alright. He on home monitor right now so his hands jive tied, and with Yo uptight I need someone to step up and hold his position and you’re the only one I feel comfortable wit’”, said Lucky Al, pausing, allowing his words to linger while staring into the core of Dirty’s pupils before continuing,

“You’re a stand-up man and you can think plus you’re loyal… I need you to pick up the slack. What you think? Can you handle the major leagues?”

“Ain’t no question, I’m wit’ ya, just point me in the right direction and I got it from there”, replied Dirty maintaining eye contact with Lucky Al.

Content with the answer given Lucky Al leaned forward and spoke in a whispered tone, “From now on you’ll be on a whole different level. You gonna have to pass the day to day street corner shit and focus on laying bricks, feel me?”

“Yeah, I feel ya I got a man to fill my shoes”, stated Dirty thinking of Nah.

“Cool, starting today you’re responsible for 150 bricks at 15 a pop, your bill is 2 and a quarter. You can do them as you choose but I suggest you only put a $5000 cushion on each one and push them for 20, it’s about the quick flip, feel me?”, asked Lucky Al after explaining a mouthful.

“Yeah, I can….”, Dirty stopped in mid-sentence as the waitress approached their table.

“Good afternoon. Are you gentlemen ready to order?”, asked the mildly attractive white waitress.

“Yes, I’d like a double order of steamed shrimp and a large lemonade”, said Lucky Al.

“Okay double steamed shrimp, large lemonade”, said the waitress jotting down the order. “and you sir, would you like to order now?”, she asked, Dirty’s eyes had wandered off landing on a familiar face three tables to his right which held his attention.

Transfixed he didn’t respond until Lucky Al spoke up, “A, Antonio you gonna order?”

“Huh… Oh yeah, my fault”, said Dirty looking away from the familiar dace and up at the waitress. “Uh, just give me the same thing he ordered.”

“Okay, thank you”, said the waitress politely as she hurried off.

Dirty’s attention immediately returned to the familiar face. He hadn’t seen her in years but he often thought of her while he was incarcerated and he even dreamed of her on occasions. She hadn’t aged a bit, her mahogany skin still shined refulgently. Her luscious lips and sensual almond shaped eyes still caused Dirty’s lustful hormones to ripple.

“Antonio… Man you still wit’ me?”, asked Lucky Al bringing Dirty’s attention back to the table.

“Oh yeah, my fault”, replied Dirty looking away from the familiar face, with a big Kool-Aid smile.

“Damn, what’s up man you smiling and shit like you just seen a goddess”, said Lucky Al hitting the nail on the head.

“Naw, see the lady over there wit’ the cream blouse on”, began Dirty looking in the direction he was referring to, “She the one represented me on my murder case.”

“Man, get the hell outta here”, replied Lucky Al in disbelief glancing at the female with the cream blouse on, “That woman looks way too young to have represented you.”

“No bullshit, her name is Patricia Smallwood. I’d never forget that face, especially them lips.”, stated Dirty staring at his old public defender.

“Man, stop staring at the woman and go say something to her, pay for her food or something, but don’t just stare.”, said Lucky Al trying to give his protégé some game.

“Yeah, that’s what I’ma do, I’ma pay for her and her girlfriends food and give her my card”, stated Dirty pulling a business card from the breast pocket on his Polo shirt jean jacket, “and let her know as a token of my appreciation from when she represented me she has a V.I.P pass to the club if she ever decides to swing by.”

“I hear ya Cutty”, smiled Lucky Al, before turning the conversation back to business.

“Look here are the keys to the storage bin, call Los and he’ll give you all the details when ya’ll hook up.”

“Bet!”, replied Dirty accepting the keys he put them in his front pant pocket.

The two men indulged in small talk until the waitress returned with their food. At which time they enjoyed their meal in silence. The shrimps and butter sauce were delicious. Once they finished eating Dirty volunteered to pick up the tab.

“I got the bill”, he said when Lucky Al waved the waitress over.

“You sure”, asked Lucky Al before standing to depart.

“Yeah I got it.”

“Alright then I’ll hit you tonight after you and Los rap and when you ready you know how to reach me, be safe”, stated Lucky Al walking pass the waitress as she approached the table.

“I’ma hit ya later, Stay up!”, replied Dirty.

“Are you ready for your bill, sir?”, asked the waitress.

“Yeah, plus I’d like to pick up the tab for the beautiful sisters at the third table over there”, said Dirty pointing towards the table where Patricia Smallwood sat with two other classy dressed females. “Can I borrow your pen for a second?”

“Oh, certainly”, replied the waitress lending him a pen.

He scribbled both of his cell phone numbers and his name on the back of the business card. Then before handing the waitress her pen back he removed a wad of money from his pocket and peeled off twenty-five 20 dollar bills and handed them to the waitress along with her pen.

“Here this is for the two bills, keep the change, thanks for your hospitality.”

“Oh, you’re welcome Sir and thank you very very much”, replied the waitress smiling from ear-to-ear knowing she’d just cashed in on the largest tip in her history as a waitress.

“No problem, just make sure their tab is paid too, okay?”, said Dirty standing to leave.

“Yes Sir, I certainly will and thanks again”, said the waitress to Dirty as he walked over to the table where the three-woman sat.

“excuse me, your name is Patricia Smallwood, right?”, asked Dirty already knowing the answer.

“well um yes”, she replied as she and her girlfriends looked up at the handsome young man who’d just stopped at their table.

Patricia immediately recognized Dirty, their eyes locking, her stomach fluttered. She’d often thought of the adolescent she’d represented when she’d first began her career as a public defender.

Ummm, he’s blossomed into quite a man, physically, thought Patricia staring into Dirty’s alluring eyes.

“I’m not sure if you remember me, it’s been years, but uh, my name is Antonio Lord. I just wanted to say thanks. Here’s my card, if you’re ever out and about you may wanna stop by my club. You can bring your friends and all of yall will be V.I.P. status, my treat just call in advance.”, said Dirty placing his card on the table in front of Patricia.

"oh, and don't worry about the tab I've taken care of it", he added as an afterthought. Then just that quick he was gone, exiting the café before she'd even parted her lips to respond.

"Damn girl who was that?", asked one of her friends with a smirk.

"How 'bout that, girl that nigga was fine, wit 'a capital F and he got his own club. What's up wit' that? You holding out on us Pat?", stated her other friend as she put her chin in her hand and rested her elbow on the table staring at Pat.

"Go 'head wit' that, girl, he's just uh... friend of mines from a while back", said Patricia still a bit shocked by the encounter. For some reason, she didn't feel the need to reveal the truth about how her and Antonio met.

"So, you gonna call him girl? Ya'll gonna get back together? Why yall break up anyway?", ranted one of her friends jumping to her own conclusions.

"For real Pat, he is fiiiiiiine. You should call him, you can use my phone", offered her other friend jokingly handing Pat her phone.

They laughed. "You two are a trip", said Pat shaking her head as she put the business card in her purse.

■■

In just 48 hours Dirty with Los assisting him had sold 10 kilos at $20,000.00 A kilo during a so- called drought where kilos sold for upwards of $30,000.00. Dirty had a strong hold on the market pushing kilos, so he no longer dealt with the day to day street operation, having passed it onto Nah. He fronted him 10 kilos at $22,000.00 a kilo, plus stipulated that Nah continued to keep all of his 'homies' on the pay docket. Nah agreed.

He then had a talk with Skiddie Box and Dirt-Dirt and offered to employ the teens as his personal gunmen who'd accompany him on all runs. They were instructed to 'shoot first, ask questions later'. The job paid $7500.00 a week and the youngsters had to agree to stop hustling on corners and enroll in Harford Institute, they happily accepted the job. As a bonus Dirty promised them cars of their choice if they obtained their G.E.D.

Aside from Skiddie Box and Dirt-Dirt, Dirty also pulled Munchie into the fold of things as the transporter, reasoning that he'd rather she be hustling then 'stripping' or 'selling her body' as rumor had her doing. At $500 a kilo she couldn't turn the transportation offer down and happily agreed to the stipulations set forth by Dirty. Which were to stop 'stripping', find a house in Baltimore county for her and her sons, and enroll her sons into a private school for 'head start'. Everyone in the four-person crew knew their position, Dirty was the voice and salesman, Munchie transported, Skiddie Box and Dirt-Dirt were the enforcers, everybody played their part accordingly. They were all on route to make a drop for 40 kilos when Dirty's phone rang.

"Yoooo, what's up?", asked Dirty answering his cell phone with his customary greetings.

"Um, hello can I speak to Antonio?", said a feminine voice.

"This is he", replied Dirty keeping his eyes on the ice blue Astro mini-van in which Munchie was driving. She drove three cars ahead of him carrying the 40 kilos on route to make the drop at fair Lanes Bowling Alley on Security boulevard.

"This is Pat, I mean Patricia Smallwood, you gave me your card at the Rain Forest café a few days ago. I've been meaning to call you but I've been busy.", explained Patricia in an apologetic tone.

"I understand. I'm glad you called though. How have you been?", asked Dirty smiling.

"I'm fine, just buried in case work", she replied. "how about you? How's life treating you?"

"I'm cool, just taking it easy", he replied, then out of curiosity asked, "Are you still a public defender?"

"Um-hm, but I work in the federal public defender's branch now", said Patricia twirling his business card around in her hand. "I see you're on the right track with a club, huh?"

"Oh yeah, I'm tryna live good, legitimately", replied Dirty.

"That's good", complimented Patricia.

Silence fell over the line for a few seconds then, “So when you gonna let me take you out to dinner or somethin’? it’s the least I can do since you helped me get such a sweet deal that helped me get my life in order”, said Dirty flattering Patricia.

“Well, I usually don’t mix business and …”, she started in a timid tone.

“Shhhh! Before you think of an excuse let me assure you that this ain’t no date, it’s more like a show of my appreciation. I’d just like to treat you to a night out, cut and dry. I know a hard-working woman like yourself could use a little unwinding after work one evening, no extra strings attached, no hidden agendas. Honestly it would make my day if you’d allow me to take you out. Don’t refuse me and steal my joy”, said Dirty in a convincing tone that burned into her soul.

Passive by nature, she loved a strong man and the confidence Dirty displayed caused her to swallow hard before responding, “Well, I suppose you do have a point but I …”

“No buts, just give me a day, we can move from there, I’ll work around your schedule”, stated Dirty.

“Well um, I guess this Friday after 5pm would be good. How about 7:30 Friday? That gives me time to get home and slip into something fresh”, said Patricia blushing, feeling like a 16-year-old school girl.

“So 7:30 it is. Where can we meet?”, he asked as Munchie followed closely by Skiddie Box and Dirt-Dirt pulling into the crowded bowling alley parking lot.

“I don’t know. Where you plan on going?”, questioned Patricia.

“We can go anywhere you wanna go. I don’t know… let’s say Fisherman’s Wharf”, blurted Dirty saying the first thing that came to mind as he pulled into the bowling alley parking lot and parked.

“Okay, I’ll meet you there at 7:30”, said Patricia smiling as she twirled a lock of her hair with her finger.

“Cool, don’t have me down there at 7:30 looking crazy and you don’t show up, either”, said Dirty climbing out of the car.

“I won’t, I promise”, she assured him.

“I hope not ‘cause I look forward to seeing your beautiful smile”, stated Dirty flirtatiously.

“He-heh-heh, I hear you”, replied Patricia laughing. “I’ll be there, you just don’t stand me up.”

“Don’t worry, I’ll be there. Take care Patricia I’ll…”

“Call me Pat, Antonio.”

“Okay, take care Pat. I’ll talk to you soon and I really look forward to seeing you.”

“You take care too, bye bye!”

“Bye”, said Dirty disconnecting their call he quickly dialed a number as he made his way into the bowling alley.

“Whoa!”, said a male voice answering on the first ring.

“Yo, I’m here, meet me in the bathroom”, said Dirty.

‘Click!’, he hung up.

By the time Dirty entered the bowling alley, Munchie was already posted up by the arcade games. Spotting Munchie, Dirty walked over and embraced her. Scanning the crowded bowling alley while wrapping his arms around her waist, he slid his hands into her back-jean pockets, retrieving the keys to the van. Smoothly he removed his hands from her back pockets and released her from his embrace before stepping in the direction of the restroom.

Pushing the men’s bathroom door in ward he quickly scanned the clean restroom for Fat Berry (a hustler out of Richmond, V.A) at one of the urinals pretending to urinate. Dirty went straight to the sink turning the water on to wash his hands. Looking in the mirror he could see Fat Berry flush the urinal and walk towards the sinks. On que, he laid the keys in the sink, nodded his head, then stepped to the side to dry his hands under the hand dryer. Fat Berry washed his hands in the sink where Dirty left the water running and grabbed the keys to his van which he’d a; owed Dirty to take earlier with the money for the kilos already in it.

Dirty casually exited the restroom and slipped out to the parking lot. He climbed into his car pulling off, followed closely by his side kicks who’d stayed in the parking lot watching the mini-van. Munchie had already left.

Later that evening he hooked up with Lucky Al and squared his bill up. Lucky Al promised him another shipment in a couple days.

Damn 150 birds in three days, fuck that corner shit, this what's happening, thought Dirty marveling at the easy with which the kilograms were sold using Los plugs.

Chapter 23

At 7:20 Friday evening Dirty pulled into a private owned parking lot to the left of Fisherman's Wharf. Parking he sat in his truck listening to 'Angel in Disguise' by Brandy vibing off the beat. A couple minutes passed then his cell phone began to vibrate, turning the car stereo down he answered it.

"Hey Miss lady", said Dirty noticing the number on his caller I.D. "where you at?"

"I'm right here but I don't know where to park", explained Patricia driving pass the Fisherman's Wharf. "I passed it."

"well, make the first right you come to and circle the block, there's a private parking lot right before you get to the wharf", explained Dirty. "What you driving? I'ma get out and stand on the corner so I can wave you down."

“I’m in a gold Camry”, replied Patricia making the right, she circled the block as Dirty had instructed.

“Alright, I’m getting out of my car now”, he stated climbing out of his car, he shut the door and stepped over to the corner of the parking lot dressed in a grey sweat suit, with his t-shirt hanging down concealing his Glock 40 on his waist.

“I see you”, they both said almost simultaneously before hanging up.

Pulling into the parking lot, Patricia parked. Dirty approached her car, reaching it just as she stepped out. She looked stunning in a navy-blue Donna Karen out fit with matching soft leather shoes, her hair styled in a flipped bob, a light coat of lip gloss shined on her lips and her nails were manicure coated with clear polish.

“You look nice Miss Lady”, said Dirty complimenting Patricia as she shut her car door.

“Thank you”, she replied turning towards him their eyes met, they held each other gaze, a magnetic force drawing them to one another.

“Come on, you ready?”, asked Dirty reaching for her hand, she gave it to him.

They walked hand in hand into Fisherman’s Wharf in silence. When they entered the dim lit restaurant the first thing they noticed was the bar, dead center. To their left there was several dark wooden tables surrounded with matching chairs. From one of the tables a female called out to Patricia.

“hey Sis, what you doin’ down here?”, questioned Patricia’s younger sibling having seen her sister and Dirty through the glass windows that covered the front of the restaurant. Turning toward the familiar voice Patricia blushed at the sight of her little sister Tawanda. Tawanda sat alone but there was a picked over seafood platter and a glass of dark liquor sitting on the table across from her, a tell-tale sign that she was with someone. Making her way over to the table, followed by Dirty, Patricia attempted to introduce her sister and Dirty unaware that the two had crossed paths before.

“Hey baby sis, how you feeling?”, said Patricia looking at her sister then to Dirty.

“Antonio this is my sister Tawanda. Tawanda this is Antonio”.

“Pat, I know who Dirty is”, said Tawanda waving to Dirty, she flashed a smile, “Hey Dirty what you doin’ with my sister?”

No sooner than the question rolled off her tongue Bucky, just finished using the bathroom, appeared from seemingly nowhere and made a big ghetto-fied outburst.

“Yoooo, Dirty Whiiite, what’s up my nigga?”, exclaimed Bucky smiling, revealing a mouth full of oversized gold teeth.

“Damn Yo, who shorty?”, he added giving Patricia, who looked shocked with her mouth wide open, a once over.

“Whoa, come here Cutty let me holla at ya really quick”, said Dirty shooting Bucky an icy glare caught by everyone before turning to Patricia, “Pardon me for one moment if you don’t mind.”

“Oh no, go right ahead, I don’t mind”, she assured him.

Draping his arm over Bucky’s shoulder he turned away from the sisters and lead Bucky away from the table before speaking.

“Yo, look you my nigga but pipe down some Cutty. That’s my old public defender from that body shit, she a jazzy older broad don’t scare her off with all that hood-ghetto shit, my nigga”. Explained Dirty looking Bucky in his eyes.

“Oh, I feel ya yo, don’t sweat it I’m bout’ to shoot out D.C. to Dreams with shorty anyway”, replied Bucky.

“My man, good lookin’ out yo”, said Dirty giving Bucky dap before returning to the table where the sisters were engaged in a shallow conversation.

“Excuse me ladies, Tawanda I hope you don’t mind if I steal your sister back.”

“Oh no, be my guess, yall go ‘head and enjoy yall self. Shit I’m happy to see her out and about it’s only been years since she’s been out”, remarked Tawanda causing her sister to blush.

“Girl shut up please!”, said Patricia a bit embarrassed.

“Bye Sis!”, said Tawanda waving her hand.

“Bye”, replied Patricia.

Leaving Bucky and Tawanda's table Dirty and Patricia eased over to a table tucked in the corner. Once seated Dirty immediately sensed something had struck an ill cord with Patricia.

She sat in silence her disposition having changed from happy-go-lucky to reserved.

"What's wrong?", he questioned looking over at Patricia.

"Aint nothing wrong", she lied.

"That's what your mouth says but your demeanor says different. Something's on your mind, you can be straight up wit' me. What's bothering you?", said Dirty looking into her eyes.

She didn't respond.

"Look I don't know what's up, but I hope the encounter with your sister and Bucky doesn't make you second guess me or somehow spoil our evening. Don't allow nothing to rain on our parade. If something's on your mind speak up. Now I'ma ask you again what's wrong?"

"I don't know", began Patricia exhaling a gust of air, "It's just the whole Dirty White thing caught me off guard. Here I am thinking I'm going to have a nice evening with Antonio Lord then I find out you're this Dirty White character. Who's Dirty White? Where'd you get that name from anyway?"

"First off let me assure you that you will have a nice evening with Antonio Lord, if you allow yourself to", said Dirty smiling.

"Now to your question, Dirty White is my nickname and has been for years, it's no different than Pat. See when I was a kid everybody use to say I looked like a little white boy because of my light skin complexion, good hair and light eyes. The twist came when I was ten, I use to climb roofs, play in alleys, flip on old mattresses, catch pigeons, a ghetto 'Dennis the Menace' and by me being so light, dirt, mud, tar and everything showed up on my skin good. I became the dirty little white boy. My homies mother's use to forbid them to hang with me like, 'don't let me catch you wit' dat dirty little white boy, don't have dat dirty little white boy in my house and so on. Then one day a junkie name Kurt-Kurt was beating my mother up in front of the whole neighborhood and even though I wasn't fond of her I couldn't see her get beat down by a man so I ran in my grandmother's and grabbed a bat and ran down on Kurt-Kurt who had his back to me, I cocked my bat back and hit him in his head wit' it using all my might. He fell out and I hit him a few more times before Blue grabbed and drug me away. After that the little and boy part went out the window and I became either Dirty White or Dirty", he explained while trying to read Patricia's thoughts, staring at her intently.

"Okay I've answered your question. Where do we go from here? Do you wanna salvage our evening or should we depart in full no cut cards, no hard feelings?"

Feeling a bit foolish due to the childish way she'd performed, Patricia began her response apologetically, "Pardon me if I offended you, it's just that this is all new to me. Not only were you once my client, but you're also several years younger than me and..."

"Hold up, slow down", interjected Dirty, "don't allow your age or profession to dictate your happiness. A few minutes ago, you were glowing, smiling and cheerful. What happened? A person recognizes me and calls me by my nickname and an alarm sounds in your head. Me being your client in the past or the age difference is irrelevant, neither stopped us from making it to this restaurant today. So why should they matter now?"

"I guess you're right let's go ahead and enjoy our evening. I apologize", said Patricia feeling drawn to Dirty White, her curiosity mounting, the taboo sucking her in gripping her mentally.

"It's nothing", said Dirty brushing her apology off.

Having smoothed the bumps out they ordered their meals and ate. They conversated discussing a vast number of topics. Patricia under estimated Dirty due to his age and wound up being thoroughly impressed with the maturity he possessed and his ability to hold an intellectual conversation.

By the end of the evening Patricia was mesmerized, almost hypnotized by the attractive young man. Especially when he walked her to her car and grabbed her left hand lifting it to his lips he kissed it sending a chill up her arm, she nearly melted.

"Thanks for accompanying me this evening, I hope you enjoyed yourself as much as I enjoyed being in your presence", said Dirty releasing her hand with a devilish grin on his face.

"Maybe you'll hang out wit' me again one day soon."

"Certainly, just say the word. I'd gladly accompany you again", said Pat smiling a Colgate smile.

"I really enjoyed myself, thanks."

"The pleasure was mines, call me when you get home and let me know you made it safely", said Dirty kissing her left hand then turning on his heels he walked over to his car and climbed in it.

Pat honked her horn when she drove by. Dirty honked back and pulled out behind her. He went straight home and got a little rest wishing Patricia could be in his bed with him.

▪▪▪

"Yo who dis?", asked Dirty wiping the cold out of his eyes.

"Hey Sweetie!", said Ms. Cookie when Dirty answered his cell phone. "I didn't mean to wake you but Smurf just called me. Him and Snuggles got locked up last night with little some boy and they got $50,000 bails. They said they can't catch Nah. What you want me to do Sweetie?"

“Call Fat Frank and tell’um get them out… hold on Ms. Cookie my phone clicking”, said Dirty clicking over.

“Yo, what’s up?”

“Please help me! They gonna kill my mother and my sister!” screamed a distorted female voice crying.

“What da fuck?” “Who dis?”, asked Dirty unable to recognize the voice.

“It’s Pa-Patricia”, she managed to say through a fit of sobs. “I need to talk to you.”

“Calm down and hold on for one minute”, said Dirty clicking over.

“Ms. Cookie, I got an important call on my other line, go ‘head and have Frank get Smurf and Snug out and do me a favor, make sure Peaches okay, you know she still acting crazy. I love you.”

“Alright Sweetie, I love you too, be safe”, replied Ms. Cookie then she hung up.

Dirty clicked back to Patricia, “Hello, you still there?”

“Um-hum”, she mumbled.

“Okay now take your time and explain what you’re talking about. What happened?”

“That guy at the restaurant who was with my sister went to my mother’s house early this morning and threatened her with a gun…”

“Did what?”, “You sure it was the dude from the restaurant?”, asked Dirty stunned.

“My mother said the ugly guy wit’ the poppy eyes and a mouth full of big gold teeth pulled a gun out on her”, said Patricia sobbing.

“Oh yeah, what happened? I mean why?”

“Something about my sister stole his jewelry and some money from him while he was sleep and he gonna kill her and my mother if he doesn’t get his stuff back”, explained through the sobbing. “You know him, please help me Antonio.”

“Alright, stop crying, I’ll do what I can. Stay by the phone and don’t call the police alright baby-girl”, that part having slipped out of his mouth.

“Okay, thanks Antonio”.

“No problem”, said Dirty hanging up, he immediately called Bucky.

“Yo, what the fuck’s going on Cutty?”, barked Dirty when Bucky answered the phone.

“What’chu talkin’ ‘bout Yo?”, questioned Bucky.

“Yo, I just got word that you runnin’ ‘round flashin’ on old women and shit ‘cause some bitch clipped you…”

“You motherfuckin’ right, that bitch stole 12G’s and damn near 50 G’s worth of jewels from me, I’m kill that bitch”, spat Bucky.

“Yo, it’s a way to do everything. I feel ya if the bitch stole your shit but don’t go threatnin’ people and pullin’ guns and shit out unless you gonna kill a motherfucka right then and there. That bitch sister work for the feds. I know you aint tryna go back to the joint behind no bullshit and still be wit' out shit. I'm trying to get your shit back just chill. I'll hit you back in a couple minutes."

"Alright yo, but if that bitch doesn't give me my shit I'ma deal wit' dat on some gutter shit", said Bucky not liking how Dirty jumped down his throat but nonetheless understanding his means of thinking.

Hanging up with Bucky he called Patricia back. "Look", he began when she answered,

"I just talked to the dude and he wants his jewelry back. She can keep the money, but he wants his jewels, it's like 50 thousand dollars' worth of jewelry and Yo aint tryna accept dat lost."

"Um-hm, I understand. I'm going to call her right now and try to get his jewelry back. Stay on the line", said Patricia, clicking over she dialed her sister's cell phone number and clicked back.

Dirty could hear the phone ringing.

"Hello", answered a female after three rings.

"Tawanda, I just talked to my friend and he called the guy and the guy said if you give him the jewelry back you can keep the money, so go head and give the jewelry back", begged Patricia.

"Pat fuck dat ugly ass nigga. I ain't giving him shit back. The motherfucka shouldn't a put his dope fiend ass hands on me."

"Tawanda, please give him his jewelry back. He threatened mommy with a gun and he said he gonna kill you and her if you don't give him his stuff", whined Patricia.

"Didn't you just hear me? I said his dope fiend ass, he sh…"

"Tawanda, look this Dirty White, just do me a favor and give this nigga his shit back. You can keep the 12 G's just give him his jewelry back before shit get ugly", said Dirty unable to maintain his silence. "and I don't wanna see dat".

"why you worrying 'bout dat nigga he don't fuck wit' you like dat, he was just tellin' me dat you crossed him by lettin' Nah a ol' eastside nigga step up over your homeboys you grew up wit'. Fuck dat nigga!", exclaimed Tawanda.

Her words stung Dirty like an open hand smack across his face but he didn't let her know and instead he continued to try and persuade her to return the jewelry.

"Look, I feel ya, I know you're upset, but do this for me and I'll owe you one, plus you can keep the money without having to look over your shoulder and if Yo ever come at you wrong again, my word, I'll deal wit' it."

Tawanda was hungry but she knew Dirty was a good man and that it would be more beneficial for her to go along with his request and return the jewelry. She may have been a fool but she wasn't a damn fool. So, she agreed to return his jewelry.

“Alright, I’ma give his bitch ass back the jewels but I’m keepin’ the money and you owe me one”, said Tawanda in a conniving tone.

“I’ma give Shaneeka his shit, she works up Foot Locker in Mondawmin. She knows you and Bucky, either one of yall can pick it up.”

“I appreciate dat yo, if you ever need my assistance just tell your sister or Munchie to get in touch wit’ me or come to the club.”

“I’ma hold you to dat”, said Tawanda.

“Go to the Footlocker around 4.”

“Alright Yo, good lookin’”, said Dirty.

Tawanda hung up and Patricia spoke again, “Thank you Antonio. I really appreciate your help. I didn’t mean to be so hysterical but…”

“Ssh”, said Dirty silencing her in mid-sentence. “I understand. How ‘bout we discuss this over dinner tonight? You choose the location this time.”

The phone was silent for a couple seconds then, “How about Houston’s in D.C? we can hook up around 8 o’clock if that’s alright with you”, said Patricia smiling.

She couldn’t help but admire the way Dirty just handled the crisis like Don Corleone then once things were under wraps he snapped back into ‘Prince Charming’.

"Alright then Baby Girl, I'll call you after I make the run up Mondawmin", stated Dirty disconnecting the call. He dialed Bucky's number and told him what was what once he answered.

■■■

Dirty picked Bucky up at 4:12. The ten-minute ride to the mall was silent for the most part. Dirty tried to push the words Tawanda spoke to the back of his mind but they kept resurfacing. He knew that Bucky had to have bad mouthed him or else Tawanda wouldn't have known about Nah being in control. Dirty loved Bucky and all his homies like family, but Nah could out think them and he was the most reliable and responsible, he reasoned. Nah had proven he was ready when he volunteered to step up to the plate when Dirty was shot up.

How the fuck Bucky gonna throw dirt on my name to a bitch, thought Dirty repeatedly throughout the ride to the mall. Fighting the urge to confront Bucky he bit his tongue. Finally, he concluded, *I ain't gonna let no bitch fuck me and my man relationship up or question Yo behind no shit a bitch said…fuck it.*

Parking the truck, Dirty whipped his pistol out and pulled the chamber on the Glock 40 back, making sure the gun was cocked and ready just in case he was walking into an ambush.

Satisfied with the sight of the hollow tip in the chamber he released it and tucked the Glock back in his waistline under the hoodie he wore, putting the hoodie on his head he climbed out of the truck.

Bucky had already got out of the truck and stood at the back of it waiting on Dirty. Together they strolled into the mall. Making their way to Footlocker a brown skin slender male dressed in all black caught Dirty's attention. He vaguely recognized the face but couldn't pinpoint from where. The dude didn't even seem to notice let alone pay Dirty any attention as he and Bucky continued. Bucky went into the store to locate Shaneeka and retrieve his jewelry. Dirty on the other hand remained at the entrance wrecking his brain trying to place where he knew the dude from staring intently at him as the dude spoke on his silver cell phone. The dude made a fatal mistake when he pulled the phone away from his ear, turned to the nail shop and gestured to someone in the shop talking with his hands, the phone in his hand slightly resembling a chrome gun.

BAM! It hit Dirty like a ton of bricks, "That's the dude T.C", he mumbled, "I got this bitch."

Stepping into Footlocker he pulled Bucky to the side right after Shaneeka handed him the bag containing his jewelry.

"Yo, here take these keys, go start the truck and pull up by the exit where we came in", he whispered handing Bucky his keys.

“What’s up Dirty?”, asked Bucky with a puzzled look on his face.

“don’t worry ‘bout dat just go start da truck up and pull in front da exit for me Yo”, demanded Dirty in a low menacing tone.

“You got dat yo”, said Bucky exiting Footlocker, he beelined straight for the truck.

Dirty lingered in the shoe store for a few seconds before exiting it. Figuring Bucky had reached the truck he slowly eased up on T.C who was engrossed in a seemingly heavy phone conversation looking in the opposite direction.

Never thinking to occasionally look around, T.C didn’t see the hooded figure approaching him.

Dirty spotted the watch on T. C’s arm, “A Cutty what time is it?”, he asked.

Turning in the direction of the voice T.C lifted his arm to look at his watch. Just then, suddenly without warning Dirty whipped the Glock 40 out from his waist with his right hand and grabbed T. C’s forearm with his left hand. A look of horror froze on T. C’s face when Dirty jabbed the gun on a diagonal angle ‘pointing upwards’ into his rib cage and squeezed the trigger.

BOOM! A shout rang out, then BOOM! Another and BOOM! Another. Three slugs in all pierced T. C’s body, traveling up and through his heart, exiting his back.

He was dead before he even hit the floor. Blood covered the shattered nail shop window and formed around his lifeless body once he fell back and slid down the glass front. Dirty never looked back as he strolled out of the mall, concealing the hot gun in his hoodie pocket. He hopped in the truck and was gone before the people who ran, ducked or hovered in fear had a chance to regroup. The hit was so public that it caught everybody off guard and no one could identify the assassin who executed the murder.

Chapter 24

Parking his truck in front of the six-unit tri-level apartment building where Star lived, Bucky eased out and strolled into the building. Eager to get next to Star he pounded on her apartment door. A couple seconds passed before a toffee brown skin female answered the door dressed in nothing but a long white t-shirt with a pair of blue thongs on. Opening the door, she smiled and spoke.

“Hey Bucky, what’s up Baby?”, said Star stepping to the side so Bucky could enter her nicely furnished apartment.

“Ain’t shit, what’s up wit cha?”, replied Bucky easing by Star, he walked over into the living room and sat down on the couch.

“Nothin’ just chillin’ waitin’ on you. Did you bring some smoke?”, she asked. After locking the door, she made her way over to the couch and sat next to Bucky.

“Don’t I always?”, replied Bucky pulling the Dutch Masters cigars and six bags of weed out.

“Um-hum”, said Star flashing a smile, hoping he’d give her the $500.00 she’d asked him for earlier.

Bucky gutted a Dutch and dumped two bags of the light green weed into it, twisted it up and lit it. They shared the blunt and talked casually. Bucky continued to gawk at Star as they talked. He’d been trying to get between her legs ever since they met at Windsor Inn weeks ago, to no avail. Still he continued to try, by showering her with money and materialistic gifts. He just knew today would be the day he got the pussy. Star on the other hand had no intentions on giving Bucky none of her goodies and in fact she secretly frowned down on him, to her Bucky was just a ‘trick ass nigga’ she could work. She’d heard the rumor that a girl named Tawanda had beat him for several G’s and reasoned that, if Tawanda did it, then she could do it too.

Thus, she played on Bucky, teasing him, she stroked his ego and pockets simultaneously.

“A Bucky you still gonna give me dat money?”, she asked running her tongue over her lips seductively.

“Yeah, I got’chu”, replied Bucky attempting to reach out for Star, but she seen it coming and quickly stood, avoiding his touch.

“I’ll be right back Yo, I’m thirsty as shit”, she said once she stood, she walked towards the kitchen. “You want something to drink?”

“Yeah, bring me somethin’”, replied Bucky staring at Star mesmerized by the way she swayed her hips when she walked.

Man, this bitch phat as a donkey, I gotta get some a dat pussy tonight, thought Bucky having popped a double stack M Ecstasy pill just before he reached Star’s apartment, his hormones were in over drive.

After pouring two glasses of Sunny Delight Star returned to the living room carrying one in each hand. She handed Bucky the full glass and sat her half empty glass on the coffee table in front them. Then she sat down, scooting back on the couch, her T-shirt hiked up, exposing her firm thighs, arousing Bucky.

“Come here girl!”, said Bucky advancing on Star before she could make any sudden moves. Grabbing her he attempted to kiss her. Unable to do much Star twisted her head to the side so Bucky couldn’t kiss her lips. By doing so she exposed the left side of her face and neck then Bucky planted his lips on her face. Panting like a dog he slivered his tongue around her neck.

“Boy get the fuck off me!”, snapped Star angrily as she tried to free herself from his grasp.

“Fuck all dat! I been lookin’ out for yo’ ass like shit and all you keep doin’ is playin’ games wit’ a nigga”, said Bucky pinning Star down by holding her wrist while laying his weight on her,

"You gonna give me some of dis pussy."

"I ain't givin' ya ugly ass shit, get the hell…"

SMACK! Before she'd finished her sentence, Bucky smacked her viciously.

"Get the FUCK off me you BITCH ASS NIGGA!!" screamed Star trying to get Bucky off, only to be smacked again.

SMACK!!

"Bitch shut the fuck up!", spat Bucky using his left hand he gripped her neck and smacked her again with his right hand. "I said shut the fuck up bitch!"

"Help Meee! Somebody help meee!", screamed Star tears streaming down her face as she thrashed about on the couch, hollering at the top of her lungs, "HELP! HELP! SOMEBODY HEEEEELP!!!"

Her pleas for help only angered Bucky causing him to rain down on the defenseless woman with a furry of blows, silencing her. The pain was so excruciating that Star passed out, her entire body was limp. In a sex induced rage, fueled by Ecstasy in his system Bucky decided to take the pussy. Ripping Star's thongs off her he tossed them to the floor, fumbled with his zipper until he'd unzipped his pants, then he pulled his dick out. Lifting Star's limp legs, he spread and positioned himself between them before stuffing his erect dick into her vagina. Savagely he raped her thrusting in and out until he ejaculated. Satisfied he stood, stuffed his dick back in his pants and zippered up before heading for his truck.

He didn't even notice the nosey old lady in the apartment below Star's peering out of her window as he climbed in his truck and pulled off. Slouching back in the leather seat one hand on the steering wheel, he headed for the city limits, his foot on the gas pedal doing nearly 70mph. just before he reached Baltimore city a Baltimore County police patrol car signaled him to pull over. Knowing he'd been speeding he assumed it was a routine traffic stop and pulled over, cursing under his breath.

This some bullshit, deez county bounties always fuckin' wit' a nigga", he said looking in his rearview mirror. He saw two white police officers climb out of their patrol car and walk toward his truck. When the police reached his door, he rolled the window down.

"What's the problem officers?"

"License and registration please sir", said the short balding officer stepping up to the truck while his tall blonde partner stood back fingering the gun in his holster.

Bucky fished the registration out of the glove compartment and handed I, along with his license which he'd retrieved from his pocket, to the officer, "Here ya go."

Taking his documents, the officer scanned them, then looked at Bucky.

"Mr. Barnes please step from the truck with your hands up."

"Do what?!", barked Bucky with his mug broke ready to protest.

“Step from the truck sir”, said the officer, his partner already on point with his gun ready, just in case Bucky tried something slick.

Wisely Bucky kept his hand visible and followed the instructions given, easing out of the truck. Once he was out of the truck, he was lead to the patrol car, ordered to put his hands on the hood of the car, legs spread and searched. After being searched he was handcuffed.

“Man, the fuck yall cuffin’ me for?”, asked Bucky when the cold steel clicked around his wrists.

“You fit the description of an assault and rape called in by the neighbor of a woman minutes ago…”, began the officer his voice fading out losing meaning to Bucky as his world started to crumble.

From that moment forward everything was ablur, from the ride to the police station behind the patrol car to the police station itself. Bucky couldn’t recall being processed, seeing the commissioner or being shipped to Baltimore County’s Detention Center in Towson. Literally everything seemed to be in slow motion, like a nightmare. He even went so far as to pinch himself hoping he’d awake from the nightmare, but it was far from a nightmare, it was harsh reality.

Looking at his charge papers he blew out a gust of hot air, “How da fuck I get myself in dis kinda position over some pussy”, he exclaimed, talking to himself as he read over the list of charges of rape, assault, battery, malicious wounding, handgun violation…, frowning he silently read the last charge over, handgun violation. Then it hit him, he had a 9 Beretta under his driver's seat.

"Shit!", he cursed, then read his bail, 350G's. he sighed with relief knowing Dirty would pay the bail.

Soon as he reached the filthy over crowded orientation block he immediately posted up to await an available phone. Grabbing the first phone that came open. Bucky quickly dialed Dirty's home number. The phone rang, holding his breath Bucky willed his homie to answer the phone, "Pick up yo, pick up…"

Hearing the phone ring Dirty ignored it and continued to slide in and out of the warm wet pussy that engulfed his swollen 'manhood'. The phone continued to ring and finally after roughly a dozen rings Dirty figured it had to be important so he reluctantly eased out of Pat's snug 'love tunnel', his dick rock hard he rolled over and grabbed the phone off the nightstand.

Thinking that Peaches might have been in labor, he spoke into the receiver, "Yo what's up? Who dis?"

"You have a collect call from "Bucky", at the Baltimore County Detention Center. If you accept this call do not use 3-way or call waiting features or you will be disconnected to accept this dial 1 now…"

Dirty pushed 1 without hesitation. "Thank You."

"Yo, what's up Cutty? Fuck you locked up for?", asked Dirty curiously, then just as quickly dismissed the question. "Never mind what you locked up for. What's your bail?"

“It’s 350G’s”, said Bucky.

“Damn, you fuckin up Yo! Your ugly ass need to pump the brakes ‘cause you movin’ entirely too fast”, warned Dirty.

“I know yo”, agreed Bucky humbly.

“Look, I’ma go ‘head and call Fat Frank. I’ll rap wit’chu when I see ya!”

“Good lookin’ yo”, said Bucky feeling a thing of guilt knowing he’d been bad mouthing the realest nigga he knew about the Nah’s situation.

“Dat’s what real homies do”, said Dirty thinking of what Tawanda had told him. “You still my nigga, Peace”, he hung up before Bucky could respond.

After hanging up with Bucky, he immediately called Fat Frank and arranged for Bucky’s bail to be paid. Then he laid back on the king size bed, his whole demeanor having changed, his dick limp. Patricia understood the unspoken and did her womanly magic. Grabbing his dick, she massaged it then lowered her head and put it in her mouth. She sucked and licked on his dick until he was ridged and hard as steel again, then she straddled him and rode him like a rodeo girl. They enjoyed each other’s bodies from several different angles, before slowing to a halt after they’d both reached the pinnacle of ecstasy.

Having made Patricia cum several times and ejaculating twice himself, Dirty left her curled up asleep on the bed and went to take a shower. The hot water felt good on his skin as he bathed. While lathering up he began to think of his position a situation.

Things were sweet. Dirty and his whole circle were doing well. He was on top of his game.

Aside from Bucky who seemed to become obsessed with flossing and tricking, the rest of Dirty's close associates were all excelling. Each of them having invested in small legal businesses. Snuggles and Smurf both owned their own houses in the county and they were partners with a car wash on Monroe and Mosher Streets and had three cleaners. Squirrel and Fatty-Pooh also owned their houses and shared a barber shop that catered to hustlers called 'Hustlers Heaven'. Nah owned a nice house in Chase, Maryland plus he'd bought his sisters a house in Essex. He also owned a pool hall on 25th street and Greenmount as well as a rim and car accessory store he and his little cousin 'Shyheem' owned on Reisterstown Road. Tracy and Munchie had both invested in small beauty shops. Even Skiddie Box and Dirt-Dirt had purchased a nice rowhouse in Northeast Baltimore together and converted the basement into a little music studio. In all, everyone was living especially Dirty who in a single year had stormed Baltimore sucking up enough illegal money to retire at 21. He owned a club, nine houses each converted into two or three apartments, plus he'd purchased a house for Mrs. Cookie. Peaches and their child had a new house at his expense although he and Peaches weren't together. At 21 Antonio 'Dirty White' Lord had reached a position most hustlers only dream of.

I got everything a nigga want, maybe it's time for me to get out da game, thought Dirty rinsing off and stepping out of the shower. *I ain't tryna fuck around and end up like A.J wit a triple life in A.D.X 'federal Supermax'...*

▪▪

Chapter 25

Celebrating the day of his release this time last year Dirty treated himself to a new pearl white 2000 Mercedes Benz S600 with ash gray leather interior. Soon as he purchased the car he turned it over to Nah and Shy's rim store where the car was fitted with chrome 20' inch Luciano rims and a complete Kenwood stereo system 26 CD changer, speakers, digital remote stereo system panel and amps. Also as an added luxury he had three Panasonic 7-inch T. V's installed, all which were hooked up to the DVD and PlayStation 2. The coup de grace was a surprise 'stash spot' in the driver's door panel where he could store his gun that Nah had installed as a gift.

Once the car was ready Nah drove Dirty to pick it up. He loved it and the first thing he did was shoot to

Snuggles and Smurf car wash to have the S600 washed, waxed and detailed. The afternoon sun had come out, weather promised to be beautiful. People were out on the sidewalks and steps in front of their rowhouses gossiping and enjoying the weather as Dirty slowly drove through the slums of Baltimore Nah right behind him.

When they finally reached the car wash they spotted Skiddie Box and Dirt-Dirt who were getting their floss on standing in front of their new vehicles. They parked and turned their keys over to A respected older gentlemen who hustled, washing cars, then they walked over to kick it with their protégé's.

"What's up big homies?", said Dirt-Dirt and Skiddie Box simultaneously.

"Aint shit, what's up wit' yall?", said Nah as they exchanged dap.

"Same ol' shit", said Skiddie Box leaning up against his STS Caddy.

"Yo Nah, Dirty, why don't ya'll invest into the rap game, it's money wit' dat shit", said an animated Dirt-Dirt.

"I was jive thinkin' 'bout it but I can't rap", said Dirty.

"Shit you ain't gotta rap, me and Skiddie nice, we can do the rappin'", said Dirt-Dirt.

"Oh yeah! Let me hear somethin'", said Dirty.

Dirt-Dirt eagerly began rapping, "Baltimore 'bout money nigga fuck what you heard/ from the Ravens to the Orioles we known for them birds/ known for toting

Glocks, spittin' shots murderin herbs/ wit' no remorse for a nigga leave'um slumped in a alley/ headbusta out for Blood like a Crip our Cali/ outlaw to the core nigga fuck O'Malley/" ... he had everyone's attention until Dirty's cell phone began to vibrate and he answered it.

"Yo, who dis?", he asked turning away from the trio, he took a few steps to his left.

"Peaches in labor Yo", shouted Keisha instantly getting his full attention.

"What hospital she in?, he asked anxiously, butterflies fluttering in the pit of his stomach.

"Saint Joseph, out York Road!"

"I'm on my way", said Dirty hanging up, he turned to Nah.

"Yo you know where Saint Joseph Hospital at?"

"Yeah it's out Towson."

"Come on Yo show me where it's at, Peaches in labor", said Dirty walking toward his car.

"Yo Mr. Skip don't worry 'bout the rest I gotta go.", he said handing the older man his normal fee along with a tip. "Good lookin'."

By the time he had climbed into the Benz and started it Nah had already pulled over to the Fulton avenue exit and was waiting on him. Rolling his window down he honked his horn and shouted to his protégé's, "I'ma holla at yall later", as he pulled behind Nah's black Harley Davidson F-150 pickup truck.

Nah pulled out of the car wash and began weaving in and out of the afternoon traffic followed closely by Dirty, who even had to run a few red lights to keep up with Nah. Finally, several minutes later they reached the elegantly manicured scenery at Saint Joseph Hospital. Parking Dirty with Nah on his heels rushed into the woman's pavilion. The inside of the nearly impeccable hospital was cold and smelled of antiseptics. Spotting a fat white woman behind a desk, Dirty approached her and asked the receptionist where the Labor and Delivery unit was located.

"Excuse me, my wife in labor here, her name is Tynisha Coleman. Can you direct me to her room?"

"Certainly Sir, can you repeat the last name again please?", asked the woman, typing the information in the computer as he gave it to her.

"Coleman, Tynisha Coleman", said Dirty.

"T-y-n-i-s-h-a C-o-l-e….."

"She's on the second floor, room 214. Walk down this hall to the elevators", said the woman pointing to her left, "Take the elevator to the second floor, the number is above the room, look for 214."

"Thanks", said Dirty over his shoulders already on route to the elevators.

While waiting on the elevator a sledge hammer seemed to be pounding on his chest, he held his breath. When the elevator opened he exhaled and he and Nah boarded. Stopping on the second floor they disembarked the elevator and veered right walking fast, reading the numbers plastered above each door until they located 214.

Keisha, Lil' Mookie, Ms. Cookie and Ms. Janice 'Peaches aunt', were already in the room when Dirty and Nah entered. Smiling Dirty stepped over to Peaches bedside and grabbed her hand. Even with her hair everywhere on her head, sweat glistening on her brows and her face contorted into a grimacing mask Peaches still looked beautiful in his eyes.

"You alright sexy?", he asked rubbing her hand as she breathed heavily.

She shook her head, yes, then groaned, "AAAAH!", a contraction gripping her followed closely one after another, "AAAH!"

"Yo, get the doctor Nah", shouted Dirty.

Nah turning on his heels bolted out of the room to find a nurse or doctor. Everyone else gathered around Peaches bed. Ms. Cookie, Ms. Janice and Keisha all instructed her to breathe slow deep breaths and relax. Dirty continued to hold her hand as she squeezed his and groaned.

A second before Nah returned with a nurse, her water broke and her cervix dilated a few centimeters. Contractions tore through her causing her to groan like a wounded animal, "Urrrrgh!"

When the nurse entered the room she immediately, with Dirty's assistance began to wheel the bed out of the room and toward the delivery room. At the entrance to the delivery room several nurses and a doctor stood, taking charge as soon as the bed reached them. Dirty at the urgency of one of the nurses got dressed in the scrubs given to him. Once dressed he washed his hands and stepped into the main part of the delivery room. Seated by narcotics, Peaches seemed to be much more stable as the doctor positioned between her legs instructed her to push.

“Push Ms. Coleman”, he said sternly. “Push!”

She pushed hard, straining, her face scrunched up, “Uuuuuuh!”

“Push Baby!”, said Dirty holding one of her hands while caressing her hair with his other hand.

“I am pushhhhhhhin’, niggaaaaaaah!”, screamed Peaches straining.

“One more time Ms. Coleman!”, instructed the doctor seeing the top of the baby’s head covered with jet black hair. “One more time!”

“Urrrrrgh!”, strained Peaches, a vein appearing in the center of her forehead as she pushed the infant out of her vagina.

The doctor grabbed the afterbirth covered newborn, the child cried.

“It’s a boy”, shouted the doctor examining the newborn after allowing Dirty to cut the umbilical cord.

The doctor then handed one of the nurses the newborn and she turned to rinse him off at the sink.

She then took the infants vital signs, weighed him, checked his length, got his foot prints and wrapped him in a blanket before handing him to his father.

“Here you go, a beautiful, healthy baby boy. He weighs 8 pounds and 7 ounces and he’s 21 inches long”, said the nurse, her eyes warm as if she was smiling under her mask.

“Thanks”, said Dirty having grabbed the bundle of joy, he smiled, holding him out from his body he gave his son a once over before cuddling him close to his chest, “Hey Lil’ White”, the baby cooed in his father’s arms.

“Let me see him Antonio”, said Peaches softly smiling at the way Dirty held their child able to see all the love and admiration in his eyes.

Dirty reluctantly gave his son to Peaches. As soon as Antonio Lord Jr. left his father’s arm he started whining.

“Boy I carried you for nine months don’t start whining wit’ me”, said Peaches kissing her son.

“He wants Daddy”, joked Dirty, leaning down he kissed Peaches and their son on their foreheads. “I love yall!”

“We love you too Antonio, we love you too”, said Peaches tears welling up in her eyes, she really missed her man and hoped he’d leave the streets alone and be with her so they could raise their child together.

▪▪▪

Darkness had just started to fall when Fatty-Pooh parked in front of his main girl Tammy's townhouse. Climbing out of the he popped the trunk and retrieved two shopping bags. Clutching both bags in his left hand, his keys in the right he walked up to the door, stuck the house key in the lock and turned it. Opening the door, he stepped into the living room. All his senses heightened due to the complete darkness in the townhome.

"Tammy!", he shouted.

Receiving no answer, he ran his hand along the wall, located the switch, flicked it up and the light came on pushing the darkness out. With the light on Fatty-Pooh could see Tammy sitting on the leather couch. In her hand, she held a large butcher knife, tears running down her face smearing her make-up. Baffled he stared at her for a few long tense seconds, she held his gaze, hatred in her eyes.

"Yo what's up wit'chu?", he asked sitting the bags down and shutting the door behind him.

Tammy didn't respond. Thinking he could coax her into releasing the knife and talking to him he attempted to ease up on her. But Tammy wasn't having it and quickly sprung up like a jack in a box, knife in hand.

"What da fuck is wrong wit'chu Yo?", asked Fatty-Pooh stopping in his tracks.

She still didn't respond. Tears continued to stream down her cheeks. Again Fatty-Pooh attempted to ease up on her hoping to disarm her.

"Come here Boo, let's talk about it", he said taking a couple steps toward Tammy.

"Don't Boo me motherfucka", shouted Tammy. "I hate you Bitch! Oooow I hate your no-good trifling ass."

"What da fuck is you talkin' 'bout?" he asked looking 10 Karat stupid.

"What the am I talkin' bout? I'm talkin' 'bout fuckin' Angie. Who the fuck is this young bitch Angie you fuckin'?", asked Tammy accusingly.

"That's a good motherfuckin' question 'because I don't know no Angie", snapped Fatty-Pooh with a blank look on his face.

"Don't fuckin lie to me Fatty, the bitch told my sister she pregnant by you motherfucka. Oooow! You make me sick!!!!...... I should cut your got damn dick off!", screamed Tammy advancing toward Fatty-Pooh welding the butcher knife.

"I'm tellin' you Tammy don't do no dumb shit wit' dat knife or I'ma make you regret it", warned Fatty-Pooh trying to maintain his composure as he sized her up. She continued to circle the marble table. So, thinking he could grab her real quick and strip her of the knife Fatty-Pooh lunged at her. However, he misjudged his footing and his right foot hit the coffee table causing him to stumble off balance into tammy. The sudden lunge startled her and with both hands around the wooden handle of the butcher knife she flinched thrusting the blade upwards. Pain exploded in Fatty-Pooh's chest as the long blade sunk into his solar plexus. Together they crashed to the floor. Tammy landed on her back and Fatty-Pooh landed on top of her, forcing the butcher knife up to its hilt, burying it in his chest.

"W-w-why?", stuttered Fatty-Pooh, a glob of blood in his mouth. He heaved and exhaled a hollow breath of air, his soul slipping from his body. He died lying on top of Tammy.

Chapter 26

At the intersection of Madison and Milton Avenue Dirty held his foot on the brake pedal, patiently he waited for the red light to turn green. While at the light he took in his surroundings, noticing the good weather of the approaching summer brought the slums of Baltimore to its apex of life. Everywhere he looked there were hustlers on the grind, junkies trying to get their blast, or hoodrats (young females from the neighborhood) in hot pants, miniskirts and booty shorts revealing their assets in hopes of catching a hustler's eyes. Dirty loved the slums, but in his heart, he felt it was time to step back, leave the game alone and raise his son. The more he thought about it, the more he conformed to the idea.

...After these last 30 birds done I'ma chill for a while and do right by my seed, thought Dirty floating forward when the light changed. *What's left anyway? Shit I did everything I set out to do. I'm rich and I can live comfortable for the rest of my life*

without ever breaking the law again..., Yeah I'ma go out wit' a bang and throw a White Out party.

Grabbing his cell phone, he started dialing numbers to inform his peeps that he was throwing a White Out party at Fat Daddy's announcing his retirement. The first number he dialed was Nah's. Unusual for Nah he didn't answer his cell phone so he dialed Snuggles number and Snuggles didn't answer either, nor did Smurf.

"I wonder what's up with them niggas not answering their phones", exclaimed Dirty out loud hitting speed dial he called Squirrel who also failed to answer his phone as did Bucky, when he called him.

Shrugging it off he continued west bound on route to his grandmother's so he could go bowling with her like they did every Monday night. She still lived on Hollins Street having refused to move when her grandson tried to buy her a house in the county, Ms. Cookie on the other hand accepted the offer.

Nearing the intersection of Madison Avenue and Martin Luther King Boulevard Dirty hit his blinkers signaling left, about to turn when....SKKKKKKRRRRRRD!, a wreck less rust colored four door 1985 Ford LTD slammed square into the rear of his S600with a thunderous metallic roar, CRRRRAAASSSSHHH!

The impact of the collision forced the S600 into the rear end of a Honda Civic directly in front of it, despite Dirty's attempt at slamming on the brakes. The airbag exploded preventing him from meeting the same fate as Fatz.

Fortunately, he hadn't been injured. Slamming the car in park, off impulse, he whipped out his blue steel 9 Ruger in case it was a kidnapping or assassination attempt. He clutched the gun, ready, looking in his rearview mirror. No one emerged from the LTD. Content he put his gun back in his dip and eased out of the Benz his face red, temper flaring.

Rushing over to the LTD, which had swerved off to the right and crashed into a red brick wall, he froze in his tracks at the sight he saw. Behind the steering wheel sat a gray haired older black man slumped over twitching, blood leaking from a gash in his head.

"Damn slim fucked up", murmured Dirty staring at the old man, mystified. Evidently someone had called 911 because the loud sirens could be heard in the distance. Hearing the sirens jolted Dirty out of the mystified state and back to the present. Shaking his head, he walked back over to his Benz assessing the damage.

"Damn this old motherfucka done fucked my shit up!" he cursed as he climbed back into his car and stashed the gun in the stash spot.

After stashing his gun in the driver's door, he eased out of his wrecked car and stepped over to the Civic he'd rear ended. The driver of the Civic happened to be a dark skin girl named Keona, one of Tracee's buddies that knew Dirty. Her nerves were shot and she was visibly shaken, but aside from that she appeared to be okay and stated such when he asked her.

“Yo, you alright?”, asked Dirty looking down in Keyona’s car.

“Yeah, I’m cool, but I ain’t getting’ out dis car. Fuck dat, I’ma sue the insurance company. I got whiplash and my back hurt”, stated Keona deviously plotting to turn the accident into a come up.

“I feel ya”, replied Dirty knowing her intentions.

When the ambulance finally arrived, they rushed the driver of the LTD off to shock trauma. Keona less visibly injured had to wait for a second ambulance. By the time one arrived several police patrol cars and even a fire truck was at the scene of the accident. The first officer to arrive filed the report on the accident an after doing so he handed Dirty his license, registration and insurance paper back, dismissing him.

“You can go Mr. Lord.”

“Thanks”, said Dirty about to step on the curb and wait for his grandmother who he’d called to come pick him up.

When a suspicious racist, white, blonde haired, blue eyed officer climbed out of his patrol car and ordered Dirty to be detained.

“Hold up Cox, there’s a U.S. Marshall’s warrant for that feller’s arrest”, said the racist pig to the young black officer. “I knew something was fishy with a young black man driving a $100,000.00 car with a big diamond neckless on, so I ran a check on him and it came back that he’s wanted by the U.S. Marshall’s”, stated the officer sardonically.

“Man, what the fuck you talkin’ bout I ain’t got no motherfuckin’ warrant”, quipped Dirty certain there had to be a mistake.

“Tell it to the Marshall’s”, said the racist officer approaching him. “Now turn around and put your hands behind your head.

Angry his eyes shot darts at the white officer nonetheless he complied with the order, turning around and putting his hands on his head. He was frisked, then handcuffed and lead to a patrol car. His world all at once seemed to be spinning out of control as the officer roughly forced him into the back of his patrol car.

What the fuck is this shit about, what the fuck do I got a warrant with the Marshall’s for… fuck it don’t matter I’ll be out wit’ one phone call, thought Dirty as he reasoned sitting back in the back seat of the patrol car with his mug broke.

Whistling Dixie, the racist officer, smiling sinisterly, periodically looked into the rearview mirror ridiculing Dirty as she navigated through the streets of Baltimore on route to Central Booking.

Arriving at the side gate leading to the intake entrance, the gates rose, they continued forward as the gates closed behind the car. Finding a parking space, the officer parked, climbed out and unlocked the back-driver’s side door.

“Come on let’s go Lord.”

Scooting to the edge of the back seat Dirty swung his feet out of the car and rose to his full height of 6 feet 1 inch. Ice grilling the officer with contempt in his eyes he fought the urge to spit in the 'pig's' face. Clutching his left bicep, the officer escorted Dirty into the intake vestibule.

"Have a seat", instructed the officer pointing to a metal bench lining the wall.

Dirty went with the flow and sat down on the bench. Sitting to his right was a dirty foul smelling dope fiend with open abscesses on his arms and legs. Also on the bench sat four other black men of various shades with white plastic hand restraints on their wrists, all waiting to be processed.

The officer disappeared and about five minutes later Big Bubba a C.O. who worked part-time as a bouncer at Fat Daddy's came to process him having got wind that Dirty had been brought in to be booked.

"Yo White come on man", motioning for Dirty to follow him. "What the hell they lock you up for man?"

"I don't know what the fucks goin' on. Some old motherfucka crashed into me and when five-o came they ran a check and I had a Marshall warrant", replied Dirty standing and walking over to where Big Bubba stood.

"A Marshall warrant, damn that's Feds White", said Big Bubba as he uncuffed Dirty and lead him through the corridor where new arrestees are strip searched.

"The Feds?", mocked Dirty.

“Yeah that’s what the Marshall’s o, they catch federal fugitives”, replied Big Bubba as they entered the strip down room.

“Goddamn, it stinks in dis bitch!”, complained Dirty.

“Huh man”, agreed Big Bubba. “Look I ain’t gonna search you just give me your belt, cell phones, jewels, and the stuff in your pockets”, said Big Bubba respectfully.

“You got dat yo”, replied Dirty handing Big Bubba his platinum chain, platinum Aqua Swiss watch, both of his cell phones, his belt and emptied his pocket, removing a wad of money, a wallet, some coins and a pack of juicy fruit chewing gum.

Big Bubba placed all Dirty things on top of the counter against the wall opposite of the stripping stalls. Then he placed his belongings into a clear plastic bag and lead him out of the room to a desk counter on the opposite side of the corridor which he saw a honey colored complexion female C.O. he recognized.

“Hey Dirty White, what you get locked up for?”, asked the female C.O. flashing a smile that revealed two gold teeth.

“Shit, your guess just as good as mines”, he replied dryly.

After his property and valuables were accounted for he was finger printed and his mug shot was taken. Then Bubba gave him free access to the phone. The first person he called was his grandmother, then he called Mrs. Cookie so the two of them could get on top of things, call his lawyer and the bail bondsman and find out what was what. Then he called Peaches and explained his situation as best he could.

Typical of her she became emotional and hysterical, crying and carrying on. Dirty did his best to sooth her and assure her that everything would be okay.

About 30-40 minutes passed before Big Bubba said anything to him. But shift was about to change and he had to secure him in a holding cell.

"Look shift 'bout to change so I gotta put you in a bull pen. I'ma put word wit' my man on the next shift to get you on the phone if the Marshalls ain't come to get you before then", said Big Bubba.

"Alright Yo", said Dirty then he spoke into the receiver.

"I gotta get off the phone, I'ma call you later… I love you too… kiss' Lil' White for me and call Ma Ma and Ms. Cookie…Alright love ya", he said hanging up. Then he followed Big Bubba to a holding cell.

"Be cool White", said Big Bubba giving him dap.

"Most definitely, you be cool too. Oh, and tell Mr. K to call my grandmother and Ms. Cookie so the club won't miss a beat", said Dirty stepping into the holding cell when Big Bubba unlocked it.

"I got'chu", said Big Bubba locking the holding cell door. "Good Luck!"

Dirty saluted him with a closed fist gesture as Big Bubba walked off. The bullpen was cold and crowded as always so he stepped over and around a few dudes who were laying on the floor a made his way to the toilet where he urinated and washed his hands. Then turning to the men on the concrete bench he asked them to slide over so he could cop a squat and sit down.

“Yo, let me squeeze up on there wit’ yall Cutty”, said Dirty looking down at the men on the bench.

The authoritative way he spoke, combined with his mannerism and the way the C.O. treated him told the men on the bench that the pretty boy standing in front of them had to be a prominent individual with pull so they didn’t hesitate to slide over. Dirty sat down and began trying to put the puzzle together.

How the fuck I get trapped off by the Feds, this shit crazy, he thought as he tried to recount all his actions. He’d sold plenty Kilo’s with Los’s assistance, but he’d been extra cautious on every drop. *Naw, it can’t be that unless Los set me up…*

Just as the thought popped I his head the bullpen door swung open. “Lord, the Marshall’s are here for ya”, said the male C.O. with a huge beer belly.

Standing Dirty exited the bullpen, following the C.O. down the hall to the vestibule through which he’d entered the Bookings. Two U.S. Marshalls whom favored Starsky and Hutch awaited him. ‘Starsky’ frisked him, then put the three-piece restraint set on him. Once he was secured in the handcuffs, shackles and lockbox the Marshalls escorted him out of the sliding vestibule door, into the parking lot where a burgundy Chevy Lumina with dark tinted windows awaited them. Dirty was instructed to get in the back seat as 'Hutch' drove.

Soon as the car pulled out of the bookings parking lot "Starksy and Hutch' started talking.

"So, Dirty White, why don't you help yourself before it's too late 'cause it won't look good for yall", said 'Starsky' turned halfway around in his seat, sarcastically referring to Antonio Lord as Dirty White.

"Yeah tell us who your supplier is and we can help you out", added 'Hutch' looking at Dirty through the rearview mirror.

"Man, yall got me fucked up", spat Dirty, perplexed, wondering, how the fuck they know my name.

Frowning he remained silent as they continued to throw help yourself, snitch, hints at him. Dirty may have been a lot of things, but a rat wasn't one of them. He'd do life or go to the gas chamber before he turned into a rat. It only took a few minutes for the Lumina to reach 101 Lombard Street, the federal courthouse. driving down into the large white building's basement, 'Hutch' pulled into the garage area and parked. Seconds later a metal gate rolled down from the ceiling enclosing the car in the small area.

Once the car was parked and secured in the garage area by the drop gate 'Starsky' climbed out of the car and put him and 'Hutch's' guns in a safe box on the wall near the elevator then he stuck a key in the elevator, beckoning it to the basement. When the elevator arrived 'Starsky' held it open and waited for his partner and Dirty.

Seeing the elevator open 'Hutch' climbed out of the car, opened the driver's side back door and helped Dirty out of the car. With shackles on his ankles he shuffled over to the elevator, 'Hutch' at his side. On the elevator, the Marshalls locked him in a small cage, pushed 6 on the control panel and the elevator lunged upwards.

Stopping on the sixth floor the elevator door opened and a burly white Marshall greeted them. The Marshalls exchanged pleasantries, then the burly one led the way into a small white room just opposite of the elevator and again Dirty was fingerprinted and his mugshot taken.

After being processed into the Marshall's system Dirty was driven to M.R.D.C.C where he'd spend the night and be arraigned the following morning. At M.R.D.C.C he went through the tiresome processing procedures for the third time that day, before being escorted to the 6th floor where federal inmates are housed. When he stepped off the elevator, bared left, walked down to the tier an entered the tier he was greeted by familiar voices.

"Yo White, up here", shouted Nah from the second tier banging on the blue metal cell door, his face pressed against the small rectangular window in the door.

"Yeah Dirty White", hollered Smurf from the left side of the lower tier, his face also pressed up against the window.

“A Snug, Squirrel they just bring White in yall”, hollered Smurf banging on the door.

Squirrel, Snuggles and Shyheem who was also on the tier all came to their cell doors shouting his name, hooping and hollering. In response, he simply gritted his teeth and shook his head in utter disgust visibly torn by the reality of his situation.

The C.O. led him to a cell on the second tier. Opening the heavy metal door, he instructed Dirty to step in, then slammed the door shut behind him with a loud clinging sound.

Being locked down like an animal in the all too familiar setting again ate at his soul. Frustrated he began to pace the cell in deep thought, *The motherfuckin Feds! Damn where the fuck did I go wrong???!!!*

One thing for certain, he’d soon find out…….

Chapter 27

In the United States District Court

For the District of Maryland

Northern Division

United States of America cr.no L1420-37

v.s

Antonio Lord a.k.a Dirty White	21 USC S 846
Naheem Kane a.k.a Nah	21 USC S 841(A)(1)
Michale Thomas a.k.a Squirrel	18 USC S 924(c)(1)
Kevin Holmes a.k.a Snuggles	18 USC S 1111
Kentroy Harris a.k.a Smurf	21 USC S 856
Shyheem Kane a.k.a Shy	
Tracy Mcknight a.k.a Tray	

COUNT 1

The Grand Jury charges:

That from on or about April 1999, the exact date to the Grand Jury being unknown and continuing thereafter to and including the return of this indictment, in the District of Maryland, the defendants, Antonio Lord a.k.a Dirty White, Naheem Kane a.k.a Nah, Michale Thomas a.k.a Squirrel, Kevin Holmes a.k.a Snuggles, Kentroy Harris a.k.a Smurf, Shyheem Kane a.k.a Shy and Tracy Mcknight a.k.a Tray, knowingly and intentionally did combine, conspire, confederate and agree together and have facet understanding with each other and various other persons both known and unknown to the Grand Jury to possess with intent to distribute and distribute 150 or more kilograms of cocaine, a Schedule II controlled substance, in violation of Title 21, United States code, section 841(A)(1);

All in violation of Title 21 United States code, section 846

COUNT 2

The Grand Jury further charges:

That on or about April 1999, the exact date to the Grand Jury being unknown in the District of Maryland, the defendants Antonio Lord a.k. a Dirty White, Naheem Kane a.k. a Nah, Michale Thomas a.k.a Squirrel, Kevin Holmes a.k.a Snuggles, Kentroy Harris a.k.a Smurf, Shyheem Kane a.k.a Shy and Tracy Mcknight a.k.a Tray did knowingly and intentionally possess with the intent to distribute 150 or more kilograms of cocaine, a schedule II controlled substance;

In violation of Title 21, United States code, section 841(A)(1)

COUNT 3

That Grand Jury further charges:

That on or about Feb.20,2000, in the District Court of Maryland, the defendant Antonio Lord a.k.a Dirty White, did knowingly use, carry and discharge a firearm during and in relation to a drug trafficking crime for which he may be prosecuted in a court of the United States to wit: conspiracy to distribute narcotics as set forth in count one of this indictment which is incorporated herein by reference, in violation of Title 18 United States code, section 924(C)(1) and in the course of this violation caused the death of a person through the use of a firearm which killing is murder as defined in Title 18, United States code, section 1111, in that the defendant, with malice aforethought, did unlawfully kill, Tavon Crocket a.k.a T.C, by shooting him with the firearm, willfully, deliberately, maliciously and with premeditation in the perpetration of the conspiracy;...

Man, these people tryna wash a nigga up for life, thought Dirty having re-read the first 3 counts of his 21-count indictment for the umpteenth time, *and they won't even give a nigga a bail so I'm stuck up in this hot ass Supermax.*

"This shit ridiculous", mumbled Dirty climbing down off the top bunk. Once on the floor he took two steps and was at the sink and toilet, pushing a button on the sink, water sprouted out of the spicket. Cupping the cool liquid in his hand he splashed some on his face, letting it run down his neck and over his bare chest attempting to cool off.

The summer heat was excruciating, even the walls seemed to be perspiring. Stepping over to the stool bolted to the ground in front of the desk in the corner of the cell he stood on it and looked out of the small metal mesh screen covered window where he could see Interstate 83, a club, a parking lot and several streets. *Damn, I 'pose to be out that bitch stuntin' in the 6 wit'*

Lil' White in his car seat, thought Dirty missing his freedom and his son.

Everyone charged on the indictment were detained, except Shyheem who was out on home monitor. Tracy was over the Women Detention Center and the rest of the co-defendants were on one of the four pods on the federal section at M.C.A.C or the Super Max as it's commonly called.

Originally designed as a lock down institution for state inmates. However due to complications at Baltimore City Detention Center in the late 90's Super Max began to house federal inmates also. The federal section is in the far east end of the building on the second floor directly above death row.

So, deplorable are the conditions at the Super Max that federal inmates have been granted departures 'sentence reduction' for conditions of confinement. In other words, the courts are aware of the horrible conditions. The food served to the inhabitants isn't fit for a dog let alone a human, sanitation is extremely poor, medical assistance is nearly unheard of, and worst of all inmates on average are forced to remain in their cells for 18-19 hours a day with temperatures sometimes reaching 100-110 degrees. Imagine being trapped in an 8x10 coffin like cell when it's 110 degrees outside and no circulating air inside. It's inhumane torture especially when one's presumed innocent until proven guilty.

Fortunately for Dirty Ms. Cookie's buddy Denise West now worked as the federal liaison in the Super Max so he was granted a few advantages, such as extra visit's here and there. Plus, he was already a tier runner even though he'd only been locked up for a little over a month. Being the tier runner afforded him access to the phone on the tier, the shower and the law computer all while the rest of the tier is locked in their cells.

Waiting patiently for the 4o'clock count to clear so he could get out of his cell and call Peaches. He continued to stare out of the small window in a daze yearning to be free.

"Lord, you got an attorney visit", said a husky voice emulating from the speaker box in the light fixture above the sink. "How long you need?"

"I'm ready when yall are", he replied.

"Well, come on out", stated the husky voice popping the cell door.

Hopping down off the stool, he grabbed a brand-new t-shirt and some burgundy state shorts and put the clothing on, then slipped his shoes on and stepped out of the cell onto the tier. Descending the stairs, he walked over to the sliding plexi glass and steel door that led to the hallway.

Standing at the door was Sgt. Colts a militant slender black man. Smitty who sat in the control booth opened the pod door. Stepping into the hallway he was escorted by Sarge around the perimeter of the control booth to the visiting booth.

Reaching the visiting booth, he smiled at his visitor from outside of the booth. Sarge opened the door, Dirty stepped in, Sarge secured the door then left the lawyer and client alone. “Hey Miss Lady, how ya feelin’?”, asked Dirty putting his hand up to the inch-thick glass partition as he sat down on the stool.

“I’m alright and you?”, replied Pat smiling as she put her hand on the glass where his was.

“I’m holdin’ on, still tryna piece this puzzle together. What’s up though? I thought we agreed that it wouldn’t be wise for you to come over here to see me”, said Dirty having told her not to jeopardize her job by visiting him.

“I know but I came to see a client and thought I’d pull you while I was here”, said Pat then dropping her voice to a whisper she leaned forward and added, “plus I needed to see you to tell you what I dug up at the office. Do the names Donte’ Barnes and Shyheem Kane ring a bell?”

Drawing his lips tight Dirty squinted his eyes and tried to read Pat’s mind while nodding his head up and down confirming that he knew the names.

“Well based on my research, all the government has in your case is the testimonies of those two individuals and two controlled buys involving Donte’ Barnes and Keith Holmes.”

“Donte Barns! Are you sure?”, he asked in disbelief.

“Yes, I’m 100 percent certain”, she confirmed. “He’s apparently been a C.I. for a couple months.”

“What’s a C.I.?”, he asked baffled.

“Confidential Informant.”

Unable to believe his ears he shook his head. “A Confidential informant, huh? And a controlled buy involving Kevin Holmes…”

“No, the controlled buy was with Keith Holmes. Yeah Keith Holmes”, she assured him after pausing for a second.

“Yo dead, that’s Snuggles twin brother Fatty Pooh”, said Dirty.

“Really? Well, that’s good, I mean it’s good for the case if he’s deceased cause all the government will have is the testimony of others, so you need to think of a way to discredit their testimony”, explained Patricia giving him sound legal advice.

“Don’t worry I’ll think of something, thanks Patricia”, he said, his mind already conjuring up a way to address the situation.

“Do me a favor and call my godmother and tell her I need to see her and Munchie as soon as possible.”

“Cookie, right?”

“Yeah.”

“Okay is there anything else you need me to do?”, she asked wanting to assist him as he’d assisted her with his sister’s crisis.

“Just keep your eyes open for me I’ll call you tonight”, replied Dirty bringing the visit to a closure he stood.

“I sure will. Make sure you call me”, said Patricia putting her belongings in her briefcase she stood and using the phone on the wall she called the front desk to have the C.O. come and unlock her side of the booth.

A minute later the C.O. arrived and unlocked the visitor's side of the booth. Patricia waved good-bye and said, "Take care", over her shoulder.

"You too", replied Dirty as he turned and pounded on the glass part of the door getting Smitty's attention in the bubble.

"Come get me, I'm finished!"

Once back on the tier his head began to ache, a sharp pain jack hammering just behind his eyes so he decided to lock in and lay down. While laying down he went over the information Patricia had dropped on him trying to digest the revelation.

I can see Shyheem Kane, but not Donte' Barns, he thought unable to believe his comrade would betray him. *The shit is unreal, naw not yo... I knew yo all my life. I went to prison for killing a nigga that robbed him. I've treated yo like my blood since we were kids. I even bought the nigga a truck and put him on his feet soon as he came uptown. When the nigga got locked up I'm the first person he called and I posted his bail with no questions asked. Naw Bucky couldn't do me like this,* he thought believing his loyalty to Bucky would generate the same from him. *But he the only one knew 'bout T.C body and that's count 3 on the indictment...*

He wanted Patricia to be wrong, but unfortunately all the pieces of the puzzle fit together perfectly. It wasn't a coincident that Bucky didn't get indicted with the rest of the team. It was planned that way. In a desperate attempt to save himself from a prison term for the rape case with the state and the felony possession of a firearm case from the same arrest which the Feds picked up Bucky decided to flip and work for the other side. Being granted immunity he helps the government make a foundation so they could build a case against the "Slum Lord Gang" the title given to Dirty White and his co-defendants by the media after a group picture taken at the Black Out party with Dirty holding the pendant on his chain up somehow wound up in the Baltimore Sun newspaper and made front page.

***

"Hey Sweetie, me and Munchie raced over here as soon as your friend called me. How's everything coming along? Is everything alright?", asked Ms. Cookie when Dirty entered the visiting booth. She was sitting, Munchie stood behind her.

"Nah shit fucked up", began Dirty sighing as he sat down.

"You won't believe what I found out, Bucky punk ass the reason I'm locked up. His whore ass started workin' wit' the Feds so he would get off that bullshit rape charge..."

"Get the fuck outta here", interjected Munchie a look of disbelief on her face.

"I just seen yo up Windsor the other night stuntin' and shit. He tried to get me to go home wit' him."

“That’s a damn shame, good as you was to that nigga. I knew somethin’ was funny though when all yall got locked up except him”, said Ms. Cookie shaking her head she angrily added,

“Somebody need to kill his ass! That’s what they did back in the 70’s and early 80’s, a nigga tell, they killed his ass.”

“My sentiments exactly! Plus, Nah cousin on home monitor tellin’ too. I don’t understand niggas, we pose’ to roll to death, but the Feds come in the picture and nigga’s fold. This shit crazy. Sammy the Bull fucked up the whole game, now niggas think that sucka shit gangsta”, ranted Dirty, venting.

“I know Sweetie, calm down, it’s gonna be alright”, said Ms. Cookie.

“I hear ya. What’s up wit’ Tray? Have yall talked to her?”, he asked fearing that as a female with two children she may flip also.

“Yeah, I talked to her”, said Munchie, “She said that the Feds tried to get her to go to profit…Naw I mean a proffer hearing to tell but she said she love you like a brother and she gonna either get out wit’chu or go down wit’chu. She on some real ride or die shit!”

“Oh yeah!”, smiled Dirty. “Next time you talk to her give her my love and regards, that’s my girl!”

“So, what else did you find out?”, asked Ms. Cookie.

“Basically, that’s all they got is Bucky and Shy’s testimony. Wit’ out that they ain’t got shit”, said Dirty looking from his godmother's face up to Munchie then back to Ms. Cookie.

"That's why I wanted Munchie to come wit' you when you came", he explained getting Munchie's full attention, he looked up at her.

"Yo Munch, I need you to get in touch wit' Dirt-Dirt and Skiddie Box for me, tell'um to take care of this situation. What's left of them 30 birds I had you go get when I first got locked up?"

"It's like 17, I think, it may be 16. Skiddie Box and Dirt-Dirt been doin' 'um wit' they lil' team on the block and bringin' me back 25 off each one", she explained.

"Why what's up?"

"Look tell Skiddie and Dirt-Dirt it's 5 joints on each of dem niggas head and I 'm eternally in their depth", said Dirty having already paid his bill with Lucky Al the 30 Kilo's he had left when he was arrested were all profits. "I can't have dem niggas make it to court, if I get convicted that's an automatic life sentence."

"Don't worry I'ma make sure everything takin' care of", Munchie assured him.

"What you want me to do wit' the rest of the joints and the money?"

"Just look out for Tracy kids and if anybody call needing anything make sure they get it, the rest is you lil' sis'", said Dirty unconcerned with the money, after all he was a millionaire, but money meant nothing if he was sentenced to life.

"Good lookin' out White, don't worry yall gonna come up out this", she assured him again.

"I promise you dat, if I gotta handle dem niggas myself".

Dirty nodded his head understanding then he looked to Ms. Cookie who'd been silent throughout him and Munchie's conversation.

"You alright Ms. Cookie?" he asked concerned with what she felt about the moves he was setting in motion.

"Yeah I'm alright Sweetie. You do what you gotta do to get up outta here like a man", she said giving her approval, then looking up at her daughter she spoke to her,

"Munchie, make sure you handle your end."

"Don't worry I am Ma", replied Munchie, then hearing keys everyone became silent.

The door on the visitor's side opened and a dark skin female C.O. appeared, "It's that time, I gave yall a few extra minutes and I hate to break yall up but it's some other visitor's downstairs tryna come up."

"Thanks Green", hollered Dirty to the C.O. he'd built a cool little relationship with since he'd been in the institution.

She waved and flashed a smile, "You welcome".

"I love yall, I'll call later", said Dirty, placing his hand on the glass.

His visitors returned the gesture and simultaneously said, “we love you too.” Then they turned on their heels to exit the booth, stopping at the door they waved. He waved back wishing he was leaving with his visitors as the door closed and they disappeared.

If things go as planned I’ll be uptown soon, he thought as he waited for C.O. Austin to get him back to the tier.

Chapter 28

The stifling summer heat began to subside slightly, the late afternoon making way to the early evening. Munchie in her purple 2000 S-type Jaguar cruised down Baltimore Street. Reaching Pulaski Street, she made a left heading southbound to Hollins Street. Rolling the automatic window down on the driver's side, she glanced up and down the poverty ridden strip, her eyes searching for Dirt-Dirt. Spotting his dwarf like figure leaning up against the navy blue 1996 Yukon he'd purchased when Skiddie Box purchased his Cadillac, she honked her horn and shouted his name, "A Dirt-Dirt!"

Catching his attention Dirt-Dirt turned his head in the direction from which the voice came. Seeing Munchie's car, he threw his hands up in a street gesture meaning, what's up, at the same time shouting the words.

"Yo, what's up Munch?"

"Come here Yo! I gotta holla at'cha!", she said turning left onto Hollins Street she double parked and waited for Dirt-Dirt to come and see what she wanted.

Pulling his camouflage shorts up which were being weighed down by the 10mm in his right pocket he stepped into the street and bopped over to the Jaguar. Reaching the car, he put his left hand up on top of the car's roof and looking in at Munchie he spoke.

"What's up? You need me to handle something?", asked the 16-year-old hustler knowing something had to be wrong for Munchie to come down the strip.

"You hollered at Dirty?"

"Yeah, that's what's up, I just came from visitin' yo a little while ago and I got a message for you and Skiddie. Get in", replied Munchie popping the automatic lock on the passenger side door.

"Hold up, let me get my keys out of my truck and turn it off". After grabbing his keys, he hollered to Moo-Moo, "I'll be back, hold shit down Cutty."

"I got'chu", replied Moo-Moo watching as Dirt-Dirt slammed the door on his truck, walked over to the Jaguar and climbed in it.

Once he was in Munchie pulled off and drove around aimlessly explaining to him everything Dirty had told her on the visit, from Bucky and Shy snitching to the payoff of 5 Kilo's on each of their heads. When she finished talking Dirt-Dirt responded smoothly in a casual monotone.

"That's done, tell yo watch the news and want for something else", said the loyal teen.

Munchie dropped him off where she'd picked him up and told him to call her when everything had been taken care of, in full. He agreed and immediately climbed into his truck, started the truck up and pulled away from the curb heading to him and Skiddie Box crib. He phoned Skiddie Box along the way and told him meet him at the house.

When Dirt-Dirt reached the crib, he spotted Skiddie Box's car indicating that he was already there. Using his Nextel, he hit Skiddie Box on the Walkie-talkie.

"Yo come out front, I'm out front", said Dirt-Dirt as he parked his truck, the message crackled out of Skiddie Box's phone.

"Here I come yo", replied Skiddie Box hitting him back.

Within minutes Skiddie Box was up in the truck. He sparked a blunt and listened as Dirt-Dirt ran the story Munchie gave him down in depth. He digested everything and contemplated for a couple minutes before suggesting they execute Shyheem first thing in the morning. Since he knew where Shyheem's mother lived and knew he was on home monitor there. Plus, if Shyheem was snitching he could very well start pointing the finger at Skiddie Box, they'd come up in the same neighborhood and Skiddie Box wasn't trying to take any chances. Dirt-Dirt agreed and they headed to Valentino's to grab a bite to eat before going to get the old Crown Victoria out of the cut.

■■

Just before the break of dawn Skiddie Box and Dirt-Dirt pulled into the peaceful working-class block of Chesterfield Avenue and parked. Dressed in identical attire that consisted of all black and matching baseball caps pulled low over their heads and black batting gloves on their hands, the teens were prepared for the encounter. Dirt-Dirt checked his 10mm making sure it was cocked and ready, then he tucked it in his waist and slid out of the car inconspicuously. The street was deserted and everything was calm as he walked over to and sat on the concrete steps in front of a red brick two story flat. Resting his elbows on his knees, he held his head down, looking at the ground, waiting patiently. It was 10 minutes to 6 o'clock, Skiddie Box had told him Shyheem's mother would be heading to work at 6 o'clock.

Checking the Stallard Arms 9mm in his hand Skiddie Box sat upright in the passenger seat of the car with the door cracked slightly. He stared intently at the white screen door next tot where Dirt-Dirt sat. one side of Skiddie Box hated the situation at hand because him and Shyheem grew up together, Shyheem had been almost like a big brother to him, but betrayal wasn't tolerated in their lifestyle, no matter what, you don't snitch, so now their bond no longer held any value. Patiently waited.

At 6:03 am the screen door Skiddie Box was eyeing opened. He sat on edge as a plump chocolate brown skin woman in her early 40's emerged from the house. Locking her front door, she turned on her heels, stepped off her porch and started down her front stairs. As soon as her heel clad feet touched the sidewalk the teens reacted. Dirt-Dirt sprung off the steps with the 10mm in hand leveled at the woman's frame. As Skiddie Box in a fluid motion flung the car door open and hopped out aiming the 9mm he was clutching at the center of the woman's torso.

"Oh my God, sweet Jesus", uttered the woman dropping her keys and purse she grabbed her chest as if she were having a heart attack, her mouth wide open.

"Sssssh! Just turn around and walk back in the house and everything will be alright", warned Skiddie Box through clenched teeth.

She didn't hesitate to cooperate walking back up the steps with Dirt-Dirt at her side gripping her right arm with his left hand, his right hand still aiming the 10mm at her mid-section. Skiddie Box quickly picked up her keys and purse and followed them up the steps.

"Open the door", said Skiddie Box handing the frightened woman her keys.

She grabbed the keys, her hand shaking she unlocked her front door and the 3 of them entered the dark living room. Skiddie Box in the rear looked over his shoulder and scanned the block.

It was deserted still and from the looks of things no one had seen what transpired. Content he shut the door behind them before speaking a whisper.

"Where Shy at?", he questioned.

“Upstairs in his room”, said the frightened woman knowing that this had something to do with her troublesome nephew Naheem and all the drug stuff she’d read about in the newspaper.

“Who else in here besides Shy?”, asked Dirt-Dirt nudging her with the barrel of his gun.

“La La and him, that’s all”, she stammered.

“Come on. What room he in?”, demanded Dirt-Dirt pushing her in the direction of the steps which lead to the second floor.

“I know where he sleeps”, said Skiddie Box before Mrs. Niecey had a chance to respond.

Being familiar with the lay out of the house from when he and Shyheem use to hang together Skiddie Box lead the way up the stairs to the second floor followed by Mrs. Niecey and Dirt-Dirt. Once on the second floor they turned right and crept down a short narrow hall, Mrs. Niecey between the two teens. Skiddie Box stopped in front of a dark wooden door and looked back at Dirt-Dirt nodding his head, Dirt-Dirt nodded back, his gun still trained on Mrs. Niecey. Skiddie Box using his left hand slowly turned the knob and pushed the door inward, a touch. It slowly creaked open revealing two sleeping figures sprawled out on a queen-sized mattress their bodies covered in a sky-blue sheet. Skiddie Box eased into the room holding his gun with both hands aimed at Shyheem.

Once Skiddie Box entered the room Dirt-Dirt forced Mrs. Niecey into the bedroom with a rough shove to the back. She stumbled forward and shouted, “Lord Jesus, please don’t kill my baby”, as she nearly slipped from the shove.

The commotion jolted Shyheem and his girlfriend awake. Stunned Shyheem sat up right in the middle of the bed, his eyes widened, his heart sank and his bowels broke at the sight of the two gunmen. He raised his hands over his head as if surrendering to the police.

“Yo Skiddie come on, don’t do this yo”, he pleaded knowing the lanky frame was Skiddie Box, his signature gold Cartier frames being a dead giveaway.

“Please yo, I had to do it. We came up together, I love yay o”.

“Man, fuck all dat”, replied Skiddie Box with no remorse as he squeezed the trigger three times.

BOOM! BOOM! BOOM! Shots rang out, hot lead projectiles leaped from the 9mm tearing into Shyheem’s chest, knocking him back to the mattress.

“Looooord my Ba…..”

BOOM! A loud roar cut Mrs. Neicey’s plea short as the bullet from Dirt-Dirt’s gun entered the base of her head just behind her right ear and exited the left side of her face blowing her left eye out.

Blood and fragments of flesh sprayed the bed as she toppled forward with a heavy thud. La La, her eyes wide with fear tried to jump out of the bed, but became tangled in the sheets and fell between the bed and the dresser. Landing on her side she turned and kicked frantically trying to free her tangled foot. Dirt-Dirt quickly stepped around the bed and fired several shots at La La's frame, shaking her foot loose, she tried to crawl under the bed, blood was everywhere. Her body was halfway under the bed when Dirt-Dirt leaned down and grabbed her ankle, yanking her back. She tried to scramble back under the bed as Dirt-Dirt pumped four bullets into her upper back, killing her.

Shyheem laid covered in blood still gasping for air, looking like a fresh fish out of water. So, to make sure the job was done and done thoroughly Skiddie Box stepped closer to the bed and placed the barrel of his gun to Shyheem's lips.

Looking him in his eyes Skiddie Box spat, "Death before dishonor bitch!", and pulled the trigger.

The youngsters scanned the room before leaving, it was a bloody mess. Shyheem, his mother and his girlfriend were all dead, they'd never testify. Satisfied with their handy work they flew out of the bedroom, down the stairs and out the front door.

People on the peaceful block having heard all the shooting were out on their porches and peeping out of their front windows trying to figure out what was going on as Skiddie Box and Dirt-Dirt exited the house. Guns in hand they briskly strolled to the Crown Victoria, climbed in and sped off without incident.

Later that evening Dirt-Dirt the better driver of the duo drove the Crown Victoria to South Baltimore, followed by Skiddie Box in the gray Lincoln they used on runs with Dirty and Munchie. Near Cherry hill they pulled behind a desolated factory and parked. Getting out of the Crown Victoria Dirt-Dirt walked around to the trunk, popped it and retrieved a red 5-gallon container filled with gas. Using the gas, he doused the entire car then stepped away from it, Skiddie Box lit the cocktail bomb he'd made and tossed it at the Crown Victoria. The car was engulfed in flames in no time.

"Let's be out Cutty", said Dirt-Dirt climbing into the driver's side of the Lincoln.

"Yeah, let's go see Munchie and try to find this nigga Bucky", replied Skiddie Box getting in the car and leaning all the way back in the reclined seat as Dirt-Dirt pulled off.

Unknown to them Bucky had already met his fate…

■■

The parking lot at the Windsor Inn was packed when Munchie arrived. Finding an empty parking spot, she pulled into it and turned her cap off. Opening the door, she slid out of the car, shut the door and looked at her reflection in the cars tinted window. In a 'hoe stroll' she may have easily been mistaken for a prostitute in the form fitting black leather Fendi mini-skirt, skin tight black Fendi shirt and matching thigh high leather boots and flaming red wig, she wore, but for Baltimore's club scene her attire was appropriate. Combing her fingers through her wig she smoothed over the synthetic hair, then applied another coat of lip gloss to her succulent lips and pulled her skirt down before walking toward the club's entrance. Smiling at the sight of Bucky's truck in the parking lot, she strolled into the dimly lit club snapping her fingers and moving her shoulders in rhythm with the music being played. After paying the admission fee she began to mingle while scanning the bar, her eyes searching for Bucky. Zeroing in him at the far-left hand side of the bar she sashayed over in that direction. Bucky having spotted Munchie when she entered the club watched her cross the floor with the stride of a model. Nearing him she smiled, revealing even pearl white teeth and waved congenially. Typical of Bucky he hopped off the bar stool he was occupying and stood in her path, obstructing her course of movement.

"What's up Munch?", asked Bucky his words slurred.

"Ain't shit just tryna find this fake ass nigga Donnie", sighed Munchie putting her hand on her hip.

"Shit where the fuck this nigga at!"

"What Donnie you talkin' bout?", asked Bucky curiously.

"Donnie from da Avenue wit' da blue Escalade…"

"What da fuck you lookin' for Yo for?", asked Bucky in a jealous tone.

"He 'pose to give me some money for my mortgage and shit", lied Munchie trying to step around and get pass Bucky. "I'll holla at you later yo".

"Hold up", said Bucky grabbing her arm.

“Boy get off me”, ordered Munchie rolling her eyes as she snatched away from him, “I gotta find this nigga ‘fore me and my sons get put out”

“Fuck dat nigga. Come on hang out wit’ me I got chu”, said Bucky.

“You got me what?”, asked Munchie tilting her head to the side and running her tongue over her lips.

This nigga so fucking predictable, she thought already knowing he’d give her the money and try to convince her to go home with him.

“I’ll give you the dough for your mortgage, dat shit ain’t nothin’”, said Bucky trying to impress Munchie and stunt as usual.

“Shit I need 3G’s. if you got that then you got my attention, if not I’ll holla at ‘cha”, snapped Munchie sardonically.

“I said I got’chu, you gonna have to ride out my crib wit’ me though ‘cause I only got ‘bout $1500 on me”, said Bucky baiting her in.

If I get her out my crib I’ma slip her a E-pill and fuck the shit outta her, plus I’ma suck dat pussy real good and turn her ass out, thought Bucky perverted-ly plotting.

“I don’t feel like going out your crib”, griped Munchie falsely, as she paused and scanned the club as if looking for someone, “but I don’t see yo and I need that bread so fuck it I’ll go”

“Shit we can go now”, offered Bucky, eager to leave, not wanting Donnie to show up and blow what he thought to be his chance.

“It’s up to you”, said Munchie shrugging her shoulders.

“Shit let’s go then”, said Bucky putting his hand on the small of Munchie’s back he pushed her forward.

She went with the flow starting in the direction of the exit. Bucky right on her heels gawked at her ass, saliva forming in the corner of his mouth. Shaking his head unable to believe his luck, he with a backwards swipe of his hand wiped the corner of his mouth catching the saliva. Together they exited the club and strolled to Bucky’s truck. Using the small black gadget on his keychain he deactivated the alarm and unlocked the doors. They climbed in the truck and Bucky sparked a blunt inhaling deeply while starting the truck, then he exhaled and pulled off. Weaving the Tahoe in and out of traffic, Bucky drove down a series of back roads and side streets constantly peeking in his rearview mirror to assure no one was following him. Several minutes passed before content that he wasn’t being tailed he hopped on the expressway and followed it towards Baltimore County.

“Damn why you keep peekin’ in your rearview mirror lookin’ all crazy?”, asked Munchie crossing her legs causing the mini-skirt to rise.

“Shit everybody locked up but me so I gotta be careful ‘cause the Feds might try to track me down”, lied Bucky the paranoia of breaking the code of silence constantly haunting him, keeping him on edge.

“I know that’s right”, chimed Munchie in agreement. “Shit you lucky they ain’t get you yet”, she added playing along with him all the while cursing him in her mind.

“Ain’t no question”, replied Bucky looking over at Munchie, sneaking a peek at her firm pecan toned thighs.

It took less than a half hour for them to reach Bucky’s elegant condo complex. He parked the truck around the corner from his building. They exited the truck and walked together up the sidewalk, each deep in their own thoughts. When they reached his building, Bucky opened the door and pointed the way to his condo out to Munchie. She entered the building and started in that direction, he followed her up the stairs. Once in front of his condo Munchie stood back as Bucky unlocked his door, twisted the knob and pushed it inward.

“Come on make yourself at home”, offered Bucky from just inside of the condo, stepping to the side so Munchie could squeeze by.

The condo was dark except for the light coming from the fish tank which casted a gloomy bluish green ray that illuminated most of the living room. As soon as Munchie entered the welling she could feel her boots sink into the plush carpet. Sashaying over to the fish tank she bent over pretending to take an interest in the fish, all the while intentionally exposing her perfectly round rump.

Hearing the door lock Munchie glanced back at Bucky, catching him staring at her with his mouth open, his eyes full of lust, “Damn Boy close your mouth”.

“A nigga can’t help but to stare at dat ass girl”, said Bucky off handedly, “Dem babies made you phat as shit yo”

“Naw dem babies made me broke that’s what dem babies did. Now is you gonna give me the money we came to get?”, cracked Munchie.

“I told ya I got’cha damn! Hold up”, said Bucky turning the living room light on, before he disappeared down the hall toward the back of the nicely furnished condo, leaving Munchie in the living room. Stopping at the bathroom he relieved himself and tried to conjure up a way to finesse Munchie out of her panties. *I got her here and she need 3 G’s, I gotta hit dat,* thought Bucky continuing to his bedroom from the bathroom. In his bedroom, he went into the walk-in closet where he kneeled in front of a heap of dirty clothes, swiping the dirty clothes to the side revealing a light gray fireproof digital safe. He removed 3G’s out of the safe, stood and stepped out of the closet.

“A Munchie, here Yo!”, he shouted.

In seconds, she appeared at the threshold of his room.

“What’s up?”, she asked.

“Huh”, said Bucky handing her the money, “it’s 3G’s like you asked for, you owe me yo.”

“Thanks Bucky Baby”, said Munchie wrapping her arms around his neck, she hugged him, her body pressed against his.

“I really needed this yo, thanks. I’ma pay you back.”

“Don’t trip on dat, we family”, said Bucky returning her embrace. His manhood began to respond stirring to life slightly.

“Thanks Buck, for real”, said Munchie puckering her lips she tilted her head to the side to kiss him on his cheek, and just at that instant Bucky twisted his head and their lips met.

A chill ran up Munchie’s spine, she wanted to vomit but held back and went with the flow returning his kiss. Bucky’s hands began to explore her body. He ran them down her back and over her soft ass lingering there for a minute before working his hand around to the front of her skirt where he ran it up between her legs. She didn’t resist, so he probed further until he could feel her silky panties. Working his finger around and under her panties he touched her warm moist pussy.

“Mmmm Buckee”, she moaned tilting her head back.

He continued to probe with his finger becoming more and more aroused. Unzippering his pants with one hand he struggled to free his ick all the while fingering Munchie. Having successfully freed himself he then grabbed Munchie’s left leg, lifted it awkwardly and tried to pull her panties to the side so he could insert himself in her.

“Slow down nigga damn”, suggested Munchie pushing him back and straightening her leg.

“Besides you know the golden rule, you gotta lick it before you stick it”, she said running her tongue over her lips.

“Shit you ain’t said nothin’ but a word”, snapped Bucky pushing Munchie back onto his bed. She sat or more like flopped down on the edge of the bed. Bucky towered over her, his dick directly in her face. He grabbed himself and aimed his dick at her face.

“Oh no nigga, it don’t work like that”, she protested as she stood, sat the money on the bed, pulled her zebra striped thongs down, stepped out of them.

“Aint gonna be no 68 and I owe you one shit, you gotta eat this pussy first and turn some music on, don’t just try to slut me out.”

“Girl, you crazy”, said Bucky as he turned the stereo on, Carl Thomas filled the room. “Is dat cool?”

“Yeah turn it up”, replied Munchie sitting back on the edge of the king-size bed.

Bucky did so then turned back to Munchie. She laid back on the bed, lifted her legs up planting her boots on the edge of the bed, then gapped her legs open revealing her shaved cunt.

“Taste dis pussy Bucky”, she moaned biting down on her lower lip as she ran her hand over her sensitive pussy lips. “Mmmm”

Bucky transfixed, watched as Munchie touched herself. A few seconds passed before he squatted at the foot of the bed and buried his face between her legs. His tongue danced around her clit, she moaned.

“Ooooh suck dis pussy oww yeees”, exclaimed Munchie drawing her knees up to her shoulders.

“Mmmm, dat’s right oooow!”

Bucky was feeling himself. After all these years, he finally had Munchie in his bed and she was climbing the wall. His ego was on overload as he lapped away at her pussy.

"Aah yes Bucky", she moaned caressing the top of his head with her left hand.

"Oh, stay right there Daddyyyy! Ooow right there, mmmm, make me cumm!"

Keeping her hand on his head she continued to moan while carefully unzippering the top of her right boot. Feeling down in the boot she felt the cold steel of the 38. Derringer strapped to her calf, she grabbed it and carefully eased it out of her boot. Once she had the gun out of her boot she lifted it up over her head and eased the hammer all the way back so both bullets would expel from the small gun with one touch of the trigger. Still moaning and caressing the top of Bucky's head she eased the gun around, removed her left hand from his head and placed the Derringer a fraction of an inch from his skull then squeezed the trigger, B-BOOM! Both bullets pierced the top of his dome at once. He sat back in a full squat before falling into the plush carpet with a muffled thud.

Munchie sprung up from the bed and stared down at Bucky's lifeless form, his blood seeping into the gray carpet. She heaved, but covered her mouth before the vomit could escape and quickly looked away. Her nerves were on end and it took a few minutes for her to recuperate, but once she calmed down and her hands ceased to tremble Munchie retrieved the latex gloves she had in her left boot and cleaned up behind herself, wiping off everything she'd touched. Then she relieved Bucky of all his jewelry and searched his pockets, taking his keys and money and before she left she ransacked his room a little, emptied his safe which he'd left opened to stage a robbery and put on a gray sweat suit she'd taken from his closet.

Content that she'd covered her tracks Munchie tip-toed to the front door, eased it open and peered out into the hallway, down the stairs and out the front door with the hoodie on her head carrying a laundry basket containing everything she'd taken from Bucky's condo. She retraced her steps back to Bucky's truck, put the laundry basket in the back seat, climbed in and pulled off. Glancing at her watch she noticed it was 4:07am when she reached Gilmore Homes, in West Baltimore. Parking the truck, she took her time wiping the areas she remembered touching, then she thoroughly wiped the Derringer off and put it in the glove compartment, placed Bucky's chain on the rearview mirror neck, leaving it to dangle, put his watch, bracelet and two diamond rings in the coin dish and climbed out of the truck. Leaving the keys in the ignition with the front door open and all the doors unlocked.

Somebody will steal it by the crack of dawn, she reasoned strolling off to catch a cab with the laundry basket under her arm. *I wonder did Dirt-Dirt and Skiddie Box get as lucky…*

Epilogue

Despite having literally no evidence against Dirty White and his co-defendants the government continued to detain them. In total, they spent nearly a year in confinement as the prosecutors tried every trick in the book to build a stable case against them. They were superseded and charged with the witness murders, but ultimately the ends didn't connect and without the cooperation of the deceased one someone in the crew there was no evidence to stand trial. The government never pulled their resources together and conducted a thorough investigation. Instead they cut corners and relied predominately on the testimony of witnesses, the infamous 5.K.1, code used by the government for a rat/snitch/informant, without which the government seldom has a case that's fit to stand trial, especially on conspiracy. So, due to the loyalty of the co-defendants on the indictment and the lack of the government's competence the prosecution had to dismiss all counts of the indictment without prejudice.

The sight was heavenly enough to inspire tears the day the media's proclaimed, most organized narcotics ring, the 'Slum Lord Gang' were all freed and bopped out of 101 Lombard Street with a George Jefferson strut to resume their lives...

Dirty White is now a successful business man, he owns 16 houses, half of club Fat Daddy's and is currently renovating a club in downtown Baltimore. He no longer hustles, but still has a powerful voice in the slums. He and Peaches reconciled, got married and are expecting another child soon. He still looks out for all his Comrades in prison and maintains a bond with all his old friends/ associates.

Nah is now serving 8 years in a state prison in Jessup for an unrelated attempted murder. He and Dirty are still close friends and he often gets visits from him and his godson Lil' White. His sisters Ra'jah and Ta'jay tend to his business and look out for him.

Snuggles is in the slums wheeling and dealing. He has a major marijuana strip in northwest Baltimore that sells 30's and 60's.

Smurf is still in the slums wheeling and dealing. He's loving life and controls Pulaski and Vine streets crack market.

Squirrel is now a die-hard Christian. He invested in a nice little church he operates with his beautiful wife.

Tracy is now the Madame of a female escort service. She also sells Ecstasy pills. Plus, she upgraded her salon which is doing well.

Munchie is no longer in the slums. She stacked enough money to be happy and left the slums alone. She now attends nursing school and intends to open a care service center for the elderly and disabled. Her and her sons are doing well.

Lucky Al is still in control of the slums. He eventually told Dirty White all about his son who was killed by the New York stick up boy that Dirty White killed, the revelation strengthened their bond. Lucky Al is like

Dirty White's surrogate father and Dirty White is like a surrogate son.

Antmoe is now home, when he was released from prison Dirty White had a 'coming home' party for him. Lucky AL gave him half of what he was worth. He moved to Montgomery County, Maryland where he resides with his girlfriend, they are trying to start their own family.

Los is in F.C.I Cumberland doing 15 years as a felon in possession armed career criminal. He's working on his appeal.

Ma Ma is still a hard-working woman despite her grandson begging her to stop working and just live life. She also still lives on Hollins Street, she insists it's the only home she knows and she feels safe there.

Ms. Cookie is still 100 percent behind her self-proclaimed godson. She tends to business for him almost like a secretary, and he takes care of her like she was his biological mother. Her house in Owings Mills is where everyone in the crew goes every three months for a get together/ family reunion.

Lil' Mookie is an honor roll student. He lives with his grandmother.

Tish and Lil' Marvin are well, they live in one of Dirty White's houses near Morgan State University. Dirty White makes sure they are okay.

Gizmo is still in prison. He stabbed an inmate to death behind a melee involving the Muslims. He was given an additional 25 years.

Mike-Mike is in Jessup with Nah. With Dirty White's assistance, he managed to get back on appeal and his sentence was commuted, he now has 20 years, instead of 50.

Patricia Smallwood is still a federal public defender. Her and Dirty White remained friends but only see each other on occasions. She's involved with a radio DJ from Washington, D.C.

Skiddie Box and Dirt-Dirt are still in the slums and have become two of Baltimore's most violent hustlers… To be continued in "Death B4 Dishonor" …

Made in the USA
Columbia, SC
13 March 2018